The Simple Truth

The Simple Truth

David Baldacci

Thorndike Press • Chivers Press
Thorndike, Maine   Bath, England

ADH - 5055

This Large Print edition is published by Thorndike Press, USA
and by Chivers Press, England.

Published in 1999 in the U.S. by arrangement with *LP*
Warner Books, Inc.   *FIC*

Published in 1999 in the U.K. by arrangement with *BALOUCC*
Simon & Schuster Ltd.

U.S. Hardcover	0-7862-1695-6	(Basic Series Edition)
U.S. Softcover	0-7862-1696-4	
U.K. Hardcover	0-7540-1244-1	(Windsor Large Print)
U.K. Softcover	0-7540-2178-5	(Paragon Large Print)

The text of this Large Print edition is unabridg[...]
Other aspects of the book may vary from the o[...]tion.

Set in 16 pt. Plantin.

Printed in the United States on permanent paper.

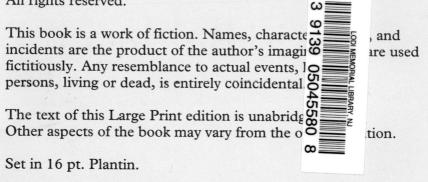

British Library Cataloguing in Publication Data available

Library of Congress Cataloging in Publication Data

Baldacci, David.
    The simple truth / David Baldacci.
       p.   cm.
    ISBN 0-7862-1695-6 (lg. print : hc : alk. paper)
    ISBN 0-7862-1696-4 (lg. print : sc : alk. paper)
    1. Large type books. I. Title.
    [PS3552.A446S56   1999]
    813´.54—dc21   98-44512

To Michelle:
The simple truth is,
my life doesn't work without you

This book is also lovingly dedicated
to the memory of Brenda Gayle Jennings,
a special child

The Truth is rarely pure and never simple.

— Oscar Wilde

ACKNOWLEDGMENTS

To Jennifer Steinberg, once more for superb research.

To Lou Saccoccio, for his able assistance on military legal matters.

To Lee Calligaro, whose stories about his tenure as a JAG attorney during the Vietnam War fascinated me, and who is also the finest trial lawyer I have ever met.

To Steve Jennings, for his astute editorial comments.

To the Warner Books family — Larry, Maureen, Mel, Emi, Tina, Heather, Jackie J. and Jackie M. and all the rest of an incredibly fine and dedicated group of people who make my life so much more enriched.

To my mother, for the finer points of southwest Virginia, an area she knows awfully well.

To Karen Spiegel, who has been with me for a long time on this story.

To attorney Ed Vaughn, for educating me on some of the finer points of Virginia law and practice.

To those other sources, for their help in enlightening me on that fascinating place, the United States Supreme Court.

To my friend and agent, Aaron Priest, who provided me, as always, with a lot of good counsel as I worked my way through this novel.

To Frances Jalet-Miller, for putting so much time, effort and spirit into helping me realize the full potential of this work. I couldn't have done it without you.

CHAPTER ONE

At this prison the doors are inches thick, steel; once factory smooth, they now carry multiple dents. Imprints of human faces, knees, elbows, teeth, residue of blood are harvested large on their gray surface. Prison hieroglyphics: pain, fear, death, all permanently recorded here, at least until a new slab of metal arrives. The doors have a square opening at eye level. The guards stare through it, use the small space to throw bright lights at the human cattle on their watch. Without warning, batons smack against the metal with the pop of gun reports. The oldies bear it well, looking down at the floor, studying nothing — meaning their lives — in a subtle act of defiance, not that anyone notices or cares. The rookies still tense when the pop or light comes; some dribble pee down their cotton pants, watch it flow over their black low-quarter shoes. They soon get over it, smack the damn door back, fight down the push of schoolboy tears and belly bile. If they want to survive.

At night, the prison cells hold the darkness of a cave but for odd shapes here and there. On this night a thunderstorm grips the area.

When a lightning bolt dips from the sky, it splashes illumination into the cells through the small Plexiglas windows. The honeycomb pattern of the chicken wire stretched tight across the glass is reproduced on the opposite wall with each burst.

During the passage of such light, the man's face emerges from the dark, as though having suddenly parted the surface of water. Unlike those in the other cells, he sits alone, thinks alone, sees no one in here. The other prisoners fear him; the guards too, even armed as they are, for he is a man of intimidating proportions. When he passes by the other cons, hardened, violent men in their own right, they quickly look away.

His name is Rufus Harms and his reputation at Fort Jackson Military Prison is that of a destroyer: He will crush you if you come at him. He never takes the first step, but he will the last. Twenty-five years of incarceration have taken a considerable toll on the man. Like the age rings of a tree, the ruts of scars on Harms's skin, the poorly healed fractures of bone on his skeleton are a chronicle of his time here. However, far worse damage lies within the soft tissue of his brain, within the centers of his humanity: memory, thought, love, hate, fear, all tainted, all turned against him. But mostly memory, a humbling tumor of iron against the tip of his spine.

There is substantial strength left in the

massive frame, though; it is evident in the long, knotty arms, the density of Harms's shoulders. Even the wide girth of his middle carries the promise of exceptional power. But Harms is still a listing oak, topped out on growth, some limbs dead or dying, beyond the cure of pruning, the roots ripped out on one side. He is a living oxymoron: a gentle man, respectful of others, faithful to his God, irreversibly cast in the image of a heartless killer. Because of this the guards and the other prisoners leave him be. And he is content with that. Until this day. What his brother has brought him. A package of gold, a surge of hope. A way out of this place.

Another burst of light shows his eyes brimming with deep red, as though bloodied, until one sees the tears that stain his dark, heavy face. As the light recedes, he smooths out the piece of paper, taking care not to make any sound, an invitation to the guards to come sniffing. Lights have been extinguished for several hours now, and he is unable to reverse that. As it has been for a quarter century, his darkness will end only with the dawn. The absence of light matters little, though. Harms has already read the letter, absorbed every word. Each syllable cuts him like the quick bite of a shiv. The insignia of the United States Army appears bold at the top of the paper. He knows the symbol well. The Army has been his employer, his warden for almost thirty years.

The Army was requesting information from Rufus Harms, a failed and forgotten private from the era of Vietnam. Detailed information. Information Harms had no way of giving. His finger navigating true even without light, Harms touched the place in the letter that had first aroused fragments of memory drifting within him all these years. These particles had generated the incapacitation of endless nightmare, but the nucleus had seemed forever beyond him. Upon first reading the letter, Harms had dipped his head low to the paper, as though trying to reveal to himself the hidden meanings in the typewritten squiggles, to solve the greatest mystery of his mortal life. Tonight, those twisted fragments had suddenly coalesced into firm recollection, into the truth. Finally.

Until he read the letter from the Army, Harms had only two distinct memories of that night twenty-five years ago: the little girl; and the rain. It had been a punishing storm, much like tonight. The girl's features were delicate; the nose only a bud of cartilage; the face as yet unlined by sun, age or worry; her staring eyes blue and innocent, the ambitions of a long life ahead still forming within their simple depths. Her skin was the white of sugar, and unblemished except for the red marks crushed upon a neck as fragile as a flower stem. The marks had been caused by the hands of Private Rufus Harms, the same hands that now clutched the letter as his mind careened dangerously close to that image once more.

Whenever he thought of the dead girl he wept, had to, couldn't help it, but he did so silently, with good reason. The guards and cons were buzzards, sharks, they sniffed blood, weakness, an opening, from a million miles away; they saw it in the twitch of your eyes, the widened pores of your skin, even in the stink of your sweat. Here, every sense was heightened. Here, strong, fast, tough, nimble equaled life. Or not.

He was kneeling beside her when the MPs found them. Her thin dress clung to her diminutive frame, which had receded into the saturated earth, as though she had been dropped from a great height to form the shallowest of graves. Harms had looked up at the MPs once, but his mind had registered nothing more than a confusion of darkened silhouettes. He had never felt such fury in his life, even as the nausea seized him, his eyes losing their focus, his pulse rate, respiration, blood pressure all bottoming out. He had gripped his head as if to prevent his bursting brain from cleaving through the bone of his skull, through tissue and hair, and exploding into the soaked air.

When he had looked down once more at the dead girl, and then at the pair of twitching hands that had ended her life, the anger had drained from him, as though someone had jerked free a plug embedded within. The functions of his body oddly abandoning him, Harms could only remain kneeling, wet and shivering, his knees sunk deeply into the mud. A black high chieftain in green fatigues presiding over a small pale-skinned sacrifice, was how one stunned witness would later describe it.

The next day he would come to learn the little girl's name: Ruth Ann Mosley, ten years old, from Columbia, South Carolina. She and her family had been visiting her brother, who was stationed at the base. On that night Harms had only known Ruth Ann Mosley as a corpse, small — tiny, in fact — compared to the stunning breadth of his six-foot-five-inch, three-hundred-pound body. The blurred image of the rifle butt that one of the MPs smashed against his skull represented the last mental sliver Harms carried from that night. The blow had dropped him to the ground right next to her. The girl's lifeless face pointed upward, collecting droplets of rain in every still crevice. His face sunken into the mud, Rufus Harms saw nothing more. Remembered nothing more.

Until tonight. He swelled his lungs with rain-drenched air and stared out the half-open window. He was suddenly that still rare beast: an innocent man in prison.

He had convinced himself over the years that such evil had been lurking, cancerlike, within him. He had even thought of suicide, to make penance for stealing the life of another, more pitiably a child's. But he was deeply religious, and not a fleeting jailhouse convert to the Lord. He thus could not commit the sin of prematurely forcing his last breath. He also knew the girl's killing had condemned him to an afterlife a thousand times worse than the one he was now enduring. He was unwilling to rush to its embrace. Better this place, this man-made prison, for now.

Now he understood that his decision to live had been right. God had known, had kept him alive for this moment. With stunning clarity he recalled the men who had come for him that night at the stockade. His mind once more clearly held every contorted face, the stripes on the uniforms some of them wore — his comrades in arms. He recalled the way they circled him, wolves to prey, emboldened only by their numbers; the telling hatred of their words. What they had done that night had caused Ruth Ann Mosley to die. And in a very real sense, Harms had died as well.

To these men Harms was an able-bodied soldier who had never fought in defense of his country. Whatever he got, he deserved, they no doubt believed. Now he was a middle-aged man slowly dying in a cage as punish-

15

ment for a crime of long-ago origin. He had no power to see that any semblance of justice was done on his behalf. And yet with all that, Rufus Harms stared into the familiar darkness of his crypt, a single passion empowering him: After twenty-five years of terrible, wrenching guilt that had relentlessly taunted him until he was just barely in possession of a ruined life, he knew that it was now their turn to suffer. He gripped the worn Bible his mother had given him, and he promised this to the God who had chosen never to abandon him.

CHAPTER TWO

The steps leading up to the United States Supreme Court building were wide and seemingly endless. Trudging up them was akin to laboring toward Mount Olympus to request an audience of Zeus, which in a real sense you were. Engraved in the facade above the main doorway were the words EQUAL JUSTICE UNDER LAW. The phrase came from no significant document or court ruling but from Cass Gilbert, the architect who had designed and built the courthouse. It was a matter of spacing: The words fit perfectly into the area designated by Gilbert for a memorable legal phrase.

The majestic building rose four stories above ground level. Ironically, Congress had appropriated the funds to construct it in 1929, the same year the stock market crashed and helped bring on the Great Depression. Almost a third of the building's $9 million cost had gone to the purchase of marble. Pure Vermont was on the exterior, hauled down by an army of freight cars; crystal-lined Georgia rock padded the four interior courts; and milky Alabama stone lay over most of the floors and walls of the interior, except in the

Great Hall. Underfoot there was a darker Italian marble, with African stone in other places. The columns in the hall had been cast from blocks of Italian marble quarried from the Montarrenti site and shipped to Knoxville, Tennessee. There ordinary men struggled to cast the blocks into thirty-foot shapes to help support the building that had been the professional home to nine men since 1935 and, since 1981, to at least one woman, all of extraordinary achievement. Its supporters deemed the building a fine example of the Corinthian style of Greek architecture. Its detractors decried it as a palace for the insane pleasures of kings, rather than a place for the rational dispensation of justice.

And yet since John Marshall's time, the Court had been the defender and interpreter of the Constitution. It could declare an act of Congress unconstitutional. These nine people could force a sitting president to turn over tapes and documents that would ultimately lead to his resignation and disgrace. Crafted alongside the legislative authority of the Congress and the executive power of the presidency by the Founding Fathers, the American judiciary, headed by the Supreme Court, was an equal branch of government. And govern it did, as the Supreme Court bent and shaped the will of the American people by virtue of its decisions on any number of significant issues.

The elderly man walking down the Great Hall carried on this honored tradition. He was tall and bony, with soft brown eyes in no need of glasses, his eyesight still excellent even after decades of reading small print. His hair was nearly gone; his shoulders had narrowed and curved over the years, and he walked with a slight limp. Still, Chief Justice Harold Ramsey had a nervous energy about him and a peerless intellect that more than compensated for any physical slide. Even his footfalls seemed to carry special purpose.

He was the highest-ranking jurist in the land, and this was his Court, his building. The "Ramsey Court," the media had long deemed it, like the Warren Court and its other predecessors — his legacy for all time. Ramsey ran his court tight and true, cobbling together a consistent majority that was now going on ten years running. He loved the wheeling and dealing that went on behind the scenes at the Court. A carefully placed word or paragraph here or there, give a little on one point with the favor to be repaid later. Waiting patiently for just the right case to come along as a vehicle for change, sometimes in ways unexpected by his colleagues. Culling together the five votes necessary for a majority was an absolute obsession with Ramsey.

He had come to the Court as an associate justice and then been elevated to the top rank a decade ago. Merely first among equals in theory, but something more than that in reality. Ramsey was a man of intense beliefs and personal philosophies. Fortunately for him, he had been nominated to the Court when the selection process had nothing of the political sophistication of today. There were no bothersome questions about a candidate's positions on specific legal issues like abortion, capital punishment and affirmative action, queries that now littered the highly politicized process of becoming a Supreme Court justice. Back then, if the president nominated you, if you possessed the requisite legal pedigree, and if there were no particularly bad skeletons lying in wait, you were in.

The Senate had confirmed Ramsey unanimously. It really had no choice. His educational and legal backgrounds were of the first order. Multiple degrees, all from Ivy League schools, and top of his class in every one of them. Next had come an award-winning stint as a law professor with original, sweeping theories on the direction the law and, by extension, humanity should take. Then he had been nominated to the federal appellate bench, quickly becoming chief judge of his circuit. During his tenure on the appellate bench, the Supreme Court had never reversed one of his majority opinions. Over the years he had built the right network of contacts, done all the necessary things in his pursuit of the position he now held as tightly as he could.

He had earned the position. Nothing had ever been given to him. That was another of his firm beliefs. If you worked hard, you would succeed in America. No one was entitled to any handouts, not the poor, not the rich, not the middle class. The United States was the land of opportunity, but you had to work for it, sweat for it, sacrifice for its bounty. Ramsey had no patience for people's excuses for not getting ahead. He had been born to abysmal poverty and an abusive, hard-drinking father. Ramsey had found no refuge with his mother; his father had crushed any maternal instincts she might have had. Not a promising start in life, and look where he now stood. If he could survive and flourish under those circumstances, then others could too. And if they didn't it was their fault, and he would not hear otherwise.

He let out a contented sigh. Another Court term had just begun. Things were going smoothly. But there was one hitch. A chain was only as strong as its weakest leak. And he had one of those. His potential Waterloo. Things might be going well now, but what about five years down the road? Those problems were better dealt with early on, before they surged out of control.

He knew he was close to meeting his match with Elizabeth Knight. She was as smart as he, and just as tough, perhaps. He had known this the day her nomination had been approved. A young-blood female on a court of old men. He had been working on her from day one. He would assign her opinions when he thought she was on the fence, with the hope that the responsibility of penning a draft that would bring together a majority would put her firmly in his camp. He had tried to place her under his wing, to guide her through the intricacies of the Court process. Still, she had shown a very stubborn independent streak. He had watched other chief justices grow complacent, let their guard down, with the result that their leadership had been usurped by others more diligent. Ramsey was determined never to join that group.

"Murphy's concerned about the *Chance* case," Michael Fiske said to Sara Evans. They were in her office on the second floor of the Court building. Michael was six-two and handsome, with the graceful proportions of the athlete he once was. Most clerks did a one-year stint at the Supreme Court before moving on to prestigious positions in private practice, public service or academia. Michael was beginning an almost unprecedented third year here as senior clerk to Justice Thomas Murphy, the Court's legendary liberal.

Michael was the possessor of a truly wondrous mind. His brain was like a money-sorting machine: Data poured into his head and was swiftly sorted and sent to its proper location. He could mentally juggle dozens of complex factual scenarios, testing each to see how it would impact on the others. At the Court he happily labored over cases of national importance, surrounded with mental sabers equal to his own. And Michael had found that, even in the context of rigorous intellectual discourse, there was time and opportunity for something deeper than what the stark words of a law proclaimed. He really didn't want to leave the Supreme Court. The outside world held no appeal for him.

Sara looked concerned. Last term, Murphy had voted to hear the *Chance* case. Oral argument was set, and the bench memo was being prepared. Sara was in her mid-twenties, about five-five, slender, but her body possessed subtle curves. Her face was nicely shaped, the eyes wide and blue. Her hair was thick and light brown — it still turned blondish in the summer — and seemed always to carry a fresh, pleasing scent. She was the senior clerk for Justice Elizabeth Knight. "I don't understand. I thought he was behind us on this. It's right up his alley. Little person against a big bureaucracy."

"He's also a firm believer in upholding precedent."

"Even if it's wrong?"

"You're preaching to the choir, Sara, but I thought I'd pass it along. Knight's not going to get five votes without him, you know that. Even with him she might fall short."

"Well, what does he want?"

This was how it went most of the time. The famed clerk network. They hustled and debated and scrounged for votes on behalf of their justices like the most shameless political hucksters. It was beneath the justices to openly lobby for votes, for a particular phrasing in an opinion, or for a specific angle, addition or deletion, but it wasn't below the clerks. In fact, most of them took great pride in the process. It was akin to an enormous, never-ending gossip column with national interests at stake. In the hands of twenty-five-year-olds at their first real job, no less.

"He doesn't necessarily disagree with Knight's position. But if she gets five votes at conference, the opinion will have to be very narrowly drawn. He's not going to give away the farm. He was in the military in World War II. He holds it in the highest regard. He believes it deserves special consideration. You need to know that when you're putting together the draft opinion."

She nodded her head in appreciation. The backgrounds of the justices played more of a role in their decision making than most people would suspect. "Thanks. But first

Knight has to get the opinion to write."

"Of course she will. Ramsey is not voting to overturn *Feres* and *Stanley*, you know that. Murphy will probably vote in favor of Chance at the conference. He's the senior associate, so he gets to assign the opinion. If she gets her five votes at conference, he'll give Knight her shot. If she delivers the goods — meaning no broad, sweeping language — we're all okay."

United States v. Chance was one of the most important cases on the docket for this term. Barbara Chance had been a private in the Army. She had been bullied, harassed and frightened into repeatedly having sexual intercourse with several of her male superiors. The case had gone through the internal channels of the Army with the result that one of the men had been court-martialed and imprisoned. Barbara Chance, however, had not been content with that. After leaving the military, she had sued the Army for damages, claiming that it had allowed this hostile environment to exist for her and other female recruits.

The case had slowly worked its way through the proper legal channels, Chance losing at each stop. The matter presented enough gray areas in the law that it had eventually been plopped like a big tuna on the doorstep of this place.

The current law said that Chance had, ironically, no chance of winning. The military was virtually immune from suit by its personnel for any damages, regardless of the cause or the element of fault. But the justices could change what the law said. And Knight and Sara Evans were working hard behind the scenes to do just that. The support of Thomas Murphy was critical to that plan. Murphy might not support overturning completely the military's immunity right, but the Chance case could at least punch a hole in the Army's wall of invincibility.

It seemed premature to be discussing resolution of a case that had not yet been heard, but in many cases and for many justices, oral argument was anticlimactic. By the time it rolled around, most had already made up their minds. The argument phase of the process was more an opportunity for the justices to showcase their positions and concerns to their colleagues, often by use of extreme hypotheticals. They were akin to mental scare tactics, as if to say, "See what could happen, Brother Justice, if you vote that way?"

Michael stood and looked down at her. It was at his urging that Sara had signed up for another term at the Court. Raised on a small farm in North Carolina and educated at Stanford, Sara had, like all the clerks here, a wonderful professional future waiting once she left the Court. Having a clerkship at the Supreme Court on one's résumé was a gold key to entry at just about anyplace an attorney would care to put down his briefcase. That had affected some clerks in a negative way, giving them inflated egos that their actual accomplishments did not quite back up. Michael and Sara, though, had remained the same people they had always been. Which was one reason, aside from her intelligence, good looks and refreshingly balanced personality, that Michael had asked her a very important question a week ago. A question he hoped to receive an answer to soon. Perhaps now. He had never been a particularly patient man.

Sara looked up at him expectantly.

"Have you given my question any thought?"

She had known it was coming. She had avoided it long enough. "That's all I've been thinking about."

"They say when it takes that long, it's a bad sign." He said this jokingly, but the humor was obviously forced.

"Michael, I like you a lot."

"*Like?* Oh boy, another bad sign." His face suddenly grew warm.

She shook her head. "I'm sorry."

He shrugged. "Probably not half as sorry as I am. I've never asked anyone to marry me before."

"You're actually my first too. And I can't tell you how flattered I am. You've got it all."

"Except for one thing." Michael looked down at his hands as they quivered a bit. His skin suddenly seemed too tight for his body. "I respect your decision. I'm not one of those who thinks you can learn to love someone over time. It's either there or not."

"You'll find someone, Michael. And that woman will be very lucky." Sara felt so awkward. "I hope this doesn't mean I'm losing my best friend on the Court."

"Probably." He held up a hand as she started to protest. "I'm just kidding." He sighed. "I don't mean this to sound egotistical, but this is the first time anybody's really turned me down for anything."

"I wish my life had been so easy." Sara smiled.

"No, you don't. It makes rejection a lot harder to accept." Michael went over to the doorway. "We're still friends, Sara. You're too much fun to be around. I'm too smart to let that go. And you'll find someone too, and he'll be very lucky." He didn't look at her when he added, "Have you found him yet, by the way?"

She started slightly. "Why do you ask that?"

"Call it a sixth sense. Losing is a little easier to accept if you know who you lost out to."

"There's no one else," she said quickly.

Michael didn't look convinced. "Talk to you later."

Sara stared after him, very troubled.

"I remember my first years on the Court." Ramsey was staring out the window, a smile working across his face.

He was seated across from Elizabeth Knight, the Court's most junior associate. Elizabeth Knight was in her mid-forties, average height, with a slender body, and long black hair tied back in a harsh, unflattering bun. Her face possessed sharply edged features, and her skin was unlined, as though she never spent any time outdoors. Knight had quickly established a reputation as one of the most vocal questioners at oral argument and as one of the most hardworking of all the justices.

"I'm sure they're still vivid." Knight leaned back in her desk chair as she mentally checked off her work schedule for the rest of the day.

"It was quite a *learning* process."

She stared at him. He was now looking directly at her, his large hands clasped behind his head.

"It took me five years just to figure out things, really," Ramsey continued.

Knight managed not to smile. "Harold, you're being much too modest. I'm sure you had it all figured out before you walked in the door."

"Seriously, it does take time. And I had

many fine examples with whom to work. Felix Abernathy, old Tom Parks. Respecting the experience of others is nothing to be ashamed of. It's an indoctrination process we all go through. Though you certainly have progressed faster than most," he quickly added. "Still, here, patience is a very cherished virtue indeed. You've been here only three years. I've called this place home for over twenty. I hope you understand my point."

Knight hid a smile. "I understand you are a little perturbed that I led the way for *U.S. v. Chance* to be put on the docket at the end of the last term."

Ramsey sat up straight. "Don't believe everything you hear around here."

"On the contrary, I've found the clerk grapevine to be extraordinarily accurate."

Ramsey sat back once more. "Well, I have to admit that I was a little surprised about it. The case presents no unsettled question of law that requires our intervention. Need I say more?" He threw up his hands.

"In your opinion?"

A tinge of red eased across Ramsey's face. "In the published opinions of this Court over the last fifty years. All I ask is that you accord the Court's precedents the respect they deserve."

"You'll find no one who holds this institution in higher regard than I do."

"Very happy to hear that."

"And I'll be delighted to entertain your thoughts further on the *Chance* case after we hear oral argument."

Ramsey looked at her dully. "It will be a very short discussion, considering that it doesn't take long to say yes or no. Bluntly speaking, at the end of the day, I'll have at least five votes and you won't."

"Well, I convinced three other justices to vote to hear the case."

Ramsey looked as though he might laugh. "You'll quickly learn that the difference between votes to hear a case and votes to decide it is enormous. Rest assured, I will have the majority."

Knight smiled pleasantly. "Your confidence is inspiring. That I *can* learn from."

Ramsey rose to leave. "Then consider this other lesson: Small mistakes tend to lead to large ones. Ours is a lifetime appointment, and all you have is your reputation. Once it's gone, it doesn't come back." Ramsey went to the door. "I wish you a productive day, Beth," he said before leaving her.

CHAPTER THREE

"Rufus?" Samuel Rider cautiously pressed the phone to his ear. "How did you track me down?"

"Ain't many lawyers up these parts, Samuel," Rufus Harms said.

"I'm not in the JAG anymore."

"Being on the outside pays good, I guess."

"Some days I miss the uniform," Rider lied. He had been a terrified draftee, fortunately with a law degree in hand, and had chosen a safe role in the Judge Advocate General's Office — or JAG — over toting a gun through the jungles of Vietnam as a pudgy, fear-soaked GI, a sure beacon for enemy fire.

"I need to see you. Don't want to say why over the phone."

"Everything okay up at Fort Jackson? I heard you were transferred there."

"Sure. Prison's just fine."

"I didn't mean that, Rufus. I was just wondering why you looked me up after all this time."

"You're still my lawyer, ain't you? Only time I ever needed one."

"My schedule's kind of tight, and I don't usually travel over that way." Rider's hand tightened on the phone with Harms's next words.

"I really need to see you tomorrow, Samuel. You think you owe me that?"

"I did all I could for you back then."

"You took the deal. Quick and easy."

"No," Rider countered, "we did the pre-trial agreement with the convening authority, and the trial counsel signed off on it, and that was the smart thing to do."

"You didn't really try to beat it none on the sentencing. Most try to do that."

"Who told you that?"

"Learn a lot in prison."

"Well, you can't waive the sentencing phase. We put on our case to the members, you know that."

"But you didn't call no witnesses, didn't really do much that I could see."

Rider now got very defensive. "I did the best I could. Remember something, Rufus, they could've executed you. A little white girl and all. They would've gone for first degree, they told me that. At least you got to live."

"Tomorrow, Samuel. I put you on my visitors' list. Around about nine A.M. Thank you. Thank you kindly. Oh, bring a little radio with you." Before Rider could ask him why he should bring such a device, or why he should even come to see him, Harms had hung up the phone.

Rider eased back in his very comfortable

chair and looked around his spacious, wood-paneled office. He practiced law in a small rural town some distance from Blacksburg, Virginia. He made a fine living: nice house, new Buick every three years, vacations twice annually. He had put the past behind him, particularly the most horrible case he had ever handled in his brief career as a military lawyer. The kind of case that had the same effect on your stomach as curdled milk, only no amount of Pepto-Bismol could right the discomfort.

Rider touched a hand to his face as his thoughts now drifted back to the early seventies, a time of chaos in the military, the country, the world. Everybody blaming everybody else for everything that had ever gone wrong in the history of the universe. Rufus Harms had sounded bitter over the phone, but he *had* killed that little girl. Brutally. Right in front of her family. Crushed her neck in a few seconds, before anyone could even attempt to stop him.

On Harms's behalf, Rider had negotiated a pretrial agreement, but then, under the rules of military law, he had the right to attempt to beat that deal in the sentencing phase. The defendant would either receive the punishment in the pretrial agreement, or the one meted out by the judge or by the members — the military counterpart of a jury — whichever involved less prison time. Harms's words gnawed at the lawyer, though, for Rider had been persuaded at the time not to put on much of a case at the sentencing phase. He had agreed with the prosecutor not to bring in any witnesses from outside the area who could attest to Harms's character and so forth. He had also agreed to rely on stipulations from the official record instead of attempting to find fresh evidence and witnesses.

That was not exactly playing by the rules, because a defendant's right to beat the deal was not supposed to be waived or bargained away in any substantive manner. But without Rider working behind the scenes like that, the prosecutor would have gone for the death penalty, and with those facts, he probably would have gotten it. It mattered little that the murder had happened so quickly that proving premeditation would have been very difficult. The cold body of a child could derail the most logical of legal analyses.

The bald truth was nobody cared about Rufus Harms. He was a black man who had spent most of his Army career locked in the stockade. His senseless murder of a child certainly had not improved his standing in the eyes of the military. Such a man was not entitled to justice, many had felt, unless it was swift, painful, and lethal. And maybe Rider was one of those who felt that way. So he hadn't exactly practiced the scorched-earth policy in his defense of the man, but Rider had gotten Rufus Harms life. That was the best any lawyer could have done.

So what could Rufus want to see him about? he wondered.

CHAPTER FOUR

As John Fiske rose from the counsel's table he glanced over at his opponent, Paul Williams. The young assistant commonwealth attorney, or ACA, had just finished confidently stating the particulars of his motion. Fiske whispered, "Your ass is grass, Paulie. You messed up."

When Fiske turned to face Judge Walters, his manner was one of subdued excitement. Fiske was broad-shouldered, though at six feet he was a couple of inches shorter than his younger brother. And unlike Michael Fiske, his features were far from classically handsome. He had chubby cheeks, a too-sharp chin and a twice-broken nose, one time from high school wrestling, the other time a carryover from his cop days. However, Fiske's black hair was swept over his forehead in an unkempt manner that somehow managed to be attractive and intimate, and his brown eyes housed an intense core.

"Your Honor, in the interest of not wasting the court's time, I would like to make an offer in open court to the Commonwealth Attorney's Office regarding its motion. If they agree to withdraw with prejudice and contribute one thousand dollars to the public defender's fund, I will withdraw my response, not file for sanctions and we can all go home."

Paul Williams leaped to his feet so quickly his eyeglasses fell off and hit the table. "Your Honor, this is outrageous!"

Judge Walters looked over his crowded courtroom, silently contemplated his equally bulging docket and flicked a weary hand at both men. "Approach."

At the sidebar, Fiske said, "Judge, I'm only trying to do the commonwealth a favor."

"The commonwealth doesn't need favors from Mr. Fiske," Williams said with disgust.

"Come on, Paulie, a thousand bucks, and you can get a beer before you go back and explain to your boss how you messed up. I'll even buy you the beer."

"Not in ten thousand years will you get a dime from us," Williams said disdainfully.

"Well, Mr. Williams, this motion is a little unusual," Judge Walters said. In the Richmond criminal courts, motions were heard before or during trial. And there weren't lengthy briefs attached to them. The sad truth was, most issues of criminal law were well settled. Only in the unusual case in which the judge was unsure of a ruling after he had heard the lawyers' oral arguments would he ask for written briefs to review before making his decision. Thus, Judge

Walters was a little bewildered by the unsolicited and lengthy brief filed by the commonwealth.

"I know, Your Honor," said Williams. "However, as I stated, this is an unusual situation."

"Unusual?" Fiske said. "Try nuts, Paulie."

Judge Walters impatiently broke in. "Mr. Fiske, I have admonished you before regarding your unorthodox behavior in my courtroom, and I will not hesitate to find you in contempt if your future actions warrant it. Get on with your response."

Williams returned to his seat and Fiske stepped to the lectern. "Your Honor, in spite of the fact that the commonwealth's 'emergency' motion was faxed to my office in the middle of the night and I haven't had time to prepare a truly proper response, I believe that if you would refer to each of the second paragraphs on pages four, six and nine of the commonwealth's memorandum, you will conclude that the facts relied upon therein, particularly with regard to the defendant's prior criminal record, the statements of the arresting officers and the two eyewitness accounts at the location of the crime allegedly committed by my client, are unsustainable with the established record in this case. Further, the principal precedent cited by the commonwealth on page ten was very recently overturned by a decision of the Virginia

Supreme Court. I've attached the pertinent materials to my response and highlighted the discrepancies for your ease of review."

As Judge Walters examined the file in front of him, Fiske leaned over to Williams and said, "See what happens when you draft this shit in the middle of the night?" Fiske dropped his reply brief in front of Williams. "Since I only had about five minutes to read your brief, I thought I'd return the favor. You can read along with the judge."

Walters finished reviewing the file and gave Williams a stare that chilled even the most casual observer in the courtroom.

"I hope the commonwealth has an appropriate response to this, Mr. Williams, although I'm at a loss as to what it could possibly be."

Williams rose from his chair. As he tried to speak, he suddenly discovered that his voice, along with his hubris, had deserted him.

"Well?" Judge Walters said expectantly. "Please say something or I've a mind to grant Mr. Fiske's motion for sanctions before I've even heard it."

When Fiske glanced over at Williams, his expression softened somewhat. You never knew when you might need a favor. "Your Honor, I'm certain the factual and legal errors in the commonwealth's motion are due to the overworked lawyers there rather than anything intentional. I'll even cut my settlement offer to five hundred dollars, but I'd like a personal apology from the commonwealth on the record. I really could've used some sleep last night." That last comment brought laughter from around the courtroom.

Suddenly a voice boomed out from the back of the courtroom. "Judge Walters, if I may intercede, the commonwealth will accept that offer."

Everyone looked at the source of the announcement, a short, almost bald, thick-bodied man dressed in a seersucker suit, his hairy neck pinched by his starchy collar. "We'll take the offer," the man said again in a gravelly voice laced with both the pleasing drawl of a lifelong Virginian and the rasp of a lifelong smoker. "And we do apologize to the *court* for taking up its valuable time."

"I'm glad you happened by when you did, Mr. Graham," Judge Walters said.

Bobby Graham, commonwealth attorney for the city of Richmond, nodded curtly before leaving through the double glass doors. He had offered no apology to Fiske; however, the defense lawyer chose not to push it. In a court of law, you rarely got everything you asked for.

Judge Walters said, "Commonwealth's motion is dismissed with prejudice." He looked at Williams. "Mr. Williams, I think you should go have that beer with Mr. Fiske, only I think you should be the one doing the buying, son."

As the next motion was called, Fiske snapped shut his briefcase and walked out of the courtroom, Williams right next to him.

"Should've taken my first offer, Paulie."

"I won't forget this, Fiske," Williams said angrily.

"Don't."

"We're still going to put Jerome Hicks away," Williams sneered. "Don't think we're not."

For Paulie Williams and most of the other assistant commonwealth attorneys Fiske faced, Fiske knew his clients were like their personal, lifelong enemies, undeserving of anything other than the harshest of punishments. In some cases, Fiske knew, they were right. But not in all.

"You know what I'm thinking?" Fiske asked Williams. "I'm thinking how fast ten thousand years can go by."

As Fiske left the third-floor courtroom, he passed police officers he had worked with when he was a Richmond cop. One of them smiled, nodded a hello, but the others refused to look at him. To them he was a traitor to the ranks, suit and briefcase traded for badge and gun. Mouthpiece for the other side. Rot in hell, Brother Fiske.

Fiske looked at one group of young black men, crewcuts so severe they looked bald, pants pushed down to the crotch, boxers showing, puffy gang jackets, bulky tennies with no laces. Their open defiance of the criminal justice system was clear; they were imperiously sulky in their sameness.

These young men crowded around their attorney, a white guy, office-chunky, sweaty, expensive pinstripe soiled at the cuffs, slick-skinned loafers on his feet, horn-rim glasses twisting a little as he hammered home a point to his scout troop. He banged his fist into his meaty palm as the young black men, abdominals racked under their silk drug-trove shirts, listened intently, the only time they figured they would need this man, would bother to even look at him other than with contempt, or through a gun sight. Until the next time they needed him. And they would. In this building, he was magic. Here Michael Jordan could not touch this white man. They were Lewis and Clark. He was their Sacajewea. Shout the mystical words, Sac. Don't let them do us.

Fiske knew what the suit was saying, knew it as if he could read the man's lips. The man specialized in defending gang members on any crime they cared to commit. The best strategy: stone silence. Seen nothing, heard nothing, remembered nothing. Gunshots? Car backfire, most likely. Remember this, boys: Thou Shalt not kill; but if thou Shalt kill, thou Shalt not rat on each other about it. He smacked his palm against his briefcase for added emphasis. The huddle broke and the game commenced.

Along another part of the hallway, sitting on the boxy gray-carpeted seating built into the wall, were three hookers, working teens of the night. A variety pack: one black, one Asian, one white, they waited their turn before justice. The Asian looked nervous, probably needing a calming smoke or the sting of a needle. The others were vets, Fiske knew. They strolled, sat, showed some thigh, the jiggle of breast occasionally when some good old boys or young turks prowled by. Why miss some business over a little court thing? This was America, after all.

Fiske took the elevator down and was just passing by the metal detector and X-ray machine, standard equipment in virtually every courthouse these days, when Bobby Graham approached him, an unlit cigarette in his hand. Fiske liked the man neither personally nor professionally. Graham selected cases for prosecution based on the size of the headlines they would garner for him. And he never took on a case he would have to work real hard to win. The public doesn't like prosecutors who lose.

"Just a little pretrial motion in a dime-a-dozen case. The big man has better things to do with his time, don't you, Bobby?" said Fiske.

"Maybe I had an inkling that you were going to chew up and spit out one of my baby lawyers. It wouldn't have been so easy if you'd been up against a real attorney."

"Who, like you?"

With a wry smile, Graham put the unlit cigarette in his mouth. "Here we are, living in arguably the damned tobacco capital of the world, the biggest cigarette manufacturing facility on the planet just a spit on down the road, and one can't even smoke in the halls of justice." He chewed on the end of his unfiltered Pall Mall, noisily sucking in the nicotine. Actually there were still designated smoking areas in the Richmond court building, only not where Graham happened to be standing.

The prosecutor let slip a triumphant grin. "Oh, by the way, Jerome Hicks was picked up this morning on suspicion of murdering a guy over on Southside. Black on black, drugs involved. Wow, what a surprise. Apparently he wanted to increase his inventory of coke and didn't want to go through the normal acquisition channels. Only your guy didn't know we had his target staked out."

Fiske wearily leaned up against the wall. Court victories were often empty, particularly when your client couldn't keep a lid on his felonious impulses. "Really? That's the first I've heard about it."

"I was coming down here anyway for a pre-trial conference, thought I'd fill you in. Professional courtesy."

"Right," Fiske said dryly. "If that's the case, why did you let Paulie's motion go forward?" When Graham didn't respond, Fiske answered his own question. "Just making me jump through the hoops?"

"A man's got to have some fun with his work."

Fiske balled up a fist, and then just as quickly he uncurled it. Graham wasn't worth it. "Well, as a professional courtesy, were there any eyewitnesses?"

"Oh, about a half dozen, murder weapon found in Jerome's car, along with Jerome. He almost ran down two policemen trying to get away. We've got blood, the drugs, the whole candy store, really. Guy shouldn't have been granted bail in the first place. Anyway, I've a mind to drop this rinky-dink distribution charge you're representing him on and just focus on this new development. Got to maximize my scarce resources. Hicks is a bad one, John. I think we're gonna have to seek a capital murder indictment on this one."

"Capital case? Come on, Bobby."

"The willful, deliberate and premeditated killing of any person in the commission of a robbery equals capital murder equals death penalty. At least that's what my Virginia statute book says."

"I don't give a shit what the law says, he's only eighteen years old."

Graham's face tensed. "Funny talk coming from a lawyer, an officer of the court."

"The law's a sieve I have to slip my facts through, because my facts always suck."

"They're scum. Come out of the womb looking to hurt people. We oughta start building baby prisons before the sonsof-bitches can really hurt anybody."

"Jerome Hicks's entire life can be summed up —"

"Right, blame it on his piss-poor child-hood," Graham interrupted. "Same old story."

"That's right, *same* old story."

Graham smiled and shook his head. "Look, I didn't grow up with a silver spoon in my mouth, okay? Wanta know my secret? I worked my ass off. If I can do it, they damn well can too. Case closed."

Fiske started to walk off and then looked back. "Let me take a look at the arrest report and I'll call you."

"We got nothing to talk about."

"Killing him won't get you the AG slot, Bobby, you know that. Aim higher." Fiske turned and walked away.

Graham twisted the cigarette between his fingers. "Try getting a real job, Fiske."

A half hour later, John Fiske was at a suburban county jail meeting with one of his clients. His practice often took him outside of Richmond, to the counties of Henrico, Chesterfield, Hanover, even Goochland. His ever-expanding pool of work was not something he was particularly pleased about, but it was like the sun rising. It would continue until the day it stopped for good.

"I've got a plea to talk to you about, Derek."

Derek Brown — or DB1, as he was known on the street — was a light-skinned black, with tattoos of hate, obscenity and poetry running down his arms. He spent enough time in jail to be buffed; wormy veins split his biceps. Fiske had once seen Derek playing basketball in the jail's recreation yard, shirt off, well muscled, more tattoos on his back and shoulders. It looked like a damn musical score from a distance. Rising from the air like a jet on takeoff, gliding smooth, held up by something Fiske couldn't see, the guards and other cons turning to look in admiration, the young man slammed the ball home, finishing with high-fives all around. Never good enough, though, to play college ball, much less NBA. So here they were looking at each other in the county lockup.

"ACA's offered malicious wounding, Class Three felony."

"Why not Class Six?"

Fiske stared at him. These guys were in and out of the criminal system so often they knew the criminal code better than most lawyers.

"Class Six is heat of the moment. Your heat came the next day."

"He had a gun. I ain't going up against Pack when he got his shooter and I ain't got mine. What, you stupid?"

Fiske wanted to reach across and wipe the man's attitude right off his face. "Sorry, the Commonwealth isn't budging from Class Three."

"How much time?" Derek said stonily. His ears were pierced, by Fiske's count twelve times.

"Five, with time already served."

"Bullshit. Five years for cutting somebody a little with a damn pocketknife?"

"Stiletto, six-inch blade. And you stabbed him ten damn times. In front of witnesses."

"Shit, he was feeling up my bitch. Ain't that a defense?"

"You're lucky you're not looking at murder in the first, Derek. The docs said it was a miracle the guy didn't bleed to death right there on the street. And if Pack weren't such a dangerous slimeball you wouldn't just be looking at malicious wounding either. You could've been looking at aggravated malicious wounding. That's twenty to life. You know that."

"Messing with my bitch." Derek leaned

49

forward and popped his bony knuckles to emphasize the absolute logic of both his legal and moral positions.

Derek had a good-paying job, Fiske knew, albeit an illegal one. He was a first lieutenant for the number two drug distribution ring in Richmond, hence his street name of DB1. Turbo was the boss, all of twenty-four years old. His empire was well organized, discipline enforced, and included the facade of legality with dry-cleaning operations, a café, a pawnshop, and a stable of accountants and lawyers to deal with the drug funds after they had been laundered. Turbo was a very smart young man, good head for numbers and business. Fiske had always wanted to ask him why he didn't try running a Fortune 500 company. The pay was almost as good, and the mortality rate was considerably lower.

Normally, Turbo would have one of his three-hundred-dollar-an-hour Main or Franklin Street lawyers take care of Derek. But Derek's offense was unrelated to Turbo's business, so that accommodation had not been made. Sloughing him off to someone like Fiske was a form of punishment for Derek doing something as stupid as losing his head over a female. Turbo had no reason to fear Derek's turning snitch. The prosecutor hadn't even made any noises along those lines, knowing it was futile. You talk, you die — in or out of prison, it made no difference.

Derek had grown up in a nice middle-class neighborhood, with nice middle-class parents, before he decided to drop out of high school and take the easy route of drug dealing over actually working for a living. He had every advantage, could have done anything with his life. There were just enough Derek Browns around to make the world largely apathetic to the horrific lives of the kids who turned to the sugar-elixir provided by people like Turbo. Which made Fiske want to take Derek out to an alley late at night with a baseball bat in hand and teach the young man some good old-fashioned values.

"The ACA doesn't give a damn about what he was doing to your girlfriend that night."

"I can't believe this shit. Buddy of mine cut up somebody last year and he got two years, half that suspended. Out in three months with time served. And I'm looking at five damn years? What kinda shitty lawyer are you?"

"Did your buddy have a prior felony conviction?" Was your good old buddy one of the top men for one of Richmond's worst diseases? Fiske wanted to ask, and he would have but it would be wasted breath. "I tell you what — I'll go back with three and time served."

Now Derek looked interested. "You think you can get that?"

Fiske stood up. "Don't know. I'm just a shitty lawyer."

On the way out, Fiske looked out the barred window and watched as a new shipment of inmates climbed from the prison van, grouped close, shackles beating a chant on the asphalt. Most were young blacks or Latinos, already sizing each other up. Slave to master. Who gets cut or scored first. The few whites looked as though they might drop and die from sheer panic before they even got to their cells. Some of these young men were probably the sons of men Patrolman John Fiske had arrested ten years ago. They would have been just kids then, maybe dreaming of something other than the public dole, no daddy at home, mother struggling through a horror of a life with no end in sight. Then again, maybe not. Reality had a way of punishing one's subconscious. Dreams weren't a reprieve, merely a continuation of the real-life nightmare.

As a cop, the dialogue he had had with many arrestees tended to repeat itself.

"Kill you, man. Kill your whole damn family," some would scream at him, drug-faced, as he put the cuffs on.

"Uh-huh. You have the right to remain silent. Think about using it."

"Come on, man, ain't my fault. My buddy done it. Screwed me."

"Where would that buddy be? And the

blood on your hands? The gun in your pants? The coke still in your nostrils? Buddy do all that? Some buddy."

Then they might eye the dead body and lose it, blubbering. "Holy shit! Sweet Jesus! My momma, where's my momma? You call her. Do that for me, oh shit, do that, will you? Momma! Oh shit!"

"You have the right to an attorney," he would calmly tell them.

And that now was John Fiske.

After a couple more court appearances downtown, Fiske left the glass and brick John Marshall Courts Building, named after the third chief justice of the United States Supreme Court. Marshall's ancestral home was still right next door, now a museum dedicated to preserving the memory of the great Virginian and American. The man would have turned over in his grave if he had known of the vile acts being debated and defended in the building that bore his name.

Fiske headed down Ninth Street toward the James River. Hot and humid the last few days, the weather patterns had angled cooler with the coming rain, and he pulled his trench coat tighter around him. As the rain started, he began to jog along the pavement, his shoes cleaving through puddles of filthy water collected in dips of asphalt and concrete.

By the time he reached his office in

Shockoe Slip, his hair and coat were soaked, the water running in miniature rivulets down his back. Eschewing the elevator, he took the steps two at a time and unlocked the door to his office. It was located in a cavernous building that had once been a tobacco warehouse, its oak and pine guts having been given the new ribs of multiple office drywall. The reek of the tobacco leaves forever lingered, however. And this wasn't the only place it could be found. Cruising on Interstate 95 south past the Philip Morris cigarette-manufacturing facility Bobby Graham had referred to, one could almost get a nicotine high without even lighting up. Fiske had often been tempted to fling a lighted match out the window as he drove by, to see if the air would simply explode.

Fiske's office was one room with a small attached bathroom, which was important, since he slept here more often than he did at his apartment. He hung up his coat to dry, and wiped his face and hair down with a towel he grabbed off the rack in the bath. He put on a pot of coffee and watched it brew while he thought about Jerome Hicks.

If Fiske did a superb job, Jerome Hicks would spend the rest of his life behind bars instead of receiving the prick of lethal injection at the Virginia death house. Killing an eighteen-year-old black kid would not win Graham the attorney general's job he coveted. A black-on-black, loser-on-loser murder wouldn't even warrant a back-page story in the newspaper.

As a Richmond cop, Fiske had survived, barely, the violence of combat. It swept through neighborhood and town, swelling large, like an aneurysm, the size of a county, leaving behind the shattered ghettos, and the soaring, dollar-consumed spires of down-town, flowing over, around and through the ill-conceived barricades of suburbia. And it wasn't just the commonwealth. Glaciers of criminal activity flowed from all the states. When they eventually met, then where would we go? Fiske wondered.

He abruptly sat down. The burn had started slowly at first; it usually did. He sensed its march from his belly up to his chest, then spreading. Finally, like lava in a trench, the sensation of impossible heat started down his arms and poured into his fingers. Fiske staggered up, locked his office door and stripped off his shirt and tie. He had a T-shirt on underneath; always wore the damn T-shirt. Through the cotton, his fingers touched the starting point of the thick-ened scar, after all these years still rough-edged. It began just below his navel and fol-lowed the meandering path of the surgeon's saw in an unbroken line, until it ended at the base of his neck.

Fiske dropped to the floor and did fifty

push-ups without ceasing, the heat in his chest and extremities surging and then diminishing with each repetition. A drop of sweat fell from his brow and hit the wooden floor. He thought he could see his reflection in it. At least it wasn't blood. He followed the push-ups with an equal number of stomach crunches. The scar rippled and flexed with each bend of his body, like a serpent unwillingly grafted to his torso. He attached a quick-release bar to the doorway leading to the bathroom and struggled through a dozen pull-ups. He used to be able to do twice that many, but his strength was slowly ebbing. What lurked beneath the fused skin would eventually overtake him, kill him, but, for now, the heat faded; the physical exertion seemed to frighten it off, letting the trespasser know that somebody was still home.

He cleaned up in the bathroom and put his shirt back on. As he sipped his coffee he looked out the window. From this vantage point he could barely make out the line of the James River. The water would grow rough as the rain picked up. He and his brother had often boated down the river, or leisurely floated down it in truck-tire inner tubes on hot summer days. That had been years ago. This was as close as Fiske got to the water these days. Leisure time was over. He had no space left for it in his shortened frame of life. He enjoyed what he did, though, at least most of the time. It wasn't the life of a Supreme Court superlawyer like his brother, but he took a certain pride in his job and how he did it. He would have no money or grand reputation when he died, but he believed he would die reasonably satisfied, reasonably fulfilled. He turned back to his work.

CHAPTER FIVE

Like a brooding hawk, Fort Jackson perched on the desolate topography of southwest Virginia, fairly equidistant from the Tennessee, Kentucky and West Virginia borders and in the middle of a remote scrap of coal country. There were few if any stand-alone military prisons in the United States; they were typically attached to a military facility, due both to tradition and to the constraints of defense dollars. Fort Jackson did have a military base component; however, the dominant feature of the place would always be the prison, where the most dangerous offenders in the United States Army silently counted down their lives.

There had never been an escape from Fort Jackson, and even if an inmate could manage to achieve his freedom without benefit of a court ruling, such liberty would be empty and short-lived. The surrounding countryside represented a prison of even greater menace, with jagged-faced, strip-mined mountains, treacherous roads with widowmaker drops, dense, unyielding forest laced with copperheads and rattlers. And along the polluted waterways awaited their more aggressive cousin, the water moccasin, anxious for panicked feet crashing its border. And the self-reliant local folk in the forgotten "toe" of Virginia — the human equivalent of razor wire — were well schooled with the gun and the knife, and unafraid to use either. And yet in the slope of the land, the breadth of forest, shrub and flower, the scent of unhurried wildlife and the quiet of ocean depths, there was much beauty here.

Attorney Samuel Rider passed through the fort's main gate, received his visitor's badge and parked his car in the visitors' lot. He nervously walked up to the flat, stone-walled entrance of the prison, his briefcase lightly tapping against his blue-clothed leg. It took him twenty minutes to go through the screening procedure, which included producing personal identification, verifying that he was on the visitors' list, a pat-down of his person, walking through a metal detector and ending with a search of his briefcase. The guards suspiciously eyed the small transistor radio, but allowed him to keep it after confirming that it contained no contraband. He was read the standard rules of visitation and to each he gave an affirmative, audible reply that he understood. Rider knew that were he to run afoul of any of these rules, the guard's polite facade would quickly disappear.

He looked around, unable to shake the oppression of fear, of extreme nervousness, as though the prison's architect had managed to craft these elements into the bones of the place. Rider's bowels clenched, and his palms were sweaty, like he was about to climb on a twenty-seat turboprop in the face of a hurricane. As a member of the military during Vietnam, Rider had never left the country, never come close to combat, to mortal danger. Damn ironic if he were to drop dead from a coronary while standing in a military prison on United States soil. He took a deep breath, mentally signaled his heart to calm down, and wondered again why he had come. Rufus Harms was in no position to make him, or anyone else, do anything. But here he was. Rider took another deep breath, clipped on his visitor's badge and gripped the comforting handle of his briefcase, his leather amulet, as a guard escorted him to the visitors' room.

Alone for a few minutes, Rider eyed the dull brown of the walls that seemed designed to depress further those who probably already lived in the throes of near-suicidal intent. He wondered how many men called this place home, entombed by their fellow man and with excellent reason. And yet they all had mothers, even the vilest among them; some, Rider assumed, even had fathers, beyond the stain of semen on egg. And still, they ended up here. Born evil? Maybe so. Probably have a genetic test soon that'll tell you if your preschooler is the second coming of Ted Bundy, Rider thought. But when they drop the bad news on you, then what the hell do you do?

Rider stopped his musings as Rufus Harms, towering over the two guards trailing him, entered the visitors' room. The quick image was that of the lord to his serfs, reality the reverse of that. Harms was the largest man Rider had ever personally encountered, a giant possessed of truly abnormal strength. Even now he seemed to fill up the room with his bulk. His chest was two slabs of rebarred concrete hung side by side, arms thicker than some trees. Harms wore shackles on both his hands and feet that forced him to do the "prison shuffle." He was accomplished at it, though; the shortened strides were graceful.

He must be close to fifty, Rider thought, but actually looked a good ten years older; he noted the facial scars, the awkward twist of bone beneath Harms's right eye. The young man Rider had represented was the owner of fine, even handsome features. Rider wondered how often Rufus had been beaten in here, what other telling evidence of abuse he carried under his clothing.

Harms sat down across from Rider at a wooden table heavily scored by thousands of nervous, desperate fingernails. He didn't look at Rider just yet, but instead eyed the guard, who remained in the room.

Rider caught Harms's silent meaning and said to the guard, "Private, I'm his lawyer, so you're going to have to give us some space here."

The reply was automatic. "This is a maximum-security prison facility and every prisoner here is classified as violent and dangerous. I'm here for your safety."

The men here *were* dangerous, both prisoners *and* guards, and that was just the way things were, Rider knew.

"I understand that," replied the lawyer. "I'm not asking you to abandon me, but I'd be obliged if you could stand farther away. Attorney-client privilege — you understand, don't you?"

The guard didn't answer, but he did move to the far end of the room, ostensibly out of earshot. Finally, Rufus Harms looked over at Rider. "You bring the radio?"

"A strange request, but one that I honored."

"Take it out and turn it on, would you?"

Rider did so. The room was immediately filled with the mournful tunes of country-western music, the lyrics contrived, shallow in the face of the genuine misery sensed at this place, Rider thought uncomfortably.

When the lawyer looked at him questioningly, Harms glanced around the room. "Lotta ears around this place, some you can't see, right?"

"Bugging the conversations of an attorney and his client is against the law."

Harms moved his hands slightly, chains rattling. "Lot of things against the law, but people still do 'em. Both in and out of this place. Right?"

Rider found himself nodding. Harms was no longer a young, scared kid. He was a man. A man in control despite being unable to control one single element of his existence. Rider also observed that each of Harms's physical movements was measured, calculated; like he was engaging in chess, reaching out slowly to touch a piece, and then drawing back with equal caution. Here, swift motion could be deadly.

The inmate leaned forward and started speaking in a tone so low that Rider had to strain to hear him above the music. "I thank you for coming. I'm surprised you did."

"Surprised the hell out of me to hear from you. But I guess it got my curiosity up too."

"You look good. The years have been kind to you."

Rider had to laugh. "I lost all my hair and put on fifty pounds, but thank you anyway."

"I won't waste your time. I got something I want you to file in court for me."

Rider's astonishment was clear. "What court?"

Harms spoke in even lower tones, despite

the cover of the music. "Biggest one there is. Supreme Court."

Rider's jaw went slack. "You got to be kidding." The look in Harms's eyes would not brook such a conclusion. "Okay, what exactly do you want me to file?"

With smooth increments of motion, despite the restraints of the manacles, Harms slid an envelope out of his shirt and held it up. In an instant, the guard stepped across and snatched it from his hand.

Rider protested immediately. "Private, that is a confidential attorney-client communication."

"Let him read it, Samuel, I got nothing to hide," Harms said evenly, eyes staring off.

The guard opened the envelope and scanned the contents of the letter. Satisfied, he returned it to Harms and resumed his post across the room.

Harms handed the envelope and letter across to Rider, who looked down at the material. When he looked back up, Harms was leaning even closer to him, and he spoke for at least ten minutes. Several times Rider's eyes widened as Harms's words spilled over him. Finished, the prisoner sat back and looked at him.

"You going to help me, ain't you?"

Rider could not answer, apparently still digesting all that he had heard. If the waist chain had not prevented such a movement,

Harms would have reached out and put his hand over Rider's, not in a threatening manner, but as a tangible plea for help from a man who had experienced none for almost thirty years. "Ain't you, Samuel?"

Finally, Rider nodded. "I'll help you, Rufus."

Harms rose and headed for the door.

Rider put the paper back in the envelope and tucked it and the radio away in his briefcase. The lawyer had no way of knowing that on the other side of a large mirror that hung on the wall of the visitors' room, someone had watched the entire exchange between prisoner and attorney. This person now rubbed his chin, lost in deep, troubled thought.

CHAPTER SIX

At ten A.M., the marshal of the Supreme Court, Richard Perkins, dressed in charcoal-gray tails, the traditional Supreme Court dress of lawyers from the Solicitor General's Office as well, stood up at one end of the massive bench, behind which sat nine high-backed leather chairs of various styles and sizes, and pounded his gavel. The packed courtroom grew silent. "The Honorable, the Chief Justice, and the Associate Justices of the United States," Perkins announced.

The long burgundy-colored curtain behind the bench parted at nine different places, and there appeared a like number of justices looking stiff and uncomfortable in their black robes, as though startled awake and discovering a crowd next to their beds. As they took their seats, Perkins continued. "Oyez, oyez, oyez. All persons having business before the Honorable, the Supreme Court of the United States, are admonished to draw near and give their attention, for the Court is now sitting. God save the United States and this honorable Court."

Perkins sat down and looked out over a courtroom with the square footage of a mansion. Its forty-four-foot ceiling made the eye look for drifting clouds. After some preliminary business and the ceremonial swearing in of new Supreme Court Bar members, the first of the day's two morning cases would be called. On this day, a Wednesday, only two cases during the morning would be heard, afternoon sessions being held only on Monday and Tuesday. No oral arguments were held on Thursday and Friday. On it would go, three days a week every two weeks, until the end of April, approximately one hundred and fifty oral argument sessions later, the justices assuming the modern-day role of Solomon for the people of the United States.

There were impressive friezes on either side of the courtroom. On the right were figures of lawgivers of the pre-Christian era. On the left, their counterparts of the Christian period. Two armies ready to have go at each other. Perhaps to determine who had gotten it right. Moses versus Napoleon, Hammurabi against Muhammad. The law, the handing down of justice, could be damn painful — bloody, even. Right above the bench were two figures carved in marble, one depicting the majesty of the law, the other the power of government. Between the two panels was a tableau of the Ten Commandments. Swirling around the vast chamber like flocks of doves were carvings — Safeguard of the Rights of

People, Genii of Wisdom and Statecraft, Defense of Human Rights — representing the role of the Court. If there ever was a stage of perfect proportion for the hearing of matters paramount, it seemed that this landscape represented it. However, topography could be deceiving.

Ramsey sat in the middle of the bench, Elizabeth Knight at the extreme right. A boom microphone was suspended from the middle of the ceiling. The moms and pops in the audience had noticeably tensed up when the justices appeared. Even their gangly, bored kids sat a little straighter. It was understandable enough even for those barely familiar with the reputation of this place. There was a discernible feeling of raw power, of important confrontations to come.

These nine black-robed justices told women when they could legally abort their fetuses; dictated to schoolchildren where they would do their learning; proclaimed what speech was obscene or not; pronounced that police could not unreasonably search and seize, or beat confessions out of people. No one elected them to their positions. They held their positions for life against virtually all challenge. And the justices operated in such levels of secrecy, in such a black hole, that it made the public personae of other venerable federal institutions seem vainglorious by comparison. They routinely confronted issues that had activist groups all over the country banging heads, bombing abortion clinics, demonstrating outside prison death houses. They judged the complex issues that would bedevil human civilization until its extinction. And they looked so calm.

The first case was called. It dealt with affirmative action in public universities — or, rather, what was left of the concept. Frank Campbell, the counsel arguing on behalf of affirmative action, barely got through his first sentence before Ramsey pounced.

The chief justice pointed out that the Fourteenth Amendment unequivocally stated that no one shall be discriminated against. Didn't that mean affirmative action of any sort was impermissible under the Constitution?

"But there are broad wrongs that are trying to be —"

"Why does diversity equate with equality?" Ramsey abruptly asked Campbell.

"It ensures that a broad and diverse body of students will be available to express different ideas, represent different cultures, which in turn will serve to break down the ignorance of stereotypes."

"Aren't you premising your entire argument on the fact that blacks and whites think differently? That a black raised by parents who are college professors in a well-to-do household in, say, San Francisco will bring a different set of values and ideas to a university than a white person who was raised in the exact same affluent environment in San Francisco?" Ramsey's tone was filled with skepticism.

"I think that everyone has differences," Campbell responded.

"Instead of basing it on skin color, doesn't it seem that the most impoverished among us have a greater right to a helping hand?" Justice Knight asked. Ramsey looked over at her curiously as she said this. "And yet your argument draws no distinction on wealth or lack thereof, does it?" Knight added.

"No," Campbell conceded.

Michael Fiske and Sara Evans sat in a special section of seats perpendicular to the bench. Michael glanced over at Sara as he listened to this line of questioning. She didn't look at him.

"You can't get around the letter of the law, can you? You would have us turn the Constitution on its head," Ramsey persisted after finally taking his eyes off Knight.

"How about the spirit behind those words?" Campbell rejoined.

"Spirits are such amorphous things, I much prefer to deal in concrete." Ramsey's words brought scattered laughter from the audience. The chief justice renewed his verbal attack, and with deadly precision he skewered Campbell's precedents and line of

70

reasoning. Knight said nothing more, staring straight ahead, her thoughts obviously far from the courtroom. As the red light on the counsel lectern came on indicating Campbell's time was up, he almost ran to his seat. As the counsel opposing affirmative action took his place at the lectern and began his argument, it didn't seem like the justices were even listening anymore.

"Boy, Ramsey is efficient," Sara remarked. She and Michael were in the Court's cafeteria, the justices having retired to their dining room for their traditional post-oral argument luncheon. "He sliced up the university's lawyer in about five seconds."

Michael swallowed a bite of sandwich. "He's been on the lookout for a case for the last three years to really blow affirmative action out of the water. Well, he found it. They should have settled the case before it got here."

"You really think Ramsey will go that far?"

"Are you kidding? Wait until you see the opinion. He'll probably write it himself, just so he can gloat. It's dead."

"I can partly see his logic," Sara said.

"Of course you can. It's evident. A conservative group brought the case, handpicked the plaintiff. White, bright, blue-collar, hardworking, never given a handout. And, even better, a woman."

"The Constitution does say no one shall discriminate."

"Sara, you know that the Fourteenth Amendment was passed right after the Civil War to ensure that blacks wouldn't be discriminated against. Now it's been forged into a bat to crush the people it was supposed to help. Well, the crushers just guaranteed their own Armageddon."

"What do you mean?"

"I mean that poor with hope starts to push back. Poor without hope lashes back. Not pretty."

"Oh." She looked at Michael, his manner so intense, so mercurial. Serious beyond his years. He climbed on the soapbox with regularity, sometimes to an embarrassing degree. It was one of the elements about him that she both admired and feared.

"My brother could tell you some stories about that," Michael added.

"I'm sure he could. I hope to meet him someday."

Michael glanced at her and then looked away. "Ramsey sees the world differently than it actually is. He made it in the world by himself, why can't everybody else? I admire the guy, though. He sticks it equally to the poor and the rich, the state and the individual. He doesn't play favorites. I'll give him that."

"You overcame a lot too."

"Yeah. I'm not blowing my own horn, but I've got an IQ over one-sixty. Not everybody has that."

"I know," Sara said wistfully. "My legal brain says what happened today was correct. My heart says it's a tragedy."

"Hey, this is the Supreme Court. It's not supposed to be easy. And by the way, what was Knight trying to do in there today?" Michael was perpetually in the loop on everything that happened at the Court, all the inner secrets, the gossip, the strategies employed by the justices and their clerks to further philosophies and points of view on cases before them. He felt behind on whatever Knight had alluded to in court this morning, though, and it bothered him.

"Michael, it was only a couple sentences."

"So what? Two sentences with a ton of potential. Rights for the poor? You saw the way Ramsey picked up on it. Is Knight posturing for something down the road? A case she was trying to set up in there?"

"I can't believe you're asking me that. It's confidential."

"We're all on the same team here, Sara."

"Right! How often do Knight and Murphy vote together? Not very. And this place has nine very separate compartments, you know that."

"Right, nine little kingdoms. But if Knight has something up her sleeve, I'd like

73

to know about it."

"You don't have to know everything that goes on at this place. Christ, you already know more than all the clerks combined, and most of the justices. I mean, how many other clerks go down to the mail room at the crack of dawn to get a jump on the appeals coming in?"

"I don't like to do anything halfway."

She looked at him, was about to say something, but then stopped herself. Why complicate things? She had already given him her answer. In reality, although a driven person herself, she could not imagine being married to someone with standards as high as Michael Fiske's. She could never reach them, sustain them. It would be unhealthy even to try.

"Well, I'm not betraying any confidences. You know as well as I do that this place is like a military campaign. Loose lips sink ships. And you have to watch your backside."

"I'm not disagreeing with you in the grand scheme of things, but I am in this case. You know Murphy, he's a throwback — a lovable throwback, but he's a pure liberal. Anything to help the poor he'd go for. He and Knight would be aligned on this, no doubt about it. He's always on the lookout to throw a wrench in Ramsey's machine. Tom Murphy led the Court before Ramsey got the upper hand. It's no fun always being on the dissenting end in your twilight years."

Sara shook her head. "I really can't go into it."

He sighed and picked at his meal. "We're just pulling away from each other at all points, aren't we?"

"That's not true. You're just trying to make it seem that way. I know I hurt you when I said no, and I'm sorry."

He suddenly grinned. "Maybe it's for the best. We're both so headstrong, we'd probably end up killing each other."

"Good old Virginia boy and a gal from Carolina," she drawled. "You're probably right."

He fiddled with his drink and eyed her. "If you think I'm stubborn, you really should meet my brother."

Sara didn't meet his gaze. "I'm sure. He was terrific during that trial we watched."

"I'm very proud of him."

Now she looked at him. "So why did we have to sneak in and out of the courtroom so he wouldn't know we were there?"

"You'd have to ask him that."

"I'm asking you."

Michael shrugged. "He's got a problem with me. He sort of banished me from his life."

"Why?"

"I actually don't know all the reasons. Maybe he doesn't either. I do know it hasn't made him very happy."

"From the little I saw, he didn't strike me as that sort of person. Depressed or anything."

"Really? How did he strike you?"

"Funny, smart, identifies well with people."

"I see he identified with you."

"He didn't even know I was there."

"You would have liked him to, though, wouldn't you?"

"What's that supposed to mean?"

"Only that I'm not blind. And I've walked in his shadow all my life."

"You're the boy genius with a limitless future."

"And he's a heroic ex-cop who now defends the very people he used to arrest. He also has a martyr quality about him that I never have been able to get around. He's a good guy who pushes himself unbelievably hard." Michael shook his head. All the time his brother had spent in the hospital. None of them knowing if he was going to make it day to day, minute to minute. He had never known such fear, the thought of losing his brother. But he had lost him anyway, it seemed, and not because of death. Not because of those bullets.

"Maybe he feels like he's living in your shadow."

"I doubt that."

"Did you ever ask him?"

"Like I said, we don't talk anymore." He paused and then added quietly, "Is he the reason you turned me down?" He had watched her as she observed his brother. She had been enraptured with John Fiske from the moment she saw him. It had seemed like a fun idea at the time, the two of them going to watch his brother. Now Michael cursed himself for doing it.

She flushed. "I don't even know him. How could I possibly have any feelings for him?"

"Are you asking me that, or yourself?"

"I'm not going to answer that." Her voice trembled. "What about you? Do you love him?"

He abruptly sat up straight and looked at her. "I will always love my brother, Sara. Always."

CHAPTER SEVEN

Rider wordlessly passed his secretary, fled to his office, opened his briefcase and slipped out the envelope. He withdrew the letter from inside, but barely glanced at it before tossing it in the wastebasket. In the letter Rufus Harms had written his last will and testament, but that was just a dodge, something innocuous for the guard to read. Rider looked at the envelope closely while he punched his intercom.

"Sheila, can you bring in the hot plate and the teakettle? Fill it with water."

"Mr. Rider, I can make tea for you."

"I don't want tea, Sheila, just bring the damned kettle and the hot plate."

Sheila didn't question this odd request or her boss's temper. She brought in the kettle and hot plate, then quietly withdrew.

Rider plugged in the hot plate and within a few minutes steam poured out of the kettle. Gingerly grasping the envelope by its edges, Rider held it over the steam and watched as the envelope began to come apart, just as Rufus Harms had told him it would. Rider fussed with the edges, and he soon had it completely laid out. Instead of an envelope, he now held two pieces of paper: one hand-written; the other a copy of the letter Harms had received from the Army.

As he turned off the hot plate, Rider marveled at how Rufus had managed to construct this device — an envelope that was actually a letter — and how he had copied and then concealed the letter from the Army in it as well. Then he recalled that Harms's father had worked at a printing press company. It would have been better for Rufus if he had followed his daddy into the printing business instead of joining the Army, Rider muttered to himself.

He let the pieces of paper dry out for a minute and then sat behind his desk while he read what Rufus had written. It didn't take long, the remarks were fairly brief, though many words were oddly formed and misspelled. Rider couldn't have known it, but Harms had scrawled it out in near darkness, stopping every time he heard the steps of the guards draw close. There wasn't a trace of saliva left in Rider's throat when he had finished reading. Then he forced himself to read the official notice from the Army. Another body blow.

"Good God!" He sank back in his chair, rubbed a trembling hand over his bald spot, and then lurched to his feet, rushed over and locked his office door. The fear spread like a mutating virus. He could barely breathe. He staggered back to his desk and hit his intercom button again. "Sheila, bring me in some water and some aspirin, please."

A minute later Sheila knocked on the door. "Mr. Rider," she said through the door, "it's locked."

He quickly unlocked the door, took the glass and aspirin from her and was about to shut the door again when Sheila said, "Are you okay?"

"Fine, fine," he replied, hustling her out the door.

He looked down at the paper Rufus wanted him to file with the United States Supreme Court. Rider happened to be a member of the largely ceremonial Supreme Court Bar, solely by virtue of the sponsorship of a former colleague in the military who had gone on to the Justice Department. If he did exactly as Rufus asked, he would be the attorney of record in Harms's appeal. Rider could envision only personal catastrophe resulting from such an arrangement. And yet he had promised Rufus.

Rider lay down on the leather sofa in one corner of his office, closed his eyes and commenced a silent deliberation. So many things hadn't added up the night Ruth Ann Mosley had been killed. Rufus didn't have a history of violence, only a constant failure to follow orders that had enraged many a superior, and, at first, had bewildered Rider as well.

Harms's inability to process even the simplest of commands had been finally explained during Rider's representation of him. But his escaping from the stockade never had. Confronted with no defense, factually, Rider had made noises about an insanity plea, which had given him just enough leverage to save his client from possible execution. And that had been the end of it. Justice had been served. At least as much as one could expect in this world.

Rider looked once more at the notice from the Army, the stark lie of the past now firmly revealed. This information should have been in Harms's military file at the time of the murder, but it wasn't. It would have constituted a completely plausible defense. Harms's military file had been tampered with, and Rider now understood why.

Harms wanted his freedom and his name cleared and he wanted it to come from the highest court in the land. And he refused to entrust the prospect of freedom to the Army. That's what Harms had said to him while the country-western music had covered his words. And could he blame him?

All things good were in Rufus's corner. He should be heard and he should be free. But despite that, Rider remained immobile on his couch of worn leather and burnished nails. It was nothing complex. It was fear — a far stronger emotion, it seemed, than any of the others bestowed upon humankind. He planned to retire in a few years to the condo he and his wife had already picked out on the Gulf Coast. Their kids were grown. Rider was weary of the frigid winters that settled into the low pockets of the area and he was tired of always chasing new pieces of business, of diligently recording his professional life in quarter-hour increments. However, as enticing as that retirement was, it wasn't quite enough to prevent Rider from helping his old client. Some things were right and some things were wrong.

Rider rose from the couch and settled behind his desk. At first he had thought the simplest way to help Rufus was to mail what he had to one of the newspapers and let the power of the press take over. But for all he knew, the paper would either toss it as a letter from some crazy, or otherwise bungle it such that Rufus might be put in danger. What had really made up Rider's mind as to his course of action was simple. Rufus was his client and he had asked his lawyer to file his appeal with the United States Supreme Court. And that's what Rider was going to do. He had failed Rufus once before; he wasn't going to do it again. The man was in dire need of a little justice, and what better place for that than the highest court in the land? If you couldn't get justice there, where the hell could you get it? Rider wondered.

As he took out a sheet of paper from his desk drawer, sunlight from the window glanced off his square gold cuff links, sending bright dots around the room helter-skelter. He pulled over his ancient typewriter, kept out of nostalgia. Rider was unfamiliar with the Supreme Court's technical filing requirements, but he assumed he would be running afoul of most of them. That didn't bother him. He just wanted to get the story out — away from him.

When he had finished typing, he started to place what he had typed, together with Harms's letter and the letter from the Army, into a mailing envelope. Then he stopped. Paranoia, spilling over from thirty years of practice, made him hustle out to the small workroom at the rear of his office suite and make copies of both Harms's handwritten letter and Rider's own typewritten one. This same uneasiness made him decide to keep, for now, the letter from the Army. When the story broke he could always produce it, again anonymously. He hid the copies in one of his desk drawers and locked it. He returned the originals to the envelope, looked up the address of the Supreme Court in his legal directory, and next typed up a label. He did not provide a return address on the envelope. That done, he put on his hat and coat and walked down to the post office at the corner.

Before he had time to change his mind, he

filled out the form to send the envelope by certified mail so he would get a return receipt, handed it to the postal clerk, completed the simple transaction and returned to his office. It was only then that it struck him. The return receipt could be a way for the Court to identify who had sent the package. He sighed. Rufus had been waiting half his life for this. And, in a way, Rider had abandoned him back then. For the rest of the day Rider lay on the couch in his office, in the dark, silently praying that he had done the right thing, and knowing, in his heart, that he had.

Chapter Eight

"Ramsey's clerks have been pestering me about the comment you made the other day, Justice Knight, about the poor being entitled to certain preferences." Sara looked over at the woman, sitting so calmly behind her desk.

A smile flickered across Knight's face as she scanned some documents. "I'm sure they have."

They both knew that Ramsey's clerks were like a well-trained commando unit. They had feelers out everywhere, looking for anything of interest to the chief justice and his agendas. Almost nothing escaped their notice. Every word, exclamation, meeting or casual corridor conversation was duly noted, analyzed and catalogued away for future use.

"So you intended for that reaction to happen?"

"Sara, as much as I may not like it, there is a certain process at this place that one must struggle through. Some call it a game, I don't choose to do so. But I can't ignore its presence. I'm not so much concerned with the chief. The positions I'm thinking about taking on are a number of cases Ramsey would never support. I know that and he knows that."

"So you were floating a trial balloon to the other justices."

"In part, yes. Oral argument is also an open, public forum."

"So, to the public." Sara thought quickly. "And the media?"

Knight put down the papers and clasped her hands together as she stared at the younger woman. "This Court is swayed more by public opinion than many would dare to confess. Some here would like to see the status quo always preserved. But the Court has to move forward."

"And this ties into the cases you've been having me research about equalizing educational rights of the poor?"

"I have a compelling interest in that." Elizabeth Knight had grown up in East Texas, the middle of nowhere, but her father had had money. Thus, her education had been first-rate, and she had often wondered how her life would have been if her father had been poor like so many of the people she had grown up with. All justices carried psychological baggage to the Court and Elizabeth Knight was no exception. "And that's all I'm really going to say right now."

"And *Blankley*?" Sara said, referring to the affirmative action case Ramsey had so thoroughly decimated.

"We haven't voted on it yet, of course, Sara, so I can't say one way or the other how it will turn out." The voting conferences took place in complete secrecy, without even a stenographer or secretary in residence. However, for those who followed the Court with any consistency, and for the clerks who lived in the place every day, it wasn't too difficult to predict how votes were lining up, although the justices had surprised people in the past. Justice Knight's depressed look made it clear, however, which way the votes were aligned on the *Blankley* case.

And Sara could read the tea leaves as well as anyone. Michael Fiske was right. The only question was how sweeping the opinion would be.

"Too bad I won't be around to see the results of my research come to fruition," Sara said.

"You never know. You came back for a second term. Michael Fiske signed up with Tommy for a third. I'd love to have you back again."

"Funny you should mention him. Michael was also asking about your remarks at oral argument. He thought Murphy might welcome anything you were trying to put together concerning preferences for the poor."

Knight smiled. "Michael would know. He

and Tommy are as close as clerk and justice can be."

"Michael knows more about the Court than just about anyone. Actually, sometimes he can be a little scary."

Knight eyed her keenly. "I thought you and Michael were close."

"We are. I mean, we're good friends." Sara blushed as Knight continued to watch her.

"We won't be getting any announcements from the two of you, will we?" Knight smiled warmly.

"What? No, no. We're just friends."

"I see. I'm sorry, Sara, it's certainly none of my business."

"It's okay. We do spend a fair amount of time together. I'm sure some people assume that there's more there than just friendship. I mean, Michael's a very attractive man, obviously very smart. Great future."

"Sara, don't take this the wrong way, but you sound like you're trying to convince yourself of something."

Sara looked down. "I guess I do, don't I?"

"Take it from someone who has two grown daughters. Don't rush it. Let it take its natural course. You have plenty of time. End of motherly advice."

Sara smiled. "Thanks."

"Now, how is the bench memo coming on *Chance v. U.S.*?"

"I know Steven's been working on it non-stop."

"Steven Wright is not holding up well here."

"Well, he's trying really hard."

"You have to help him, Sara. You're the senior clerk. I should have had that memo two weeks ago. Ramsey has his ammo bag filled and the precedents are completely on his side. I need to be at least equal to that if I'm going to have a shot."

"I'll make it a top priority."

"Good."

Sara rose to leave. "And I think you'll handle the chief justice just fine."

The women exchanged smiles. Elizabeth Knight had become almost a second mother to Sara Evans, replacing the one she had lost as a young child.

As Sara walked out the door, Knight sat back in her chair. Where she was now was the culmination of a lifetime of work and sacrifice, luck and skill. She was married to a well-respected United States senator, a man she loved and who loved her. She was one of only three women who had ever donned the robes of a Supreme Court justice. She felt humble and empowered at the same time. The president who had nominated her was still in office. He had seen her as a reliable middle-of-the-road jurist. She had not been that active politically, so he could not exactly expect her to toe his party's line, but he probably expected her to be judicially passive, letting the solution to the really important questions fall to the people's elected representatives.

She had no deep-set philosophies like Ramsey or Murphy. They decided cases not so much on the facts of each one, but on the broad positions each case represented. Murphy would never vote to uphold or reverse any case in favor of capital punishment. Ramsey would wither and die before he would side with a defendant in a criminal rights case. Knight could not choose her sides in that manner. She took each case, each party, as they came. She agonized over the facts. While she thought about the broader impact of the court's decisions, she also worried about the fairness to the actual parties. It often meant she was the swing vote on a lot of cases, and she didn't really mind that. She was no wallflower, and she had come here to make a difference.

Only now was she seeing what a very great impact she could have. And the responsibility that came with such power was what humbled her. And frightened her. Made her stare at the ceiling wide awake as her husband slept soundly beside her. Still, she thought with a smile, there was no other place she would rather be; no other way she would rather be spending her life.

CHAPTER NINE

John Fiske walked into the building located in the West End of Richmond. The place was officially called a rest home, but, plain and simple, it was a place for the elderly to come to die. Fiske tried to ignore the moans and cries as he strode down the corridor. He saw the feeble bodies, heads dipping low, limbs useless, encased in the wheelchairs, stacked like shopping carts against the wall, waiting for a dance partner who was never going to show up.

It had taken all the resolve he and his father had in order to move John's mother into this place. Michael Fiske had never faced up to the fact that their mother's mind was gone, eaten away by Alzheimer's. The good times were easy to enjoy. The real worth of a person came from how he acted during the bad times. As far as John Fiske was concerned, his brother Mike had failed that test miserably.

He checked in at the desk. "How is she today?" he asked the assistant administrator. As a frequent visitor here, he knew all the staff.

"She's had better ones, John, but your

being here will perk her up," the woman answered.

"Right," Fiske muttered as he walked to the visitors' room.

His mother awaited him there, dressed, as always, in her housecoat and slippers. Her eyes wandered aimlessly, her mouth moving, but no words coming out. When Fiske appeared at the doorway, she looked at him, a smile breaking across her face. He walked over and sat down across from her.

"How's my Mikey?" Gladys Fiske asked, tenderly rubbing his face. "How's Momma's baby?"

Fiske took a deep breath. It was the same damn thing, for the last two years. In Gladys Fiske's devastated mind he was Mike, he would always be his brother until the very end of his mother's life. John Fiske had somehow completely vanished from her memory, as if he had never been born.

He gently touched her hands, doing his best to quiet the absolute frustration inside him. "I'm fine. Doing good. Pop's good too." He then added quietly, "Johnny's doing good too, he asked about you. Always does."

Her stare was blank. "Johnny?"

Fiske attempted this every time, and every time the response was the same. Why did she forget him and not his brother? There had to have been some deep-rooted facet in her that had allowed the Alzheimer's to erase his identity from her life. Was his existence never that strong, never that important to her? And yet he had been the son who had always been there for his parents. He had helped them as a boy, and continued to be there for them as a man. Everything from giving them a large part of his income to getting up on the roof on a suffocating August day, in the middle of a hellish trial, to help his old man shingle their house, because he didn't have the cash to pay someone to do it. And Mike, always the favorite, always the one to go his own way, his own selfish way, Fiske thought . . . Mike was always hailed as the great one, the one who would do the family proud. In reality, his parents had never been that extreme in their views of their sons; Fiske knew that. But his anger had skewed that truth, empowering the bad and subverting the good.

"Mikey?" she said anxiously. "How are the children?"

"They're fine, they're good, growing like weeds. They look just like you." Having to pretend that he was his brother and had fathered children made Fiske want to collapse to the floor bawling.

She smiled and touched her hair.

He picked up on that. "Looks good. Pop says you're prettier than ever." Gladys Fiske had been an attractive woman for most of her life, and her appearance had been very important to her. The effects of the Alzheimer's had, in her case, accelerated the aging process. She would have been terribly upset with how she looked now, Fiske knew. He hoped his mother still saw herself as twenty years old and the prettiest she would ever be.

He held out a package he had brought. She seized it with the glee of a child and tore off the wrapping. She touched the brush delicately and then ran it through her hair very carefully.

"It's the most beautiful thing I've ever seen."

She said that about everything he brought her. Tissues, lipstick, a picture book. The most beautiful thing she had ever seen. Mike. Every time he came here, his brother scored brownie points. Fiske forced these thoughts away and spent a very pleasant hour with his mother. He loved her so much. He would rip from her the disease that had destroyed her brain if he could. Since he couldn't, he would do anything to spend time with her. Even under another's name.

Fiske left the rest home and drove to his father's house. As he turned onto the familiar street, he looked around the disintegrating boundaries of his first eighteen years of life: dilapidated homes with peeling paint and crumbling porches, sagging wire fences, and dirt front yards running down to narrow, cracked streets where twin streams of ancient, battered Fords and Chevys docked. Fifty years ago, the neighborhood had been a typical starter community for the post–World War II masses filled with the unshakable confidence that life would only get better. For those who hadn't crossed that bridge of prosperity, the most visible change in their worn-out lives was a wooden wheelchair ramp grafted over the front stoop. As he looked at one of the ramps, Fiske knew he would choose a wheelchair over the rot of his mother's brain.

He pulled into the driveway of his father's well-kept home. The more the neighborhood fell apart around him, the harder his old man worked to keep it at bay. Perhaps to keep the past alive a little longer. Maybe hoping his wife would come home twenty years old again with a fresh, healthy mind. The old Buick was in the driveway, its body rusted a little, but the engine in mint condition thanks to its owner's skills as a master mechanic. Fiske saw his father in the garage, dressed in his usual outfit of white T-shirt and blue work pants, hunkered over some piece of equipment. Retired now, Ed Fiske was at his happiest with his fingers full of grease, the guts of some complex machinery strewn out helter-skelter in front of him.

"Cold beer's in the fridge," Ed said without looking up.

Fiske opened the old refrigerator his father

kept in the garage and pulled out a Miller. He sat down on a rickety old kitchen chair and watched his father work, just as he had done as a young boy. He had always been fascinated with the skill of his father's hands, the way the man confidently knew where every piece went.

"Saw Mom today."

With a practiced roll of his tongue, Ed pushed the cigarette he was puffing on to the right side of his mouth. His muscular forearms flexed and then relaxed as he ratcheted a bolt tight.

"I'm going tomorrow. Thought I'd get all dressed up, bring some flowers, a little boxed dinner Ida is going to make up. Make it real special. Just me and her."

Ida German was the next-door neighbor. She had lived in the neighborhood longer than anyone else. She had been good company to his father ever since his wife had gone away.

"She'll love that." Fiske sipped on his beer and smiled at the picture the two would make together.

Ed finished up what he was doing and took a minute to clean up, using gasoline and a rag to get the grease off his hands. He grabbed a beer and sat down on an old toolbox across from his son.

"Talked to Mike yesterday," he said.

"Is that right?" Fiske said with no interest.

"He's doing good up there at the Court. You know they asked him back for another year. He must be good."

"I'm sure he's the best they've ever had." Fiske stood up and went over to the open doorway. He took a deep breath, letting his lungs fill with the scent of freshly cut grass. Every Saturday growing up, he and his brother would mow the lawn, do the chores and then the family would pile into the mammoth station wagon for the weekly trip to the A&P grocery store. If they had been really good, done all their chores correctly, not clipped the grass too short, they'd get a soda from the machine next to the paper box outside the A&P. To the boys it was liquid gold. Fiske and his brother would think all week about getting that cold soda. They had been so close growing up. Carried the morning *Times Dispatch* together, played sports together, though John was three years older than his brother. Mike was so gifted physically that he had played varsity sports as a freshman. The Fiske brothers. Everybody knew them, respected them. Those were happy times. Those times were over. He turned back and looked at his father.

Ed shook his head. "Did you know Mike turned down a teaching job at one of them big law schools, Harvard or something, to stay at the Court? He got a slew of offers from big law firms. He showed me 'em. Lord, they were talking money I can't even believe." The pride in his voice was obvious.

"More power to him," Fiske said dryly.

Ed suddenly slapped his thigh. "What's wrong with you, Johnny? What the hell do you have against your brother?"

"I've got nothing against him."

"Then why the hell don't you two get along like you used to? I've talked to Mike. It's not on account of him."

"Look, Pop, he's got his life and I've got mine. I don't remember you being all touchy-feely with Uncle Ben."

"My brother was a bum and a drunk. Your brother ain't either of those."

"Being a drunk and a bum aren't the only vices in the world."

"Damn, I just don't understand you, son."

"Join the crowd."

Ed put out his cigarette on the concrete floor, stood and leaned against one of the garage's exposed wall studs. "Jealousy ain't right between brothers. You should feel good about what he's done with his life."

"Oh, so you think I'm jealous?"

"Are you?"

Fiske took another sip of beer and looked over at the belly-button-high wire fence surrounding his father's small backyard. It was currently painted dark green. Over the years it had seen many different colors. John and Mike had painted it each summer, the color being whatever the trucking firm Ed worked for had left over from its annual office repainting. Fiske looked over at the apple tree that spread over one corner of the yard. He motioned with his beer. "You've got caterpillars. Get me a flare."

"I'll get to it."

"Pop, you don't even like standing on a chair."

Fiske took off his jacket, grabbed a ladder from the garage and took the flare his father handed him. He ignited it, positioned the ladder under the bulging nest and climbed up. It took a few minutes, but the nest slowly dissolved under the heat of the flare. Fiske climbed back down and stamped out the flare while his father raked up the remains of the nest.

"And you just saw my problem with Mike."

"What?" Ed looked confused.

"When was the last time Mike was down here to help? Hell, just to see you or Mom?"

Ed scratched at his beard stubble and fumbled in his pants pocket for another cigarette. "He's busy. He gets down when he can."

"Sure he does."

"He's got important work to do for the government. Up there helping all them judges. It's the damn highest court in the land, you know that."

"Well, guess what, Pop, I keep pretty busy too."

"I know that, son. But —"

"But, I know, it's different." Fiske threw his jacket over his shoulder, wiped the sweat from his eyes. The mosquitoes would be out soon. That made him think of water. His father kept a trailer at a campground down by the Mattaponi River. "You been down to the trailer lately?"

Ed shook his head, relieved at the change in subject. "Naw, planning to go soon, though. Take the boat out before it gets too cold."

Fiske rubbed another bead of sweat off his forehead. "Let me know, I might run down with you."

Ed scrutinized his eldest son. "How you doing?"

"Professionally? Lost two, won two this week. I take that as an acceptable batting average these days."

"You be careful, son. I know you believe in what you're doing and all, but that's a damn rough bunch you're lawyering for. Some of them might remember you from your cop days. I lie awake at night thinking about that."

Fiske smiled. He loved his father as much as he did his mother, and, in some subtle ways of men, even more. The thought of his father still losing sleep over him was very reassuring. He slapped his father on the back.

"Don't worry, Pop, I never let my guard down."

"How about the other thing?"

Fiske unconsciously touched his chest. "Doing just fine. Hell, probably live to be a hundred."

"I hope you do, son," his father said with great conviction as he watched his boy leave.

Ed shook his head as he thought of how far his sons had drifted apart and his being unable to do anything about it. "Damn," was all he could think of to say before sitting down on the toolbox to finish his beer.

CHAPTER TEN

It was early in the morning as Michael Fiske quietly hummed his way through the broad, high-ceilinged hallway toward the clerks' mail room. As he entered the room, a clerk looked up. "You picked a good time, Michael. We just got in a shipment."

"Any con mail?" Michael asked, referring to the ever-growing number of petitions from prisoners. Most of them were filed *in forma pauperis,* meaning, literally, in the form of a pauper. There was a separate docket kept for these petitions, and it was so large that one clerk was specially designated to manage the filings. The IFPs, as they were termed by Court personnel, were usually a place to discover either humor over some ridiculous claim or occasionally a case worthy of the Court's attention. Michael knew that some of the most important Court decisions ever had resulted from IFP cases — thus his early morning ritual of panning for appellate gold in the paper piles.

"From the hand scribblings I've tried to decipher so far, I'd say that was a good bet," the clerk responded.

Michael dragged a box over to one corner.

Within its confines was an array of complaints, penned miseries, a procession of claimed injustice of varying content and description. But none of them could be simply shrugged off. Many were from death row inmates; for them, the Supreme Court represented the last hope before legal extermination.

For the next two hours Michael dug through the box. He was very accomplished at this now. It was like expertly shucking corn, his mind scanning the lengthy documents with ease, effortlessly probing through the legalese to the important points, comparing them to pending cases as well as precedents from fifty years ago pulled from his encyclopedic memory; then filing them away and moving on. However, at the end of two hours he had not found much of great interest.

He was thinking of heading up to his office when his hand closed around the plain manila envelope. The address label was typewritten, but the envelope had no return address. That was strange, Michael thought. People seeking to plead their case before the Court normally wanted the justices to know where to find them in the rare event that their plea was answered. There was, however, the left side of a postal return receipt card affixed to it. He slid open the envelope and removed the two sheets of paper. One of the functions of the clerks' mail room was to ensure that all filings met the strict standards of the Court. For parties claiming indigent status, if their petitions were granted, the Court would waive certain filing requirements and fees, and even engage and pick up some of the expenses of counsel, although the attorney would not bill for his or her time. It was an honor simply to stand before the Court as an advocate. Two of the forms required to achieve indigent status were a motion for leave to file as a pauper, and an affidavit signed by the prisoner, basically swearing to the person's impoverished status. Neither was in the envelope, Michael quickly noted. The appeal would have to be kicked back.

When Michael started reading what *was* in the envelope, all thoughts of any filing deficiencies vanished. After he finished, he could see the sweat from his palms leach onto the paper. At first Michael wanted to put the pages back in the envelope and forget he had ever seen them. But, as though he had now witnessed a crime himself, he felt he had to do something.

"Hey, Michael, Murphy's chambers just called down for you," the clerk said. When Michael didn't answer, the clerk said again, "Michael? Justice Murphy is looking for you."

Michael nodded, finally managing to focus on something other than the papers in his hand. When the clerk turned back to his work, Michael put the pages back in the manila envelope. He hesitated an instant. His entire legal career, his entire life, could be decided in the next second or so. Finally, as though his hands were acting independently from his thoughts, he slipped the envelope into his briefcase. By doing so before the petition had been officially processed with the Court, he had just committed, among other crimes, theft of federal property, a felony.

As he raced out of the mail room, he almost collided head-on with Sara Evans.

She smiled at first, but the look changed quickly when she saw his face. "Michael, what's wrong?"

"Nothing. I'm fine."

She gripped his arm. "You're not fine. You're shaking and your face is white as a sheet."

"I think I'm coming down with something."

"Well, then you should go home."

"I'll grab some aspirin from the nurse. I'll be okay."

"Are you sure?"

"Sara, I really have to go." He pulled away, leaving her staring worriedly after him.

The rest of the day moved at a glacial pace for Michael and he repeatedly found himself staring at his briefcase, thinking of the contents. Late that night, his day's work at the

Court finally completed, he furiously rode his bike back to his apartment on Capitol Hill. He locked the door behind him and took out the envelope once more. He grabbed a yellow legal pad from his briefcase and carried everything over to the small dinette table.

An hour later he sat back and stared at the numerous notes he had made. He opened his laptop and rewrote these notes onto his hard drive, changing, tinkering, rethinking as he did so, a longtime habit of his. He had decided to attack this problem as he would any other. He would check out the information in the petition as carefully as he could. Most important, he would have to confirm that the names listed on the petition were actually the people he thought they were. If it seemed legitimate, he would return the appeal to the clerks' mail room. If it was clearly frivolous, the work of an unbalanced mind or a prisoner blindly lashing out, he had made up his mind to destroy it.

Michael looked out the window and across the street at the cluttered line of row houses that had been converted into apartments just like his. Young disciples of government were honeycombed in this neighborhood. Half were still at work, the rest in bed, nightmaring through a list of uncompleted tasks of national importance, at least until the five A.M. awakening. The darkness Michael stared into was interrupted only by the wash of a corner streetlight. The wind had gained strength, and the temperature had dropped, in readiness for an advancing storm. The boiler in the old building was not yet engaged, and a sudden chill hit Michael through the window. He pulled a sweatshirt from his closet, threw it on, and returned to stare out to the street.

He had never heard of Rufus Harms. According to the dates in the letter, the man had been incarcerated when Michael was only five years old. The spelling in the letter was abysmal, the formation of the letters and words clumsy, resembling a child's humorous first attempts at penmanship. The typewritten letter explained some of the background of the case and was obviously composed by a far better educated person. A lawyer, perhaps, Michael thought. The language had a legal air to it, although it was as though the person typing it had intended his professional — together with his personal — identity, to remain unknown. The notice from the Army, according to the typewritten letter, had requested certain information from Rufus Harms. However, Rufus Harms denied ever being in the program the Army's records apparently indicated he was in. It had been a cover, Harms was alleging, for a crime that had resulted in a horrific miscarriage of justice — a legal fiasco that had caused a quarter century of his life to disappear.

Suddenly warm, Michael pressed his face into the coolness of the window and took a deep breath, the air frosting the glass. What he was doing amounted to blatant interference with a party's right to seek his day in court. All of his life Michael had believed in a person's inalienable franchise to have access to the law, no matter how rich or poor. It was not scrip that could be revoked or declared worthless. He comforted himself somewhat with the knowledge that the appeal would have been defeated via a host of technical deficiencies.

But this case was different. Even if false, it could still do terrible damage to the reputations of some very important people. If it was true? He closed his eyes. Please, God, do not let it be, he prayed.

He turned his head and eyed the phone. He suddenly wondered if he should call and seek his brother's advice. John was savvy in ways his younger brother was not. He might know how to handle the situation better. Michael hesitated for a moment longer, reluctant to admit that he needed any help, especially from that troubling, estranged source. But it also might be a way back into his brother's life. The fault was not entirely on one side; Michael had matured enough to comprehend the elusiveness of blame.

He picked up the phone and dialed. He got the answering machine, a result that pleased a certain part of him. He left a message asking for his brother's help but revealing nothing. He hung up, and returned to the window once more. It was probably better that John had not been there to take the call. His brother tended to see things only in rigid lines of black and white, a telling facet of the way he lived his life.

Toward the early hours of the morning, Michael drifted off to sleep, growing ever more confident that he could handle this potential nightmare, however it turned out.

CHAPTER ELEVEN

Three days after Michael Fiske had taken the file from the clerks' mail room, Rufus Harms placed another call to Sam Rider's office, but was told the attorney was out of town on business. As he was escorted back to his cell, Rufus passed a man in the corridor.

"Lot of phone calls lately, Harms. What, you have a mail-order business going or something?" The guards laughed loudly at the man's words. Vic Tremaine was a little under six feet, had white-blond, close-cropped hair, weathered features and was molded like a gun turret. He was the second-in-command of Fort Jackson, and he had made it his personal mission to compress as much misery into Harms's life as he could. Harms said nothing, but stood there patiently as Tremaine looked him up and down.

"What'd your lawyer want? He coming up with another defense for you slaughtering that little girl? Is that it?" Tremaine drew closer to the prisoner. "You still see her in your sleep? I hope you do. I listen to you crying in your cell, you know." Tremaine's tone was openly taunting, the muscles in his arms and shoulders tensing with each word, neck veins pulling taut, as though he were hoping Harms would crack, try something, and that would be the end of the prisoner's life tenure here. "Crying like a damn baby. I bet that little girl's momma and daddy cried too. I bet they wanted to wrap their fingers around your throat. Like you did to their baby. You ever think about that?"

Harms did not flinch. His lips remained in a straight line, his eyes looking past Tremaine. Harms had been through isolation, solitary, taunts, physical and mental abuse; everything one man could do to another out of cruelty, fear and hatred, he had endured. Tremaine's words, no matter their content or how they were delivered, could not break through the wall that encased him, kept him alive.

Sensing this, Tremaine took a step back. "Get him out of my sight." As the group headed off, Tremaine called after them, "Go back to reading your Bible, Harms. That's as close as you're ever getting to heaven."

John Fiske hustled after the woman walking down the hallway of the court building.

"Hey, Janet, got a minute?"

Janet Ryan was a very experienced prosecutor currently doing her best to send one of Fiske's clients away for a long time. She was

111

also attractive and divorced. She smiled when she turned to him. "For you, two minutes."

"About Rodney —"

"Wait, refresh my memory. I've got lots of Rodneys."

"Burglary, electronics store, north side."

"Firearm involved, police chase, priors — now I remember."

"Right. Anyway, neither one of us wants to take this sucker to trial."

"Translation, John: Your case stinks and mine is overwhelming."

Fiske shook his head. "You might have a chain-of-custody problem with some of the evidence."

"*Might* is such a funny word, don't you think?"

"And that confession has holes."

"They always do. But the fact is your guy is a career crim. And I'll get a jury who'll put him away for a long time."

"So why waste the taxpayers' money, then?"

"What's your deal?"

"Plead to the burglary, possession of stolen property. Drop the nasty little firearm count. We end up with five years with credit for time served."

Janet started walking. "See you in court."

"Okay, okay, eight, but I need to talk with my guy."

She turned around and ticked off the points on her fingers. "He pleads to all of it, including the 'nasty little firearm' count, he gets ten years, forget the time served, and he punches the whole ticket. Probation for another five after that. If he pees funny, he goes back for another ten, no questions asked. If he goes to trial you're looking at a slam-dunk of twenty. And I want an answer right now."

"Damn, Janet, where's the compassion?"

"Saving it for somebody who deserves it. As you can probably guess, my list is very short. Besides, it's a sweetheart deal. Yes or no?"

Fiske tapped his fingers against his briefcase.

"Going once, going twice," Ryan said.

"Okay, okay, deal."

"Good doing business with you, John. By the way, why don't you call me sometime. You know, off hours?"

"Don't you think there might be a conflict lurking there somewhere?"

"Not at all. I'm always hardest on my friends."

She walked off humming while Fiske leaned up against the wall and shook his head.

An hour later, he returned to his office and tossed down his briefcase. He picked up the phone and checked his messages at home, listening to the recorded voices at the same time he wrote down notes for an upcoming hearing. When he heard his brother's voice, he didn't even stop writing. One finger flicked out and erased the message. It was rare but not unheard-of for Mike to call. Fiske had never called him back. Now he thought his brother was doing it just to antagonize him. As soon as he completed this thought, he knew it was not true. He rose and went over to a bookcase jammed with trial notebooks and legal tomes. He slid out the framed photograph. It was an old picture. He was in his policeman's uniform, Mike stood next to him. Proud little brother just entering manhood and stern-faced big brother, who had already seen a lot of evil in life and expected to see a lot more before he was done. In reality he had experienced firsthand the ugly side of humanity, and was still, but now he did so without the uniform. Just a briefcase, a cheap suit and a fast mouth. Bullets exchanged for words. Till the end of his days. He put the photo back and sat down. However, he looked over at the photo, suddenly unable to concentrate.

A few days later, Sara Evans knocked and then opened the door to Michael Fiske's office. It was empty. Michael had borrowed a book and she needed it back. She looked around the room but didn't see it lying any-where. Then she spotted his briefcase under-neath the kneehole of his desk. She picked it up. From the weight, she knew there was something inside. The briefcase was locked, but she knew the combination from having borrowed his briefcase a couple of times before. She opened it and immediately saw two books and the papers inside. Neither book was the one she was looking for though. She was going to close it back up but then stopped. She pulled the papers out and then looked at the envelope they had come in. Addressed to the clerks' office. She had just glanced at the handwritten page and then the typewritten letter when she heard footsteps. She put the papers back, closed the briefcase and slid it back under the desk. A moment later Michael walked in.

"Sara, what are you doing here?"

Sara did her best to look normal. "I just came looking for that book I had lent you last week."

"I've got it at home."

"Well, maybe I can come over for dinner and get it."

"I'm kind of busy."

"We're all busy, Michael. But you've really been keeping to yourself lately. Are you sure you're okay? Not cracking under the strain?" She smiled to show she was kidding. But Michael did look like he was cracking.

"I'm fine, really. I'll bring the book tomorrow."

"It's not that big a deal."

"I'll bring it tomorrow," he said a little angrily, his face flushing, but he calmed down quickly. "I've really got a lot of work to do." He looked at the door.

Sara went over and put her hand on the knob, then looked back. "Michael, if you need to talk about anything, I'm here for you."

"Yeah, okay, thanks." He ushered her out and closed and locked the door. He went over to his desk and pulled out the briefcase. He looked at the contents and then over at the door.

Later that night, Sara pulled her car down the gravel drive and stopped in front of the small cottage located off the George Washington Parkway, a truly beautiful stretch of road. The cottage was the first thing she had ever owned and she had put a lot of work into fixing up the place. A stairway led down to the Potomac, where her small sailboat was docked. She and Michael had spent their rare free time sailing across the river to the Maryland side and then north under Memorial Bridge and then on to Georgetown. It was a haven of calm for them both, surrounded as they were by a sea of crisis at work. Michael had turned down her last offer to go sailing.

In fact, he had turned down all of her get-together ideas the past week. At first she thought it was due to her rejecting his marriage offer, but after the encounter at his office, she knew that was not it. She struggled to remember precisely what she had seen in the briefcase. It was a filing, she was sure of that. And she had seen a name on the type-written letter. It was Harms. She hadn't remembered the first name. From the little she had been able to read before Michael walked in, apparently Harms was filing some sort of appeal with the Court. She didn't know what about. There had been no signature at the bottom of the typewritten letter.

She had gone directly to the clerks' office to see if any case with the name Harms had been logged in. It hadn't. She couldn't believe she was thinking this, but had Michael taken an appeal before it had been processed and put into the system? If he had, that was a very serious crime. He could be fired from the Court — sent to jail, even.

She went inside, changed into jeans and a T-shirt and walked back outside. It was already dark. Supreme Court clerks rarely made it home while it was still light, unless it was daybreak and they were coming home to shower and change clothes before going back to work. She walked down the stairs to the dock and sat on her boat. If only Michael would confide in her, she could help. Despite his words to the contrary, Michael had pulled back from her. He had not taken rejection well. Who would? she told herself.

She abruptly jumped up and raced to the house, picked up the phone and started to dial his number, but then stopped. Michael Fiske was a stubborn man. If she confronted him on what she had seen, that could very well make matters worse. She put the phone back down. She would have to let him come to her. She went back outside and looked at the water. A jet flew by and she automatically waved to it, a ritual of hers. Indeed, the planes were so low at this point that, had it been light, a passenger on the plane could have seen her waving. When her hand dropped back down, she felt more depressed than she had since her father had passed away, leaving her all alone.

After that loss, she had started life anew. Gone to the West Coast for law school, where she had excelled, clerked at the Ninth Circuit Court of Appeals and then taken a job with the Supreme Court. That's when she had sold the farm in North Carolina and bought this place. She wasn't running from her old life, or from the sadness that gripped her whenever she dwelled on her parents not being around either to see her accomplishments, or to simply hold her. At least she didn't think she was. When the day came for her to leave the Court, she had no idea what she wanted to do. In the legal arena, she could go anywhere. The trouble was, she didn't even know if she wanted the law to be part of her life. Three years of law school, a year at the court of appeals, starting on her second year up here, she was creeping close to burnout.

She thought of her father, a farmer and also the town's justice of the peace. He had no fancy courtroom. He often dispensed sound and fair justice while perched on his tractor in the field or while washing up for dinner. To Sara, that was what the law was, what it meant to most people, or at least what it should mean. A search for the truth, and then the handing down of justice after that truth was found. No hidden agendas, no word games, simply common sense applied to the facts. She sighed. But it was never that simple. She knew that better than most.

She went back inside, stood on a chair and snared a pack of cigarettes off the top of the cabinet in the kitchen. She sat on the glider on the back porch overlooking the water. She looked up at the clear sky and located the Big Dipper. Her dad had been an avid, if amateur, astronomer, and had taught her many of the constellations. Sara often used the stars to sail by, a practice she had picked up while at Stanford. On a clear night, you could never lose the stars, and with them you could never be truly lost. That was comforting. As she smoked her cigarette, she hoped Michael knew what he was doing.

Her next thoughts turned to another Fiske: John. Michael's comment about his brother had been close to the mark despite her protests. At the very first instant she had seen John Fiske, something had clicked in all the important conduits of her heart, brain and soul that she simply had no way to explain. She did not believe that significant emotions could be aroused to such an intensity that quickly. It just didn't happen. But that was why she was so confused, because, in a way, that's exactly what had occurred to her. Every movement John Fiske made, every word he spoke, every time he made eye contact with someone, or simply laughed, smiled or frowned, she felt as though she could watch him forever and never grow tired of it. She almost laughed at the absurdity. But then again, how crazy could it be when it was how she felt?

And that wasn't her only observation of the man. Unknown to Michael, she had checked with a friend at the courthouse in Richmond and found out Fiske's trial schedule for a two-week period. She had been amazed at how often the man was in court. She had gone down once more during the summer when things were slower at the Supreme Court, and watched John Fiske argue at a sentencing hearing. She had worn a scarf and glasses, just in case she was ever introduced to him later on, or in case he had seen her the first time she had come to watch him with Michael.

She had listened to him argue forcefully for his client. As soon as he had finished, the judge had put the man away for life. His client led away to begin his prison term, Fiske packed his briefcase and left the courtroom. Outside, Sara had watched as Fiske had attempted to comfort the man's family. The wife was thin and sickly, her face covered with bruises and welts.

Fiske spoke a few words to the wife, hugged her and then turned to the oldest son, a young man of fourteen who already looked to be a committed slave of the street.

"You're the man of the house now, Lucas. You have to look after your family," said Fiske.

Sara studied the teenager. The anger in his face was painful to see. How could someone so young have all that hostility inside him?

"Uh-huh," Lucas said, staring at the wall. He was dressed for gang work, a bandanna covered his head. He wore clothes one could not afford flipping burgers at McDonald's.

Fiske knelt down and looked at the other son. Enis was six years old, cute as the devil and usually bubbly.

"Hey, Enis, how you doing?" Fiske asked, holding out his hand.

Enis warily shook Fiske's hand. "Where's my daddy?"

"He had to go away for a while."

"Why's that?"

"Cause he kill —" Lucas started to say before Fiske cut him off with the sharpest of looks. Lucas muttered an expletive, threw off his mother's shaky hand and stalked away.

Fiske looked back at Enis. "Your daddy did something he's not too proud of. Now he's going away to make up for it."

"Jail?" Enis asked. Fiske nodded.

As Sara observed this exchange it occurred to her that today Fiske, and adults in general, probably felt foolish and inadequate in these situations, like sitcom characters from the 1950s trying to deal with a second millennium child. Even at six years old Enis probably knew a great deal about the criminal justice system. In fact, the little boy probably knew far more about the evil parts of life than many adults ever would.

"When's he getting out?" Enis asked.

Fiske looked up at the wife and then back at the little boy. "Not for a real long time, Enis. But your mom's going to be here."

"Okay, then," Enis said with little emotion. He took his mom's hand and they left.

Sara watched as Fiske looked after the pair for a moment. Again, she could almost feel what he was thinking. One son perhaps lost forever, the other casually leaving his father behind, like a stray dog on the street.

Finally, Fiske had loosened his tie and walked off.

Sara wasn't exactly sure why, but she decided to follow him. Fiske kept a slow pace, and she easily was able to keep him in sight. The bar he entered was a little slit in the wall, its windows dark. Sara hesitated and then went in.

Fiske was at the bar. He had obviously already ordered because the bartender was sliding a beer across to him. She quickly went to a back booth and sat down. Despite its dingy appearance, the bar was fairly full and it was barely five o'clock. There was an interesting mixture of working class and downtown office dwellers in here. Fiske sat between two construction workers, their yellow hard hats on the bar in front of them. Fiske slipped his jacket off and sat on it. His shoulders were as broad as the burly men's next to him. Sara noted that his shirt was untucked and fell over the back of his pants. The way his dark hair covered the back of his neck and touched the white of his shirt held her gaze for some time.

He was talking to the men on either side of him. The workers laughed heartily at something Fiske had said, and Sara felt herself smile even though she hadn't heard it. A waitress finally came over and Sara ordered a ginger ale. She continued to watch Fiske sitting at the bar. He was not joking around anymore. He stared at the wall so intently Sara caught herself looking at it too. All she saw were bottles of beer and liquor, neatly arranged; Fiske obviously observed far more. He had already ordered a second beer, and when it arrived he held the bottle to his lips until it was empty. She noticed that his hands were large, the fingers thick and strong-looking. They didn't look like the hands of someone who spent all his time punching a pencil or sitting in front of a computer screen.

Fiske slapped some money down, grabbed his jacket and turned around. For an instant Sara thought she felt his eyes upon her. He hesitated a moment and then pulled his jacket on. The corner she was in was dark. She didn't believe he had seen her, but why had he hesitated? A little nervous now, she waited an extra minute or so before she rose and left, leaving a couple of singles behind for her drink.

She didn't see him as she came back out into the sunlight. Just like that, as though in a dream, he was gone. On an impulse she went back into the bar and asked the bartender if he knew John. He shook his head. She wanted to ask some more questions, but the bartender's expression signaled that he would not be communicative if she did.

The construction workers eyed her with a great deal of interest. She decided to leave before things turned uncomfortable for her. Sara walked back to her car and climbed in. Half of her had wanted to run into Fiske somehow, the other part of her was glad that she hadn't. What would she say anyway? Hello, I work with your brother and I'm sort of stalking you?

She had driven back to northern Virginia that night, had two beers herself, and fallen asleep in the glider on her rear deck. The same one she was sitting in right now as she smoked her cigarette and watched the sky. That had been the last time she had seen John Fiske, almost four months ago.

She couldn't be in love with him, since she didn't even know the man; infatuation was far more likely. Maybe if she ever did meet Fiske it would destroy her impression of him.

She wasn't a believer in destiny, though. If anything was going to happen between them, it would probably be up to her to make the first move. She was just totally confused as to what that first move should be.

Sara put out her cigarette and stared at the sky. She felt like going for a sail. She wanted to feel the wind in her hair, the tickle of water spray against her skin, the sting of rope against her palm. But right now, she didn't want to experience any of those things alone. She wanted to do them with someone, someone in particular. But with what little Michael had told her about John Fiske, and what she had seen of the man herself, she doubted that would ever happen.

A hundred miles south, John Fiske too gazed up at the sky for a moment as he got out of his car. The Buick wasn't in the driveway, but Fiske had not come to see his father anyway. The neighborhood was quiet other than a couple of teenagers two doors down working on a Chevy with an engine so big it looked like it had ruptured through the car's hood.

Fiske had just spent all day in a trial. He had presented his case, warts and all, as best he could. The ACA had vigorously represented the commonwealth. Eight hours of intense sparring, and Fiske had barely had time to go to the john to take a leak before the jury came back with a guilty verdict. It was his guy's third strike. He was gone for good. The ironic thing was Fiske really believed him innocent of this particular charge — not something he could say with most of his clients. But his guy had beat so many other raps, maybe the jury was just unconsciously evening the score. To top it off, he'd die of old age waiting for the rest of his legal fee to come. Prisoners for life seldom bothered about settling their debts, particularly debts to their loser attorneys.

Fiske went into the backyard, opened the side door to the garage, went in and pulled a beer from the fridge. The humidity still lay over them like a damp blanket, and he held the cold bottle against his temple, letting the chill sink deep. At the very rear of the yard was a small stand of bent trees and a long-dead grapevine still tightly wrapped around rusty poles and wire. Fiske went back there and leaned up against one of the elms. He looked down at a recessed spot in the grass. Here was buried Bo, the Belgian shepherd the Fiske brothers had grown up with. Their father had brought the dog home one day when Bo was no bigger than his fist. Within a year or so he had grown into a big-chested, sixty-pound, black and white beauty that both boys adored, Mike especially. Bo would follow them on their morning paper routes, taking turns with the two boys. They had had almost nine years of intense pleasure together before Bo had toppled over from a stroke while Mike was playing with him. John had never seen anyone cry that hard in his whole life. Neither his mother nor his father could console Mike. He had sat in the backyard bawling, holding the dog's bushy coat, trying to make him stand up again, to go play with him in the sunshine. John had held his brother tightly that day, cried with him, stroked the still head of their beloved shepherd.

When Mike had gone to school the next day, John had stayed behind with his father to bury the dog here. When Mike had come home they all had attended a little service in the backyard for Bo. Mike had read with great conviction from the Bible and the brothers had placed a little headstone, actually a chunk of cinder block, with Bo's name scrawled on it in pen, at the head of the simple grave. The piece of cinder block was still there, though the ink had long since vanished.

Fiske knelt down and ran his hand along the grass, so smooth and fine in this shaded spot. Damn, they had loved that dog so much. Why did the past have to recede so quickly? Why did one always recall the good times as being so brief? He shook his head, and then the voice startled him.

"I remember that old dog like it was yesterday."

He looked up at Ida German, who stood on the other side of the fence staring at him. He rose, looking a little embarrassed. "It was a long time ago, Ms. German."

The woman smelled perpetually of beef and onions, as did her house, Fiske knew. A widow for nearly thirty years now, she moved slowly, her body shrunken, squat and thick. Her long housecoat covered veiny, splotched legs and bloated ankles. But at nearly ninety years old, her mind was still clear, her words crisp.

"Everything's a long time ago with me. Not

128

with you. Not just yet. How's your momma?"

"Holding her own."

"I've been meaning to get over there to see her soon, but this old body just doesn't have the get up and go it used to."

"I'm sure she'd love seeing you."

"Your daddy went out a while ago. American Legion or VFW, I think."

"Good, I'm glad to see he's getting out. And I appreciate you keeping him company."

"Isn't any fun being alone. I've outlived three of my own children. Hardest thing in the world for a parent to do is bury their babies. Ain't natural. How's Mike? Don't see him much."

"He keeps pretty busy."

"Who would've thought that chubby-cheeked little towhead would've gone on to do what he's done? Mind-boggling, if you ask me."

"He's earned it." Fiske stopped for a moment. That had just slipped out. But his brother *had* earned it.

"You both have."

"I think Mike hit it a little higher than I did."

"Huh. Don't you go believing that. Your daddy brags about you a mile a minute. I mean, he talks about Mike too, but you're the king of the hill with him."

"Well, he and Mom brought us up right. Sacrificed everything for us. You don't forget that." Maybe Mike had, but he never would, Fiske told himself.

"Well, Mike had three fine examples to follow." Fiske looked at her curiously. "That boy worshiped the ground you walked on."

"People change."

"You think so, do you?"

A few drops of rain started to fall. "You better get back inside, Ms. German, it looks like it might pour."

"You know you can call me Ida if you want."

Fiske smiled. "Some things don't change, Ms. German."

He watched her until she made it inside. The neighborhood wasn't nearly as safe as it had once been. He and his father had installed deadbolts on her doors, sash locks on her windows and a peephole in her front door. The elderly carried a bull's-eye on them when it came to crime.

Fiske looked down once more at Bo's grave, the vision of his brother crying his eyes out over a dead dog cemented in his mind.

CHAPTER TWELVE

"How are you, Mom?" Michael Fiske touched his mother's face. It was early in the morning and Gladys was not in a good mood. Her face darkened and she pulled back from his touch. He looked at her a moment, deep sadness in his eyes as he saw the open hostility in hers.

"I brought you something." He opened the bag he carried and pulled out a gift-wrapped box. When she made no move to open it, he did so for her. He showed her the blouse, her favorite shade of lavender. He held it out to her, but she wouldn't take it. It was like this every time he came to visit. She would rarely talk to him, her mood always foul. And his gifts were never accepted. He repeatedly tried to draw her out in conversation, but she refused.

He sat back and sighed. He had told his father about this, that his mother absolutely refused to have anything to do with him. But his old man was powerless to change things. No one could control who Gladys was nice to. Michael's visits had grown less and less frequent because of it. He had tried to talk to his brother about it, but John had refused to discuss it with him. His mother would never treat John that way, Michael knew. To her, he was the golden child. Michael Fiske could be elected the president of the United States or win the Nobel Prize, and in her eyes he would still always be second to his older brother. He left the blouse on the table, gave his mother a quick kiss and left.

Outside, the rain had started to come down. Michael pulled up the collar on his trench coat and got back in his car. He had a very long drive ahead of him. The visit to his mother was not the only reason he had driven south. He was now headed to southwest Virginia. To Fort Jackson. To see Rufus Harms. For a moment, he debated whether to stop and see his brother. John had not returned his phone call, which was no surprise. But the journey he was about to undertake had some personal risk to it, and Michael wouldn't have minded having his brother's advice and perhaps presence. But then he shook his head. John Fiske was a very busy attorney and he didn't have time to run around the state chasing wild theories of his younger brother's. He would just have to deal with it alone.

As she often did, Elizabeth Knight rose early, did some stretching exercises on the floor and then ran on the treadmill in the spare bedroom of her and her husband Senator Jordan Knight's Watergate apartment.

She showered, dressed, fixed some coffee and toast and looked over some bench memos in preparation for oral argument next week. Since it was Friday, the justices would spend part of the day in conference, where they would vote on cases they had already heard. Ramsey ran the conferences on a tight schedule. To her disappointment, there was little debate at these meetings. Ramsey would summarize the salient points of each case, cast his vote orally, and wait while the other justices did the same. If Ramsey was in the majority, which he usually was, he assigned the opinion. If he wasn't, the most senior associate justice in the majority, usually Murphy — ideological opposites, he and Ramsey rarely if ever voted the same way — would assign the opinion.

As Knight finished her coffee, she thought back over her first three years on the Court. It had been a whirlwind, really. Because of her gender, she was automatically seen as not only a champion of women's rights but also of causes that many women traditionally supported. People never considered this stereotyping, although it was a blatant form of it, Knight knew. She was a judge, not a politician. She had to look at each case separately, just as she had done as a trial court judge. And yet, even she had to own up to the fact that the Supreme Court was different. The impact of its decisions was so far-reaching that the justices were forced to go beyond the four corners of each case and look at the effect of the decision on everyone else. That had been one of the hardest things for her to do.

She looked around the luxurious apartment. She and her husband had a good life together. They were routinely touted as the capital's number one power couple. And in a way they were. She carried that mantle as well as she could, even as she combated the isolation that each justice had to endure. When you went on the Court, friends stopped calling, people treated you differently, were careful, guarded in what they said around you. Knight had always been gregarious, outgoing. Now she felt much less so. She clung to her husband's professional life as a way to lessen the impact of this abrupt change. Sometimes she felt like a nun with eight monks as her lifelong companions.

As if in answer to her thoughts, Jordan Knight, still dressed in his pajamas, came up behind her and gave her a hug.

"You know, there's no rule that says you have to start every day at the crack of dawn. Snuggling in bed is good for the soul," he said.

She kissed his hand and turned to give him a hug back.

"I don't recall you being a late sleeper either, Senator."

"We should both make a concerted effort to do it, I think. Who knows what it could lead to? I've heard sex is the best defense against aging."

Jordan Knight was tall and heavily built, with thinning gray hair and a tanned face scored with lines. In the inequitable way of the world regarding the physical appearances of men and women, he would be considered handsome even with the wrinkles and the extra pounds. He cut quite a figure on the pages of the *Post* and local magazines, and on national TV shows where even the most experienced political pundits were often overwhelmed by his wit, experience and intelligence.

"You certainly have some interesting opinions."

He poured himself a cup of coffee while she looked over her papers.

"Ramsey still grooming you to become a good member of his camp?"

"Oh, he's pushing all the right buttons, saying all the right things. However, I'm afraid some of my recent actions aren't sitting all that well with him."

"You go your own way, Beth, just like always. You're smarter than all of them. Hell, you should be chief justice."

She put an arm around his thick shoulders. "Like maybe you should be president?"

He shrugged. "I think the U.S. Senate is

challenge enough for me. Who knows, this might be the last roundup for yours truly."

She pulled her arm away. "We really haven't talked about it."

"I know. We're both busy. Too many demands on our time. When things settle down, we'll talk. I think we have to."

"You sound serious."

"Can't keep on the treadmill forever, Beth."

She let out a troubled laugh. "I'm afraid I signed on for life."

"Good thing about politics. You can always decide not to run again. Or you can lose your seat."

"I thought there was a lot more you wanted to accomplish."

"It's not going to happen. Too many obstacles. Too many games. To tell you the truth, I'm getting kind of tired."

Beth Knight started to say something and then stopped. She had jumped firmly into the "game" of the Supreme Court.

Jordan Knight picked up his coffee and kissed her on the cheek. "Go get 'em, Ms. Justice."

As the senator walked off, she rubbed her face where he had kissed it. She tried to study her papers once more, but found she couldn't. She simply sat there, her mind suddenly whirling in many different directions.

John Fiske held the photo of himself and his brother. He had sat there for almost twenty minutes with it, not even looking at it for much of that time. Finally he stood it up on his bookcase, went over to the phone and dialed his brother's number. There was no answer and Fiske didn't bother leaving a message. He then called the Supreme Court, but was told Michael was not yet in. He called thirty minutes later and was told by another person that Michael would not be in at all that day. Figures, he thought. He couldn't get hold of his brother when he had at last gotten up the nerve to call him. Was that what it was — nerve? He sat down at his desk and tried to work, but his eyes kept stealing over to that photo.

Finally, he packed his briefcase, grateful that he had to go to court, grateful to get away from some nagging feelings.

In the course of the morning, he had two hearings back to back. One he won convincingly; with the other he was torn apart by the judge, who seemingly took every opportunity to ridicule his legal arguments, while the assistant commonwealth attorney stood by politely, holding back the smiles; you had to maintain the professional facade, because it could be your butt being put through the wringer the next time. Everyone here understood that. Or at least those who stuck with it did.

He next went to the Richmond city jail and then the county jail in Henrico to speak with clients. With one, he discussed strategy for the man's upcoming trial. His inmate client offered to go on the witness stand and lie. Sorry, you won't be doing that, Fiske told him. With another client the talk was about the ubiquitous plea bargain. Months, years, decades. How much time? Will I have a shot at parole? Suspended sentence? Help me out, man. I got a woman and kids. I got bizness to take care of. Okay, right. What's a little murder and mayhem compared to that?

With the last client, things took a very different turn. "We're not in good shape here, Leon. I think we should plead," Fiske advised.

"Nope. We go to trial."

"They've got two eyewitnesses."

"Is that right?"

Leon had been charged with the shooting of a child. It had been a dispute between two gangs of skinheads, and the little girl had gotten in the way — a fairly common tragedy these days. "Well, they're not going to hurt me if they don't testify, are they?"

"Why won't they testify?" Fiske said evenly. He had been down this road before. How many times as a cop had cases disappeared before his eyes because the witnesses suddenly forgot what they had so clearly seen and remembered before?

Leon shrugged. "You know, things come up. People don't keep their appointments."

"The police took their statements."

Leon gave him a sharp glance. "Right, but I get to face people testifying against me, right? So's you can trip 'em up on the witness stand, right?"

"You certainly know your Constitution," Fiske said dryly. He took a deep breath. He was so tired of the game of witness intimidation. "Come on, Leon, tell me — I'm your attorney, it's all privileged. Why won't they testify against you?"

Leon cracked a smile. "You don't need to know."

"Yes, I do. I don't need any surprises. You never know what a prosecutor is going to try. Believe me, I've seen it happen before. If something goes down and I'm not prepared for it, your ass could go up the river."

Now Leon looked a little worried. He obviously hadn't thought of that. He rubbed at the swastika on his forearm. "Privileged, right? That's what you said."

"That's right." Fiske leaned forward. "Between you, me and God."

Leon laughed. "God? Shit, that's a good one." He hunched forward and spoke in a low voice. "Got me a couple of friends. They gonna pay a little visit to these witnesses. Make sure they forget their way to the courthouse. It's all set up."

Fiske slumped back. "Aw hell, now you've done it."

"Done what?"

"Told me the one damn thing I have to go to the judge with."

"What the hell you talking about?"

"Legally, and ethically, I can't divulge any information given to me by a client."

"So, what's the problem? I'm your client and I just gave you the damn information."

"Right, but you see, there's an important exception to that rule. You just told me about a crime you've planned for the future. That's the one thing I have to tell the court. I can't let you commit the crime. I have to advise you not to do it. Consider yourself so advised. If you'd already done it, we'd be okay. What the hell were you thinking about, telling me that?" Fiske looked disgusted.

"I didn't know that was the law. Shit, I ain't no damn lawyer."

"Come on, Leon, you know the law better than most lawyers. Now you've gone and screwed up your own case. Now we have to plead."

"What the hell do you mean?"

"If we go to trial and the witnesses don't show, I have to tell the court what you told me. If the witnesses show, your ass is cooked."

"Well, then don't you go telling nobody nothing."

"That's not an option, Leon. If I don't and it comes out somehow, I lose my license to practice. And while I like you a lot, no client is worth that. Without my license I don't eat. And you screwed up, man, not me."

"I don't believe this shit. I thought you could tell your damn attorney anything."

"I'll see what I can do on the plea. You're going to spend some time in jail, Leon, no way around that." Fiske stood and patted the prisoner on the back. "Don't worry, I'll cut you the best deal I can."

As Fiske walked out of the visitors' room he smiled for the first time all day.

CHAPTER THIRTEEN

Michael Fiske looked up ahead nervously as he drove. His wipers struggled to maintain visibility in the face of the pouring rain. Headed west, he had passed places with names like Pulaski, Bland and even something called Hungry Mothers State Park, which had conjured up in his mind a discomforting vision of huddled masses of women and children begging for food along the park's trails. For a while winds swirling off nearby Big A Mountain buffeted the car. Even though he had been born and raised in Virginia, Fiske had never been west of Roanoke, and he had only ventured there to take the bar exam. Up to this point he had made good time, because the trip had been all highway. Once he had exited Interstate 81 and headed in a northwesterly direction, that had abruptly changed. Now the terrain was rugged and unforgiving, the roads narrow and serpentine.

He glanced over at the briefcase next to him on the front seat, drawing a long breath as he did so. He had learned a lot since reading Rufus Harms's plea for help.

Harms had murdered a young girl, who

was visiting the military base where Harms had been stationed at the end of the Vietnam War. He had been in the stockade at the time but had somehow broken out. There was no motive; it just seemed a random act of violence by a madman. Those facts were uncontroverted. As a Supreme Court clerk, Michael had many information resources to turn to, and he had used all of them in compiling the background facts. However, the military wouldn't acknowledge that such a program as described in Harms's petition even existed. Michael slapped the steering wheel. If only Harms or his attorney had included the letter from the Army in his filing.

Michael had finally decided that he needed to hear the account from its source: Rufus Harms. He had tried to do it through channels other than direct confrontation. He had tracked down Samuel Rider through the postal trail, but had received no reply to his calls. Was he the author of the typewritten paper? Michael believed it was a strong possibility. He had called the prison to try to talk with Harms on the phone, but his request had been denied. That had only increased his suspicions. If an innocent man was in prison, it was Michael's job — his *duty*, he corrected himself — to see that that man became free.

And there was a final reason for this trip.

Some of the names listed in the petition, the people allegedly involved in the little girl's death, were names well known to Michael. If it turned out Rufus Harms was telling the truth . . . he shuddered as one nightmarish scenario after another rolled through his thoughts.

On the seat next to him was a road atlas and a sheet of written directions he had made up for himself showing precisely the way to the prison. Over the next hour or so, he traveled through miles of back roads and over corroded wooden bridges, blackened by weather and car exhaust, through towns that weren't big enough to justify the title, and past battered house trailers tucked into narrow crevices of rock along the foothills of the Appalachians. He was passed by muddy pickup trucks with miniature Confederate flags flapping from radio antennae, and shotguns and deer rifles slung across racks in the rear window. As he drew closer to the prison, the tight, weathered faces of the few people he saw grew more and more taciturn, their eyes filled with a constant, irreversible suspicion.

As Michael rounded a curve, the prison facility loomed before him. The stone walls were thick, towering and vast, like a medieval castle transported to this miserably poor stretch of rocky soil. He wondered for a moment if the stone had been quarried by the prisoners into the assemblage of their own tombs.

He received his visitor's card, passed through the main gate and was then directed to the prison's visitors' parking. He explained his purpose to the guard at the entrance.

"You're not on the visitors' list," the young guard said. He eyed Michael's dark blue suit and intelligent features with contempt. *A rich, smartass, pretty boy from the city*, Michael could read in the man's eyes.

"I called several times, but I never got through to anyone who could tell me the procedure for being put on the list."

"Up to the prisoner. Generally speaking, if he wants you to visit, you do. If he don't, you don't. Only control these boys got." The guard cracked a grin.

"If you tell him that an attorney is here to see him, I'm sure he'll put me on his visitors' list."

"You're his lawyer?"

"I'm involved with an appeal of his right now," Michael said evasively.

The guard looked down at his ledger. "Rufus Harms," he said, evidently confused. "He's been here since before I was even born. Exactly what sort of appeal could somebody like him have going after all this time?"

"I'm not at liberty to discuss that," Michael said. "My work is covered by attor-

145

ney-client privilege and is absolutely confidential."

"I know that. What, you think I'm stupid?"

"Not at all."

"If I let you in and it turns out I wasn't supposed to, then my keester's in a lot of trouble."

"Well, I was just thinking that you might want to check with your superior. That way, it's not your call and you can't get in trouble."

The guard picked up his phone. "I was already going to do that," he said in a very unfriendly tone.

He spoke into the phone for a couple minutes and then hung up.

"Somebody's coming on down." Michael nodded. "Where you from?" the guard asked.

"Washington, D.C."

"How much does somebody like you get paid?" It was clear that whatever sum Michael stated would be too much.

He took a deep breath as he observed the approach of the uniformed officer. "Actually, not nearly enough."

The young guard quickly stood and saluted his superior officer. The officer turned to Michael. "Please come with me, Mr. Fiske." The man was in his fifties, with the lean build, calm but serious manner and closely cut gray hair that helped mark him as career military.

146

Michael followed the man's precise strides down the hallway to a small office. For five minutes Michael patiently explained what he was doing there without really revealing any information of substance. He could do the lawyer-speak with the best of them.

"If you tell Mr. Harms that I'm here, he'll see me."

The man twirled a pen between his fingers, his eyes dead center on the young lawyer. "This is rather puzzling. Rufus Harms just received a visit from his lawyer not too long ago. And that person wasn't you."

"Is that right? Was his name Samuel Rider?" The man didn't answer, but the momentary surprise on his features made Michael inwardly smile. His hunch had proven correct. Harms's former military counsel had enclosed the typewritten sheet of paper. "A person can have more than one lawyer, sir."

"Not someone like Rufus Harms. He hasn't had anyone for the last twenty-five years. Oh, his brother visits pretty regularly, but all this interest in the man has us puzzled. I'm sure you can appreciate that."

Michael smiled pleasantly, but his next words were spoken in a firm manner. "I hope you can appreciate the fact that a prisoner is entitled to speak with an attorney."

The officer stared at him for a few moments and then picked up the phone and spoke into it. He hung up and looked back at Michael without speaking. Five minutes passed before the phone rang again. When the man put it back down, he nodded at Michael and said curtly, "He'll see you."

CHAPTER FOURTEEN

When Rufus Harms appeared in the doorway of the visitors' room, he looked confused as his gaze settled on the young man. He shuffled forward. Michael rose to greet him and was met with a bark by the guard behind Rufus.

"Sit down."

Michael did so immediately.

The guard watched closely until Rufus took a seat across from Michael, and turned to the lawyer. "You were previously instructed as to the rules of conduct during visitation. In case you forgot any of them, they're posted clearly right over there." He pointed to a large sign on the wall. "No physical contact is permitted at any time. And you are to remain seated at all times. Do you understand?"

"Yes. Do you have to stay in the room? There is such a thing as attorney-client confidentiality. Also, does he have to be chained like that?" Michael asked.

"You wouldn't ask that if you'd seen what he did to a bunch of guys inside this place. Even all chained up he could snap your skinny little neck in half in two seconds." The guard moved closer to Michael. "Maybe at other prisons you get some more privacy, but this isn't like other prisons. We only got the biggest and the baddest here, and we have our own set of rules to operate by. This is an unscheduled visit, so you got twenty minutes before the big bad wolf here has to go to work cleaning toilets. And we got some real messy ones today."

"Then I'd appreciate your letting us get started," said Michael.

The guard said nothing else and moved over to his post against the door.

When Michael looked at Rufus he found the big man's gaze squarely on him.

"Good afternoon, Mr. Harms. My name is Michael Fiske."

"That name don't mean nothing to me."

"I know, but I'm here to ask you some questions."

"They said you were my lawyer. You're not my lawyer."

"I didn't say I was. They just assumed that. I'm not associated with Mr. Rider."

Rufus's eyes narrowed. "How do you know about Samuel?"

"That's really not relevant. I'm here to ask you questions, because I received your writ for certiorari."

"You did what?"

"Your appeal." Michael lowered his voice.

"I work at the United States Supreme Court."

Rufus's mouth fell open. "Then what the hell are you doing here?"

Michael nervously cleared his throat. "I know this isn't actually orthodox. But I read your appeal, and I wanted to ask you some questions about it. It makes a number of very damaging allegations against some very prominent people." As he looked into Rufus's astonished eyes, Michael suddenly regretted ever coming here. "I looked into the background of your case and some things don't make sense to me. I wanted to ask you some questions and then, if things check out, we can get your appeal going."

"Why isn't it going already? It got to the damned Court, didn't it?"

"Yes, but it also had a number of technical deficiencies that would have caused it to be denied processing. I can try to help you with those. But what I want to avoid is a scandal. You have to understand, Mr. Harms, that the Court receives bags of appeals from prisoners every year that have no merit."

Rufus's eyes narrowed. "Are you saying I'm lying? Is that what you're saying? Why don't you spend twenty-five years in this place for something that wasn't your fault and then come here and tell me that?"

"I'm not saying you're lying. I actually think there's something to all of this or, believe me, I wouldn't have come here." He looked around the grim room. He had never been near a place like this, sitting across from a man like Rufus. He suddenly felt like a first-grader getting off the bus and realizing he was somehow in high school. "Believe me," he said again. "I just need to talk to you."

"You got some ID shows you are who you say you are? I ain't been in a real trusting mood for the last thirty years."

Supreme Court clerks were not issued ID badges. The security personnel at the Court were required to learn to recognize them by sight. However, the Court did publish an official directory with the clerks' names and photos. That was one way to help the guards get to know their faces. Michael pulled this from his pocket and showed it to Rufus. Rufus studied it intently, looked over at the guard, then turned back to Michael. "You got a radio in your briefcase?"

"A radio?" Michael shook his head.

Rufus lowered his voice even more. "Then start humming."

"What?" Michael said, bewildered. "I can't really . . . I mean, I'm not really musical."

Rufus shook his head impatiently. "Then you got a pen?"

Michael nodded dumbly.

"Then pull it out and start tapping on the table. They've probably heard all they need to hear by now anyway, but we'll leave 'em a few surprises."

When Michael started to say something, Rufus interrupted. "No words, just tap. And listen."

Michael began to tap the table with his pen. The guard glanced over but said nothing.

Rufus spoke so softly that Michael had to strain to hear him. "You shouldn't have come here at all. You don't know the chance I took to get that piece of paper out of this place. If you read it, you know why. Killing some old black con who strangled a little white girl, people wouldn't give a damn. Don't think they would."

Michael stopped tapping. "That was all a long time ago. Things have changed."

Rufus let out a grunt. "Is that right? Why don't you go knock on Medgar Evers's or Martin Luther King's coffin and tell 'em that? Things have changed, yes sir, everything be all right now. Praise the Lord."

"That's not what I meant."

"If the people I talked about in that letter were black, and I was white — and I didn't call this place home — would you be here right now 'checking up' on my story?"

Michael looked down. When he looked back up, his expression was pained. "Maybe not."

"Sure as hell not! Start tapping, and don't stop."

Michael did so. "Believe it or not, I want to help you. If the things you described in your letter did happen, then I want to see justice served."

"Why the hell you care about somebody like me?"

"Because I care about the truth," Michael said simply. "If you're telling the truth, then I will do everything in my power to get you out of this place."

"That's sure easy enough to say, ain't it?"

"Mr. Harms, I like to use my brains, my skills, to help people less fortunate than I am. I feel it's my duty."

"Well, that's real nice of you, son, but don't go patting me on the head. I might bite your hand off."

Michael blinked in confusion, and then it registered. "I'm sorry, I didn't mean to be condescending. Look, if you've been wrongly imprisoned, then I want to help you get your freedom. That's all."

Rufus didn't say anything for a minute, as though attempting to gauge the sincerity of the young man's words. When he finally leaned forward again, his features were softer, but his manner remained guarded.

"It ain't safe to talk about this stuff here."

"Where else can we talk?"

"No place that I know of. They don't let

people like me out for vacation. But everything I said is true."

"You made reference to a let—"

"Shut up!" Rufus said. He looked around again, his eyes locking for a moment on the large mirror. "Wasn't it with what was filed?"

"No."

"All right, you know my attorney. You said his name before."

Michael nodded. "Samuel Rider. I tried to call him, but he didn't call me back."

"Tap louder." Michael picked up the beat. Rufus glanced around and then began speaking. "I'll tell him to talk to you. Whatever you need to know, he'll tell you."

"Mr. Harms, why did you file your appeal with the Supreme Court?"

"Ain't no higher one, is there?"

"No."

"Didn't think so. We get newspapers in here. Some TV, radio. I've been watching them people over the years. In here you think a lot about courts and such. Faces change, but them judges can do anything. Anything they want to. I seen it. Whole country's seen it."

"But from a purely legal technical point of view there are other avenues you really have to pursue in the lower courts before your appeal can be heard there. You don't even have a lower court ruling from which you're appealing, for instance. In sum, your appeal

155

has numerous flaws."

Rufus shook his head wearily. "I been in this place half my life. I ain't got all that much time left. I ain't never been married, I ain't never gonna have no kids. The last thing I'm gonna do is spend years messing around with lawyers and courts and such. I want out of here, and I want out of here just as fast as I can. I want to be free. Them big judges, they can get me outta here, if they believe in doing the right thing. That's the right thing, you go back and tell 'em that. They call 'em justices, well, that's justice."

Michael looked at him curiously. "Are you sure there's not another reason you filed it with the Supreme Court?"

Rufus looked blankly at him. "Like what?"

Michael let out a breath he hadn't realized he was holding. It was certainly possible that Rufus wouldn't know the positions now held by some of the men named in his appeal. "Never mind."

Rufus sat back and stared at Michael. "So what do them judges think about all this? They sent you down here, didn't they?"

Michael stopped tapping and said nervously, "Actually, they don't know I'm here."

"What?"

"I haven't actually shown anyone your appeal, Mr. Harms. I . . . I wanted to be sure, you know, that it was all aboveboard."

"You're the only one that's seen it?"

"For now, but like I said —"

Rufus looked at Michael's briefcase. "You didn't bring my letter with you, did you?"

Michael followed his gaze to the briefcase. "Well, I wanted to ask you some questions about it. You see —"

"Lord help us," Rufus said so violently that the guard braced himself to pounce.

"Did they take your briefcase when you come in? Because two of the men I wrote about are at this prison. One of them is in charge of the whole damn place."

"They're here?" Michael went pale. He had confirmed that the men named in the appeal were in the Army back in the seventies. He knew the current whereabouts of two of them, but he hadn't bothered to locate the others. He froze, suddenly realizing that he had just made a potentially fatal mistake.

"Did they take your damn briefcase?"

Michael stammered, "Just — just for a couple of minutes. But I put the documents in a sealed envelope, and it's still sealed."

"You done killed us both," Rufus screamed. Like a hot geyser, he exploded upward, flipping the heavy table over as though it were made of balsa wood. Michael leaped out of the way and slid across the floor. The guard blew his whistle and grabbed Rufus from behind in a choke hold. Michael watched as the giant prisoner, shackled as he was, flipped the two-hundred-pound guard off like a bothersome gnat. A half dozen other guards poured into the room and went at the man, swinging their batons. Rufus kept tossing them off like a moose against a pack of wolves, for a good five minutes, until he finally went down. They dragged him from the room, first screaming and then gagging as a baton was wedged against his throat. Right before Rufus disappeared, he stared at Michael, horror and betrayal in his eyes.

After an exhausting struggle that had continued all the way down the hallway, the guards managed to strap Rufus to a gurney.

"Get him to the infirmary," somebody screamed. "I think he's going into convulsions."

Even with the shackles and thick leather restraints on, Rufus wildly gyrated, the gurney rocking back and forth. He kept screaming until someone stuffed a cloth into his mouth.

"Hurry up, dammit," the same man said.

The group burst through the double doors and into the infirmary.

"Good God!" The physician on duty pointed to a clear space. "Over here, men."

They swung the gurney around and slid it into the empty spot. As the doctor approached, one of Rufus's thrashing feet almost clipped him in the gut.

"Take that out of his mouth," the doctor said, pointing at the handkerchief balled up in Rufus's mouth. The prisoner's face was turning a deep purple.

One of the guards looked at him warily. "You better take care, Doc, he's gone nuts. If he can reach you, he'll hurt you. He already took out three of my men. Crazy SOB." The guard looked menacingly at Rufus. As soon as the cloth was pulled from his mouth, Rufus's screams filled the room.

"Get a monitor on him," the doctor said to one of the attending nurses. Seconds after they managed to attach the sensors to Rufus, the doctor was closely watching the erratic rise and fall of Rufus's blood pressure and pulse. He looked at one of the nurses. "Get an IV over here." To another nurse he said, "An amp of lidocaine, stat, before he goes into cardiac arrest or has a stroke."

Both guards and medical personnel crowded around the gurney.

"Can't your men get out of here?" the doctor yelled into the ear of one of the guards.

The man shook his head. "He's strong enough to maybe break those restraints, and if he does and we're not here, then he could kill everybody in this room within a minute. Believe me, he could."

The doctor eyed the portable IV stand as it was placed next to the gurney. The other nurse raced up with the amp of lidocaine. The doctor nodded at the guards. "We're going to need your help to hold him down. We need a good vein to get the IV started, and from the looks of things we're only going to get one shot at it."

The men gathered around Rufus, holding him down. Even with their combined weight, it was barely enough.

Rufus looked back at them, so enraged, so terrified, he could barely keep his senses. Just like the night when Ruth Ann Mosley had perished. They ripped his shirtsleeve up, exposing his sinewy forearm, the veins strong and pronounced. He shut his eyes and then opened them again as he saw the shiny needle coming his way. He shut his eyes one more time. When he opened them he was no longer in the infirmary at Fort Jackson. He was in the stockade in South Carolina a quarter of a century ago. The door burst open and a group of men walked in like they owned the place, like they owned him. There was only one he didn't know by sight. He had expected to see the batons come out, to feel the sharp thrusts into his ribs, against his buttocks and forearms. It had become a morning and evening ritual. As he absorbed the blows in silence, his mind would recite a Bible prayer, his spiritual side carrying him past the physical torture.

Instead, a gun was placed against his head.

He was told to kneel down on the floor and to close his eyes. That's when it happened. He remembered the surprise, the shock he had felt as he stared up at the grinning, triumphant group. The smiles vanished when, a few minutes later, Harms rose, threw off the men as though they were weightless, burst through his cell door, bowled over the guard on duty and was out of the stockade, running wild.

Rufus blinked again and he was back in the infirmary, looking at the faces, the bodies bearing down on him. He saw the needle coming closer to his forearm. He was looking up, the only person doing that. That's when he saw the second needle puncture the IV bag, the fluid from the hypodermic flowing into the lidocaine solution.

Vic Tremaine had carried out his task calmly and efficiently, as though he were watering flowers instead of committing murder. He didn't even look at his victim. Rufus jerked his head back around and eyed the IV needle held by the doctor. It was just about to puncture his skin, discharging into his body whatever poison Tremaine had chosen to kill him with. They had taken half his life already. He was not about to let them take the rest, not yet.

Rufus timed it as best as he could.

"Shit!" the doctor yelled, as Rufus ripped free from the restraint, grabbed his hand and

161

whipped it across his body. The IV stand came tumbling down; the IV bag hit the floor and burst. A furious Tremaine took the opportunity to quickly leave the infirmary. Rufus's chest suddenly tightened, and his breathing became constricted. When the doctor managed to stagger up, he looked at Rufus. So still was the prisoner that the doctor had to check the monitor to make sure he was still alive. As he stared at vital signs that had dropped to dangerously low levels, he said, "Nobody can take this many extremes. He could be going into shock." He turned to a nurse. "Get a medevac helicopter up here." He looked at the head guard. "We're not equipped to handle this kind of situation. We'll stabilize him and then fly him to the hospital in Roanoke. But we need to move fast. I assume you're sending a guard with him."

The guard rubbed his bruised jaw and looked at the docile Rufus. "I'd send a whole platoon if they could fit in the damn chopper."

CHAPTER FIFTEEN

Escorted by an armed guard, Michael Fiske walked unsteadily down the hallway. Waiting at the end of the corridor was the uniformed officer who had questioned him earlier. Michael could see that he was holding two pieces of paper.

"Mr. Fiske, I didn't identify myself when we first met. My name is Colonel Frank Rayfield. I'm the commanding officer here."

Michael licked his lips. Frank Rayfield was one of the men Rufus had named in his appeal. The name had meant nothing to Michael at the time. Inside this prison, it meant that he was going to die. Who could have imagined that two of the men Rufus had accused of, essentially, murder in his appeal would be here of all places? But now that he thought about it, this would be a perfect place for them to keep close watch on Rufus Harms.

Focusing on Rayfield once more, Michael wondered where they would dump his body. As he had done as a child, he suddenly found himself wishing that his big brother would appear to help him. He looked on dully as Rayfield handed him the papers and motioned the guard to leave. As Michael clutched the papers, Rayfield looked apologetic.

"I'm afraid my men were a little over-zealous," said Rayfield. "We don't usually photocopy documents in a sealed envelope." Actually, Rayfield had opened the envelope and photocopied its contents himself. None of his men had seen the documents.

Michael looked down at the papers. "I don't understand. The envelope was still sealed."

"The envelope is a very common one. They just put it back in a new one and sealed it."

Michael inwardly cursed himself for missing something that obvious.

Rayfield broke into a chuckle.

"What's so funny?" Michael demanded.

"This is the fifth time Rufus Harms has named me in some cockamamie lawsuit, Mr. Fiske. What else am I supposed to do but laugh?"

"Excuse me?"

"He's never gone as high as the United States Supreme Court before — that's who you're with, isn't it?"

"I don't have to answer that."

"Okay. But if you are, then your presence here is a little unusual."

"That's my business."

"And my business is running this prison in

a precise, military way," Rayfield snapped back. But then his voice softened. "I don't blame you, though. Harms is slick. Looks like he conned his old military lawyer to help him this time, and Sam Rider should know better."

"You're saying Rufus Harms makes a practice of filing frivolous lawsuits?"

"You think that's unusual for prisoners? Too much time on their hands. Anyway, last year he accused the president of the United States, the Secretary of Defense and yours truly of conspiring to frame him for a murder he committed, and which was witnessed by at least a half dozen people."

"Really?" Michael looked skeptical.

"Yes, really. It was finally dismissed, but it cost a few thousand bucks in government attorney time to get it done. I know the courts are open to everybody, Mr. Fiske. But a nuisance suit is a nuisance suit and, quite frankly, I'm getting tired of them."

"But he said in his petition —"

"Right, I read it. Two years ago, he claimed it was Agent Orange suffered in combat that caused him to do it. And you know what? Rufus Harms was never exposed to Agent Orange, because he was never in combat. He spent most of his two-year Army career in the stockade for insubordination, among other things. It's no secret — look it up yourself if you want. That is, if you haven't already done so." He gazed at Michael, who was looking down. "Now take your little papers, go back to Washington and let it work its way through the system. It'll get dismissed like all the others. Some innocent people are going to get embarrassed as hell, but that's the American way. I guess it's why I fought for this country: to sustain all those freedoms. Even when they're abused."

"You're just going to let me go?"

"You're not a prisoner here. I've got a lot of real inmates to worry about, including one that just beat the crap out of three of my guards. You're going to have to answer some questions that one of my men will be here shortly to ask you. It will relate to what happened in the visitors' room. We need it for our incident report."

"But that means it will go into the official record. My being here, everything."

"That's right, it will. It was your choice to come here, not mine. You have to live with the consequences."

"I know. But I wasn't counting on any of this."

"Well, life is full of little surprises."

"Look, do you really have to file anything?"

"Your presence here is a matter of official record anyway, Mr. Fiske, regardless of what happened in that visitors' room. You are in the visitation book with an assigned badge number."

"I guess I hadn't thought that all the way through."

"I guess not. I take it you're not really experienced in military matters?" While Michael stood there looking miserable, Rayfield thought for a moment. "Look, we need to fill out the report, but other things being equal, I may not officially file it. Maybe your presence here at the prison gets expunged too."

Michael breathed a sigh of relief. "Could you do that?"

"Maybe. You're a lawyer. What about a *quid pro quo?*"

"What do you mean?"

"I throw away the report and you throw away that appeal." He paused as he stared at the young man. "It would save the government another lawyer bill. I mean, God bless anybody's rights to seek their day in court, but this is getting a little old."

Michael looked away. "I'll have to think about that. It has some technical deficiencies anyway. Maybe you're right."

"I am right. I'm not looking to mess up your career. We'll just forget this ever happened. And hopefully I won't be reading about this case in the papers. If I do, then maybe your being down here has to come out too. Now, if you'll excuse me." Rayfield turned on his heel and walked off, leaving behind a visibly distressed Michael Fiske.

Rayfield went directly to his office. Rufus's suspicions had been well founded; a listening device designed to blend in with the wood grain had been planted on the underside of the table in the visitors' room. Rayfield listened once more to the conversation between Michael and Rufus. Some of it had been disrupted by Michael tapping his pen. The radio had obliterated all of Rufus's earlier conversation with Rider. Rufus was no idiot. But Rayfield had heard and read enough to know that potentially they had a big problem. And his conversation with Michael had not solved the dilemma, at least not permanently. He picked up the phone and placed a call. In concise sentences Rayfield recounted the events to the party at the other end.

"Holy shit, I can't believe this."

"I know."

"All of this happened today?"

"Well, I told you about Rider coming in earlier, but yes, all of these events happened just now."

"Why the hell did you let him in to see Harms?"

"If I didn't, don't you think he would've gotten more suspicious? After reading what Harms had written in his damn letter to the Court, what choice did I have?"

"You should have taken care of the sonofabitch before this. You've had twenty-five years to do it, Frank."

"That was the plan twenty-five years ago, to kill him," Rayfield fired back. "And look what happened. Tremaine and I have spent half our lives watching over his ass."

"You two aren't exactly doing it for free. What's your little nest egg up to so far? A million? Retirement's going to be awfully nice. But it won't be, for any of us, if this gets out."

"It's not like I haven't tried to kill the guy. Hell, Tremaine tried to do him today in the infirmary, but damn, it's like the guy's got a sixth sense. Rufus Harms is as mean as a snake when his back's against the wall. The guards will only go so far and we've got people looking over our shoulder, surprise inspections, the damn ACLU. The bastard just won't die. Why don't you come down here and try?"

"All right, all right, there's no use us arguing about it. You're sure we were all named in the letter? How is that possible? He didn't even know who I was."

Rayfield didn't hesitate. The person he was speaking with had *not* been named in Rufus's letter, but Rayfield wasn't going to tell him that. Everybody was on the hook for this one. "How should I know? He's had twenty-five years to think about it."

"So how did he get the letter out?"

"That blows my mind. The guard saw the

damn thing. It was his last will and testament, that was it."

"But he got it out somehow."

"Sam Rider is involved. That's for sure. He brought a radio with him and the noise messed up the bug we installed, so I couldn't hear what they said to each other. That should've told me something was up."

"I never trusted that guy. Except for Rider's insanity BS, Harms would've been dead a long time ago, courtesy of the Army."

"The second letter we found in Fiske's briefcase had been done on a typewriter. There were no initials at the bottom, you know, like when it's typed by a personal secretary, so Rider probably did it himself. They were both original documents, by the way."

"Dammit, why now? After all this time?"

"Harms received a letter from the Army. He referenced it in the paper he filed. Maybe that jogged his memory. I can tell you that up to now he either didn't remember what happened, or he's been keeping it inside for the last twenty-five years."

"Why would he do that? And why in the hell would the Army be sending him anything after all this time?"

"I don't know," Rayfield said nervously. He actually did know. The reason had been referenced in Rufus's court petition. But Rayfield was going to keep that card hidden for now.

"And of course you don't have this mysterious letter from the Army, do you?"

"No. I mean, not yet."

"It must be in his cell, although I can't imagine how it slipped through." The voice was again accusatory.

"Sometimes I think the guy's a magician," said Rayfield.

"Has he had any other visitors?"

"Just his brother, Josh Harms. He comes about once a month."

"And what about Rufus?"

"Looks like he's just about bought it. Stroke or heart attack. Even if he makes it, he probably won't be the same."

"Where is he?"

"En route to the hospital in Roanoke."

"Why the hell did you let him out?"

"The doc ordered it. He has an obligation to save the man's life, prisoner or not. If I overruled him, don't you think it would raise suspicion?"

"Well, keep on top of it, and pray his heart blows up. And if it doesn't, make it."

"Come on, who'd believe him?"

"You might be surprised. This Michael Fiske? He's the only other one who knows, besides Rider?"

"That's right. At least I think so. He came here to check out Harms's story. Didn't tell anybody — at least that's what he told Harms. We caught a big break there,"

Rayfield said. "I gave him the song and dance about Harms being a chronic jailhouse lawyer. I think he bought it. We got leverage because he could get in big trouble for being here. I don't think he's going to let the appeal go through."

The voice on the other end went up a few decibels. "Are you nuts? Fiske isn't going to have a choice in the matter."

"He's a Supreme Court clerk, for chrissakes. I heard him tell Harms."

"I know that. I damn well know that. But let me tell you exactly what you're going to do. You're going to take care of Fiske and Rider. And you're going to do it pronto."

Rayfield paled. "You want me to kill a Supreme Court clerk and a local lawyer? Come on, they don't have any proof of this. They can't hurt us."

"You don't know that. You don't know what was in the letter from the Army. You don't know what new information Fiske or Rider might have found out in the interim. And Rider's been practicing law for thirty years. He wouldn't have filed something he thought was frivolous, not with the damn Supreme Court. And maybe you're not aware of this, but Supreme Court clerks aren't exactly dummies. Fiske didn't drive all the way down there because he thought Harms was a lunatic. From what you told me, the contents of the letters were very specific on what happened in that stockade."

"They were," Rayfield conceded.

"So there you are. But that's not the biggest hole in all this. Remember, Harms isn't a jailhouse lawyer. He's never filed anything else in court. If Fiske checks out your claim, he'll find out you lied. And when Fiske does that — and I have to believe he will — then everything blows up."

"It's not like I had a lot of time to think up a plan," Rayfield said hotly.

"I'm not saying otherwise. But by lying to him, you just made him a big liability. And we have yet another problem."

"What's that?"

"Everything Harms said in his appeal happens to be true. Did you forget that? The truth is funny. You start looking here and there and all of a sudden the wall of lies starts to topple over. Guess where it's going to land? Do you really want to take that chance? Because when that wall comes down, the only place you're going to be retiring to is Fort Jackson. And this time on the other side of the prison cell door. That sound good to you, Frank?"

Rayfield took a weary breath and checked his watch.

"Shit, I'd take Nam over this any day."

"I guess we all got a little too comfortable. Well, it's time to earn your money, Frank. You and Tremaine just get it done. And while you're taking care of business, remember this: We all either survive this together, or we all go down together."

Thirty minutes later, after his debriefing by Rayfield's assistant, Michael left the prison building and walked in the light rain to his car. What a sucker he'd been. He felt like tearing up the appeal papers, but he wouldn't. Maybe he'd put them back into the process. Still, he felt sorry for Rufus Harms. All those years in prison had taken their toll. As Michael pulled out of the parking lot, he had no way of knowing that most of his radiator fluid had been collected in a bucket and poured into the nearby woods.

Five minutes later he looked on in dismay as the steam poured out from the hood of his car. He got out, gingerly raised the hood and then jumped back as a cloud of steam momentarily engulfed him. Swearing angrily, he looked around: not a car or human in sight. He thought for a moment. He could walk back to the prison, use the phone and call a towing service. As if on cue, the rain picked up in intensity.

As he looked up ahead of him, his spirits brightened. A van was approaching from the direction of the prison. He waved his arms to flag it down. As he did so he looked back at the car, steam still pouring out. Funny — he had just had it serviced in preparation for the trip. As he looked back at the van, his heart started to beat rapidly. He looked around, and then turned and sprinted away from the van. It sped up and quickly overtook him, blocking his way. He was about to race into the woods when the window came down and a gun was pointed at him.

"Get in," Victor Tremaine ordered.

CHAPTER SIXTEEN

It was Saturday afternoon when Sara Evans drove to Michael's apartment and looked at the cars parked on the street. His Honda wasn't there. He had called in sick on Friday, something she had never known him to do before. She had called his apartment, but he hadn't answered the phone. She parked, went in the building and knocked on his door. There was no answer. She didn't have a key. She went around to the rear of the building and climbed up the fire escape. She looked in the window of his small kitchen. Nothing. She tried the door, but it was locked. She drove back to the Court, her worries increased tenfold. Michael was not sick, she knew that. All this had something to do with the papers she had seen in his briefcase, she was sure of it. She silently prayed that he was not in over his head. That he was safe, and would be back to work on Monday.

She went back to work for the rest of the day and then had a late dinner with some of the other clerks at a restaurant near Union Station. They all wanted to talk shop, except for Sara. Usually a devoted fan of this ritual, she simply could not get into the conversations. At one point she wanted to run screaming from the room, sick of the endless strategizing, predictions, case selections, the subtlest nuances analyzed to death; mushroom clouds from mere mushrooms.

Later that night she lingered on the rear deck of her home. Then she made up her mind and took her boat out for a late-night sail on the river. She counted the stars, made funny pictures from them in her mind. She thought of Michael's offer of marriage and the reasons she had refused it. Her colleagues would be amazed that she had. It would be a brilliant match, they would say. They would have a wonderful, dynamic life together, with the almost absolute certainty that their children would be highly intelligent, ambitious and athletically gifted. Sara herself had been a scholarship lacrosse player in college, although Michael was the better athlete of the two.

She wondered whom he would ultimately marry. Or if he even would. Her rejection might cause him to remain a bachelor the rest of his life. As she sailed along, she had to smile. She was giving herself far too much credit. In a year's time, Michael would be off doing something incredibly fantastic. She would be lucky if he even remembered who she was five years from now.

As she docked her boat and wrapped the sails, she stopped for a moment to catch one last breeze off the water before she headed back to the house. Barely a twenty-minute non-rush-hour trip due north would deliver her to the most powerful city on earth, to her place with the most awe-inspiring legal minds of her time. And yet all she really wanted to do right now was snuggle under her blanket with the lights off and pretend she never had to go back there. Reasonably ambitious all her life, she suddenly had no drive to accomplish anything else of note in her professional life. It was like she had used up all her energy in getting to this point. Marriage and being a mom? Was that what she wanted? She had no siblings and had been pretty spoiled growing up. She wasn't used to being around kids all that much, but something pulled at her in this direction. Something very strong. But even so, she wasn't sure. And shouldn't she be by now?

As she went inside, undressed and climbed into bed, she realized that having a family required one thing to start: finding someone to love. She had just turned down one opportunity to do so with a truly exceptional man. Would another chance come along? Did she want a man in her life right now? Still, sometimes one shot was all you got. One shot. That was her last thought before falling asleep.

CHAPTER SEVENTEEN

It was Monday and John Fiske sat at his desk, digesting yet another arrest report on one of his clients. By now he was extremely adept at this process. He was only halfway through the report and he could already tell the sort of deal the guy could expect to get. Well, it was nice being good at something.

The knock on his office door startled him. His right hand slid open the top drawer of his desk. Inside was a 9mm, a leftover from his cop days. His clientele were not the most trustworthy. So while he would represent them zealously, he was not naïve enough to turn his back on them either. Some of his clients had shown up at his door drugged or drunk, with a grudge against him for some perceived wrong. Thus, his spirits were lifted considerably by the feel of hard steel against his palm.

"Come on in, door's unlocked."

The uniformed police officer who stepped through the doorway brought a smile to Fiske's lips, and he closed his desk drawer. "Hey, Billy, how you doing?"

"I've been better, John," Officer Billy Hawkins said.

As Hawkins came forward and sat down, Fiske saw the multicolored bruises on his friend's face. "What the hell happened to you?"

Hawkins touched one of the bruises. "Guy went nuts at a bar the other night, popped me a couple of good ones." He added quickly, "That's not why I'm here, John."

Fiske knew Hawkins to be a good-natured sort who didn't let the constant pressures of his job overwhelm him. He was always as reliable and serious about his job as he was casual and friendly off duty.

Hawkins glanced nervously at Fiske.

"It's not anything with Bonnie or the kids, is it?" Fiske asked.

"It's not about *my* family, John."

"Is that right?" As he looked into Hawkins's troubled eyes, Fiske's gut clenched.

"Damn, John, you know how much we hated going around to the next of kin, and we didn't even know them."

Fiske slowly stood up, his mouth instantly dry. "Next of kin? Oh my God, not my mom? My dad?"

"No, John, it's not them."

"Just tell me what the hell you need to tell me, Billy."

Hawkins licked his lips and then started speaking quickly. "We got a call from the police up in D.C."

Fiske looked confused for an instant. "D.C.?" As soon as he said it, his body froze. "Mike?"

Hawkins nodded.

"Was it a car accident?"

"No accident." Hawkins paused for a moment and cleared his throat. "It was a homicide, John. Looks like a robbery gone bad. They found his car in an alley. Bad part of town, I understand."

Fiske let this horrific news sink in for a long minute. As a cop and now a lawyer, he had seen the results of many murders on other people, other families. This was new territory. "You haven't told my dad, have you?" he said quietly.

Hawkins shook his head. "Figured you'd want to do that. And what with your momma the way she is."

"I'll take care of it," Fiske said.

His thoughts were interrupted by Hawkins's next words.

"The detective in charge has requested an ID from next of kin, John."

As a police officer, how many times had Fiske told a grieving parent that same thing?

"I'll go on up."

"I'm so sorry, John."

"I know, Billy, I know."

After Hawkins had left, Fiske walked over to the photo of him and his brother and picked it up. His hands were shaking. It was not possible, what Hawkins had just told him. He had survived two gunshot wounds and spent nearly a month in the hospital, his mother and his little brother next to him for much of that time. If John Fiske could survive that, if he could be alive right now, how could his brother be dead? He put the photo back down. He tried to move to get his coat, but his legs were frozen. He just stood there.

CHAPTER EIGHTEEN

Rufus Harms slowly opened his eyes. The room was dim, shadowy. However, he was accustomed to seeing without benefit of light, becoming, over the years, an expert of sorts. The years in prison had also boosted the acuity of his hearing such that he could almost hear someone thinking. You did both a lot in prison: listening and thinking.

He shifted slowly on his hospital bed. His arms and legs were still in restraints. He knew there was a guard right outside the door to his room. Rufus had seen him several times now, as people had come and gone from his room. The guard was not a cop; he was in fatigues, and he was armed. Regular Army or maybe reserves, Harms couldn't be sure. He took a shallow breath. Over the course of the last two days, Harms had listened to the doctors checking him. He had not suffered a heart attack, although apparently he had come close. He couldn't remember what the doctors had called it, but his heartbeat had been irregular enough for him to stay in intensive care awhile.

He thought back to his last hour at Fort Jackson. He wondered if Michael Fiske had even made it out of the prison before they killed him. Ironically, Rufus's near heart attack had saved his life. At least he was out of Fort Jackson. For now. But when his condition improved, they would send him back. And then he would die. Unless they killed him in here first.

He had scrutinized each of the doctors and nurses attending him. Anyone administering drugs to him was given special attention. He was confident that, if he thought himself in danger, he could rip the sides of the hospital bed off. For now, all he could do was get his strength back, wait, watch, and hope. If he could not gain his freedom through the court system, then he would obtain it another way. He was not going back to Fort Jackson. Not while he was still breathing.

For the next two hours he watched people come and go. Every time the door to his room opened, he would look at the guard outside. A young kid, looking very self-important in his uniform and wearing his gun. Two guards had flown with him on the helicopter, but neither was the one posted outside now. Perhaps they were doing a rotation. When the door opened, the guard would nod and smile at the person entering or leaving, especially if the person happened to be young and female. When the guard had occasionally looked into the room, Rufus had seen two emotions in his eyes: hatred and fear. That was good. That meant he had a chance. Both could lead to the one thing Rufus desperately needed the guard to commit: a mistake.

Leaving a single guard, they must think him pretty well incapacitated, Rufus figured; only he wasn't. The monitors with their numbers and jumpy lines meant nothing to him. They were metal-cased buzzards waiting for him to fade before moving in. But he could feel his strength returning; that was something tangible. He curled and uncurled his hands in anticipation of being able eventually to fully move his arms.

Two hours later he heard the door swing inward, and then the light came on. The nurse carried a metal clipboard and smiled at him as she checked his monitor. She was in her mid-forties, he guessed. Pretty, with a full figure. Looking at her wide hips, he figured she had been through several childbirths.

"You're doing better today," she said when she noticed him watching her.

"I'm sorry to hear that."

She stared at him openmouthed. "You better believe a lot of people in this place would love to have that kind of prognosis."

"Where exactly am I?"

"Roanoke, Virginia."

"Never been to Roanoke."

"It's a pretty town."

"Not as pretty as you," said Rufus with an

embarrassed smile, the words having slipped through his lips. He had not been this close to a woman in almost three decades. The last woman he had ever seen in person was his mother, weeping at his side as they carried him off to serve his life sentence. She had died within the week. Something exploded in her brain, his brother had told him. But he knew his mother had died from a broken heart.

His nose wrinkled up as the scent touched it. It seemed out of place in a hospital. At first, Harms did not realize that he was simply smelling the nurse's scent, a mixture of slight perfume, moisturizing lotion and woman. Damn. What else had he forgotten about living a real life? A tear started to tremble at the corner of his right eye as he thought this.

She looked down at him, her eyebrows raised, a hand on one hip. "They told me to be careful around you."

He looked at her. "I'd never hurt you, ma'am." His tone was solemn, sincere. She saw the tear barely clinging to his eye. She didn't really know what to say next.

"Can't you put on that chart that I'm dying or something?"

"Are you crazy? I can't do that. Don't you want to get better?"

"Soon as I do, I go right back to Fort Jackson."

186

"Not a nice place, I take it."

"I been in the same cell there for over twenty years. Kind of nice seeing something else for a change. Not much to do there except count your heartbeats and stare at the concrete."

She looked surprised. "Twenty years? How old are you?"

Rufus thought for a moment. "I don't know exactly, to tell you the truth. Not over fifty."

"Come on, you don't know how old you are?"

He eyed her steadily. "The only cons who keep a calendar are the ones getting out someday. I'm serving a life sentence, ma'am. Ain't never getting out. What's it matter how old I am?" He said this so matter-of-factly that the nurse felt her cheeks flush.

"Oh." Her voice quavered. "I guess I see your point."

He shifted his body slightly. The shackles pinged against the metal sides of the bed. She drew back.

"Can you call somebody for me, ma'am?"

"Who? Your wife?"

"I don't got no wife. My brother. He don't know where I am. Wanted to let him know."

"I think I have to check with the guard first."

Rufus looked past her. "That little boy out there? What's he got to do with my brother?

He don't look like he can go pee-pee by hisself."

She laughed. "Well, they sent him to guard big old you, now, didn't they?"

"My brother's name is Joshua. Joshua Harms. He goes by Josh. I can tell you his phone number if you got yourself a pencil. Just call him and tell him where I am. Gets kind of lonely in here. He don't live all that far away. Who knows, he might come on over and see me."

"It does get lonely here," she said a little wistfully. She looked down at him, at his tall, strong body, all covered with tubes and patches. And the shackles — they held her attention.

Rufus noted her staring. Chains on a man usually had that effect on people, he had found.

"What'd you do anyway? To be in prison for."

"What's your name?"

"Why?"

"Just like to know. My name's Rufus. Rufus Harms."

"I knew that. It's on your chart."

"Well, I ain't got no chart to look up your name."

She hesitated for a moment, looked around at the door and then back at him. "My name's Cassandra," she said.

"Real pretty name." His eyes passed over

her figure. "It fits you."

"Thank you. So you're not going to tell me what you did?"

"Why you want to know?"

"Just curious."

"I killed somebody. A long time ago."

"Why'd you do it? Were they trying to hurt you?"

"Didn't do nothing to me."

"So why'd you do it?"

"Didn't know what I was doing. Was out of my mind."

"Is that right?" She drew back a little farther as he said this. "Isn't that what they all say?"

"Just happens to be the truth with me. You gonna call my brother?"

"I don't know. Maybe."

"Tell you what, I'll give you the number. If you don't, you don't. If you do, then I thank you very much."

She looked at him curiously. "You don't act like a murderer."

"You ought to be careful about that. It's the sweet-talking ones end up hurting you. I seen enough of that kind."

"So I shouldn't trust you, then?"

His eyes seized on hers. "You got to make up your own mind on that."

She considered this for a moment. "So what's your brother's number?"

She took down the telephone number,

slipped it in her pocket and turned to leave.

"Hey, Ms. Cassandra?" She turned back around. "You're right. I ain't no killer. You come back and talk to me some more . . . if you want to, that is." He managed a weak smile and rattled the shackles. "I ain't going nowhere."

She eyed him from across the room and he thought he saw a smile flicker across her mouth. Then she turned and went out the door. Rufus craned his neck to see if she spoke to the guard, but she walked right past him. Rufus lay back and stared at the ceiling. He inhaled deeply, letting the remnants of her scent soak into him. A few moments later a smile spread across his face. As did, finally, the tears.

CHAPTER NINETEEN

It was an unusual gathering of all of the clerks and the justices. Marshal of the Court Richard Perkins and Supreme Court Police Chief Leo Dellasandro were there too, looking stonily around the table in the large room. Elizabeth Knight's eyes were moist and she dabbed continually at them with a handkerchief.

As Sara Evans looked at the grim-faced justices, her eyes stopped on Thomas Murphy. Murphy was short and flabby, with white hair and tufted eyebrows. His face held cheekbones the shape of almonds. He still favored three-piece suits and wore large, showy cuff links. His dress, however, did not attract Sara's attention; rather it was his expression of complete mourning. She quickly finished checking the occupants of the room: Michael Fiske was not there. She felt the blood rush to her head. When Harold Ramsey rose from the head of the table, his deep voice was oddly subdued; she could not really hear him that well, but she knew exactly what he was saying, as though reading his lips.

"This is terrible, terrible news. In fact, I can't remember anything like it." Ramsey surveyed the room, his hands making fists in his anxiety, his tall frame shaking.

He took a heavy breath. "Michael Fiske is dead."

The justices obviously already knew. All the clerks, however, collectively missed a breath.

Ramsey started to say something else but then stopped. He motioned to Leo Dellasandro, who nodded and stepped forward while the chief justice collapsed into his chair.

Dellasandro was about five-ten, face wide, with flat cheeks and a pug nose, and a layer of fat over a muscular physique. He had an olive complexion, with wiry black and gray hair. Arising from his pores was the smell of cigar. He wore his uniform with a proud air, his thick fingers tucked inside the gun belt. The other man in uniform standing immediately behind him was Ron Klaus, his second-in-command. Klaus was trim and professional in appearance, the darting activity of his blue eyes suggesting a nimble mind. He and Dellasandro were the watchdogs of this place. They seemed to move about in tandem. Most people who worked at the Court could not think of one man without the other.

"The details are sketchy right now, but apparently Michael was the victim of a robbery. He was found in his car in an alley in

Southeast near the Anacostia River His family has been notified, and one of them is coming up to officially identify the body. However, there's no question that it's Michael." He looked down for a moment. "When they learned he was employed here, the police brought over a photograph."

One nervous-looking clerk raised his hand. "Are they sure it was a robbery? It didn't have to do with his working here?"

Sara looked over at him angrily. Not the question you really wanted to hear five seconds after learning someone you worked with, cared about, was dead. But then she supposed violent death did that to people: made them instinctively fear for their own lives.

Dellasandro put up his big calming hands. "We have heard nothing that would make us believe that his death had anything whatsoever to do with the Court. However, out of an abundance of caution, we are increasing security around here, and should anyone notice anything suspicious or out of the ordinary, please contact either myself or Mr. Klaus. We'll make available to you any future details about this situation at the appropriate time." He looked over at Ramsey, who had his head bowed in his hands and was making no move to get up. Dellasandro stood there awkwardly until Elizabeth Knight rose.

"I know this has been a terrible shock to all of us. Michael was one of the most popular people ever to work here. His loss touches us all, especially those who had become close to him." She paused and looked at Sara for a moment. "If any of you wishes to talk about anything, please feel free to do so with your justice. Or you can stop by and see me. I'm not sure how we can continue to function, but the work of the Court must go on, despite this horrible, horrible . . ." Knight stopped again and gripped the table to stop herself from collapsing to the floor. Dellasandro quickly took her arm, but she motioned him away.

Knight rallied herself enough to call an end to the meeting and the room quickly cleared. Except for Sara Evans. She sat there, numb, staring at the spot where Knight had stood. The tears freely streamed down her face. Michael was dead. He had taken an appeal, acted very strangely for over a week, and now he was dead. Murdered. A robbery, they said. She didn't believe the answer was that simple. But right now it didn't matter. All that mattered was she had lost someone very close to her. Someone who, under different circumstances perhaps, she might have gladly spent her life with. She put her head down on the table as the sobs burst from her.

From the doorway, Elizabeth Knight watched her.

CHAPTER TWENTY

A little over three hours after Billy Hawkins had announced his brother's death, John Fiske was walking through the hallways of the D.C. morgue, a white-coated intake specialist leading the way. Fiske had had to show identification and prove to the man that he was really Michael Fiske's brother. He had been prepared for that and had brought pictures of the two together. He had tried to reach his father before leaving town, but there had been no answer. Fiske had driven by the house, but no one had been home. He left a note for his dad, including no details. He had to be sure it was his brother, and the only way to be certain was where he was headed.

Fiske was surprised when they entered an office, and even more puzzled when the morgue attendant pulled a Polaroid from a file and held it out to him.

"I'm not identifying a photo. I want to see the body."

"That's not the procedure we have here, sir. We're in the process of installing a video system so that IDs can be made via remote television, but it's not functional yet. Until then, it's done with a Polaroid."

"Not this time."

The man tapped the photo against his palm as though trying to arouse Fiske's curiosity in it. "Most people would much prefer to do it with a photograph. This is very unusual."

"I'm not 'most people,' and having a brother murdered is unusual. At least it is for me."

The attendant picked up the phone and conveyed instructions to prepare the body for viewing. Then he opened the door to his office, motioning Fiske to follow him. After a short walk, they entered a small room that carried a medicinal smell several times stronger than that in a hospital. In the center of the room stood a gurney. From under the white sheet rose a number of edges representing the head, nose, shoulders, knees and feet of the body. As Fiske headed toward the gurney, he clutched at the same irrational hope that everyone in his position would leap for: that the person under the sheet was not his brother, that his family was still reasonably intact.

As the attendant gripped the edge of the sheet, Fiske slid one hand around the metal side of the gurney and squeezed tightly. As the sheet rose upward, exposing the head and upper torso of the deceased, Fiske closed his eyes, looked upward and mouthed a silent prayer. He took a deep breath, held it, opened his eyes and then looked down. Before he knew it, he was nodding.

He tried to look away but couldn't. Even a stranger could have looked at the slope of the forehead, the arrangement of the eyes and mouth, the flow of the chin, and concluded that the two men held some close familial bond. "That's my brother."

The sheet was replaced and the attendant gave Fiske the ID card to sign. "Other than the items the police have retained, we'll release his personal effects to you." The attendant glanced at the gurney. "We've had a busy week, and we're backed up with bodies, but we should have autopsy results fairly soon. This one looks pretty simple anyway."

Anger flared on Fiske's face but then quickly faded. The man was not paid to be tactful. "Did they find the bullet that killed him?"

"Only the autopsy can determine cause of death."

"Don't bullshit me." The attendant looked startled. "I saw the exit wound on the left side of his head. Did they find it?"

"No. At least not yet."

"I heard it was a robbery," said Fiske. The attendant nodded. "He was found in his car?"

"Right, wallet gone. We had to trace his

identity through his license plate."

"So if a robbery, why didn't they take the car? Carjacking's the hot thing right now. Beat the victim's ATM password out of him or her, kill them, take the car and hit a few banks, load up on money, ditch the car and go on to the next one. Why not with this one?"

"I don't know anything about that."

"Who's handling the case?"

"It happened in D.C. Must be D.C. Homicide Division."

"My brother was a federal employee. United States Supreme Court. Maybe the FBI will be involved too."

"Again, I don't know anything about that."

"I'd like the name of the detective at D.C. Homicide."

The attendant didn't answer, but jotted some notes down in the file, perhaps hoping that if he remained quiet Fiske would just go away.

"I'd really like that name, please," Fiske said, edging a step closer.

The attendant finally sighed, pulled a business card out of the file and handed it to Fiske. "Buford Chandler. He'll probably want to talk to you anyway. He's a good guy. Probably'll catch the person who did this."

Fiske looked briefly at the card before putting it in his coat pocket. He settled a clear-eyed gaze on the attendant. "Oh, we're going to get whoever did this." The odd tone in his voice made the attendant look up from his file. "Now I'd like some time alone with my brother."

The attendant glanced over at the gurney. "Sure, I'll be outside. Just let me know when you're done."

After the man left, Fiske pulled a chair next to the gurney and sat down. He had not shed a tear since learning of his brother's death. He told himself it was because positive ID had not been made yet, but now it had and still no tears. On the drive up, he had caught himself counting out-of-state license plates, a game the brothers had played growing up. A game Mike Fiske had usually won.

He lifted the side of the sheet and took one of his brother's hands. It was cold, but the fingers were supple. He squeezed them gently. Fiske looked down at the concrete floor and closed his eyes. When he reopened them a few minutes later only two tears had collected on the concrete. He quickly looked up and a gush of air came out of his lungs. It felt forced, all of it, and he suddenly felt unworthy to be here.

As a cop, he had sat with the parents of too many drunken kids who had wrapped themselves around a tree or telephone pole. He had consoled them, expressed empathy, even held them. He had truly believed that he had approached, even touched the depths of their despair. He often wondered what it would feel like when it happened to him. He plainly knew this was not it.

He forced himself to think about his parents. How exactly would he tell his father that his golden child was dead? And his mother? At least there was an easy answer to that question: He couldn't and shouldn't tell her.

Raised Catholic, but not a religious man, Fiske chose to speak with his brother instead of God. He pressed his brother's hand against his chest and talked to him of things he was sorry for, of how much he loved him, how much he wanted him not to be dead, in case his brother's spirit was lingering behind, waiting for this communication, this quiet rupture of guilt and remorse from his older brother. Then Fiske fell silent, his eyes closed again. He could hear each solid drum of his heart, a sound that was somehow dwarfed by the stillness of the body next to his.

The attendant poked his head in. "Mr. Fiske, we need to take your brother on down. It's been half an hour."

Fiske rose and passed the attendant without a word. His brother's body was going to a terrifying place, where strangers would forage through his remains for clues as to who had killed him. As they wheeled the gurney away, Fiske walked back out into the sunlight and left his little brother behind.

CHAPTER TWENTY-ONE

"You're sure you covered your tracks?"

Rayfield nodded into the phone. "Every record of his being here has been expunged. I've already transferred all the personnel who saw Fiske to other facilities. Even if someone figures out somehow that he came here, there won't be anyone left to tell them anything."

"And no one saw you dump the body?"

"Vic drove his car back. I followed him. We picked a good place. The police will think it was a robbery. Nobody saw us. And even if they did, it's not the sort of place where people are real cooperative with the law."

"Nothing left in the car?"

"We took his wallet to further the robbery angle. His briefcase too. A map. There wasn't anything else. Of course we filled the radiator back up with fluid."

"And Harms?"

"He's still in the hospital. Looks like he's going to make it."

"Damn. Just our luck."

"Don't sweat it. When he comes back here, we'll deal with him. Weak heart and all, you never know what might happen to you."

"Don't wait too long. You can't hit him in the hospital?"

"Too dangerous. Too many people around."

"And you've got him well guarded?"

"He's chained to the bed with a guard posted twenty-four hours a day outside his door. He's being released tomorrow morning. By tomorrow night he'll be dead. Vic's already working on the details."

"And there's nobody out there who can help him? You're sure?"

Rayfield laughed. "Hell, no one even knows he's there. He's got nobody. Never has, never will."

"No mistakes, Frank."

"I'll call you when he's dead."

Fiske sat in the car and cranked up the air-conditioning, which, in his fourteen-year-old Ford, merely caused the slow movement of muggy air from left to right. Sweat trickling down his face and staining his shirt collar, Fiske finally eased down the window as he stared at the building. Average-looking on the outside, it was not on the inside. There, the people spent all of their time searching for those who killed other people. And Fiske was trying to decide whether to join them in their pursuit or drive back home. He had identified his brother's remains, his official duty as next of kin completed. He could go home, tell his father, make the funeral arrangements, see to his brother's final affairs, bury him and then get on with his life. That's what everyone else did.

Instead, Fiske pulled himself out of the car and into the muggy air, and entered the building at 300 Indiana Avenue, home to the D.C. Police Homicide Division. After passing through security and being directed by a uniformed police officer, he stopped at a desk. He had tried his father once again from the morgue, but still no answer. Frustrated, he was now also worried that his father had somehow found out and was on his way up here.

He looked down at the card the attendant at the morgue had given him. "Detective Buford Chandler, please," he said, looking down at the young woman behind the desk.

"And you are?" The sharp angle of her neck, and her superior tone, immediately made Fiske want to stuff her in one of her own desk drawers.

"John Fiske. Detective Chandler is investigating my brother's . . . my brother's murder. His name was Michael Fiske." She stared at him, no recognition on her features. "He was a clerk at the Supreme Court," he added.

She glanced at some papers on her desk. "And somebody killed him?"

"This is the Homicide Division, isn't it?" She settled her gaze back on him, her look of annoyance pronounced. He continued: "Yes, somebody killed him" — he glanced down at the nameplate on her desk — "Ms. Baxter."

"Well, what exactly can I do for you?"

"I'd like to see Detective Chandler."

"Is he expecting you?"

Fiske leaned forward and spoke in a low voice. "Not exactly, but —"

"Then I'm afraid he's not in," she said, cutting him off.

"I think if you put a call into —" Fiske stopped and watched as she turned away from him and started typing on her computer. "Look, I really need to see Detective Chandler."

She typed as she spoke. "Let me educate you on the situation here, okay? We have lots of cases and not too many detectives. We don't have time for every drop-in off the street. We have to have priorities. I'm sure you can understand that." Her voice drifted off as she looked at the computer screen.

Fiske leaned forward until his face was only a couple of inches from the woman. When she looked around, they were eye to eye. "Let me make you understand something. I came up from Richmond to identify the remains of my brother at *Detective Chandler's* request. I did that. My brother is dead. And right about now the medical examiner is cutting a Y incision in his chest so that he can lift out his insides, organ by organ. Then he's going to take a saw and cut an intermastoid incision like a wedge of pie through his skull, right about here." Fiske made an imaginary cut along Ms. Baxter's head with his finger, overcoming a very strong impulse to snatch up a handful of the woman's permed blond hair. "That's so he can lift out his brain and trace the path of the bullet that killed him and perhaps get some shell fragments. Now, I thought I'd come and have a chat with Detective Chandler and see if he and I can come up with some leads on who might have killed him."

She said coldly, "Well, that's not your job, is it? We have enough problems without family members getting involved in police investigations. I'm sure Detective Chandler will be in touch if he needs you." She again turned away from him.

Fiske gripped the edge of her desk and took a deep breath, trying his best not to lose it. "Look, I can understand the caseload problem you must have here, and the fact that you don't know me from Adam —"

"I'm really busy right now, sir. So if you have a problem, I suggest you put it in writing."

"All I want to do is talk to the man!"

"Am I going to have to call a guard, or what?"

Fiske slammed his hand down on the desk. "My brother is dead! And I would really appreciate if you would take that piss-poor attitude you're wearing and replace it with just an ounce of compassion. And if you can't force yourself to mean it, lady, then just pretend."

"I'm Buford Chandler."

Both Fiske and Baxter turned. Chandler was black, in his early fifties, with curly white hair, a matching mustache and a tall, thickened frame that managed to retain a certain athleticism from his youth. He wore an empty shoulder holster, a smudge of pistol oil on his shirt where the grip had lain against it. He looked Fiske up and down from behind a pair of trifocals.

"I'm John Fiske."

"I heard. In fact I've been standing over here listening to the whole thing."

"Then you know what he said to me, Detective Chandler?" Baxter said.

"Every word."

"And don't you have something to say?"

"Yes, I do."

Baxter looked over at Fiske with a look of satisfaction on her face. "Well?"

"I think this young man gave you some pretty good advice." Chandler hooked a finger at Fiske. "Let's talk."

Chandler and Fiske made their way through busy hallways to a small, cluttered office. "Have a seat." Chandler pointed to the only chair in the room other than the one behind his desk. There were files stacked on the chair. "Just put those on the floor." Chandler held up a warning finger. "Be careful you don't taint any evidence. These days if I belch while I'm looking at tissue samples, all I'm going to hear is, 'Inadmissible! Free my mass-murdering sonofabitch of a client.' "

Fiske very carefully moved the files while Chandler settled behind his desk.

"Now, I don't want you feeling sorry for what you said to Judy Baxter."

"I wasn't planning on it."

Chandler suppressed a smile. "Okay, first things first. I'm sorry about your brother."

"Thank you," Fiske said in a subdued manner.

"Probably the first time you heard that since arriving up here, isn't it?"

"Actually, it is."

"So you were in law enforcement?" Chandler casually remarked, then smiled at Fiske's surprise. "The average citizen doesn't usually know about Y incisions and intermastoid cuts. With the way you got in Ms. Baxter's face, the manner in which you carry yourself, and your build, I'd say you were a patrolman."

"Past tense?"

"If you were still on the force the folks in Richmond would've told me when we contacted them. And besides, I know very few

207

police officers who wear suits off duty."

"Right on all counts. I'm glad you were assigned to this case, Detective Chandler."

"You and forty-two other active cases." Fiske shook his head, and Chandler continued: "Budgetary cuts and all. I don't even have a partner anymore."

"So in other words, don't expect any miracles?"

"I will do my best to catch whoever killed your brother. But I can give no guarantees."

"Then how about a little unofficial help?"

"How do you mean?"

"I worked a lot of homicides with the detectives down in Richmond. Learned a lot, remember a lot. Maybe I can be your new partner."

"Officially, that's absolutely impossible."

"Officially, I absolutely understand."

"What do you do now?"

"I'm a criminal defense attorney," said Fiske. Chandler rolled his eyes. "And I take pride in my work too, Detective Chandler."

Chandler nodded over Fiske's shoulder toward the door. "Shut that, will you?" He remained silent until Fiske did so and returned to his seat.

"Now, despite my better judgment, I will take your offer of assistance under advisement."

Fiske shook his head. "I'm here now. Considering that after forty-eight hours the success rate on homicides heads to China, that's not going to cut it." Fiske thought this might set the man off, but Chandler remained calm.

"You got a business card where you can be reached?" Chandler asked.

Fiske passed across his card after writing his home number on the back.

In return, Chandler handed him a card with a series of phone numbers on it. "Office, home, beeper, fax, cell phone — when I remember to carry it, which I never do."

Chandler opened a file on his desk and studied it. Reading upside down, Fiske saw his brother's name on the label.

"I was told he was killed during a robbery."

"That's what the prelim indicated anyway."

Fiske caught the odd tone in Chandler's voice. "And has that opinion changed?"

"It was only a prelim to begin with." He closed the file and looked at Fiske. "The facts of this case, at least what we know so far, are pretty simple. Your brother was found in the front seat of his car in an alleyway near the Anacostia River with a gunshot contact wound to the right side of his head and an exit wound on the left. Looked to be fairly heavy caliber. We have not found the slug, but that search continues. The killer could have found it and taken it with him so that we couldn't do a ballistics test, if we ever get a gun to do a match."

"It would take a cool hand to root around in an alley looking for a slug while a dead body is sitting a few feet away."

"I agree. But again, the bullet may still be found."

"I understand his wallet was missing."

"Let's put it another way. No wallet was found on him. Was he in the habit of not carrying one?"

Fiske looked away for an instant. "We haven't seen each other much the last few years, but I think you can assume he was carrying a wallet. So you didn't find it in his apartment?"

"Give me a little slack, John. Your brother's body was only found yesterday." Chandler opened his notebook and picked up a pen. "The alley where he was found is a high-use drug area, among other things. To your knowledge was he a drug user? Casual or otherwise?"

"No. He was not a drug user."

"But you can't be sure, can you? You just said you hadn't seen much of each other. Right?"

"My brother set the highest goals for himself with everything he did, and then he surpassed those goals. Drugs did not enter into that equation."

"Any idea why he would've been in that area?"

"No, but he could have been kidnapped

somewhere else and driven there."

"Any reason why someone would want him dead?"

"I can't think of a one."

"No enemies? Jealous boyfriends? Money problems?"

"No. But again I'm probably not the best source for that. Do you have a prelim on the time of death?"

"Pretty vague. I'm waiting on the official word. Why?"

"I just came from the morgue. I felt my brother's hand. It was soft, supple. Rigor had long since passed. What was the condition of the body when it was found last night?"

"Let's just say he had been there awhile."

"That's surprising. From what you said, it's not an isolated area."

"True, but in that area dead bodies in alleys aren't all that uncommon. Then again, about ninety-nine percent of the homicides in that area involve black victims for the very simple fact that whites just don't frequent the place."

"So my brother should have stood out, you're saying. Any ATM withdrawals? Credit card purchases?"

"We're checking all that. When did you last speak with your brother?"

"He called me over a week ago."

"What'd he say?"

"I wasn't in. He left a message. Said he

needed my advice on something."

"Did you call him back?"

"Not until recently."

"Why'd you wait?"

"It wasn't high on my priority list."

"Is that right?" Chandler twirled his pen between his fingers. "Tell me something. Did you even like your brother?"

Fiske looked at him squarely. "Somebody killed my brother. I want to catch whoever did it. And that's really all I'm going to say about it."

The look in Fiske's eyes made Chandler decide to move on. "Maybe he wanted to talk about something to do with work? See, what makes this case intriguing is your brother's occupation."

"Meaning, is his murder related to something at the Supreme Court?"

"It's a long shot, absolutely, but what you just told me about your brother's phone call might just make it slightly less of a long shot than it seemed a minute ago."

"I doubt if he wanted my two cents on the latest abortion case."

"Then what? How to pick up women?"

"You must not have seen a picture of him. He never needed help with that one."

"I have seen a picture of him, but the dead don't photograph all that well. But he said he wanted some advice. Maybe it was legal."

"Well, you can always make a trip to the

Court to see if there are any conspiracies going on up there."

"We have to tread lightly, you know."

"*We?*"

"I'm sure your brother has personal effects there, and it would not be unusual for next of kin to visit his place of work. I'm assuming you've been there before?"

"Once, when Mike first started. My dad and I."

"And your mother?"

"Alzheimer's."

"Sorry to hear that."

"Any other developments?"

In answer, Chandler rose, took down his jacket from a hanger on the back of the door and slipped it on. "I'd like to take you down to your brother's car."

"And after that?"

Chandler checked his watch before looking up and smiling. "Then we'll have just enough time to go to Court, Counselor."

CHAPTER TWENTY-TWO

Rufus watched the door as it slowly opened. He braced himself for the sight of a mass of men in green fatigues moving in on him, but then his apprehension slid away when he saw who it was.

"Time to check me again?"

Cassandra came and stood next to the bed. "Now, isn't that a woman's plight in life, always checking up on men?" Her words were funny, her tone was not. She looked at the monitors and made some notations in his chart, glancing at him as she did so.

"It feels good. I ain't used to that." He took care not to rattle his restraints as he sat up a little.

"I called your brother."

Rufus's expression grew serious. "Is that right? What'd he say?"

"He said he'd be coming to see you."

"He say when?"

"Sooner than later. Today, in fact."

"What all did you tell him?"

"I told him you were sick, but getting better fast."

"He tell you anything else?"

"I found him to be a man of few words,"

Cassandra remarked.

"That's Josh."

"Is he as big as you?"

"Nah. He's a little guy. Six-three or so, not much over two hundred pounds." Cassandra shook her head and turned to leave. "You got time to sit and talk?" Rufus asked.

"I'm supposed to be on my break. I just came to tell you about your brother. I've got to go." She seemed a little unfriendly.

"You okay?"

"Even if I'm not, there isn't anything you can do about it." Her tone was now edgy, rough.

Rufus studied her for a moment. "Is there a Bible around here?"

She turned back, surprised. "Why?"

"I read the Bible every day. Have for as long as I can remember."

She looked over at the table next to the bed, went across and pulled out a Gideon's Bible. "I can't give it to you. Can't get that close. The people from the prison were real, real clear on that point."

"You don't have to give it to me. If you would, I'd appreciate if you could read a passage to me."

"Read to you?"

"You don't have to," he said quickly. "You may not even be interested, you know, in the Bible and churchgoing."

She looked down at him, one hand on her

hip, the other closed around the green Bible. "I sing in the choir. My husband, God rest his soul, was a lay minister."

"That's real good, Cassandra. And your kids?"

"How do you know I have kids? Because I'm not skinny?"

"Uh-uh."

"What, then?"

"You look like you're used to loving little things."

His words startled her, a smile quickly breaking through the cloud over her features. "I *am* going to have to watch you." She noted that he looked at the Bible like he was thirsty and needed a drink, and she was holding the freshest, coldest glass of water in the history of the world.

"What do you want me to read?"

"Hundred and third Psalm."

Cassandra debated for a moment and then pulled up a chair and sat down.

Rufus lay back on the bed. "Thank you, Cassandra."

As she read, she glanced at him. His eyes were closed. She read a few more words, looked up and saw his lips moving and then stopping. She looked at the next sentence, quickly memorized it, and read it, while watching him. Rufus was silently mouthing each of the words at the same time she was saying them. She stopped, but he continued to the end of the sentence. When she did not start up again, he opened his eyes. "You know the Psalm by heart?" she asked.

"Know most of the Bible by heart. All the Psalms and Proverbs."

"That's pretty impressive."

"I've had a long time to work on it."

"Why did you want me to read it to you, then, if you already knew it?"

"Looked like you were a little troubled. I thought visiting the scriptures might help you some."

"Help me?" Cassandra looked down at the page and read to herself. "He forgives all my sins. He heals me. He ransoms me from Hell. He surrounds me with loving kindness and tender mercies." Work was depressing. Her teenage children were more and more beyond her control every day. She was on the north side of forty, fifty pounds overweight, and there wasn't an eligible man in sight. With all that, as she watched this prisoner, this chained-up killer who was going to die in prison, she felt like bursting into tears in the face of his kindness, his unsolicited consideration for her plight.

The Hundred and Third Psalm also held special appeal for Rufus, one line in particular. He mouthed it to himself: "He gives justice to all who are treated unfairly."

"Recognize it?" Chandler asked as they

approached the 1987 silver Honda sedan parked in the police lot.

Fiske nodded. "We got it for him when he graduated from college. We all chipped in, my parents and me."

"I've got five brothers. They never did that for me."

Chandler unlocked the driver's-side door and stepped back for Fiske to look inside.

"Where did you find the car keys?"

"On the front seat."

"Any other personal items?" Chandler shook his head. Fiske examined the front seat, dash, windshield and side windows, his puzzlement clear. "Has it been cleaned?"

"No. Just like we found it, except for the occupant."

Fisk straightened back up and looked at the detective.

"If you put a heavy-caliber pistol flush against somebody's temple and pull the trigger in a confined space like this you'll have blood splatters on the seat, steering wheel, windshield. You'd also have bone and tissue throw-off. All I see are a few stains here and there, probably where his head was touching the seat."

Chandler looked amused. "Is that right?"

Fiske clenched his jaw. "I'm not telling you anything you didn't already know. I take it this was another little test of yours?"

Chandler nodded slowly. "Could be.

Could be another reason. Remember I said I had five brothers?"

"Yeah."

"Well, I started out with six. One of my brothers was murdered thirty-five years ago. Working at a gas station and some punk came in and popped him for the twelve bucks in the register. I was only sixteen at the time, but I remember every detail like it was maybe five minutes ago. Anyway, most families who come in to identify their loved ones don't head over to my office and offer their services. They grieve and console each other, which is entirely proper. Oh, they rant and rave for a while about wanting to catch the SOB who did it, but they don't really want to get involved in the process. I mean, who would? And they don't usually have a law enforcement background Add it all up, and I spotted you as somebody who might be able to really contribute. And you just proved it.

"I can understand the rage you must be feeling, John, whether you liked your brother or not. Somebody took something from you, something important — ripped it from you, in fact. It's been thirty-five years and I still feel that rage."

Fiske looked around at all the civilian cars in the police lot. He assumed each hunk of metal was waiting its turn to spill the secrets of another tragedy. He turned back to Chandler. "I guess rage will do." He added quietly,

219

looking down, "Until something else comes along." His tone did not hold out much hope.

"Fair enough." Chandler continued his analysis. "The absence of all the physical evidence you just mentioned does have me puzzled."

"It doesn't look like he was killed in the car."

"That's right. It looks like he was killed somewhere else and his body was then put in the front seat. Now, that single conclusion takes us into a whole new realm of possibilities."

"Then we're talking about something more deliberate than a random kidnapping and murder."

"Possibly, although some punks could have kidnapped him, taken him out of the car to maybe hit an ATM. He refuses, they pop him. Get scared and then dump him back in his car."

"Then there would have been some physical evidence at the ATM. Any sign of that?"

"No, but there are a lot of ATMs."

"And a lot of people use them. If it's been at least a day, you'd think someone would have noticed."

"You'd think, but you can't be sure. We're trying to isolate your brother's movements and whereabouts for the last forty-eight hours. He was last seen at his apartment on Thursday night. After that, nada."

"If somebody carjacked him, what about prints? Most perps looking for ATM cards aren't sophisticated enough to wear gloves."

"We're still processing that."

"Would you like another observation?"

"Fire away."

Fiske held open the car door and pointed at the inside part of the doorjamb, the section that you don't see when the door is closed. Chandler fumbled for his glasses, put them on and saw what Fiske was pointing at. Chandler slapped on a pair of latex gloves he pulled from his coat pocket, gently lifted the small piece of sticky plastic off and held it in his palm, observing it carefully.

"Your brother just had his car serviced at Wal-Mart."

"It recommends that the next oil service takes place in three months or three thousand miles, whichever comes first. They put the future date and future mileage reading on that sticker as a reminder for when you're supposed to come back in. According to the date on that sticker, and subtracting out three months, my brother went in for service three days before his body was found. Now look at the mileage for when the next service is recommended and subtract three thousand miles from it. That'll give you approximately what the odometer should read right now."

Chandler swiftly did the math. "Eighty-six thousand, five hundred and forty-three."

"Now look at the Honda's current odometer reading."

Chandler leaned back in the car and checked. Then he looked back at Fiske, his eyes slightly wide. "Somebody put about eight hundred miles on this car in the last three days."

"That's right," Fiske said.

"Where the hell did he go?"

"The sticker doesn't have which Wal-Mart he used, but probably it was one close to his home. You should call around, they might be able to tell us something useful."

"Right. Can't believe we missed this," said Chandler. He slipped the plastic sticker in a clear zippered bag he pulled from his coat pocket and wrote some information on the outside of it. "Oh, and John?"

"Yeah?"

He held up the zippered bag. "No more tests, okay?"

CHAPTER TWENTY-THREE

A half hour later, Chandler and Fiske walked through the front entrance of the United States Supreme Court.

Inside, the place was large and intimidating. What really engaged Fiske's attention, though, was the quiet, so extreme as to be unsettling. It seemed to border on the hallucinatory — trying to imagine a functioning world right outside the doors. Fiske thought of the last very silent place he had been today: the morgue.

He said, "Who are we supposed to be meeting?"

Chandler pointed to a group of men walking purposefully down the hallway toward them. "Them." As they drew nearer, their collective footsteps became the boom of cannon in this acoustical tunnel. One of the men wore a suit; the other two were in uniforms and carried sidearms.

"Detective Chandler?" The man in the suit extended his hand. "I'm Richard Perkins, marshal of the United States Supreme Court." Perkins was about five-nine, skinny, with the stuck-out ears of a boy, and white hair combed straight over his forehead like a frozen waterfall. He introduced his companions. "Chief of Police Leo Dellasandro; his second-in-command, Ron Klaus."

"Good to meet you," Chandler said, and he watched Perkins look expectantly over at Fiske. He added, "John Fiske. Michael Fiske's brother."

All of them rushed to provide their condolences.

"A tragedy. A mindless tragedy," Perkins said. "Michael was so highly thought of. He'll be sorely missed."

Fiske managed an appreciative demeanor in the face of all this instant sympathy.

"You've locked up Michael Fiske's office, as I requested?" Chandler asked.

Dellasandro nodded. "It was difficult, because he shared it with another clerk. Two to an office is the norm."

"Let's hope we won't need to keep it off limits long."

"We can meet in my office if you'd like and go over your agenda, Detective Chandler," Perkins offered. "It's right down the hallway."

"Let's do it."

As Fiske started off with them, Perkins stopped and looked at Chandler.

"I'm sorry. I was assuming that Mr. Fiske was here for another reason unrelated to your investigation."

"He's helping me out with some background information on his brother," Chandler said.

Perkins looked at Fiske with what Fiske gauged as unfriendly eyes.

"I didn't even know Michael had a brother," said Perkins. "He never mentioned you."

"That's okay, he never mentioned you either," Fiske replied.

Perkins's office was right off the hallway leading to the courtroom. It was furnished in an old-fashioned colonial style, the architecture and craftsmanship from an era of government unburdened with trillion-dollar national debts and budgets awash in red.

At a side table of Perkins's office sat a man in his late forties. His blond hair was cut very short, and his long narrow face carried an unshakable air of authority. His self-assured manner suggested that he enjoyed the exercise of that authority. When he rose, Fiske noted that he was well over six feet tall and looked as though he spent regular time in the gym.

"Detective Chandler?" The man extended one hand and with the other flashed his identification card. "FBI Special Agent Warren McKenna."

Chandler looked at Perkins. "I wasn't aware that the Bureau had been brought in on this."

Perkins started to say something, but

McKenna said briskly, "As I'm sure you know, the attorney general and the FBI have the legal right to fully investigate the murder of any person employed by the United States government. However, the Bureau is not looking to take over the investigation or step on your toes."

"That's good, because even the tiniest bit of unwanted pressure and I just go nuts." Chandler smiled.

McKenna's expression remained unchanged. "I'll try to keep that in mind."

Fiske held out his hand. "John Fiske, Agent McKenna. Michael Fiske was my brother."

"I'm sorry, Mr. Fiske. I know it must be damn tough for you," McKenna said, shaking his hand. The FBI agent focused again on Chandler. "If conditions dictate a more active role for the Bureau, then we would expect your full cooperation. Remember that the victim was a federal employee." He looked around the room. "Employed by one of the most revered institutions in the world. And perhaps one of the most feared."

"Fear out of ignorance," Perkins pointed out.

"But feared nonetheless. After Waco, the World Trade Center and Oklahoma City, we've learned to be extra careful," McKenna said.

"Too bad you people weren't faster learners," Chandler said dryly. "But turf battles are big wastes of time. I do believe in share and share alike, though, okay?"

"Of course," McKenna said.

Chandler asked a half hour's worth of questions, trying basically to establish if any case Michael Fiske had been working on at the Court could have led to his murder. The same answer kept coming back to him from each of the Court representatives: "Impossible."

McKenna asked very few questions but listened intently to the ones asked by Chandler.

"The precise details of cases pending before the Court are so well insulated from the public that there would be no way anyone could know what a specific clerk is or isn't working on." Perkins smacked the tabletop with his palm to emphasize the point.

"Unless that clerk told someone."

Perkins shook his head. "I personally run them through the drill on security and confidentiality as part of their orientation. The ethical rules which apply to them are very stringent. They're even provided with a handbook on the subject. No leaks are permitted."

Chandler looked unconvinced. "What's the average age of the clerks here? Twenty-five? Twenty-six?"

"Something like that."

"They're kids, working at the highest court in the land. You telling me that it's impossible that they might let something slip? Not even to impress a date?"

"I've been around long enough to know better than to use the word *impossible* to ever describe anything."

"I'm a homicide detective, Mr. Perkins, and believe you me, I got the same damn problem."

"Could we back up to square one here?" Dellasandro said. "From what I know about the case, it seemed that robbery was the motive." He spread his hands and looked expectantly at Chandler. "How does that involve the Court? Have you searched his apartment yet?"

"Not yet. I'm sending a team over tomorrow."

"How do we know it's not something connected to his personal life?" Dellasandro asked.

Everyone looked at Chandler for an answer. The detective glanced down at his notes without really focusing on them. "I'm just covering all the bases. Going to a homicide victim's place of work and asking questions is not even remotely unusual, gentlemen."

"Certainly," Perkins said. "You can count

on our full cooperation."

"Now why don't we have a look at Mr. Fiske's office," Chandler said.

CHAPTER TWENTY-FOUR

The man glided cat-smooth down the corridor. He was six-foot-three, lean but strongly built, with wide shoulders fanning out from a thick neck. He had a long and narrow face; the skin chestnut brown and smooth, except for deep tracings of lines at the eyes and mouth, like the whorls of a fingerprint. He wore a crumpled Virginia Tech baseball cap. A short-haired black and gray beard outlined his jaw. He was dressed in worn jeans and a faded, sweat-stained denim shirt with the sleeves rolled up, showing off a pair of thick, veiny forearms. A pack of Pall Malls poked out of the shirt's front pocket. He approached the end of the hallway and rounded the corner. As soon as he did so, the soldier sitting next to the doorway of the last room on the hall rose and held up a hand.

"Sorry, sir, this area is off limits to everyone except necessary medical personnel."

"My brother's in there," Joshua Harms said. "And I'm going to see him."

"I'm afraid that's impossible."

Harms eyed the soldier's name tag. "I'm afraid it ain't, Private Brown. I visit him at the prison all the time. Now you let me in there, you hear me?"

"I don't think so."

"Well, then I'm gonna go round up the head of this hospital and the local police and the damn commandant over at Fort Jackson and tell 'em you refused to allow a family member to visit a dying relative. Then they'll all take turns kicking your butt on down the road, soldier boy. Did I mention I spent three years in Vietnam and got me enough medals to cover your whole damn body? Now you gonna let me in or we gonna have to go down that other street? I want your answer and I want it right this damned minute."

An unnerved Brown looked around for a minute, unsure of what to do. "I need to call somebody."

"No, you don't. You can search me, but I'm going on in there. Won't be long. But it's gonna be right now."

"What's your name?"

"Josh Harms." He pulled out his wallet. "Here's my driver's license. I been over the prison a lot over the years, but I don't recall ever seeing you."

"I don't work at the prison," he said. "I'm on temporary assignment here. I'm in the reserves."

"The reserves? Pulling guard duty on a prisoner?"

"The correctional facility specialists who flew in with your brother went back yesterday. They're bringing in some replacements tomorrow morning."

"Hallelujah for them. Now, we ready to get this done?"

Private Brown stared at him for another few seconds. "Turn around," he said finally.

Josh did so. Brown started to pat him down. Right before he reached his front pants pocket, Josh said, "Don't get excited, but there's a pocketknife in there. Just pull it out and hold it for me. You hold it good and tight, son, I'm right partial to that knife."

Private Brown finished the pat-down and straightened. "You got ten minutes, and that's it. And I'm going in with you."

"You go in with me, then you're deserting your post. You desert your post in the Army or the reserves and you gonna end up where my brother is." He looked at the man's youthful features. A wannabe weekend warrior, he concluded. Probably pushed a pencil Monday through Friday before slipping on his fatigues and gun looking for adventure. "And let me tell you, prison ain't where somebody looks like you wants to be."

Private Brown swallowed nervously. "Ten minutes."

The two men locked eyes. "Thank you kindly," Josh Harms said, not meaning one word of it.

He entered the room and closed the door behind him.

"Rufus," he said quietly.

"Didn't think you were gonna get here so quick, brother."

Josh went over to the side of the bed and stared down at him. "What in the hell happened to you?"

"Ain't sure you want to know."

"It's all about that damn letter you got, ain't it?" Josh pulled a chair over next to the bed.

"How long the guard give you?"

"Ten minutes, but I ain't worried about him."

"Ten minutes ain't going to be long enough to tell you much. But I'll tell you this. I go back to Fort Jackson and they're gonna kill me soon as I step inside."

"Who's 'they'?"

Rufus shook his head. "I tell you, then they gonna just come after you."

"I'm in here with you, ain't I? That baby soldier out there is stupid, but he ain't that stupid. He's gonna put me down on the visitors' roster. You know that."

Rufus swallowed with difficulty. "I know, probably never should've got you to come on down here."

"I'm here now. So start talking."

Rufus thought about it for a minute. "Look, Josh, that letter from the Army, when I got it, I remembered everything that happened that night. I mean everything. It was like somebody shot it right into my head."

"You talking about the girl?"

Rufus was already nodding. "Everything. I know why I did it. And the fact is, it wasn't my fault."

His brother looked at him skeptically. "Come on, now, Rufus, you did kill that little girl. No way around that."

"Killing and meaning to kill's two different things. Anyway, I got my lawyer from back then —"

"You mean your piss-poor excuse for a lawyer."

"You read the letter?"

"Sure I did. Came to my house, didn't it? Guess that was the last civilian address the Army had for you. Big, dumb carcass, didn't know it had you smack in one of its own damn prisons."

"Well, I got Rider to file something for me. In court."

"What'd he file?"

"A letter I wrote."

"Letter? How'd you get it out?"

"Same way you got the letter from the Army in."

Both men smiled.

Rufus said, "They got a printing operation inside the prison. The machinery's hot and dirty, so the guards give you a little space. Let me work my magic."

"So you think the Court's gonna look at

your case? I wouldn't bet my life on it, little brother."

"Don't look like the Court's gonna do nothing."

"Well, gee, that's a big-ass surprise."

Rufus looked past his brother at the door. "When the guards coming back from the prison?"

"Boy said tomorrow morning."

"Well, that means I got to get out of here tonight."

"Woman who called me said you had some kind of heart problem. Look at you, all strapped to this crap. How far you think you can run?"

"How far you think I can run dead?"

"You really think they gonna try and kill you?"

"They don't want this to come out. You said you read the letter from the Army."

"Yep."

"Well, I was never in the program they said I was."

Josh eyed him hard. "How you mean?"

"Just what I said. Somebody put me in the records. They wanted me to look like I was in it, to cover up what they did to me. Why I killed that little girl. In case somebody checked, I reckon they had to do it. They thought I was going to be dead."

Josh took this in slowly until the truth hit him. "Jesus Lord Almighty. Why would they do that shit to you?"

"You asking me that? They hated me. Thought I was the biggest screw-up in the world. Wanted me dead."

"If I had known all that was happening, I sure as hell would've come back and kicked some butt."

"You were busy trying to keep the VC from tearing you up. But I go back to prison now, they gonna make sure they get me this time."

Josh looked at the door and then down at his brother's restraints.

"I need your help to do this, Josh."

"You're damn right you do, Rufus."

"You ain't gotta help me. You can turn and walk straight out of here. I still love you. You stood by me all these years. What I'm asking ain't fair, I know that. You worked hard, you got yourself a good life. I'd understand."

"Then you don't know your brother."

Rufus slowly reached out and took his brother's hand. They gripped each other tightly, as though trying to give strength and resolve to one another for what lay ahead.

"Anybody see you come in?"

"Nobody except the guard. I didn't exactly come in the front door."

"Then I can pretend to knock you out, get out of here on my own. They know I'm a crazy SOB. Kill my own brother and never think twice about it."

"Bullshit. That dog just won't hunt, Rufus.

236

You wouldn't even know where the hell to go. They'd catch your butt in ten minutes. I worked on repairs at this hospital for almost two years, know it like the back of my hand. Way I came in is supposed to be locked, only the nurses taped over the lock. They sneak their smokes out there."

"How you wanta work it, then?"

"We just go back out the way I came in. It's right down the hall on the left. Don't pass no nurses' station or nothing. My truck's right outside the door. I got a buddy thirty minutes from here. He owes me a favor. I'll leave my truck in one of his old barns and borrow his rig for a while. He won't ask no questions and he won't answer any if the police come along. We hit the road and don't look back."

"You sure you want to do this? How about your kids?"

"They all gone. Don't see 'em much."

"What about Louise?"

Josh looked down for a moment. "Louise walked out the door five years ago and I ain't seen her since."

"You never told me that!"

"What you gonna do about it if I had?"

"I'm sorry."

"I'm damn sorry about a lot of things. I ain't the easiest person to live with. Can't say I blame any of them." Josh shrugged his shoulders. "So it's just the two of us again.

Make Momma happy if she was alive."

"You sure?"

"Don't ask me that again, Rufus."

Rufus raised his manacled hands. "What about these?"

His brother was already sliding something out of his boot. When he straightened back up he was holding a slender piece of metal with a slight hook at one end.

"Don't tell me that boy didn't search you?"

"Shit, like he knew where to look. Once he took my pocketknife, he figured he had all my *dangerous* weapons. Didn't even bother to do my boots." Josh grinned and then inserted the metal in the lock on the restraints.

"You think you can pick it?"

Josh stopped and looked at his brother with contempt. "If I can escape from the damn Viet Cong, I can sure as hell pick an Army-issued pair of handcuffs."

Out in the hallway, Private Brown looked at his watch. The ten minutes were up. He cracked open the door to the room. "All right, Harms, time's up." He pushed the door open farther. "Mr. Harms? Did you hear me? Time's up."

Brown heard a small groan. He drew his pistol and pushed the door all the way open. "What's going on in here?"

The groaning became louder. Brown looked around for the light switch. That's when he stumbled over something. He knelt down and touched the man's face as his vision focused.

"Mr. Harms? Mr. Harms, you okay?"

Josh opened his eyes. "I'm fine. How 'bout you?"

Then a big hand clamped down on Brown's gun and stripped it clean away. The other hand went around his mouth and he was lifted completely off the floor, one massive fist colliding with his jaw and knocking him out.

Rufus put Brown in the bed, covering him with the sheet. Josh put the restraints around the unconscious soldier's arms and legs and locked them up tight. Then he used adhesive tape and gauze he found in one of the cabinets to tape his mouth shut. The last thing he did was search the soldier and retrieve his pocketknife.

As Josh turned toward him, Rufus wrapped his arms around his brother and squeezed tight. Josh returned the hug, the first time the men had been able to do this in twenty-five years. His eyes moist, Rufus shook a little as Josh finally pulled away.

"Now, don't get too mushy on me. We ain't got no time for that."

Rufus smiled. "Still feels good to hold you, Josh."

Josh put a hand on his brother's shoulder. "Never thought we'd get a chance to ever do that. Never gonna take that for granted again."

"So what now?"

"You can't see where the boy was sitting from the hallway. But they got private security here." Josh checked his watch. "When I was working here they made rounds every hour on the hour. It's quarter past now. Those boys are on the six-singles-an-hour plan and don't give much of a shit about guarding bedpans, but they'll probably notice he's gone at some point. You ready?"

Rufus had already pulled on his prison pants and shoes. He had left off the shirt, opting for just his T-shirt instead. He had one thing clutched in his hand: the Gideon Bible. He didn't feel free yet, but he was only seconds from it. "Twenty-five years' worth of ready."

CHAPTER TWENTY-FIVE

Chandler looked around Michael Fiske's office. Located on the second floor of the building, it was large, with high ceilings, and half-foot-wide moldings. There were two massive wooden desks, each with a computer workstation, shelves filled with volumes of law books and case reports, and a portable book caddy. There were wooden cabinets and stacks of files placed on the desks. The place was organized in a disorderly fashion, he concluded.

Perkins looked at Chandler. "There has to be someone from the Court present while you search. There are many confidential documents in here. Drafts of opinions, memos from justices and other clerks, that sort of thing, pertaining to undecided cases."

"All right. We won't remove anything that may relate to pending cases."

"But how can you know if it does or not?"

"I'll ask you."

"I don't know. I'm not even a lawyer."

Chandler said, "Well, then get somebody down here who is, because I'm going through this office."

"It may not be possible today. Can it wait

until tomorrow? I believe all the clerks have gone home. Chief Justice Ramsey didn't think they should work late considering what happened."

"Some of the justices are still here, Richard," Klaus said.

Perkins cast an unfriendly glance at Klaus, who looked over at Dellasandro. "I didn't want to bring the justices into this until it was absolutely necessary. But let me see what I can do," he said. "I'm afraid I'll have to lock this door until I get back."

Chandler took a step closer to Perkins. "Look, Richard, I'm the police. Now, maybe I'm wrong and you don't mean what I thought you did by that very stupid remark."

Perkins's face flushed, but he left the door unlocked, motioned to Klaus to accompany him, and they walked off. Dellasandro stayed behind, talking to McKenna.

Chandler went over to Fiske. "I get the feeling this has all been scripted out long before we got here."

"McKenna knew your name before you were introduced."

"They've obviously already done some digging."

"Well, I guess you can't blame them."

"I'm gonna go over and talk to McKenna," said Chandler. "Never know when we might need a favor from the Feds."

Fiske leaned back against the wall and

checked his watch. He still hadn't reached his father.

The door a short way down the hall from his brother's office opened and a young man came out.

Fiske nodded his head. "Busy place."

"Are you with the police?"

Fiske shook his head and extended his hand. "Just an observer. I'm John Fiske. Mike was my brother."

The young man went pale. "Oh God, it's awful. Awful. I'm so sorry." He shook Fiske's hand. "I'm Steven Wright."

"Did you know Mike well?"

"Not really. I just started this session. I clerk for Justice Knight. I know everyone thought the world of him."

Fiske looked at the door Wright had come out of. "Is that your office?" Wright nodded. "I guess there's been a lot of activity at my brother's office."

"You bet. People have been in and out all day."

"Like Mr. Perkins, Chief Dellasandro?"

"And that gentleman over there."

Fiske looked to where he was pointing. "That's Agent McKenna from the FBI," Fiske said.

Wright shook his head sadly. "I've never known anyone who's been . . ." He stopped and looked embarrassed.

"It's okay. I know what you mean." Suddenly all of Fiske's attention was trained on a pair of people walking toward him. His focus, actually, was on only one. Despite her obvious physical attractiveness, the woman looked, Fiske concluded, like the tomboy next door. Someone you could play touch football or chess with. And end up losing.

Sara Evans eyed Fiske. She had seen him come into the building earlier and guessed what he was here for. She had stayed close by in case they needed one of the clerks to talk to. That's why Perkins had "found" her so quickly. She stopped directly in front of Fiske, causing Perkins to abruptly do the same.

"Oh," he said, "John Fiske, this is Sara Evans."

"You're Michael's brother?"

"Let me guess, he never mentioned me," said Fiske.

"As a matter of fact, he did."

They shared a firm handshake. The whites of her eyes were smudged with red, as was the tip of her nose. Her voice sounded tired. Fiske noted that she clutched a handkerchief in her other hand. He had the feeling they had met before.

"I'm very, very sorry about Michael," she said.

"Thank you. It came as a tremendous shock." Fiske blinked. Was there something in her eyes when he said that? Something that said it wasn't all that shocking to her?

Perkins looked at Wright. "I didn't know you were in your office."

"You might have tried knocking," Fiske suggested.

Perkins cast him an unfriendly glance and walked over to Chandler and McKenna.

"Hi, Sara," Wright said, a smile breaking across his face.

From the way Wright was looking at her, it was obvious to Fiske that he was infatuated with the woman.

"Hello, Steven. How are you holding up?"

"I don't think anyone's gotten much work done today. I'm thinking about leaving soon."

Sara looked at Fiske. "Everyone thought the world of your brother. It's rocked all of us, from the chief justice on down. But it doesn't come close to equaling your loss, I know."

She said this so strangely that Fiske did a double-take. Before he could say anything, Perkins rejoined them.

"All right, Detective Chandler from D.C. Homicide is waiting along with a gentleman from the FBI," Perkins said to Sara.

"Why do they want to search Michael's office?"

Perkins's tone was blunt. "That's none of our business."

"It's part of the investigation, Ms. Evans,"

Fiske explained, "in case there's a connection with his murder."

"I thought it was a robbery."

"It was a robbery, and the sooner we can convince Detective Chandler that it has nothing whatsoever to do with the Court, the better," Perkins said huffily.

"If that happens to be the case," Fiske said.

"Of course, but it is the case." Perkins turned to Sara. "As I explained on the way down, your task is to ensure that no confidential documents are seen or taken."

"Confidential meaning exactly what?" she asked.

"You know, anything having to do with pending court cases, opinions, memos, that sort of thing."

"Shouldn't I be involved in that decision, Richard," came a new voice, "or is that outside my jurisdiction?"

Fiske easily recognized the man approaching them. Harold Ramsey strode toward them like a vintage ocean liner grandly pulling into harbor.

"Chief, I didn't see you there," Perkins said nervously.

"Obviously not." Ramsey looked at Fiske. "I don't believe we've met."

"Michael's brother, John Fiske," offered Sara.

Ramsey held out his hand; his long, bony fingers seemed to wrap twice around Fiske's.

"I cannot tell you how sorry I am. Michael was a very special young man. I know that you and your family must feel his loss terribly. If there's anything we can do, please let us know."

Fiske acknowledged Ramsey's sentiments, feeling like a stranger at a wake, awkwardly receiving condolences for a deceased he could not name.

"I will," he said solemnly.

Ramsey looked at Perkins and inclined his head toward Chandler and McKenna. "Who are those men and what do they want?"

Perkins explained the situation in a fairly efficient manner, although it was clear that Ramsey had already thought five steps ahead by the time Perkins finished his account.

"Would you ask Detective Chandler and Agent McKenna to step over here, please, Richard?"

When introductions had been made, Ramsey turned to Chandler. "It seems to me that the better way of approaching the problem is to sit down with Justice Murphy and his clerks and take an oral inventory of the cases on which Michael was engaged. Understand that I'm trying to balance your right to investigate this crime with the Court's responsibility to keep confidential its opinions, until such time as they become publicly known."

"Okay." And I don't want anyone trying to

pin any leak on me, Chandler thought to himself.

Ramsey continued. "I see no reason why you can't examine Michael's personal effects, if he kept any here. I only ask that any documents pertaining to the Court's work be set aside until you have had your discussion with Justice Murphy. Then, should there appear to be a connection between a case Michael was working on and his death, arrangements can be made for you to investigate any link thoroughly."

"All right, Mr. Chief Justice," Chandler said. "I've actually already spoken briefly with Justice Murphy."

McKenna quickly agreed with this approach.

Ramsey turned to Perkins. "Richard, please advise Justice Murphy and his clerks that Detective Chandler will want to meet with them as soon as possible. I'm assuming tomorrow after oral argument would do?"

"That'll be fine," Chandler replied.

"I'll also make available the Court's legal counsel to assist you in coordinating matters and addressing any concerns of confidentiality that may arise. Sara, you'll be available tomorrow, won't you? You were close with Michael."

Fiske eyed her. How close? he wondered.

Ramsey once again extended his hand to Fiske. "I would also appreciate being advised of funeral arrangements."

Ramsey then turned to Perkins. "Richard, after you speak with Justice Murphy, please come to my office." The meaning in his tone was clear.

After Ramsey and Perkins had left, Chandler watched as McKenna looked into Michael Fiske's office again. "Chief Dellasandro," Chandler said, "to be as least disruptive as possible, I'll bring a team in tomorrow to search the office, so we only have to do it once."

"We appreciate that," Dellasandro replied.

"However, I want this door locked until I come back," Chandler continued. "Nobody goes in, and that means you, or Mr. Perkins, or" — he looked pointedly at Agent McKenna — "anybody else."

McKenna glared at Chandler as Dellasandro nodded his agreement.

Fiske looked around and caught Wright staring at Chandler. Wright abruptly closed his office door, and Fiske heard the lock turn. Smart man, he thought.

As Fiske and Chandler were leaving the building, a voice made them stop.

"Do you mind if I see you out?" Sara said.

"Okay with me," Chandler said. "John?"

Fiske shrugged noncommittally.

Chandler smiled as they walked along. "Why do I have the feeling we were just in the presence of the Almighty?"

Sara smiled. "The chief has that effect on people."

"So you clerk for Justice Knight?" Fiske asked.

"Going on my second year."

As they rounded a corner, they almost collided with Elizabeth and Jordan Knight.

"Oh, Justice Knight, we were just talking about you," Sara said. She made introductions all around.

"Senator," Chandler said, "we appreciate what you're doing for the District. Without the special funding you just pushed through for the police department, I'd be conducting homicide investigations via bicycle."

"We've got a lot more to do, as you know. The problems were built up over a long time, and they're going to take just as long to correct," Knight said in a political stumping tone. He looked at Fiske and his voice softened. "I am sorry about your brother, John. I didn't personally know him. I don't make it up to the Court much. If I have lunch with my wife too often the media thinks I'm trying to influence her decision making. I guess they forget we share the same house and bed. But please accept my heartfelt condolences to you and your family."

Fiske thanked him and then added, "For what it's worth, I voted for you."

"Every vote counts." He looked over at his wife and smiled warmly. "Just like it does up here, right, Mrs. Justice? How did Brennan put it? You need five votes to do anything? God, if I only had five votes to worry about I'd be thirty pounds lighter and my hair would still be black."

Elizabeth Knight didn't smile. Her eyes were as red as Sara's, her skin paler than usual. "Sara," she said, "I'd like to meet with you after the afternoon session tomorrow." She cleared her throat. "And I'd like you to speak with Steven about the bench memo on *Chance*. I have to have it by tomorrow at the latest. If he has to work through the night, I have to have it." Her voice was almost shrill.

Sara looked shaken. "I'll tell him right away, Justice Knight."

Knight gripped one of Sara's hands. "Thank you." She swallowed with difficulty. "Please also remember that the dinner for Judge Wilkinson is tomorrow night at seven o'clock at my home."

"It's on my calendar," Sara said a little reluctantly.

Elizabeth Knight finally looked at Fiske. "Your brother was a very gifted lawyer, Mr. Fiske. I know it may sound callous discussing these details, but the business of the Court stops for no one." She added a little wearily, "I learned that lesson a long time ago. Again, I'm very sorry." She checked her watch. "Jordan, you're going to be late for your meeting on the Hill. And I have some work to finish." She looked at Fiske. "If you'll excuse us."

Fiske shrugged. "Like you said, the machine stops for no one."

After the Knights had departed, Sara commented, "Justice Knight is tough, but fair." She glanced quickly at Fiske. "I'm sure she didn't mean it to sound that way."

"Sure she did," Fiske said.

Chandler stepped in. "Well, she probably had to work three times as hard as a man to get where she is. You don't ever forget that sort of experience."

"That's a very liberated mind-set," Sara said.

"If you knew my wife, you'd understand."

Sara smiled. "Ramsey and Knight are from different walks of life, although they tend to work together on many issues. He seems overly accommodating to her. Maybe he doesn't like confrontation with women. He's from a different generation."

"I don't think gender has anything to do with it," Fiske remarked bluntly.

"She's a brilliant jurist," Sara said defensively.

They all heard the beeping sound. Chandler reached down to his belt, held up the pager and looked at the number on its screen. "Can I use a phone?" he asked Sara.

She led the way.

Chandler rejoined them a minute later and

shook his head wearily. "Couple of new customers for me to interview. Shotgun wounds to the heads. Lucky, lucky me."

"Can you take me back to the station so I can pick up my car?" Fiske asked.

"Actually, I was heading the other way."

"I can drive you," Sara said quickly. Both men looked at her. "I'm finished for the day. Not that I got much accomplished." She looked down and smiled a little wistfully. "The ironic thing is, I know Michael wouldn't approve. I've never seen anyone so dedicated, so hardworking." She looked at Fiske keenly, as though giving added strength to her words.

"Grab some dinner or something," Chandler suggested. "You two might find a lot to talk about."

Fiske glanced around, clearly uncomfortable with this suggestion, but he finally nodded. "You ready?"

"Give me a minute." She shook her head wearily. "I have to tell Steven he has to work all night," she said, and headed off.

Chandler said, "John, find out what you can. She was close to your brother." He added, "Unlike you."

"I'm not real good at spying," Fiske said, feeling guilty about plotting like this behind Sara's back. He had to catch himself, though; he didn't even know the woman.

As if he were privy to Fiske's thoughts,

Chandler said, "John, I know she's smart and pretty, and she worked with your brother and she's shook up about his death. But remember one thing."

"What's that?"

"Those are *not* reasons to trust her." With that parting comment, Chandler walked off.

CHAPTER TWENTY-SIX

Jordan Knight stood in the doorway of his wife's office and watched her. Elizabeth Knight's head was bowed as she sat at her desk. Several books were open in front of her, but she was obviously not reading any of them.

"Why don't you call it a day, honey?"

She looked up, startled. "Jordan, I thought you had left for your meeting."

He came over and stood next to her, massaging the back of her neck with one hand. "I canceled it. And now it's time to go home."

"But I have some more work to go. We're all behind. It's so hard —"

He put a hand under her arm and helped her up. "Beth, no matter how important it is, it's not that important. Let's go home," he said firmly.

A few minutes later they were being driven in a government car to their apartment. After a relaxing shower, something to eat and a glass of wine, Elizabeth Knight finally started to feel halfway normal again as she lay on her bed. Her husband came in and sat down next to her, putting her feet on his lap and rubbing them.

"Sometimes I think we're too hard on our clerks. Work them too hard. Expect too much from them," she said after a while.

"Is that right?" Jordan Knight cupped her chin in one hand. "What, are you somehow trying to blame yourself for Michael Fiske's death? He wasn't working late the night he was probably killed. You told me he called in sick. His being in an alleyway in a bad part of town has nothing to do with you or the Court. Somebody, some piece of street trash, killed him. Maybe it was a robbery, or maybe he was just in the wrong place at the wrong time, but you had nothing to do with it."

"The police think it was a robbery."

"I'm sure it's early on in the investigation, but it'll be given the highest priority."

"One of the clerks today asked if Michael's death might be connected to the Court somehow."

Jordan Knight considered this for a moment. "Look, I suppose it's possible, but I can't see how." He suddenly looked worried. "If it is, though, I'm going to make sure you have added protection. I'll make a call tomorrow and you'll have your own Secret Service or FBI agent, round the clock."

"Jordan, you don't have to do that."

"What, make sure that some nut doesn't take you away from me? I think about that a lot, Beth. Some of the Court's decisions are very unpopular. You all get death threats from time to time. You can't ignore that."

"I don't. I just try not to think about it."

"Fine, but don't get upset if I do."

She smiled, touched his face. "You take much too good care of me, you know."

He smiled. "When you have something precious, that's the only way to go."

They tenderly kissed and then Jordan pulled the covers up over her, turned out the light and left to finish up some work in his study. Elizabeth Knight didn't go to sleep right away. She stared into the darkness, a series of emotions hitting her. Right when they all threatened to overwhelm her, she thankfully drifted off.

"I can't imagine what you're going through, John. I know how badly I'm feeling, and I'd only known Michael for a relatively short time."

They were in Sara's car and had just crossed over the Potomac River and into Virginia. Fiske wondered if she was trying to impress upon him that she had little information to provide.

"So how long did you two work together?"

"A year. Michael talked me into coming back for a second year."

"Ramsey said you and Michael were close. How close?"

She looked sharply at him. "What are you implying?"

257

"I just want to gather facts about my brother. I want to know who his friends were. If he was seeing anyone." He glanced over at her to gauge her reaction. If she had one, she wasn't showing it.

"You only lived two hours away and you know nothing about his life?"

"Is that your opinion or someone else's?"

"I can actually make observations all by myself."

"Well, that's a two-way street."

"The observations, or the two-hour drive?"

"Both."

They pulled into the parking lot of a restaurant in northern Virginia. They went inside, got a table and ordered their drinks and food. A minute later, Fiske took a swallow of his Corona; Sara sipped on a margarita.

Fiske wiped his mouth. "So, do you come from a family of lawyers? We tend to run in packs."

She smiled and shook her head. "I'm from a farm in North Carolina. Single-stoplight town. But my father had a connection to law."

Fiske looked mildly interested. "What was that?"

"He was the justice of the peace for the area. Officially, his courtroom was a little space in the back of the jail. More often he'd hear cases while sitting on his John Deere tractor in the middle of the field."

"Is that what got you interested in law?"

She nodded. "My dad looked more like a judge sitting on dusty farm equipment than some others I've seen in the fanciest courts."

"Including the one you're in now?"

Sara blinked and suddenly looked away. Fiske felt guilty for having made the comment. "I bet your dad was a good JP. Common sense, fair in his decisions. Man of the soil."

She glanced at him to see if he was being sarcastic, but Fiske's look was genuine. "That's exactly what he was. He mostly dealt with poachers and traffic tickets, but I don't think anyone walked away feeling they had been treated unfairly."

"You see him often?"

"He died six years ago."

"I'm sorry. Is your mom still around?"

"She died before Dad. Rural life can be rough."

"Sisters or brothers?"

She shook her head and seemed relieved to see their food arrive.

"It just occurred to me that I haven't eaten today," Fiske said as he took a large bite of his tortilla.

"I do that a lot. I think I had an apple this morning."

"Not good." His gaze swept over her. "You don't have a lot of excess on you."

She looked him over. Despite his broad

shoulders and full cheeks, he almost looked gaunt, his shirt collar loose against his neck, his waist a little too small for his size. "Neither do you."

Twenty minutes later Fiske pushed away his empty plate and sat back. "I know you're busy, so I won't waste your time. My brother and I didn't see a lot of each other. There's an information void I need to fill if I'm going to find out who did this."

"I thought that was Detective Chandler's job."

"Unofficially, it's mine."

"Your cop background?" Sara asked. Fiske arched his eyebrows. "Michael told me a lot about you."

"Is that right?"

"Yes, that's right. He was very proud of you. From cop to criminal defense attorney. Michael and I had some interesting discussions about that."

"Look, it bothers me that someone I don't know has been having discussions about my life."

"There's no reason to get upset. We just thought it was an interesting career change."

Fiske shrugged. "When I was a cop I spent all my time getting criminals off the streets. Now I make my living defending them. To tell you the truth, I was starting to feel sorry for them."

"I don't think I've ever heard a cop admit that."

"Really? How many cops have you dealt with?"

"I have a heavy foot. I get lots of traffic tickets." She smiled teasingly. "Seriously, why did you make the switch?"

He absently played with his knife for a moment. "I busted a guy who was carrying a brick of coke. He was a mule for some drug runners, a real minor role; just transport the stuff from point A to point B. I had other probable cause to do a stop and search. I turn up the brick and then the guy, with the vocabulary of a first-grader, tells me he thought it was a hunk of cheese." Fiske looked directly at her. "Can you believe that? He would've been better off claiming he didn't know how it got in there. Then his attorney could've at least had a shot at raising reasonable doubt on the possession charge. Trying to sell a jury on the fact that somebody who looks, acts and talks like a slimeball really thought ten thousand bucks worth of misery for their kids was a chuck of Swiss, well, you got problems." He shook his head. "You put ten of these guys in jail, there's a hundred more just waiting to take their place. They've got nowhere else to go. If they had, they would. The thing is, you don't give people hope, they don't care what they do to themselves or each other."

Sara smiled. "What's so funny?" he asked.

"You sound a lot like your brother."

Fiske paused and rubbed his hand across a water ring on the table. "You spent a lot of time with Mike?"

"Yes, quite a lot."

"Socially too?"

"We had drinks, dinner, outings." She took a sip of her drink and smiled. "I've never been deposed before."

"Depositions can actually be quite painful."

"Really?"

"Yes, like this for instance: Something tells me Mike's death didn't seem to surprise you all that much. Is that true?"

Sara instantly dropped her casual manner. "No. I was horrified."

"Horrified, yes. But surprised?"

The waitress stopped by and asked if they would like some dessert or coffee. Fiske asked for the bill.

Then they were back in the car and heading toward the District. A light rain had begun to fall. October was a quirky month, weather-wise, for the area. It could be hot, cold or mild during any given stretch. Right now it was very hot and humid outside, and Sara had the AC on high.

Fiske looked at her expectantly. She caught his gaze, took a troubled breath and started speaking slowly.

"Recently, Michael did seem nervous, distracted."

"Was that unusual?"

"For the last six weeks we've been cranking out bench memos. Everybody's short-fused, but Michael thrived under those conditions."

"You think it was related to something at the Court?"

"Michael didn't have much of a life outside the Court."

"Other than you?"

She glanced at him sharply but said nothing.

"Any big controversial cases pending?" he asked.

"Every case is big and controversial."

"But he never mentioned specifics to you?"

Sara stared ahead but again chose not to answer.

"Whatever you can tell me will help, Sara."

She slowed the car slightly. "Your brother was funny. Do you know that he would go down to the clerks' mail room at the crack of dawn to get an early jump on any interesting cases?"

"I'm not surprised. He never did things halfway. How are the appeals normally processed?"

"The clerks' mail room is where the filings are opened and processed. Each filing goes to a case analyst to make sure that it complies with the requirements of the rules of the

Court, and so forth. If it's handwritten, like a lot of the *in forma pauperis* appeals are, they even make sure the handwriting is legible. Then the information goes into a database under the last name of the party filing the appeal. Lastly, the filing is copied and sent to all the justices' chambers."

"Mike once told me how many appeals the Court gets. The justices can't possibly read all of them."

"They don't. The petitions are divided up among the justices' chambers, and the clerks are assigned to do certorari pool memos on them. For example, we might get in a hundred or so appeals in a week's time. There are nine justices, so each chamber gets roughly a dozen appeals. Of the dozen appeals sent to Justice Knight's chambers, I might write a memo on three. That memo is circulated to all the chambers. Then the other justices' clerks look over my memo and make a recommendation to their justice on whether the Court should grant cert or not."

"You clerks have a lot of power."

"In some areas, but not really with the opinions. A clerk's draft of an opinion is mostly a recap of the facts of the case and then stringing together cites. The justices just use the clerks to get the grunt work done, the paper pulp. We have the greatest impact in the screening of the appeals."

Fiske looked thoughtful. "So a justice may

not even see the actual documents filed with the Court before deciding whether to hear the case or not? He'd just read the pool memo and the clerk's recommendation."

"Maybe not even the memo, perhaps just the clerk's recommendation. The justices hold discussion conferences usually twice a week. That's when all the petitions screened by the clerks are discussed and voted upon to see if there are at least four votes, the minimum you need, to hear the case."

"So the first person to actually see an appeal filed with the Court would be someone in the clerks' mail room?"

"That's normally the case."

"What do you mean, 'normally'?"

"I mean there's no guarantee that things will always be done by the rules."

Fiske thought about this for a moment. "Are you suggesting that my brother might have taken an appeal before the clerks' mail room could process it?"

Sara let out a muffled groan but quickly composed herself. "I can only tell you this in confidence, John."

He shook his head. "I'm not going to promise you something I can't deliver."

Sara sighed and in concise sentences told Fiske about finding the papers in his brother's briefcase. "I didn't really mean to snoop. But he had been acting strangely, and I was worried about him. I ran into him one morning coming from the clerks' mail room. He looked really distraught. I think he had just taken the appeal I found in his briefcase."

"The filing you saw, was it the original or a copy?"

"Original. One of the pages was hand-written, the other typewritten."

"Are originals normally circulated?"

"No. Only copies. And the copied files certainly don't have the original envelope the filing came in."

"I remember Mike telling me that clerks sometimes take home files, even originals sometimes."

"That's true."

"So maybe that was the case here."

She shook her head. "It wasn't set up like a normal case file. There was no return address on the envelope, and the typewritten page had no signature at the bottom. The hand-written page made me think it was an *in forma pauperis* petition, but there was no motion or affidavit of indigency that I could see."

"Did you see any name on the papers, anything that could identify who was involved?"

"I did. That's why I knew Michael had taken a filing."

"How?"

"I managed to glance at the first sentence of the typewritten page. The person identified as the party filing the appeal was named there. As soon as I left Michael's office I checked the Court's filing database. There was no one by that name listed."

"What was the name?"

"The last name was Harms."

"First name?"

"I didn't see it."

"Do you remember anything else?"

"No."

Fiske eased back in his seat. "The thing is, if Mike took the appeal, he had to be sure that no one would call up about the disappearance of the file. Like the attorney who filed it, if an attorney did."

"Well, the envelope had a return receipt requested label. The sending party would've gotten notice that it was delivered to the Court."

"Okay. And why one handwritten page and one typewritten page?"

"Two different people. Maybe the person didn't want to be recognized, but still wanted to help Harms."

"From all the appeals the Court gets, Mike takes this one. Why?"

She glanced at him nervously. "Oh God, if it turns out that this had anything to do with Michael's death. I never thought . . ." She suddenly looked as though she would burst into tears.

"I'm not going to tell anyone about this. For now. You took a risk for Mike. I appreciate that." There was a lengthy silence until

Fiske said, "It's getting late."

As they drove along, Fiske finally said, "We've been able to ascertain that Mike put eight hundred or so miles on his car in the last couple of days. Any idea where he might have gone?"

"No. I don't think he liked driving. He rode his bike to work."

"How was he perceived by the other clerks?"

"Highly respected. He was incredibly motivated. I guess all Supreme Court clerks are, but Michael seemed incapable of turning it off. I consider myself a hard worker too, but I think a balance in life is good."

"Mike was always that way," Fiske said a little wearily. "He started at perfection and moved up from there."

"Must run in the family. Michael told me that, growing up, you worked two and three jobs almost all the time."

"I like to have spending money."

The money had not remained long in Fiske's pocket. It had gone to his father, who had never earned more than fifteen lousy grand a year in over forty years of working his ass off. Now it went to his mother and her massive health bills.

"You also went to college while working as a cop."

Fiske impatiently tapped his fingers against the car window. "Good old Virginia Commonwealth University, the Stanford of the next century."

"And you read for the law." Fiske looked at her angrily. "Please don't get upset, John. I'm just curious."

Fiske sighed. "I apprenticed to a Richmond criminal defense attorney. Learned a lot. Got my certificate and passed the bar." He added dryly, "It's the only way to become a lawyer if you're too dumb to score high enough on the LSATs."

"You're not dumb."

"Thanks, but how would you know?"

"We watched you do a trial."

He turned to look at her. "Excuse me?"

"Over the summer, Michael and I came down to Richmond and watched you do a trial in circuit court." She was not going to mention her second trip to watch him in court.

"Why didn't you let me know you were there?"

Sara shrugged. "Michael thought you'd be upset."

"Why would I be upset at seeing my brother?"

"Why are you asking me? He was your brother." When Fiske said nothing, Sara continued, "I was really impressed. I think you might have motivated me to become a criminal defense lawyer someday. At least for a while, try it out, see what it's really like."

"Oh, you think you'd like to do that?"

"Why not? The law can still be a noble calling. Defending the rights of others. The poor. I'd love to hear about some of your cases."

"Would you really?"

"Absolutely," she said enthusiastically.

He settled down, pretended to think hard. "Let's see, there was Ronald James. That was his real name, but he preferred to be called Backdoor Daddy. That referred to his sexual position of choice with the six women he brutally raped. I plea-bargained that one, even though all six women identified him from a police lineup. I had some leverage, though. Four of the women couldn't face Backdoor in court. That's what terror will do for you. Or *to* you. The fifth victim had a few nasties in her past that maybe we could've used to attack her credibility. The last woman wanted nothing less than to crucify him. But one good witness isn't the same as a half dozen. Bottom line: The prosecutor got cold feet and Backdoor got twenty years with a shot at parole.

"Then there was Jenny, a nice kid who put a cleaver into her grandmother's skull because, as she tearfully explained to me, the old, dumb bitch wouldn't let her go to the mall with her friends. Jenny's mother, the daughter of the woman little Jenny butchered, is paying my legal bill in installments of two bucks a month."

"I think I get the point," Sara said tersely.

"Now, I don't want to disillusion you. The guy I just got off for burglary paid my bill in full, probably with the cash he got from fencing the property he stole. I've learned not to ask. So my rent's paid for the month, and I haven't had to pull a gun on one of my clients in a long time. And tomorrow's always a new day." Fiske leaned back. "Go get 'em, Ms. Evans."

"You really enjoy shocking people, don't you?"

"You asked."

"So why the hell do you do it, then?"

"Someone has to."

"That wasn't exactly the answer I was expecting, but let's just drop it," she said harshly. "Thanks for bursting my balloon, though, I really appreciate it."

"If I burst your little balloon, you should thank me," he said angrily. Then he added more calmly, "Look, Sara, I'm no white knight. Most of my clients are guilty. I know that, they know that, everybody knows that. Ninety percent of my cases are plea-bargained for that very reason. If somebody actually came to me proclaiming their innocence, I'd probably die of a heart attack. I'm not a defender of anybody, I'm a negotiator of sentencing. My job is to make sure that the prison time is fair relative to what everybody else gets. On the rare occasion I do go to trial, the trick there is to blow enough smoke around that a jury just loses the energy to figure it all out and gives up. Like they really want to sit around debating the fate of somebody they don't even know, and could give a shit about."

"Gee, whatever happened to the truth?"

"Sometimes the truth is a lawyer's biggest enemy. You can't spin it. Nine times out of ten, with the truth I lose. Now, I'm not paid to lose, but I try to be fair. So we all do our little shuffle during the day, the tuna nets go out at night and catch a batch of fresh meat, and we all come back and do the dance again. And on and on it goes."

"Your version of real life?" she asked.

"Don't worry, you're never going to see it. You'll be teaching at Harvard, or working at some gold-plated New York law firm. If I'm ever up there, I'll be sure to wave to you from the Dumpster."

"Can you please stop?" Sara exclaimed.

They drove on in silence until something occurred to Fiske.

"If you had already seen me at the trial, why did you make a show of not knowing who I was back at the Court when Perkins intro-duced us?"

Sara took a short breath. "I don't know. I guess because in front of Perkins, I couldn't think of a clever way to tell you how I had already seen you."

"Why did it have to be clever?"

"You know what they say about first impressions." She shook her head at the thought now. *Christ!*

As Fiske watched her, the last of his hostility faded. "Don't let my cynical ass dampen your enthusiasm, Sara." He added quietly, "Nobody has that right. I'm sorry."

Sara looked over at him. "I think you care more than you let on." She hesitated for a moment, debating whether to tell him or not. "You know a little boy named Enis, don't you?" Fiske stared over at her. "I saw you talking to him."

It finally hit Fiske. "The bar. I knew I had seen you before. What were you doing, following me?"

"Yes."

Her frankness caught Fiske off guard. "Why?" he asked quietly.

She spoke slowly. "That's a little difficult to explain. I don't think I'm up to it right now. I wasn't spying on you. I could see how difficult it was for you, talking to Enis and his family."

"Best thing that ever happened to them. Next time the old man might have killed them."

"Still, to lose your father like that . . ."

"He wasn't Enis's father."

"I'm sorry, I thought he was."

"Oh, Enis is his son. But that doesn't make somebody your father. Fathers don't do what that guy did to his family."

"What'll happen to them?"

Fiske shrugged. "I give Lucas two more years before they find him in some alley with a dozen holes in him. The really sad thing is, he knows it too."

"Maybe he'll surprise you."

"Yeah. Maybe."

"And Enis?"

"I don't know about Enis. And I don't want to talk about it anymore."

They remained silent until they pulled up in front of the Homicide building.

"I'm parked right in front."

Sara looked at him in surprise. "Pretty lucky. In the two years I've lived in this city, I don't think I've ever found an empty parking space on the street."

Fiske stared at one spot. "I could've sworn I parked right here."

Sara looked out the window. "You mean right next to that tow-away zone sign?"

Fiske jumped out of the car just as the rain picked up, and looked at the sign and then at the space where his car used to be. He climbed back in her car, leaned back against the seat and closed his eyes. Water droplets clung to his face and hair. "I really can't believe this day."

"They have a number you can call to get

your car back." Sara picked up the cell phone and punched in the numbers as she read them off the street sign. The phone rang ten times, but no one answered. She hung up. "It doesn't look like you're going to get your car back tonight."

"I can't go to sleep until my dad knows."

"Oh." She thought for a moment. "Well, I'll drive you."

Fiske looked outside at the pouring rain. "You sure?"

She put the car in gear. "Let's go find your dad."

"Can we make one stop first?"

"Sure, just tell me where."

"My brother's apartment."

"John, I'm not sure that's a good idea."

"I think it's a great idea."

"We can't get in."

"I've got a key," said Fiske. She looked puzzled. "I helped move him in when he started working at the Court."

"Won't the police have it taped off or anything?"

"Chandler said he was going to go over it tomorrow." He looked at her. "Don't worry, you're staying in the car. If anything happens, just take off."

"And if maybe the person who killed Michael is there?"

"You got a tire iron in the trunk?"

"Yes."

"Then it's my lucky day."

Sara took a shallow breath. "I hope you know what you're doing."

Me too, Fiske thought.

CHAPTER TWENTY-SEVEN

When they reached Michael Fiske's apartment, Sara pulled into a parking space around the corner. "Pop the trunk," Fiske said, before getting out.

She could hear him rummaging through the compartment for a moment. She was startled for an instant when he appeared at her window. She quickly rolled it down.

"Keep the car doors locked, the engine running and your eyes open, okay?" he said.

She nodded, noting the tire iron in one hand and a flashlight in his other.

"If you get nervous or anything, just leave. I'm a big boy. I'll get to Richmond okay."

She shook her head stubbornly. "I'll be right here."

As she watched him head around the corner, a thought occurred to her. She waited a minute or so to allow him time to get into the building, then she pulled around the corner, back onto Michael's street and parked across from the row house. She picked up her cell phone and held it ready. If she spotted anything remotely suspicious, she was going to call the apartment and warn Fiske. A good emergency plan, but one she hoped she wouldn't have to use.

Fiske closed the door behind him, clicked on the flashlight and looked around. He saw no obvious signs that anyone had searched the place.

He entered the small kitchen, which was separated from the living room by a waist-high bar. He looked for and found a couple of plastic baggies in one of the kitchen drawers and covered his hands with them, so as not to leave any prints. There was a small door leading to the pantry, but Fiske didn't bother with it. His brother wasn't the type to have neatly arranged rows of canned corn and peas. It was no doubt empty.

He went through the living room, checked the small coat closet, but there was nothing in any of the coat pockets. Next he headed to the single bedroom at the rear of the apartment. The floors were worn tongue-in-groove and the creaks followed him with each step. He pushed open the door and looked in. Bed was unmade, clothes here and there. He checked the pockets — nothing. There was a small desk in the corner. He searched it carefully but came up empty. Hidden behind the desk he saw a power cord plugged into the wall and frowned as he held up the other end. He looked next to the desk but didn't see what he had expected to see there: the laptop computer the cord should have been attached to. And his brother's briefcase; Fiske had actually bought it for Mike upon his graduation from law school. He made a mental note to ask Sara about both the briefcase and the laptop.

Finished with the bedroom, he moved back down the hallway and toward the kitchen. He stopped for a moment, listening intently. As he did so, he tightly gripped the tire iron. With a sudden lunge he jerked open the pantry door, the tire iron raised, the light shining directly into the small space.

The man burst out and hit Fiske right in the stomach with his shoulder. Fiske grunted, the flashlight flew away, but he held his ground and managed to clip the man across the neck with the tire iron. He heard a pained cry; but the man recovered more quickly than Fiske had anticipated, lifted him off the floor and threw him over the bar. Fiske landed hard and felt his shoulder go numb. Even so, he managed to twist sideways and kick the legs out from under the guy as he hurtled past, going for the door. He swung with the tire iron again, but in the darkness missed and it hit the floor instead. A fist connected with his jaw. Fiske swung out and hit solid flesh as well.

The guy was on his feet and through the door in a few seconds. Fiske finally lurched up and raced to the door, holding his shoulder. He heard feet clattering down the steps. He hustled after the man and heard the front door to the building crash open. Ten seconds later Fiske was out on the street. He looked right and left. A horn blew.

Sara rolled down her window and pointed to the right. Fiske sprinted hard through the rain in that direction and turned the corner. Sara put the car in gear, but had to wait for two cars to pass, and then she spun rubber after him. She turned the corner, raced down the next block but didn't see anyone. She backed the car up and turned down another side street, and then another, growing more and more frantic. She let out a shriek of relief when she saw Fiske in the middle of the street, sucking in air.

She jumped out of the car and ran over to him.

"John, thank God you're okay."

Fiske was furious that the man had gotten away. He stomped around in tight circles. "Dammit! Shit!"

"What the hell was that all about?"

Fiske calmed down. "Bad guys one, good guys zip."

Sara put an arm around his waist and walked him over to the car. She eased him into it. Then she climbed in the driver's side and they started off. "You need to see a doctor."

"No! It's just a stinger. Did you see the guy?"

280

Sara shook her head. "Not really. He came out so fast, I thought it was you."

"My size? Distinguishing clothing? White, black?"

Sara thought hard for a moment, trying to visualize what she had seen. "I don't know about his age. He was close to your size. He had on dark clothing and a mask, I think." She sighed. "It happened so fast. Where was he?"

"In the pantry. I didn't hear him on my first pass through, but I heard the floor squeak on my way back out." He rubbed his shoulder. "And now comes the hard part." He picked up her cell phone and pulled a business card from his wallet. "Telling Chandler what just happened."

Fiske paged Chandler and the detective called back a few minutes later. When Fiske told him what he had done, he had to hold the phone away from his ear.

"Slightly upset?" Sara asked.

"Yeah, like Mount Saint Helens *slightly* erupted." Fiske brought the receiver back to his ear. "Look, Buford —"

"What the hell were you thinking, doing something that stupid?" yelled Chandler. "You were a cop."

"That's how I was thinking. Like I was still a cop."

"Well, you're not a damn cop anymore."

"Do you want the description of the guy or not?"

"I'm not finished with you yet."

"I know, but there's plenty of me to go around."

"Give me the damn description," Chandler said.

After Fiske finished, Chandler said, "I'll get a squad car over there right now to secure it, and I'll request a tech team ASAP to go over the place."

"My brother's briefcase wasn't at his apartment. Was it in his car?"

"No, I told you we found no personal items."

Fiske looked at Sara. "Is the briefcase in his office? I don't remember seeing it. Or his laptop computer."

She shook her head. "I don't remember seeing the briefcase. And he usually didn't bring his laptop to work, since we all have desktops."

Fiske spoke back into the phone. "Looks like his briefcase is missing. And so is his computer; I found the power cord to it."

"Did the guy maybe have either of the items on him?"

"He was empty-handed. I know. He clocked me good with one of those empty hands."

"Okay, so we got a missing briefcase, missing laptop and a dumb-as-shit ex-police officer who I've got half a mind to arrest right this instant."

"Come on, you guys already towed my car."

"Put Ms. Evans on the line."

"Why?"

"Just do it."

Fiske handed the phone over to a perplexed Sara.

"Yes, Detective Chandler?" she said, nervously twirling a strand of her hair.

"Ms. Evans," he began politely, "I thought you were simply going to drive Mr. Fiske to his car and maybe get a little dinner, not engage in filming a James Bond movie."

"But you see, his car was towed and —"

Chandler's tone quickly changed. "I don't appreciate you two making my job even more difficult. Where are you?"

"About a mile from Michael's apartment."

"And where are you headed?"

"To Richmond. To tell John's father about Michael."

"Okay, then you drive him to Richmond, Ms. Evans. Don't let him out of your sight. If he wants to play Sherlock Holmes again, you call me, and I will come directly over and shoot him myself. Do I make myself clear?"

"Yes, Detective Chandler. Absolutely."

"And I expect to see both of you back in D.C. tomorrow. Is that also understood?"

"Yes, we'll be back."

"Good, Tonto, now put the Lone Ranger back on."

Fiske took back the phone. "Look, I know it was stupid, but I was only trying to help."

"Do me a favor, don't try to help anymore unless I'm with you. Okay?"

"Okay."

"John, any number of things could've happened tonight, most of them bad. Not only to you, but to Ms. Evans."

Fiske rubbed his shoulder and glanced over at the woman. "I know," he said quietly.

"Give my condolences to your father."

Fiske put down the phone.

"Can we go to Richmond now?" Sara asked.

"Yes, we can go to Richmond now."

CHAPTER TWENTY-EIGHT

In his friend's pickup truck, Josh Harms drove along the deserted country road. The dense forest bracketing the narrow lanes gave him a certain comfort. Isolation, a buffer between himself and those who would hassle him, had been Josh's one constant goal in life. As a carpenter of considerable skill, he worked alone. When he was not working, he was either hunting or fishing, again alone. He did not desire the conversation of others, and he very rarely offered any of his own. All of that had changed now. The responsibility he had just acquired had not yet fully sunk in, but he knew it was considerable. And he also knew his decision had been the right one.

The truck had a camper and his brother was back there supposedly resting, although Josh had doubts as to whether the man could really be sleeping. The back of the camper was also filled with a month's worth of food and bottled water, two deer rifles and a semi-automatic pistol in addition to the one he had tucked in his belt. That arsenal was insignificant compared to what would soon be coming after them, but he had faced long odds before and survived.

He lit a cigarette and blew the smoke cleanly out the window. They were already two hundred miles from Roanoke and he was putting as much distance between it and them as he could. The escape would have been discovered by now, he knew. The road-blocks would be set up, but not out this far, he figured. They had gotten a head start, but that gap would quickly close. The boys in green had a big advantage in manpower and equipment. But Josh had fished and hunted around the area for the last twenty years. He knew all the abandoned cabins, all the hidden valleys, the smallest opening in otherwise solid forest. His survival skills had been honed as much from scraping for an existence in America as from dodging death halfway around the world in Vietnam.

Even with his outright distrust of all authority, he didn't break the law lightly. He had never figured his little brother for some crazed killer. Rufus never should have joined the Army, wasn't cut out for it. Ironically, Josh had been the decorated war hero, and he had been drafted. His brother had volunteered and had spent his career in the stockade. Josh hadn't been too thrilled about taking up a rifle for a country that had largely failed him and anyone his color. But once in the service he had fought with great distinction. He had done it for himself and the men in his company, and for no other reason. He had no other motivation to fight and kill men with whom he had no personal quarrel.

Josh slowed the truck and turned down a dirt road that led deeper into the woods. Rufus had filled him in on some of the details of what had happened twenty-five years ago, what those men had done to him. Josh felt his face grow hot as he now recalled an incident he had kept buried. It was principally what drove the anger, the hatred in him. What their little town in Alabama had done to the Harms family after the news of Rufus's crime. He had tried to protect his mother then, but had failed. Let me meet up with the men who did this to my brother. *You hear that one, God? You listening?*

His plan was to hide out for a while and then hit the road again when the pressure died down. Maybe try to get to Mexico and disappear. Josh wasn't leaving all that much behind. A disintegrated family, a carpentry business that was always on the wrong side of profitability despite his skill. He guessed Rufus was all the family he had left. And he was certainly all Rufus ever would have. They had been cut off from each other for a quarter century. Now, in middle age, they had a chance to be closer than brothers normally were at this time in their lives. If Josh and Rufus could survive. He tossed out the cigarette and kept on driving.

In the back of the camper, Rufus was,

indeed, not asleep. He lay on his back, a black tarp partially over him — Josh's doing, the tarp designed to blend in with the dark truck bed liner under him. Stacked around him were boxes of food, secured by bungie cords — also Josh's doing, a wall to prevent anyone from seeing in. He tried to stretch out a little, relax. The motion of the truck was unsettling. He had not been in a civilian automobile since Richard Nixon had been president. Could that really be? How many presidents ago was that? The Army had always transported him between prisons via helicopters, apparently unwilling to let him get this close to the road, to freedom. When you escape from a chopper, there wasn't much place to go except down.

Rufus tried to peek between cardboard, out at the passing night. Too dark now. Freedom. He often wondered what it would feel like. He still did not know. He was too scared. People, lots of them, looking for him. Wanting to kill him. And now his brother. His fingers gripped the unfamiliar texture of the hospital Bible. The one his mother had given him was back in the cell. He had kept it beside him all these years, turned again and again to the scriptures as sustenance against all that was his existence. He felt empty of brain and heart without it. Too late now. He felt his heart start to accelerate. He figured that was bad — too much strain on it. From memory he recited comforting words from the Bible's bounty. How many nights had he mumbled the Proverbs, all thirty-one chapters, the one hundred and fifty Psalms, each one telling and forceful, each one with particular meaning, insight into elements of his existence.

When he finished his "readings," he half rose and slid open the window of the camper. From this angle he could see his brother's face in the reflection of the rearview mirror.

"I thought you were sleeping," Josh said.

"Can't."

"How's your heart feel?"

"My heart ain't troubling me none. If I die, it ain't gonna be because of my heart."

"Not unless it's a bullet ripping through it."

"Where we headed?"

"A little place in the middle of nowhere. I figure we stay there a bit, let things die down, and then we head out again when it's dark. They probably think we're shooting south, going for the Mexican border, so we're going north to Pennsylvania, at least for now."

"Sounds good."

"Hey, you said Rayfield and that other sonofabitch —"

"Tremaine. Old Vic."

"Yeah, you said they've been watching over you all this time. After all those years went by, how come they were still hanging in there? Didn't they figure if you remembered what happened you would've said something before now? Like maybe at your trial?"

"Been thinking about that. They maybe thought I couldn't remember nothing then, but maybe I might one day. Not that I could prove nothing, but just me saying stuff might get them in trouble or at least get people looking around. Easiest thing was to kill me. Believe me, they tried that, but it didn't work. Maybe they thought I was messing with 'em, playing dumb and hoping they'd give up the guard, and then I start talking. With them at the prison, they pretty much had me under their thumb. Read my mail, checked out people coming to see me. Anything look funny, then they just take me out. Probably felt better about doing it like that. After so many years, though, they got a little lazy, I guess. Let Samuel and that fellow from the Court come see me."

"I figured that. But I still got that letter from the Army in to you. I didn't know all this shit was going on, but I didn't want them having a look-see at it either."

The two stayed quiet for a while. Josh was naturally reserved and Rufus wasn't used to having anyone to talk to. The silence was both liberating and oppressive to him. He had a lot he wanted to say. During Josh's thirty-minute visits at the prison each month, he would talk and his brother would mostly listen, as though he sensed the accumulation of words, of thoughts in Rufus's head.

"I don't think I ever asked you: You been back home?"

Josh shifted in his seat. "Home? What home?"

Rufus started slightly. "Where we was born, Josh!"

"Why the hell would I want to go back to that place?"

"Momma's grave is there, ain't it?" Rufus said quietly.

Josh considered this for a moment and then nodded. "Yeah, it's there, all right. She owned the dirt, she had the burial insurance. They couldn't *not* bury her there, although they sure as hell tried."

"Is it a nice grave? Who's keeping it up?"

"Look, Rufus, Momma's dead, okay? Long time now. Ain't no way in hell she's knowing nothing about how her grave looks. And I ain't going all the way down to damn Alabama to brush some leaves off the damn ground, not after what happened down there. Not after what that town done to the Harms family. I hope they all burn in hell for it, every last damn one of 'em. If there is a God, and I got me some big-ass doubts on that, then that's what the Big Man should do. If you want to worry about the dead, you go right ahead. I'm gonna stick to what counts: keeping you and me alive."

Rufus continued to watch his brother. There is a God, he wanted to tell him. That same God had kept Rufus going all these years when he had wanted to just curl up and sink into oblivion. And one should respect the dead and their final resting place. If he lived through this, Rufus would go see to his mother's grave. They would meet up again. For all eternity.

"I talk to God every day."

Josh grunted. "That's real good. I'm glad He's keeping company with somebody."

They fell silent until Josh said, "Hey, what was the name of that fella come visit you?"

"Samuel Rider?"

"No, no, the young fella."

Harms thought for a moment. "Michael somebody."

"From the Supreme Court, you said?" Rufus nodded. "Well, they killed him. Michael *Fiske*. Anyway, I guess they killed him. Saw it on the TV right before I came to get you."

Rufus looked down. "Damn. I figured that would happen."

"Stupid thing he did, coming to the prison like that."

"He was just trying to help me. Damn," Rufus said again, and then fell silent as the truck rolled on.

CHAPTER TWENTY-NINE

With Fiske directing her, Sara drove to his father's neighborhood on the outskirts of Richmond and pulled into the gravel driveway. The grass was brown in spots after another heat- and humidity-filled Richmond summer, but fronting the house there were carefully tended flower beds that had benefited from consistent watering.

"You grew up in this house?"

"Only house my parents have ever owned." Fiske looked around, shaking his head. "I don't see his car."

"Maybe it's in the garage."

"There's no room. He was a mechanic for forty years, and accumulated a lot of junk. He parks in the driveway." He looked at his watch. "Where the hell is he?" He got out of the car. Sara did as well.

He looked at her over the roof of the car. "You can stay here if you want."

"I'll come in with you," she said quickly.

Fiske unlocked the front door and they went in. He turned on a light, and they moved through the small living room and into the adjacent dining room, where Sara stared at a collection of photos on the dining

293

room table. There was one of Fiske in his football uniform; a little blood on the face, grass stains on the knees, sweaty. Very sexy. She caught herself and looked away, suddenly feeling guilty.

She looked at some of the other pictures. "You two played a lot of sports."

"Mike was the natural athlete of the family. Every record I set, he broke. Easily."

"Quite the jock family."

"He was also valedictorian of his class, a GPA on the north side of four-point-oh, and a near-perfect score on the SATs and LSATs."

"You sound like the proud big brother."

"A lot of people were proud of him," Fiske said.

"And you?"

He looked at her steadily. "I was proud of him for some things, and not proud of him for others. Okay?"

Sara picked up a photo. "Your parents?"

Fiske stood beside her. "Their thirtieth anniversary. Before Mom got sick."

"They look happy."

"They were happy," he said quickly. He was growing very uncomfortable with her seeing these items from his past. "Wait here." Fiske went to the back room, which had once been the brothers' shared bedroom and now had been turned into a small den. He checked the answering machine. His father had not listened to his messages. He was about to leave the room when he saw the baseball glove on the shelf. He picked it up. It was his brother's, the pocket ribbing torn, but the leather well oiled — by his father, obviously. Mike was a lefty, but the family had no money to buy a special glove for him, so Mike had learned to field the ball, pull off his glove and throw. He had gotten so good that he could do it all faster than a righty could. Fiske recalled that blur of efficiency, no obstacle his brother couldn't overcome. He put the glove down and rejoined Sara.

"He hasn't listened to my phone messages."

"Any idea where he could've gone?"

Fiske thought a moment and then snapped his fingers. "Pop usually tells Ms. German."

While he was gone, Sara looked around the room some more. She eyed a small framed letter, set on a wooden pedestal. Wrapped around it was a medal. She picked up the frame and read the letter. The medal was for valor, awarded to Patrolman John Fiske, and the letter commemorated the event. She looked at the date it had been given. Quickly calculating, she concluded that the award would have been given at about the time Fiske had left the force. She still didn't know why he had, and Michael never would say. When she heard the back door open, she quickly put the letter and medal down.

Fiske entered the room. "He's at the trailer."

"What trailer?"

"Down by the river. He goes there to fish. Go boating."

"Can you call the trailer?"

Fiske shook his head. "No phone."

"Okay, so we drive. Where is it?"

"You've gone way beyond the call of duty already."

"I don't mind, John."

"It's about another hour and a half from here."

"The night's sort of shot anyway."

"You mind if I drive? It's off the beaten path."

She tossed him the keys. "I thought you'd never ask."

CHAPTER THIRTY

"Let me get this right: On top of everything else that's happened, you let him escape."

"First of all, I didn't *let* him do anything. I thought the guy had just had a friggin' heart attack. He was chained to the damn bed. He had an armed guard outside his door, and nobody was supposed to know he was even there," Rayfield snapped back into the telephone. "I still don't know how his brother found out."

"And his brother's some kind of war hero, I understand. Superbly trained in all forms of eluding capture. That's just great."

"It is for our purposes."

"Why don't you explain that one to me, Frank?"

"I've ordered my men to shoot to kill. They'll put a bullet into both of them as soon as they get a chance."

"What if he tells somebody first?"

"Tells them what? That he got a letter from the Army that says something he has no way to prove? Now we've got a dead Supreme Court clerk on our hands. That just makes our job a lot tougher."

"Well, we were supposed to have a dead

country lawyer too, but, funny, I haven't read his obituary anywhere."

"Rider went out of town."

"Oh, good, we'll just wait until he gets back from vacation and hope he's not in discussions with the FBI."

"I don't know where he is," Rayfield said angrily.

"The Army has an intelligence component, Frank. What do you say you try to use some of it? Take care of Rider and then concentrate on finding Harms and his brother. And when you do, you put them six feet under. I hope that's clear enough for you." The phone went dead.

Rayfield slammed the receiver down and stared up at Vic Tremaine.

"This is going to hell in a handbasket."

Tremaine shrugged his shoulders. "We take Rider out and then those two black SOBs, we're home free," he said in a gravelly voice that seemed perfectly calibrated to command men to fight.

"I don't like it. We're not in a war here."

"We are at war, Frank."

"The killing never did bother you, did it, Vic?"

"All I care about is the success of my mission."

"Do you mean to tell me that right before you pulled the trigger on Fiske you didn't feel anything?"

"Mission accomplished." Tremaine put his palms down on Rayfield's desk and leaned forward. "Frank, we've been through a lot together, combat and otherwise. But let me tell you something. I've spent thirty years in the Army, the last twenty-five in various military prisons just like this one when I could've gotten a civilian job that paid a lot more. We all made a pact that was supposed to protect us from a stupid thing we did a long time ago. I've kept my end of the bargain. I've baby-sat Rufus Harms while the others went on with their lives.

"Now, in addition to my military pension, I've got over one million bucks sitting in an offshore account. In case you've forgotten, you've got the same little nest egg. That's our comp for all these years of doing this crap. And after all the shit I've been through, no one and nothing is going to keep me from enjoying that money. The best thing Rufus Harms ever did for me is escape. Because now I've got a bulletproof reason to blow his sorry ass away and nobody'll ask any questions. And as soon as that sonofabitch has breathed his last, this uniform I'm wearing goes into mothballs. For good."

Tremaine straightened up. "And, Frank, I will destroy anyone who even remotely tries to mess that up." His eyes became black dots as he said the next word. "Anyone."

CHAPTER THIRTY-ONE

On the drive to the trailer, Fiske stopped at an all-night convenience store. Sara waited in the car. A rusty Esso sign clanked back and forth from the force of a semi sailing past and made her jump. When Fiske got back in the car, Sara stared at the two six-packs of Budweiser. "You intend to drink your sorrows away?"

He ignored the question. "Once we get down there, there's really no way for you to get back by yourself. It's really in the middle of nowhere; sometimes *I* get lost."

"I'm prepared to sleep in the car."

About thirty minutes later, Fiske slowed the car, turned into a narrow gravel drive and drove up to a small, darkened cottage. "You're supposed to check in here and pay the guest fee before going into the grounds," he explained. "I'll do it before we leave tomorrow."

He pulled the car past the cottage and into the middle of the campground. Sara looked at the trailers, which were laid out in a street grid style. Most of them were brilliantly outlined with Christmas lights and had flagpoles either attached to the trailer or porch, or sunk into concrete. With the strings of lights and the moonlight, the area was surprisingly well illuminated. They passed late-blooming flower beds of impatiens, and red and pink mums. Clumpy vines of clematis gripped the sides of some homes. Everywhere Sara looked were outdoor sculptures of metal, marble and resin. There were a number of cinder-block grills and a large smoke pit; the commingled smells of cooked meat and charcoal lingered tantalizingly in the hot, humid air.

"This place is like a little gingerbread town built by gnomes," Sara said. She eyed the numerous flagpoles and added, "Patriotic gnomes."

"A lot of the people are from the American Legion and VFW crowd. My dad has one of the tallest flagpoles. He was in the Navy in World War II. The all-year Christmas lights became sort of a tradition a long while back."

"Did you and Michael spend much time here?"

"My dad only got a week's vacation, but Mom would bring us down for a couple weeks at a time during the summer. Some of the old guys taught us to sail, swim and fish. Things Pop never had time to do. He's made up for it since he retired."

He stopped the car in front of one trailer. It had bright Christmas lights and was painted a soothing, muted blue. His father's Buick, with a SUPPORT YOUR LOCAL POLICE bumper sticker, was parked next to the trailer. Fronting the trailer was a bed of bulky plantation hostas. Next to the Buick was a golf cart. The flagpole in front of the trailer went a good thirty feet into the air.

Fiske eyed the Buick. "At least he's here." Well, this is it, John, no more reprieves, he thought.

"Is there a golf course nearby?"

Fiske glanced at her. "No, why?"

"So what's with the golf cart?"

"The owners of the trailer park buy them secondhand from golf courses. The roads are pretty narrow here and, while you can drive your car to your trailer, you can't drive it around the grounds. And the people down here are elderly, for the most part. They use the golf carts to get around."

Fiske got out of the car with the two six-packs. Sara didn't move to join him. He looked at her questioningly.

"I thought you might want to talk to your dad alone."

"After everything we've been through tonight, I think you've earned the right to see it through. I'll understand if you don't want to." He looked over at the trailer and felt his nerves slowly disintegrate. He turned back to her. "I could sort of use the company."

She nodded. "Okay, give me a minute."

She flipped down the visor mirror and

checked her face and hair. She grimaced and reached for her purse, doing the best she could with lipstick and a small hairbrush. She was sweaty and sticky too, her dress clingy, her hair beyond salvation thanks to the rain and humidity. As trivial as worrying about her appearance seemed under the circumstances, she felt like such a fifth wheel that it was the only thing she could think to address.

With a sigh, she flipped the visor back up, opened the door and got out. As they headed up the wooden porch, she smoothed down her dress and fiddled some more with her hair.

Fiske noted this and said, "He's not going to care how you look. Not after I tell him."

She sighed. "I know. I guess I just didn't want to look like too much of a disaster."

Fiske took a deep breath and knocked on the door. He waited and knocked again. "Pop." He waited a moment and knocked again, louder this time. "Pop," he called out, and kept knocking.

They finally heard movement in the trailer and then a light came on. The door opened and Fiske's father, Ed, peered out. Sara looked at him closely. He was as tall as his son, and very lean, although he had vestiges of the powerful musculature shared by both his boys. His forearms were enormous, like thick pieces of sun-baked wood. Sara was able to observe this because he had on a tank-top shirt. He was deeply tanned, his face lined and starting to sag, but she could see he had been handsome as a younger man. His hair was thinning and curly and almost totally gray except for small flecks of black at the temples. She fixed for a moment on his long sideburns, a holdover from the seventies, she guessed. He had on a pair of pants halfway zipped up, the clasp unbuttoned so that his striped boxers were clearly in sight. He was barefoot.

"Johnny? What the hell you doing here?" A broad smile cracked his face. When he registered Sara, he looked startled and quickly turned so his back was to them. They watched him fumble with his pants until they were right. Then he turned back to face them.

"Pop, I need to talk to you."

Ed Fiske glanced over at Sara again.

"I'm sorry — Sara Evans, Ed Fiske," John said.

"Hello, Mr. Fiske," she said, trying to sound both pleasant and neutral at the same time. She awkwardly held out her hand.

He shook it. "Call me Ed, Sara, pleased to meet you." He looked back at his son curiously. "So what's up? You two getting married or something?"

Fiske glanced at Sara. "No! She worked with Mike at the Supreme Court."

"Oh, well, hell, where are my manners,

come on in. I got the air going, sticky as the damn devil out there."

They went inside. Ed pointed to a worn sofa and Fiske and Sara sat down there. Ed pulled a metal chair from the small dinette and sat down opposite them.

"Sorry I took so long. Just nodded off to sleep."

Sara looked around the small space. It was paneled with thin plywood stained dark. Several stuffed fish were mounted on plaques and hung on the wall. Slung across a rack on another wall was a shotgun. In the corner she saw a long, round container with one end of a rod and reel poking out. A folded newspaper was lying on the dinette table. Next to that was a small kitchen area with a sink and a little refrigerator. There was a worn-out recliner in one corner, a small TV across from it. There was one window. Mounted on the ceiling was an air conditioner that was making the room deliciously cool. She actually shivered as she adjusted to the temperature. The floor was cheap, uneven linoleum with a thin rug covering a portion of it.

Sara sniffed and then coughed. She could almost see the cigarette smoke lingering in the air. As if in response to her thoughts, Ed pulled a pack of Marlboros from a knicked-up side table and deftly popped a cigarette in his mouth, taking a moment to light up, then blew the smoke to the nicotine-coated ceiling. He grabbed a small ashtray off the same table and tapped his cigarette in it. He put his hands on his knees and leaned forward. She noted that his fingers were abnormally thick, the nails cracked, and blackened in spots from what looked like grease. He had been a mechanic, she recalled.

"So what brings you two down here so late?"

Fiske handed his father a six-pack. "Not good news."

The elder Fiske tensed, and he squinted at them through the smoke. "It's not your mom. I just saw her, she's okay." As soon as he said this, he shot a glance at Sara. The look on his face was clear: She "worked" with Mike.

He looked back at John. "Why don't you tell me whatever the hell it is you need to tell me, son."

"Mike's dead, Pop." As he finished saying it, it was as though he were hearing the news for the first time. He could feel his face grow hot as though he had leaned too close to a fire. Perhaps he had waited to see his father, to join his grief with his. He could believe that, couldn't he?

Fiske could sense Sara looking at him, but he kept his gaze on his father. As he watched the devastation wash over the man, Fiske suddenly found he could barely breathe.

Ed took the cigarette out of his mouth and dropped the ashtray, his fingers shaking. "How?"

"Robbery. At least they think so." Fiske paused and then added the obvious, since he knew his father was going to ask anyway. "Somebody shot him."

Ed tore off one of the Buds from the plastic holder and popped the tab. He drank it down almost in one swallow, his Adam's apple moving up and down.

Ed crushed the beer can against his leg and threw it against the wall. He stood up and went over to the small window and looked out, the cigarette dangling from his mouth, his big hands closing and opening, the veins in his forearms swelling and then diminishing.

"Have you seen him?" he asked without turning around.

"I went up to identify the body this afternoon."

His father whirled around, furious. "This afternoon? Why the hell did you wait so long to come tell me, boy?"

Fiske stood up. "I've been trying to track you down all day. I left messages on your answering machine. I only knew you were here because I asked Mrs. German."

"That should've been the first damn place you started," his father countered. "Ida always knows where I am. You know that."

He took a step toward them, one fist balled up.

Sara, who had risen along with Fiske, shrank back. She glanced over at the shotgun and suddenly wondered if it was loaded.

Fiske moved closer to his father. "Pop, as soon as I found out, I called you. Then I went by your house. After that I had to go up to the morgue. It wasn't any fun identifying Mike's body, but I did it. And the rest of the day has been pretty much downhill from there." He swallowed hard, suddenly feeling guilty that his father's angry reaction was more painful to him than his brother's death. "Let's not argue about the timing, okay? That's not going to bring Mike back."

All the anger seemed to go out of Ed as he listened to those words. Calm, rational words that did nothing to explain or reduce the anguish he was feeling. They hadn't invented the words that could do that, or the person to deliver them. Ed sat back down, his head swinging loosely from side to side. When he looked back up, there were tears in his eyes. "I always said you never had to chase bad news, it always got to you faster than anything good. A helluva lot faster." There was a catch in his throat when he spoke. He absently crushed his cigarette out on the carpet.

"I know, Pop. I know."

"Do they got whoever did this?"

"Not yet. They're working on it. The detective in charge is first-rate. I'm sort of helping him."

"D.C.?"

"Yes."

"I never liked Mike being up there."

He glared at Sara, who completely froze in the face of that accusing look.

He pointed a thick finger at her. "People kill you for nothing up there. Crazy bastards."

"Pop, they'll do that anywhere these days."

Sara managed to find her voice. "I liked and deeply respected your son. Everyone at the Court thought he was wonderful. I'm so, so very sorry about this."

"He was wonderful," Ed said. "He damn sure was. Never figured out how we turned out such a one as Mike."

Fiske looked down at the floor. Sara picked up on the pained expression on his face.

Ed looked around the trailer's interior, memories of good times with his family nudging him from all corners. "Got his mother's brains." His lower lip trembled for an instant. "Least the one she used to have." A low sob escaped from his mouth and he slumped to the floor.

Fiske knelt down next to his father and wrapped his arms around him, their shoulders shaking together.

Sara looked on, unsure of what to do. She

was embarrassed at witnessing such a private moment, and wondered if she should just get up and flee to her car. Finally she simply looked down and closed her eyes, silently releasing her own tears onto the cheap carpet.

Thirty minutes later, Sara sat on the porch and sipped on a warm can of beer. She was barefoot, her shoes next to her. She absently rubbed her toes and stared out into a darkness that was occasionally broken by the wink of a lightning bug. She swatted at a mosquito and then swiped off a trickle of sweat that meandered down her leg. Holding the beer can to her forehead, she contemplated getting into her car, cranking up the AC and trying to fall asleep.

The door opened and Fiske appeared. He had changed into faded jeans and an untucked short-sleeved shirt. He was barefoot as well. He held a plastic package strip with two beers dangling from it. He sat down beside her.

"How is he?"

Fiske shrugged. "Sleeping, or at least trying to."

"Does he want to come back with us?"

Fiske shook his head. "He's going to come over to my place tomorrow night." He glanced at his watch and realized that dawn was not very far away. "I mean tonight. I need to stop by my apartment on the way back so I can pick up some clean clothes."

Sara looked down at her dress. "Tell me about it. Where'd you get those?"

"I left them down here from the last fishing trip."

She wiped her forehead. "God, it's so humid."

Fiske looked toward the woods. "Well, there's a cooler breeze down by the water." He led her over to the golf cart. As they drove along the quiet dirt roads, Fiske handed her a beer. "This one is cold."

She popped it open. It felt good going down, and managed to lift her spirits a little. She held the can next to her cheek.

The narrow road took them through a mass of scrub pine, holly, oak and river birch with its bark unraveling like pencil shavings. Then the land opened up and Sara could see a wooden dock with several boats tied to it. She watched as the wooden structure moved up and down with the lap of the water.

"It's a floating dock; rests on fifty-gallon drums," Fiske explained.

"I gathered. Is that a boat ramp?" she asked, pointing to a place where the road angled sharply into the water.

Fiske nodded. "The people bring their cars up another road to get here. Pop has a little motorboat. That one over there." He pointed to a white boat with red stripes that bobbed in the water. "They usually pull them out at night. He must have forgotten. He got it cheap; we spent a year fixing it up. It's no yacht, but it'll get you where you want to go."

"What river is this?"

"Do you remember on the drive down 95 seeing signs for the Matta, the Po and the Ni Rivers?" Sara nodded. "Well, up near Fort A. P. Hill, southeast of Fredericksburg, they converge and it's called the Mattaponi River." He looked out at the water. There were few things more relaxing than skimming along the water, and he could think out there. "There's a full moon, the boat has running lights and a guide beacon and I know this part of the river real well. And it's a lot cooler on the water." He looked at her questioningly.

Sara didn't hesitate. "Sounds good."

They walked out to the boat and Fiske helped her in.

"Do you know how to cast off?" he asked.

"I actually did some competitive racing when I was an undergrad at Stanford."

Fiske watched her expertly undo the knots and cast off the line. "The old Mattaponi must seem pretty dull, then."

"It's all in who you're doing it with."

She sat next to Fiske, who stuck his hand into a storage compartment next to the captain's chair and pulled out a set of keys. He started the engine and they slowly pulled away from the dock. They got out into the middle of the river and he eased the throttle forward until they were moving at a fairly decent clip. The temperature was about twenty degrees cooler on the water. Fiske kept one hand on the wheel, his beer in the other. Sara folded her legs up under her and then raised herself up so that her upper torso was above the low-slung windshield. She held her arms out from her sides and let the wind grip her.

"God, this feels wonderful."

Fiske looked out over the water. "Mike and I would race each other across the river. It gets pretty wide at some points. Couple of times I thought one or the other of us was surely going to drown. But one thing kept us going."

"What was that?"

"We couldn't bear the thought of the other winning."

Sara sat back down and swung her chair around until she was facing him, smoothing out her hair as she did so.

"Do you mind a really personal question?"

Fiske stiffened slightly. "Probably."

"You won't take this the wrong way?"

"I will now."

"Why weren't you and Michael closer?"

"There's no law that says siblings have to be close."

"But you and Michael seemed to have so much in common. He spoke so highly of you, and you obviously were proud of him. I sense you had some differences. I'm just confused as to what went wrong."

Fiske shut the engine down and allowed the boat to drift. He cut off the beacon and the moon became their only source of light. The river was very calm, and they were at one of the widest points. Fiske pulled his pants legs up, went to the side of the boat, sat on the edge and swung his feet into the water.

Sara sat down next to him, hiked her skirt up a little and lowered her feet in.

Fiske gazed out over the river, sipping his beer.

"John, I'm really not trying to pry."

"I'm not really in the mood to talk about it, okay?"

"But —"

Fiske sliced the air with his hand. "Sara, it's not the place to do it, and it's damn sure not the time, okay?"

"Okay, I'm sorry. I just care. About all of you."

They sat there as the boat drifted along, the noise of the cicadas barely reaching them from shore.

Fiske finally stirred. "You know, Virginia's such a beautiful place. You've got water, mountains, forest, beaches, history, culture, high-tech centers and old battlefields. People move a little slower, enjoy life a little more here. I can't imagine living anywhere else.

Hell, I've never been anywhere else."

"And they have really nice trailer parks," Sara said.

Fiske smiled. "That too."

"So does your segue into the travelogue mean the topic of you and your brother is officially closed?" Sara bit her tongue when she finished. Stupid mouth, she berated herself.

"Guess so." Fiske abruptly stood up. The boat rocked and Sara almost ended up in the river. Fiske's hand shot out and gripped her arm. He squeezed tightly and looked down at her. She looked up at him, her eyes as big as the moon over them, her legs splayed out and gently drifting in the water, her dress wet where the river had touched it.

"How about a swim?" she said. "To cool off?"

"I don't have any swimsuits," he said.

"My clothes are wet enough."

He pulled her up into the boat and then went over and started the engine, destroying the peace. "Okay."

"Why not swim here?"

"Current's a little too strong."

He swung the boat around and headed toward the dock. Three-quarters of the way there, he cut across and headed to the shoreline. Here the bank sloped gradually down to the water, and as they drew closer Sara could make out fifty-gallon drums floating about twenty feet apart. As they kept heading in, she could see that they were tied together by mesh rope forming a huge rectangular-shaped pool.

Fiske cut the engine near one of the drums and let the boat's momentum propel them along until he could reach out and touch the big container. Then he tied a line to a hook mounted on the drum and dropped a small anchor, actually a gallon paint bucket filled with concrete, over the side for added security.

"It's about eight feet at its deepest point inside the ropes. There's a fence of wire mesh that circles the whole area and goes all the way to the bottom. That way if the current catches you, you won't end up in the Atlantic."

When Sara started to slip out of her dress, Fiske quickly turned around.

She smiled. "John, don't be a prude. My bikini shows more than this." In her panties and bra, she dove over the side, coming up a moment later treading water.

She called out, "I'll turn *my* back, if you're too embarrassed."

"I think I'll sit this one out."

"Oh, come on, I won't bite."

"I'm a little old for skinny-dipping, Sara."

"Water's really great."

"It looks it." He still made no move to join her.

A disappointed look on her face, she finally turned and swam away from him, her arms cutting powerful strokes through the smooth surface.

As Fiske watched her, he absently ran his finger the length of the wound, touching the two circular humps of burned flesh where the bullets had entered him. He abruptly removed his hand and sat down.

The name "Harms" kept reverberating in his head. An *in forma pauperis* petition probably would have come from a prisoner, if that's what the handwritten document amounted to. He shifted in his seat and once more looked in Sara's direction. Under the moonlight he could barely make her out, in the shallow end, drifting. Whether she was looking at him or not, he couldn't tell.

He looked out over the river, his mind taking him back. There was splashing in the water, the two young men swimming for all they were worth, one pulling ahead a bit and then the other. Sometimes Mike would win, other times John. Then they would race back. Day after day, growing more tan, leaner and stronger. So much fun. No real worries, no heartaches. Swim, explore the woods, devour bologna-and-mayo sandwiches for lunch; for dinner, skewered hot dogs on straightened hangers and cooked over the coals until the meat split open. So much damn fun. Fiske looked away from the water and forced himself to concentrate.

If Harms was a prisoner, finding him would be easy. As a former police officer, Fiske knew that there were no categories of humanity better monitored than America's inmate population of nearly two million. The country might not know where all its children or homeless were, but it religiously kept track of the cons. And most of the information was on computer database now. He looked back over and saw Sara swimming toward the boat. He didn't notice the glow of a burning cigarette as someone sat on the shore and watched them.

A couple minutes later Fiske was helping Sara into the boat. She sat on the deck, breathing deeply. "I haven't swum that much in a long time."

Fiske held out a towel he had pulled from the small cabin, averting his eyes as he did so. She quickly toweled down and then slipped her dress on. When she handed him back the towel, their arms brushed. That made him look at her. She was still breathing deeply from her swim, the rise and fall of her eyelids hypnotic.

He studied her face in silence for a moment, then looked past her at something in the sky. She turned her head to look too. Pink swirls were lapping against the dark edges of the sky as dawn began to break. Everywhere they looked, the soft glow of the coming light was apparent. The trees, the leaves, the water were cast as a shimmering facade, as the boat gently rocked them.

"It's beautiful," she said in a hushed tone.

"Yes, it is," he said.

As she turned back to him, she reached up her hand, slowly at first, her eyes searching his for some reaction to what she was doing. Her fingers touched his chin, cupping it, his beard stubble rough against her skin. Her hand moved higher, tracing his cheeks, his eyes and then pressing against his hair, each touch gentle, unhurried. As she gripped the back of his neck and pulled his head toward her, she felt him flinch. Her lips trembled when she saw his glistening eyes. Sara removed her hand and stepped back.

Fiske suddenly looked out over the water, as though still seeing two young boys swimming their hearts out. He turned back to her. "My brother's dead, Sara," he said simply, his voice shaking slightly. "I'm just really messed up right now." He tried to say something else, but the words would not come.

Sara slowly walked over and sat in one of the seats. She wiped at her eyes and then self-consciously gripped the hemline of her skirt, trying to smooth it, to wring out some of the wetness. The breeze had picked up and the river bounced them. She glanced up at Fiske.

"I really did like your brother. And I'm so

damned sorry that he's gone." She looked down, as though searching at her feet for the right words. "And I'm sorry for what I just did."

He looked away. "I could have said something to you before now." He glanced up at her, bewilderment on his features. "I'm not sure why I didn't."

She stood up, wrapped her arms around her shoulders. "I'm a little cold. We should go back now, shouldn't we?"

Fiske hauled up the anchor while Sara cast off, and then he fired up the motor and they headed back to the dock, each unable to look at the other, for fear of what might happen, of what their bodies might do, despite the words they had just spoken.

On the shore, the owner of the glowing cigarette had departed just as Sara had drawn close to Fiske.

CHAPTER THIRTY-TWO

Fiske and Sara docked the boat, walked in silence to the golf cart and climbed in. The footsteps made Fiske look around. "Pop? What are you doing here?"

His father didn't answer but kept coming toward them. Fiske walked to him, his arms outstretched. "Pop, you okay?"

A puzzled Sara watched from the golf cart.

The men were about a foot apart when the elder Fiske lunged forward and punched his son in the jaw.

"You bastard," Ed shouted.

Fiske fell back from the blow, as Ed pounced on his son and hammered away with both fists.

Fiske pushed himself away from his father and staggered backward, blood coming from his mouth and nose. "What the hell is wrong with you?" he screamed.

Sara was halfway out of the cart, but she froze when Ed pointed at her.

"Get that slut and your ass out of here! Get the hell out of here, you hear me?"

"Pop, what are you talking about?"

Enraged, Ed rushed his son again. This time Fiske sidestepped the charge, wrapping his arms around his father and holding tight as the older man spun wildly, trying with all his might to hit him again.

"I saw you, damn you both. Half naked, kissing, while your brother lies dead on some slab. Your brother!" He screamed the words so loudly his voice broke.

Fiske's voice cracked as he realized what his father had seen. Or thought he had seen. "Pop, nothing happened."

"You bastard." He tried to pull his son's hair, clothing, anything to get at him again. "You heartless sonofabitch," he kept screaming, his face brick red, his breathing becoming more and more labored, his movements sluggish.

"Stop it, Pop, stop it. You're gonna have a coronary."

The two men struggled fiercely as they slipped, pitched and swung around in the loose dirt and gravel.

"My own son doing that. I don't have a son. Both my sons are dead. Both my sons are dead." Ed spat out these words in a crescendo of fury.

Fiske let his father go, and the old man spun around and dropped to the ground in exhaustion. He tried to rise, but then slumped back down, his T-shirt stained with the sweat of his efforts, the merged smells of alcohol and tobacco enveloping him. Fiske stood over him, chest heaving, his blood mixed with salty tears.

A horrified Sara stepped out of the cart, knelt down next to Ed and put a hand gently on his shoulder. She didn't know what to say.

Ed swung his arms around blindly and struck Sara on the thigh.

She gasped in pain.

"Get the hell out of here. Both of you. *Now!*" Ed screamed.

Fiske gripped Sara's arm and pulled her up. "Let's go, Sara." He looked at his father. "Dad, take the cart back." As they entered the forest, Fiske and Sara could still hear the screams of the old man.

Her leg aching, her tears half blinding her, Sara said, "Oh, my God, John, this is all my fault."

Fiske didn't answer. His insides were on fire. The pain had never been this bad, and he was scared. The dispassionate warnings of scores of doctors engulfed him. He kept walking faster and faster, until Sara had to half trot to keep up.

"John, John, please say something."

She reached over to wipe some blood from his chin, but he quickly pushed her hand away. Then, without warning, he started to run.

"John!" Sara started to run too, but she had never seen anyone accelerate as Fiske had. "John," she screamed, "please come back. Stop! Please!"

In the next moment, he had rounded a bend in the forest path and disappeared completely from her sight.

She slowed down, her own chest burning now. Then she stepped on a loose clod of dirt and fell heavily to the ground amid the scattered pine needles. She sat there sobbing, her thigh already bruised and aching from where Ed had hit her.

A minute later she started as a hand touched her shoulder. Terrified, she looked up, certain that Ed had come to beat her too, for blackening the memory of his dead son.

Fiske was breathing hard, his T-shirt soaked in sweat, the blood already hardened on his face. "Are you okay?"

She nodded and stood up, gritting her teeth as the pain in her leg increased. If Ed's blind swipe at her leg had caused so much hurt, she could hardly imagine what John was feeling, after taking a direct blow to the face. She balanced against him while he bent down, edged her skirt up and examined her thigh.

Fiske shook his head. "It's bruised pretty good. He didn't know what he was doing. I'm sorry."

"I deserved it."

With Fiske's help she was able to walk pretty normally.

"I'm sorry, John," she said. "This . . . this is a nightmare."

As they neared the trailer, she heard him say something. At first she thought he was talking to her, but he wasn't.

He said it again, in a low voice, his eyes straight ahead, his head slowly turning in disbelief. "I'm sorry."

The apology was not directed toward her, she instinctively knew. Perhaps to the screaming man back at the dock. And maybe to the dead brother?

When they reached the trailer, Sara sat down on the steps while Fiske went inside. He came back out a minute later with some ice and a roll of paper towels. While she held the ice wrapped in a paper towel against her bruised thigh, she used one of the ice cubes and another paper towel to wipe the blood from his face and clean the cut on his lip. After she had finished, he stood, went down the steps and headed down the dirt road.

"Where are you going?" she asked.

"To get my father," he said without turning around.

She watched until he disappeared into the forest. While he was gone, Sara limped into the trailer and cleaned herself up in the small bathroom. She spotted Fiske's suit and shoes and carried them out to her car. She ran her hand along the smooth metal surface of the flagpole and wondered if Ed would manage to raise the Stars and Stripes today. Maybe he would, at half-mast, in memory of his son.

Perhaps mourning *both* sons?

She began trembling with that thought, moved away from the flagpole and leaned up against her car. She scanned the woods nervously as though anticipating the abrupt charge of all sorts of terror from its underbelly.

An elderly woman came out of the trailer next door and stopped when she saw Sara.

Sara smiled in an embarrassed fashion. "I'm, uh, a friend of John Fiske's."

The woman nodded. "Well, good morning."

"Good morning to you too."

The woman disappeared down the road toward the cottage.

Sara looked anxiously back toward the woods, clutching her hands together. "Come on, John. Please, come on."

Fifteen minutes later the golf cart came into view. Fiske was driving. His father was slumped in the rear, apparently asleep.

Fiske pulled up to the trailer, got out, carefully lifted his father and put him over his shoulder. He marched up the steps and disappeared inside. He came out a few minutes later carrying the shotgun.

"He's asleep," Fiske said.

"What's that for?" Sara pointed at the weapon.

"I'm not leaving it here with him."

"You don't think he'd shoot anybody."

326

"No, but I don't want him sticking it in his mouth and pulling the trigger either. Guns, alcohol and bad news don't mix real well." He put the shotgun in the back seat of the car. "You'd better let me drive."

"Your clothes are in the trunk."

They climbed in the car and a minute later were back at the owner's cottage. Fiske went in and slapped four singles down for the guest fee. He bought some pastries and a couple cartons of orange juice.

The woman who had greeted Sara was also there. "I saw your lady friend, John. Real cute girl."

"Uh-huh."

"You leaving already?"

"Yep."

"I'll bet your daddy wishes you were staying longer."

Fiske paid for the food and didn't wait for a bag. "I'll take that bet," he told the puzzled woman, before heading back out to the car.

CHAPTER THIRTY-THREE

Samuel Rider arrived at his office early after being away a few days for business. Sheila hadn't come in yet. It was just as well, since Rider wanted to be alone. He picked up his phone and called Fort Jackson, identified himself as Harms's attorney and asked to speak with him.

"He's no longer here."

"Excuse me? He's serving a life sentence. Where exactly could he have gone?"

"I'm sorry, but I'm not allowed to give out that information over the phone. If you would like to come down in person or make an official inquiry in writing —"

Rider slammed down the phone and collapsed in his chair. Was Rufus dead? Had they somehow discovered what he was up to? Once Rider had filed the appeal with the Supreme Court, Rufus should have had instant security.

Rider clamped his fingers around the edge of his desk. *If* it had reached the Court. He tore open his desk drawer and pulled out the white receipt with the tracking number on it. The green receipt should have come back to his office. Sheila! He jumped up and raced to

Sheila's work area. Normally, any return receipts would be included in the appropriate case file. However, there was no case file for Rufus Harms. What could she have done with the damn receipt?

As if in answer to his thoughts, the woman herself walked in the door. She was surprised to see him.

"Why, you're in awful early, Mr. Rider."

Rider assumed a casual tone. "Trying to catch up on a few things." He edged away from her desk; however, she had picked up on his intentions.

"Are you looking for something?"

"Well, now that you mention it, I was, actually. I had sent a letter out and, you know, I had sent it return receipt requested, and then it occurred to me that I hadn't told you anything about it. Stupid of me."

Her next words brought an inward sigh of relief.

"So that's what that was. At first I thought I had forgotten to open a case file. I was meaning to ask you about it when you got back."

"So you got it back, then," Rider said, trying to veil his eagerness.

Sheila opened a drawer of her desk and pulled out a green receipt. "The United States Supreme Court," she said with awe, passing it over to him. "I remember thinking, are we going to be doing something with them or what?"

Rider put on his best lawyer's face. "Naw, Sheila, just something to do with a bar function. We don't need to look to Washington for our daily bread."

"Oh, here are your phone messages that came in while you were out of town. I tried to prioritize them for you."

He gave her hand a nice squeeze. "You're the essence of efficiency," he said gallantly.

She smiled and started to fuss at her desk.

Rider went back to his office, closed the door and looked down at the receipt. The filing had been delivered. The signature was right there. But then where was Rufus?

Rider planned to spend much of the morning in meetings discussing the possible development of a shopping mall on a vast tract of land that had been used since the forties as an auto wrecking yard. One of the men he was meeting with had flown a prop plane into Blacksburg, Virginia, from Washington early that morning and was driving over to Rider's office. With everything on his mind it was all Rider could do to act normal when the man arrived at his office a while later. The man had brought with him a copy of the morning's *Washington Post*. While the man accepted a cup of coffee from Sheila, Rider idly ran his eye over the *Post*'s headlines. One in particular caught his attention. The man noticed what Rider was doing.

"Damn shame," he said, nodding at the story Rider was focused on. "One of the best and brightest," he said as Rider silently mouthed the headline again: SUPREME COURT CLERK SLAIN.

"Did you know him?" Rider asked. It couldn't be connected. There was no way in hell.

"No. But if he was clerking up there, you know he had to be top of the top. Murdered too. Shows you how dangerous times have become. Nobody's safe anymore."

Rider stared at him for a moment, and then looked down at the paper and the accompanying photo. Michael Fiske, age thirty. He had earned a Ph.D. from Columbia University and then gone on to the University of Virginia Law School, where he had been editor-in-chief of the *Law Review*. He was the senior law clerk for Justice Thomas Murphy. No suspects, no clues, other than a missing wallet. *Nobody's safe anymore.* He tightly gripped the paper as he stared at the grainy, depressing photo of the dead man. It couldn't be. However, there was one way to find out.

He excused himself and slipped into his office, where he called the Supreme Court clerks' office.

"We have no case with the name Harms, sir, either on the regular or IFP docket."

"But I've got a return receipt that shows it

was delivered to you people." The voice on the other end again delivered the perfunctory message.

"Don't you have some way of keeping track of your mail up there?" The polite answer Rider received did not sit well with him. He yelled into the phone. "Rufus Harms is rotting in the damn stockade and you people can't keep track of your mail." He threw down the phone.

Somewhere between its arrival and the point where a case was actually placed in the official system, Rufus Harms's filing had apparently disappeared. And so had Rufus Harms. Rider suddenly felt chilled.

Rider looked down once more at the newspaper. And a Supreme Court clerk had been murdered. It all seemed so far-fetched, but then so had the story Rufus told him. Then another thought hit him even harder: If they had killed Rufus and the clerk, they surely wouldn't stop there. If they had what Rider had filed with the Court, then they would know that Rider had played a role in all of it. That meant he could be next on their hit list.

But come on, he told himself, you're just being paranoid. And that's when it finally dawned on him. The sheaf of phone messages that Sheila had collected while he had been away. He had idly skimmed through them, returning the ones he felt were most important. The name, the damn name.

He clawed through his desk until he found the pink pieces of paper. His hands flew through them, scanning, scanning, finally ripping the pile apart in his rising anxiety, until he found it. He looked down at the name, the blood slowly draining from his face. Michael Fiske had called him. Twice.

Oh, my God. In an avalanche of thought, visions of his wife, the condo in Florida, his grown children, all the years of billable hours, flew through his mind. Well, damn if he was waiting around for them to come get him. He punched his intercom and told Sheila he wasn't feeling well, to convey that to his visitor and the other gentlemen who would shortly arrive, and accommodate them any way she could.

"I won't be back today," he told her as he hurried through the reception area. I hope I will someday. And not in a coffin, he added silently.

"All right, Mr. Rider, you take care."

He almost laughed at her remark. He had phoned his house before leaving the office, but his wife wasn't in. As he drove along, he had already made up his mind what he was going to do. The two had kicked around the idea of taking a late fall vacation, maybe down to the islands, one last dose of sun and water before the ice set in. Only they might stay awhile. He'd prefer to pour his savings into staying alive than into securing the view of a Florida sunset he might never get a chance to see.

They could drive to Roanoke, hop a commuter flight and take it into Washington or Richmond. From there they could go anywhere. He would explain it to his wife by saying he was just being spontaneous, something she had said he never was and never could be. Good old steady, reliable Sam Rider. Did nothing more with his life than work hard, pay his bills, raise his kids, love his wife and try to catch a few strands of happiness along the way. Lord, I'm already writing my obituary, he realized.

He wouldn't be in a position to help Rufus, but he figured the man was probably dead anyway. I'm sorry, Rufus, he thought. But you're in a much better place, far better than the one those bastards saddled you with on this earth.

A sudden thought made him almost turn the car around. He had left the copies of the filing he had made for Rufus back at the office. Should he go back? He finally decided that his life was worth more than a few pieces of paper. What could he do with them now anyway?

He concentrated on the road. There wasn't much between his office and his home except windy roads, birds and the occasional deer or black bear. The isolation had never bothered Rider until now. At this moment, it terrified him. He had a shotgun at home that he used for quail hunting. He wished he had it with him.

He rounded an elbow-shaped bend in the road, a rusted guardrail the only thing standing between him and a five-hundred-foot drop. As he tapped his brakes to slow down, his breath caught in his throat. His brakes. Oh, my God, I've lost my brakes! He started to scream. But then the brakes held. Don't let your senses run away from you, Sam, he cautioned himself. A few minutes later he turned the last corner and saw his mailbox. A minute after that he pulled the car into his garage. His wife's car was next to his.

As he passed by her car, he glanced at the front seat. His feet seemed to sink right into the concrete floor. His wife was lying facedown in the front seat. Even from where he was standing, Rider could see the blood pouring from the head wound. That was the next to last memory Rider would have. The hand came around and clamped across his face a large cloth that had a sickening medicinal odor. Another hand slipped something into Rider's hand. As the lawyer looked down with eyes that were already beginning to close, he saw and felt the still-warm pistol as his fingers were wrapped around it by a pair of latex-gloved hands. It was Rider's pistol, one he used for target shooting. The one he now also knew had been used to kill his wife. From the heat left in the metal, they must have done it as soon as he turned into the driveway. They must have been watching for him. He arched his head and stared into the cold, clear eyes of Victor Tremaine as his face was thrust deeper and deeper into the clutches of unconsciousness. This man had killed her, but Rider would be blamed for it. Not that it would matter much to him. He was dead too. As he finished this thought, Samuel Rider's eyes closed for the last time.

CHAPTER THIRTY-FOUR

Driving down the George Washington Parkway south of Old Town Alexandria, Fiske glimpsed a bike rider as he flitted, phantom-like, among the line of trees that ran along the asphalt bike path paralleling the river. Fiske nudged Sara awake and she told him where to turn off the parkway. She glanced quickly at him. The encounter with his father had not been mentioned on the drive back. It was as though they had silently agreed not to discuss it.

With Sara directing, Fiske pulled down another blacktop road, and then turned right onto a gravel lane that ran steeply down toward the water. He stopped the car in front of the small, wood-framed cottage, which stood there prim and dour among the untidy backdrop of tree, bramble and wildflower, like the preacher's wife at a church picnic turned rowdy. The clapboard was layered with fifty years' worth of white paint; the structure also had black shutters, and a wide brick chimney the color of terra-cotta. Fiske watched as a squirrel sprinted across the phone line, leaped to the roof and cork-screwed up the chimney.

Anchoring one corner of the property was a crape myrtle in full bloom, its bark the texture and color of deerskin. Wedged against the other side of the cottage was a twenty-foot holly, red berries peeping out, ornamentlike, from among the dark green leaves. In between was a hedge of burning bush, the ground underneath it sprinkled with cardinal-red leaves. Behind the house Fiske noted the stairway angling down to the water. From there he thought he saw the bob of a sail mast. From the back seat, he grabbed the clean clothes he had gotten from his apartment. They got out of the car.

"Nice place," he commented.

Sara stretched and yawned deeply. "When I got the clerkship at the Court, I flew in to look at housing. I thought I'd just rent at first, but found this place and fell in love with it. So I went down to North Carolina, sold the farm, and bought this."

"Must have been hard selling the homestead."

Sara shook her head. "The two reasons it was important to me were dead. All that was left was a bunch of dirt that I couldn't do anything with."

Still stretching, she headed to the house. "I'll get the coffee going." She looked at her watch and moaned. "I'm going to be late for oral argument. I should call in, but I'm afraid to."

"I'm sure they'll understand, given the circumstances."

"You'd think so, wouldn't you," she said doubtfully.

Fiske hesitated. "Do you have a map around here?"

"What kind?"

"Eastern half of the United States."

She thought a moment. "Check the glove compartment."

He did so and pulled out the map. As they went into the house she asked, "What are you looking for?"

"I've been thinking about the eight hundred miles that were on Mike's car."

"You want to see what's eight hundred miles from here?"

"No, four hundred." Sara looked puzzled. "Four hundred miles out, but he, or someone else, had to drive back to D.C."

"Although it could be a number of smaller trips, a hundred miles here and there."

Fiske shook his head. "Human remains inside a trunk on a hot day aren't real pleasant to be around. I've found a couple that way," he added grimly.

While she fixed coffee in the kitchen, Fiske looked out the window that faced the river. From this vantage point he could now see the pressure-treated lumber dock and the sailboat tied up to it.

"You get to sail much?"

"Black or cream?"

"Black."

She got out two cups. "Not as much as I used to. Where I lived in North Carolina was pretty landlocked. Some fishing with my dad, swimming at a pond a few miles down the road. But out at Stanford, I really got into it. You never know how big something can be until you see the Pacific Ocean. It dwarfs everything else I've ever experienced."

"Never been there."

"Let me know if you ever decide to. I could show you around." She wiped the hair out of her eyes, poured his coffee and handed him his cup.

"I'll put that on my list," he said dryly.

"I've only got one bathroom, so we'll have to take turns showering."

"You go first. I want to check out this map."

"If I'm not down in twenty minutes, pound on the door; I'll probably have fallen asleep in the shower."

Fiske was looking at the map, sipping his coffee, and didn't comment. Sara paused on the stairs.

"John?" He looked up. "I hope you can forgive me for last night." She stopped, as though mulling over what she had just said. "The problem is, I don't think I deserve to be forgiven."

Fiske put his cup down and stared at her.

The sunlight poured through the window at a graceful angle, falling full upon her face, accentuating the sparkle of her eyes, the sensual margins of her lips. Her hair was limp from the river water, sweat and sleeping on it. The little makeup she wore had long since lost its life, staining her eyelids and cheeks, her entire body pushed to the point of exhaustion. This woman had been the source of a major, perhaps cataclysmic rift between him and his father, a man he worshiped. And yet Fiske had to fight the impulse to slip off her clothes and lie down next to her right there on the floor.

"Everybody deserves to be forgiven," he finally said, and then looked back at the map.

While Sara was showering, Fiske went into a room off the kitchen. She obviously used it as a home office of sorts, since it had a desk, computer, bookshelf full of law books and a printer. He spread the map out on the desk. He found the scale at the bottom, converting inches into miles, and rummaged around in the desk drawer until he found a ruler. Using Washington as the epicenter, he drew lines outward in north, west and southerly directions and then drew a line attaching the end points. He ignored the east, since four hundred miles out would put him well into the Atlantic. He made a list of the various states within this rough circumference, picked up the phone and called directory assistance.

Within a minute he was on the phone with someone from the Federal Bureau of Prisons. He gave the name Harms to the person on the other end, along with the geographic radius he might be within. It had occurred to Fiske that his brother may have gone to visit Harms in prison. The call his brother had made to him seeking some advice would then make sense. John Fiske knew a lot more about prisons than his younger brother did.

When the bureau representative came back on the line with the results, Fiske's face sagged. "You sure there's no prisoner with that last name in any federal prison in the geographic area I gave you?"

"I even went out an extra couple hundred miles."

"Well, how about state prisons, then?"

"I can give you the phone numbers for each state. You'll have to contact them separately. Do you know which ones are in that area?"

Fiske looked at the map and rattled them off. There were over a dozen. Fiske wrote down the telephone numbers he was given and hung up.

He thought for a moment and then decided to check messages at his home and office. One was from an insurance agent. Fiske returned the call to the agent, who was located in the D.C. metropolitan area.

"I was very sorry to read about your brother's death, Mr. Fiske," the woman said.

"I didn't know my brother had any life insurance."

"Sometimes the beneficiaries aren't aware. In fact, it's not the insurance company's obligation to notify the beneficiaries even if we're aware of the insured's death. Bluntly speaking, insurers don't go out of their way to pay out claims."

"So why did you call me?"

"Because I was horrified by Michael's death."

"When did he take the policy out?"

"About six months ago."

"He had no wife or kids. Why did he need insurance?"

"Well, it's why I called you. He said he wanted you to have the money in case anything happened to him."

Fiske felt a catch in his throat and he held the phone away for a moment. "Our parents could use the money a lot more than me," he finally managed to say.

"He told me you'd probably give the money to them, but he wanted you to use some of it for yourself. And he thought you'd know better than your parents how to deal with it."

"I see. Well, how much money are we talking about?"

"A half million dollars." She read his address to him to confirm that it was still accurate. "For what it's worth, I write a lot of

343

policies for people, for a lot of different reasons, not all of them good, but in case you didn't realize it, your brother loved you very much. I wished I was as close to my brother."

As Fiske hung up the phone, he realized that he was not on the verge of tears. He was on the verge of putting his fist through a wall.

He got up, put the list in his pocket and went outside, down the stairway, past the vertical rise of cattail on one side, the sprawl of fern on the other, his feet taking him to the small dock. The sky was deep blue, with dabs of cloud, the breeze encouraging, the humidity vanished for now. He looked to the north, to the four-story reach of the million-dollar town houses on the outer ring of the Old Town Alexandria area, and then at the long, serpentine shape of the Woodrow Wilson Bridge. Across the water he made out the Maryland shore, a tree-lined mirror image of the Virginia side. A jet powered by, its landing gear down as it headed into National Airport a few miles distant. The fuselage was so close to the earth that Fiske almost could have hit it with a rock.

As the plane passed by and the silence returned, he stepped onto the bow of the sailboat. The craft gently swayed under him; the sunlight stroked his face. He sat down and put his head against the mast, sniffed the canvas of the unfurled sail and closed his eyes. He was so damn tired.

"You look awfully comfortable."

Startled awake, Fiske looked around before turning and seeing Sara standing there. She wore a black two-piece business suit; a white silk blouse peeked out at the neckline. Her neck was encircled with a small strand of pearls, her hair tied in a simple bun, a touch of makeup and pale red lipstick tinting her face.

She smiled. "I'm sorry I had to wake you. You were sleeping so peacefully."

"Have you been watching me long?" Fiske asked, and then wondered why he had.

"Long enough. You can take your shower now."

He stood up and stepped back from the dock. "Nice boat."

"I'm lucky, the riverbank drops off steeply here. I don't have to keep it at one of the marinas. I'll take you out if you want. We have time left before it has to be winterized."

"Maybe."

He walked past her toward the cottage.

"John?" He turned back. She put one hand on the stair rail and looked over at her sailboat, as though hoping to carve a wedge of calm from its tranquil frame.

"If it's the last thing I ever do, I will make it right with your father," she said.

"It's my problem. You don't have to do that."

"Yes, John, I do," she said firmly.

Thirty minutes later, Fiske drove the car out onto the private road leading to the parkway. The two black sedans flashing in front of their car made Fiske slam on the brakes. Sara screamed. Fiske jumped out of the car. He stopped as soon as he saw the guns pointed at him.

"Hands in the air," one of the men barked.

Fiske immediately put his hands up.

Sara climbed out of the car in time to see Perkins emerge from one vehicle and Agent McKenna from the other.

Perkins spotted Sara. "Holster your weapons," he said to the two men in suits.

McKenna's voice boomed out. "Those men are under my command, not yours. They will holster their weapons upon my order only." McKenna stopped directly in front of Fiske.

"Are you all right, Sara?" Perkins asked.

"Of course I'm all right. What the hell is going on?"

"I left an urgent message with you."

"I didn't check my messages. What's wrong?"

McKenna's eye caught the shotgun lying in the back seat. Now he pulled his own weapon and pointed it directly at Fiske. He studied Fiske's injured face. "Is this man holding you against your will?" McKenna asked Sara.

"Will you stop with the dramatic crap?" said Fiske. He lowered his hands and caught a sucker punch in the gut from McKenna. Fiske dropped to his knees, gasping. Sara raced to him, helping him lean back against the car tire.

"Keep your hands up until the lady answers the question." McKenna reached down and jerked Fiske's hands up in the air. "Keep your damn hands up."

Sara screamed, "No, for God's sake, he's not holding me. Stop it. Leave him alone!" She pushed McKenna's hand away.

Perkins stepped forward. "Agent McKenna —" he began, but McKenna cut him off with a cold stare.

"He's got a shotgun in the car," McKenna said. "You want to take a chance with your men, fine. I don't operate that way."

Another sedan pulled up and Chandler and two uniformed Virginia police officers climbed out, guns drawn.

"Everybody freeze!" Chandler boomed out.

McKenna looked around. "Tell your men to put away their weapons, Chandler. I've got the situation under control."

Chandler walked right up to McKenna. "Tell your men to holster their weapons right now, McKenna. Right now or I'll have these officers arrest you on the spot for assault and battery." McKenna didn't move. Chandler leaned directly in his face. "Right now, Special Agent Warren McKenna, or you'll be calling the Bureau's legal counsel from a Virginia lockup. You really want that in your record?"

Finally, the man flinched. "Holster your weapons," McKenna ordered his men.

"Now move the hell away from him," Chandler ordered.

McKenna very slowly edged away from the fallen Fiske, his eyes burning into Chandler's with every backward step.

Chandler knelt down and gripped Fiske's shoulder. "John, you okay?"

Fiske nodded painfully, his eyes on McKenna.

"Will someone please tell us what is going on?" Sara cried out.

"Steven Wright was found murdered," Chandler said.

CHAPTER THIRTY-FIVE

The shack rested in the center of a heavy forest in a remote part of southwestern Pennsylvania, where it notched into West Virginia. A muddy, tire-gouged strip of dirt was the only way in or out. Josh came in the front door, his 9mm poking out of his waistband, red clay and pine needles sticking to his boots. The truck was parked under a leafy shield of a soaring walnut tree, but Josh had taken the added precaution of covering the vehicle with camouflage netting. His biggest worry was being spotted from overhead. Luckily, the nights were still warm. He couldn't risk building a fire; you couldn't control where smoke went.

Rufus sat on the floor, his broad back resting against the wall, his Bible in his lap. He was drinking a soda, the remains of his lunch beside him. He had changed into some clothes that his brother had brought him.

"Everything okay?"

"Just us and the squirrels. How you feeling?"

"Happy as hell and scared as the devil." Rufus shook his head and smiled. "Feels good to be free, sitting here drinking a Coke, not having to worry about somebody trying to get the jump on me every second of my life."

"The guards or the other cons?"

"What do you think?"

"I think both. I was on the inside for a while too, you know. We could probably write us a book."

"How long we gonna stay here?"

"A couple of days. Let things die down a little. Then we'll head on, make our way down to Mexico. Live good on a tenth of what it takes up here. Went a few times after the war. Got some old Army buddies who live there. They'll help us get in and then set us up. Find us a boat, do some fishing, live on the beach. That sound good to you?"

"Living in the sewer would sound good to me." Rufus stood up. "Got a question for you."

His brother leaned against the wall and started carving up an apple with his pocketknife. "I'm listening."

"Your truck was full of groceries, two rifles and that pistol you're carrying. And the clothes I'm wearing."

"So?"

"So you just happen to be carrying all that stuff when you come visit me?"

Josh swallowed a slice of apple. "I got to eat. That means I got to go to the store, now, don't it?"

"Yeah, but you didn't buy nothing that'd go bad, no milk or eggs, stuff like that. All cans and boxes."

"I ate out of a can in the Army. I guess I just fell in love with meals ready to eat."

"And you always carry all them guns with you?"

"Maybe I'm still screwed up from Nam, got some syndrome or other."

Rufus tugged at his shirt, which was the size of a blanket. "My size don't exactly come off the rack. You came ready to bust me out, didn't you, Josh?"

Josh finished working on his apple and then threw the core out the open window. He wiped the apple juice from his hands onto his jeans before facing his brother.

"Look, Rufus, I never knew why you killed that little girl. But I knew you weren't right in the head when you done it. When I got that letter from the Army it crossed my mind there was something there. Now, I didn't know it was some cover for what they done to you. But the fact is, nowadays, people go crazy and do bad shit, they stick 'em in the nuthouse, and when they're better, they just let 'em go. You been in prison for twenty-five years for something I know for a fact you didn't even mean to do. Let's just say I took it on myself to say that was long enough. You served your time, you know, 'paid your debt to society' crap. It was time for you to get

351

out, and I was gonna bring the key. If you hadn't wanted to come, I was going to make you change your way of thinking. Call me right or wrong, I don't give a damn. It's what I made up my mind to do."

The two brothers looked at each other for at least a minute without speaking.

"You a good brother, Josh."

"You damn right I am."

Rufus sat on the floor again and picked up the Bible, his hands gently turning the pages until he found the part he wanted. Josh eyed him.

"You still reading that stuff after all this time?"

Rufus looked up at him. "Gonna read it all my life."

Josh snorted. "You do what you want with your time, but wasting it ain't such a good idea if you ask me."

Rufus eyed him stonily. "The word of the Lord kept me alive all these years. That ain't no waste of time."

Josh shook his head, looked out the window and then back at Rufus. He touched the grip of his pistol. "This is God. Or a knife, or a stick of dynamite, or a don't-piss-on-me attitude. Not some holy book full of people killing each other, men taking other men's women, just about every sin you can think of —"

"Sins of man, not God."

"God ain't the one busted you out. I did."

"God sent you to me, Josh. His will is everywhere."

"So you're saying God made me come get you?"

"Why did you come?"

"I told you. Get you out."

" 'Cause you love me?"

Josh appeared a little startled. "Yes," he said.

"That's the will of God, Josh. You love me, you help me. That's God's way of working."

Josh shook his head and looked away. Rufus went back to his reading.

A squawking sound came from Josh's portable police scanner, which he had set on the floor along with his radio. Josh had managed to tune in a radio station from southwest Virginia for any local news on Rufus's escape.

"Heard your name on the police band anymore?" Josh asked.

Rufus Harms had been mentioned in the news the day before. All the military authorities would say was that Harms was a convicted murderer who had a history of violence inside prison. He had escaped with the help of his brother, a dangerous man in his own right. The standard lingo was used, namely that both men were believed to be armed and dangerous. Translation: No one should be surprised or ask any questions when the authorities dragged their corpses in.

"A little," Rufus replied. "They're looking south, like you thought."

Just then the afternoon news came on the radio. The first two news stories meant nothing to either brother. The third news story was a late-breaking one and it made both brothers stare at the radio. Josh hustled over and turned up the sound. The story only lasted about a minute and when it was over Josh turned the radio off. "Rider and his wife," he said.

"Made it look like he killed her and then turned the gun on himself," Rufus added, his head shaking slowly in disbelief. "Two men come to see me and now they're both dead."

Josh stared over at his brother. He knew exactly what he was thinking. "Rufus, you can't bring him back, you can't bring none of them back."

"It's my fault they're dead. For trying to help me. And Rider's wife, she didn't know nothing about any of this."

"You didn't ask that Fiske boy to come down to the prison."

"But I asked Samuel. He'd be alive except for me."

"He owed you, Rufus. Why you think he came on down in the first place? He felt guilty. He knew he didn't fight hard for you back then. He was trying to make up for that."

"He's still dead, ain't he? Because of me."

"Supposing that's true, you can't do nothing about it."

Rufus looked over at him. "I can make sure they didn't die for nothing. Them folks took most of my life away. And now they took these other peoples' lives. You say we'll be okay in Mexico, but they ain't never gonna stop looking for us. Vic Tremaine is crazy as hell. Just have to look in the man's eyes to see that. Old Vic been trying to get me all these years. Probably think he's got his chance now. Fill us both up with lead."

"The Army catches up with us before the police do, they'll damn sure keep firing till their mags are empty," Josh agreed. He pulled out his Pall Malls and lit up, blowing smoke across the room. "Well, I can shoot straight too. They'll know they been in a damn fight if they don't know nothing else."

Rufus shook his head stubbornly. "Nobody should be able to get away with what they done."

Josh flicked cigarette ash to the floor and stared at him. "Well, exactly what are you gonna do? March in to the police and say, 'Listen up, boys, I got some story to tell. Now y'all come on help a brother put these big-important white folk away'?" Josh took the cigarette out of his mouth and spit on the dirt floor. "Shit, Rufus."

"I need to get me that letter from the Army."

"Where'd you leave it?"

"I hid it back in my cell."

"Well, we ain't going back to the prison. You try to do that, I'll shoot you myself."

"I ain't going back to Fort Jackson."

"What, then?"

"Samuel was a lawyer. Lawyers make copies of things."

Josh arched his eyebrows. "You wanta go to Rider's office?"

"We got to, Josh."

Josh smoked his Pall Mall down to the filter before answering. "*I* ain't got to do nothing, Rufus. The whole damn United States Army is out looking for your ass. And mine too. You can't exactly melt into the crowd. Hell, you'd make George Foreman look like a damn sissy."

"We still got to do it, Josh. Least I got to do it. If I can get that letter, then maybe I can get it to somebody who can help. Maybe write another letter to the Court."

"Yeah, look at all the good it done you last time. Them big-ass judges just come running to help you, didn't they?"

"It don't matter if you don't want to come, Josh. But I got to do it."

"What about Mexico? Damn, Rufus, you free. For now. We try poking around this thing, they gonna take you back to prison or most likely shoot you down first. We got to go while we got the chance, man."

"I want to be free. But I can't leave it like this. I go to Mexico now and I'll die of guilt, if the Lord don't strike me down before then."

"Guilt? You done twenty-five years for nothing. When you die you going to heaven and you gonna be sitting in God's lap. You a lock for that."

"No good, Josh. You ain't changing my mind."

Josh spit again and looked out the dirty, cracked window. "You sonofabitchin' crazy. Prison's screwed you for good. Damn!"

"Maybe I am crazy."

Josh glared at him. "Where the hell is Rider's office?"

"About thirty minutes outside Blacksburg. That's all I know. Shouldn't be hard to find out where it is exactly."

"Probably crawling with cops."

"Maybe not, if they think Samuel done it all."

"Shit." Josh violently kicked the wall and then turned to his brother. "Okay, we'll wait until nightfall and then head on out."

"Thanks, Josh."

"Don't thank me for helping us both get killed. That kind of thanks I surely don't want."

CHAPTER THIRTY-SIX

The flag at the United States Supreme Court was flying at half-mast. Newspaper, TV and radio reports nationwide were filled with accounts of the two murdered clerks. The phones in the Court's Public Information Office refused to stop ringing. The adjoining press room was standing room only. Major TV and radio networks were broadcasting live from booths on the ground floor of the Court. Supreme Court police, reinforced by fifty D.C. police officers, National Guardsmen and FBI agents, ringed the Court's perimeter.

The private hallways outside the justices' chambers were filled with clusters of people nervously talking. Most of the justices were secluded inside their chambers, having barely made it through the oral argument sessions, their minds far from the advocates and issues before them. The young faces of the law clerks too bore the terror inspired by the killings.

The small first-floor room normally used for the justices' conferences was filled. The walls were dark-paneled and lined with bookshelves containing the bound volumes of two hundred years of the Court's decisions. Another wall held a fireplace, unlit on this very warm day. A grand chandelier hung overhead. Ramsey sat at the head of the table. Justices Knight and Murphy sat in their regular chairs.

While Knight's gaze darted around the table, Murphy, fiddling with an old pocket watch strung on a chain across his puffy middle, kept his eyes downcast. Also present were Chandler, Fiske, Perkins, Ron Klaus, and McKenna. Fiske and McKenna occasionally made eye contact, but Fiske had kept his temper under control.

Wright had been found in a park a half dozen blocks from his Capitol Hills apartment, with a single gunshot wound to the head. His wallet, like Michael Fiske's, was missing. Robbery was the superficial motive, although no one in the room believed the answer could be that simple. Preliminary indications were that Wright had been killed between midnight and two in the morning.

On the ride over to the Court, Chandler had filled Fiske in on recent developments. He had had Michael Fiske's autopsy expedited, although he was still awaiting the official report and the exact time of death. The cause of Michael Fiske's death, however, had definitely been a single gunshot to the head. Chandler had tracked down the northern Virginia Wal-Mart where Fiske had had his car serviced, but no one there could give them any useful information.

Fiske had had one thought that prompted him and Chandler to make a short detour on the way to the Court: They had returned to the car impoundment lot to have another look at Michael's Honda. Fiske had looked in the back pockets of the front seat.

"He kept a map in here, always did. He had this weird fear of getting lost. Had to plot out his whole trip before he set foot on the road. There's no map here, but there is this." He held up a couple of yellow Post-its that he had found wadded up at the bottom of the seat pocket. There was writing on them, names of interstates and roads — directions, given the faded condition of the ink, from some trip taken long ago.

Chandler looked at the pieces of yellow paper. "So why take the map book?"

"He would've had the directions to wherever he was going in there."

"So the miles had something to do with his death."

Fiske hesitated for a moment, debating whether to tell Chandler about the Harms filing. Revealing that information would open a can of worms that he didn't want to deal with right now. "Maybe," he finally said.

After that, he and Chandler had driven to the Court.

Now they were all in the conference room staring at each other. Without disclosing how he had come by the information, Chandler had just reported that there had been an intruder at Michael Fiske's apartment the night before.

"We're in your hands, Detective Chandler," Ramsey said. "Although now I think it much more likely that we have some madman at work with a grudge against the Court, rather than it pertaining to some matter Michael was working on."

McKenna said, "I want you to know that the Bureau has assigned a hundred agents to this matter. We've also arranged around-the-clock protection for the justices."

"What about the clerks?" Fiske said. "They're the ones getting killed."

Chandler stepped in. "I've compiled the home addresses of all the clerks. I've beefed up patrols in those areas. Most of them live on Capitol Hill close to the Court. We've offered to house any clerk who so chooses at a local hotel where full-time security is available. I've also instructed one of our experts to talk to the clerks about ways to keep safe, be on the lookout for suspicious persons, avoid going out alone or at night, that sort of thing." He looked around for a moment. "By the way, where is Dellasandro?"

"He's trying to coordinate all the new security measures," Klaus reported. "I've never

361

seen him this worried. I think he's taking it personally."

"I've been on the Court for almost thirty-three years, and I never thought I would ever see the likes of this," Justice Murphy said sadly.

"None of us did, Tommy," Knight said forcefully. She looked pointedly at Chandler. "You have no leads at all?"

"I wouldn't go that far. We have several things to go on. I'm talking about Michael Fiske's death. With Wright's murder it's still too early to say."

"But you believe them to be connected?" Ramsey said.

"I really don't have a belief on that one way or the other."

"What do you recommend that we do?"

"That you go about your business as usual. If this is the work of some nut out to disrupt the Court, then you'd be playing into his hands by canceling your docket."

"Or we could risk infuriating whoever's doing this, with the result that he will strike again," Knight said.

"That's always a possibility, Justice Knight," Chandler conceded. "But I'm not convinced that what the Court does or doesn't do will have any effect on that. *If* the cases are connected." He looked at Ramsey. "I do think it's worth going over the cases both clerks were involved in, just to cover that base. I know it's a long shot, but I could end up kicking myself later on if I don't address it now."

"I understand."

Chandler turned to Justice Murphy. "Will you and your other clerks still be available today to go over cases Michael Fiske was handling?"

"Yes," Murphy replied quickly.

"And I would appreciate if all of you would confer with the other justices and try to determine if any one case you've heard over the last few years may have prompted some action like this," said Chandler.

Knight looked at him and shook her head. "Detective Chandler, many of the cases we deal with stir incredible emotions in people. It would be impossible to know where to start."

"I see your point. I guess you've all been lucky that no one's tried to do something like this before."

"Well, if you want us to go about our normal routines, then I suppose that the dinner honoring Judge Wilkinson will go forward tonight," Knight said.

Murphy sat straight up in protest. "Beth, if nothing else, I think the murders of two Court personnel would dictate that the dinner be put off."

"That's easy enough to say, Tommy, but you didn't happen to plan the event. I did.

Kenneth Wilkinson is eighty-five years old and he has pancreatic cancer. I won't risk putting it off, unfortunate as the timing may be. This is very important to him."

"And to you as well, correct, Beth?" Ramsey said. "And your husband?"

"That's right. Are we going to have another debate on legal ethics, Harold? In front of all these people?"

"No," he said. "You know my feelings on the subject."

"Yes, I do, and the dinner will proceed."

Fiske was fascinated by the exchange. He thought he saw a hint of a smile pass across Ramsey's face as the man said, "All right, Beth. Far be it from me to attempt to change your mind on any matter of importance, much less those bordering on the trivial."

CHAPTER THIRTY-SEVEN

Tremaine set the Army helicopter down in the grassy field. As the circling of the copter blades slowed, he and Rayfield looked over at the sedan parked near the edge of the tree line. They lifted off their seat harnesses, climbed out and, torsos bent forward as they passed beneath the blades, headed toward the car. When they reached it, Rayfield sat in the front seat while Tremaine slipped into the back.

"Glad you could make it," said the man in the driver's seat, turning to face Rayfield.

The colonel's jaw fell. "What happened to you?"

The bruises were purplish in the center, leaching out to yellow around the edges. One clung to the side of his right eye, the two others spread out from his collar.

"Fiske," he answered.

"Fiske? He's dead."

"His brother, John," the man said impatiently. "He caught me at his brother's apartment."

"Did he recognize you?"

"I was wearing a mask."

"What was he doing at his brother's apartment?"

"Same thing I was, looking for anything that the cops could use to find out the truth."

"Did he find anything?"

"Nothing to find. We'd already gotten Fiske's laptop." He looked at Tremaine. "And you got his briefcase from his car before you killed him, right?" Tremaine nodded. "Where is it?" the man asked.

"A pile of ash."

"Good."

"Is this brother a problem?" Rayfield wanted to know.

"Maybe. He's an ex-cop. He and one of the other clerks are snooping around. He's helping the detective investigate the clerks' murders."

Rayfield started. "Murders? More than one?"

"Steven Wright."

"What the hell's going on?" Rayfield demanded.

"Wright saw someone come out of Michael Fiske's office. He also heard something he shouldn't have. We couldn't trust him to be quiet, so I had to bluff him out of the building and kill him. We're okay on that one."

"Are you nuts? This thing is totally out of control," Rayfield said angrily.

The man looked at Tremaine. "Hey, Vic, tell your superior to stay cool. I think Nam took away some of your nerve, Frank. You've never been the same since."

"Four murders, and you say stay cool? And Harms and his brother are still out there."

"So we've got two more bodies to go. The two most important. You understand that, don't you, Vic?"

"I do," Tremaine answered.

The man looked over at Rayfield with a pair of very cold eyes.

Rayfield swallowed nervously. "I guess there's no going back now."

"You're right there."

"John Fiske and this clerk: What are you doing about them? If Fiske is on some mission to find his brother's killer, he may be a problem."

"He already is a problem. They're on a real short leash. And they'll stay there until we decide what to do with them."

"Meaning?" Rayfield asked.

"Meaning we might have four more bodies to go instead of two."

Sara sat in her new office. Chandler had declared the space she shared with Wright off limits, but he had allowed Court personnel to move Sara's computer and work files to this overflow space. She had taken the list of state prison agencies Fiske had given her and started calling. At the end of a half an hour she hung up the phone, depressed. There was no one with the last name Harms in any prison in any of those states. She tried to remember any other helpful word or phrase from the documents she had seen, but she finally gave that up.

Suddenly she had a mental flash: the letter *R* sticking in her mind. Harms's first name started with an *R;* she had seen that in the filing. It was maddening that she couldn't remember anything else.

She stood, and that's when it caught her eye. She had just grabbed a stack of files with her abrupt move and hadn't noticed it until now. It was the *Chance* bench memo. The one she had told Wright he had to work on last night until he finished. A handwritten note was attached asking Sara to review it.

She sat down and her head sank to the desktop. What if there really was some psychopath targeting clerks? Was it just chance that Wright had been killed instead of her? For a minute she sat there, frozen. Come on, Sara, you can beat this. You have to beat this, she urged herself. Using every bit of resolve she could marshal, she stood and walked out the door.

A minute later, she entered the clerks' office, and went over to a clerk who was manning one of the Court's computer database terminals. The question she was about to ask was one she had asked earlier, but she wanted to be absolutely certain.

"Could you check and see if there's any case at the Court with the name Harms as one of the parties?"

The clerk nodded and started tapping buttons. After about a minute he shook his head.

"I'm not finding anything. When was it filed?"

"Recently. Within the last couple of weeks or so."

"I've gone back six months — there's nothing coming up. Didn't you ask me about this a while ago?"

Before Sara could answer, another voice spoke.

"Did you say Harms?"

Sara stared at the other clerk. "Yes. Harms was the last name."

"That's strange."

Sara's skin started to tingle. "What?"

"I got a call early this morning from a man asking about an appeal and he used that name. I told him we didn't have any case filing with that name."

"Harms? You're sure?" The clerk nodded. "How about a first name?" Sara asked, trying to suppress her excitement.

The clerk thought a moment.

"Maybe starting with an *R?*" Sara prompted.

The clerk snapped his fingers. "That's right. Rufus, Rufus Harms. Sounds like a hick."

"Did the caller identify himself?"

"No. He got pretty upset."

"Anything else you can remember?"

The man thought a bit longer. "He said something about the guy rotting in a stockade, whatever that meant."

Sara's eyes opened wide and she started to race out.

"What's this all about, Sara? Does this have anything to do with the murders?" the clerk asked. Sara kept going without answering. The clerk hesitated for a moment and then looked around to see if anyone was watching. Then he picked up his phone and dialed a number. When it was answered, he spoke quietly into the receiver.

Sara almost sprinted up the stairs. The reference to the *stockade* had shown her that there was a big hole in Fiske's list. She reached her office, grabbed a card from her Rolodex and dialed the number. She was calling Military Police Operations. Fiske had covered both the federal and state prison populations, but he had not thought of the military. Sara's favorite uncle had retired from the Army as a brigadier general. She knew very well what a stockade was: Rufus Harms was a prisoner of the United States Army.

She got through to Master Sergeant Dillard, the corrections specialist on duty. "I don't have his prison ID number, but I believe he's incarcerated at a military facility within four hundred miles or so of Washington," she said.

"I can't give you that information. The official procedure is to send a written request to the deputy chief of staff for operations and plans. Then that department, in turn, will send your request to the Freedom of Information Act people. They may or may not answer your request depending on the circumstances."

"The thing is, I really need the information now."

"Are you from the media?"

"No, I'm calling from the United States Supreme Court."

"Right. How do I know that?"

Sara thought for a moment. "Call directory assistance for the general number for the Supreme Court. Then call the number they give you and ask for me. My name is Sara Evans."

Dillard sounded skeptical. "This is highly unusual."

"Please, Sergeant Dillard, it's really important."

There was silence on the other end of the line for a few seconds. "Give me a few minutes."

Five very long minutes later the call was put through to Sara's phone. "You know, Sergeant Dillard, I've gotten information from your office before about military prisoners without going through the FOIA process."

"Well, sometimes the people here are a little generous with the information."

"I just want to know where Rufus Harms is, that's all."

"Actually, it wouldn't really be a problem with any other prisoner."

"I don't understand. Why is Rufus Harms so special?"

"Haven't you been reading your newspaper?"

"Not today, no, why?"

"Maybe it's not real big news, but the public ought to know, for its own safety if nothing else."

"The public ought to know what?"

"That Rufus Harms escaped." In concise sentences, Dillard filled her in on the details.

"Where was he incarcerated?"

"Fort Jackson."

"Where is that?"

Dillard told her and Sara wrote down the location.

"Now I got a question for you, Ms. Evans. Why is the Supreme Court interested in Rufus Harms?"

"He filed an appeal with the Court."

"What sort of appeal?"

"I'm sorry, Sergeant Dillard, but that's all I can tell you. I have rules to go by too."

"All right, but I tell you what. If I were you, I'd hold off working on his appeal. The courts aren't open to dead people, are they?"

"Actually, they can be. What exactly did the man do?"

"You'll have to check his military file."

"How do I do that?"

"You're a lawyer, aren't you?"

"Yes, but I don't do a lot of work with the military."

She could hear him muttering a bit over the phone.

"Since he's a prisoner of the military, Rufus Harms is no longer technically in the United States Army. Along with his conviction he would have been given either a dishonorable or a bad-conduct discharge. His military records would have been sent to the St. Louis Military Personnel Records office. Hard copies are kept there. It's not on a computer database or anything. Harms was convicted about twenty-five years ago, so his records should have been transferred to microfilm, although the personnel office is a little behind on that process. If you or anyone other than Harms wants his records, you have to use a subpoena."

Sara wrote all of this down. "Thank you again, Sergeant Dillard, you've been a huge help."

She had map software on her computer. Sara brought the screen up and, using her mouse, drew a distance line from Washington, D.C., to the approximate location of Fort Jackson.

"Almost four hundred miles exactly," she said to herself. She hurried upstairs to the Court's third-floor library and went on-line via one of the computer terminals there. None of the law clerks' office terminals were connected to phone modems for obvious reasons of security and confidentiality. But the library terminals had on-line access. Using an Internet explorer service she typed in Rufus Harms's name. She looked around at the hand-carved oak paneling as she waited for the computer to sprinkle its technological pixie dust.

A few minutes later she was reading all the latest news accounts on Rufus Harms, his background and that of his brother. She printed out all of these. One of the stories had a quote from the newspaper editor in Harms's hometown. Using an Internet telephone directory, she looked up the man's number. He still lived in the same small town near Mobile, Alabama, where both brothers had grown up.

The phone was answered after three rings. Sara introduced herself to the man, George Barker, still editor-in-chief of the local paper.

"I already talked to the papers about that," he said flatly.

His deep southern drawl made Sara think

of braying coon dogs and clear jugs of 'shine. "I'd appreciate if you could answer a few questions for me, that's all."

"Who are you with again?"

"An independent news service. I'm a freelancer."

"Well, what exactly do you want to know?"

"I've read that Rufus Harms was convicted of killing a young girl on the military base where he was stationed." She glanced at the news accounts she had printed out. "Fort Plessy."

"Killed a little *white* girl. He's a Negro, you know."

"Yes, I know," Sara said curtly. "Do you know the name of the attorney who represented him at the trial?"

"Wasn't really a trial. He did a plea arrangement. I covered the story some, because Rufus was local, sort of the reverse of the local boy makes good."

"So you know the name of his attorney?"

"Well, I'd have to look it up. Give me your number and I can call you back."

Evans gave him her home number. "If I'm not there, just leave it on the answering machine. What else can you tell me about Rufus and his brother?"

"Well, the most noticeable thing about Rufus was his size. He must have already been six-foot-three by the time he was fourteen. And he wasn't skinny or lanky or anything. He already had a man's body."

"Good student? bad? In trouble with the police?"

"From what I recall, he wasn't a good student. He never graduated high school, although he was real good with his hands. He worked at a little printing press with his daddy growing up. His brother did too. Why, I remember one time the press at my newspaper broke down. They sent Rufus over to fix it. He couldn't have been much more'n sixteen. I gave him the manual for the machinery, but he wouldn't take it. 'Words just mess me up, Mr. Barker,' he said, or something to that effect. He went in there and within one hour he had the whole damn thing up and running, good as new."

"That's pretty impressive."

"And he was never in trouble with the police. His momma wouldn't have let him. You got to understand, this is one small town, no more than a thousand souls have ever lived here, even fewer today. I'm pushing eighty, still run the newspaper. Nobody's been here longer than me. Now, the Harmses lived in the colored section of town, of course, but we still knew 'em. Now, I don't have colored folk over to my house, but they seemed like good people. She worked at the meat processing factory here just like most everybody else. Cleaning crew, not one of the good-paying jobs. But she took care of her boys."

"What happened to their father?"

"He was a good man, not prone to drink or wild living like so many of their kind. He worked hard, too hard, because one day he just didn't wake up. Heart attack."

"You have a good memory."

"I wrote out his obituary."

"What about his brother?"

"Now, Josh was a different story. Around here, he's what we call a bad black. Hotheaded, arrogant, trying to be better than he was. Now, I'm not prejudiced or anything and I don't tolerate the use of the *n* word in my presence, but if I did use that particular word I'd use it to describe Josh Harms. He rubbed a lot of people the wrong way."

"I read that he fought in Vietnam and was actually a war hero."

"Sure, that's right," Barker conceded quickly. "He was the most decorated war hero to ever come out of this town, by a long shot. People were damn surprised about that, let me tell you. But he could fight, I'll give the man that."

"What else?"

"Well, Josh actually graduated high school." Barker's voice changed. "But where he really showed up everybody was in sports. I'm a one-man shop here and I cover all the news. Josh Harms was the greatest pure athlete I have ever had the privilege to see.

White, black, green or purple, that boy could run faster, jump higher, stronger, quicker than anybody else. Now, I know the coloreds can do all that really well anyway, but Josh was truly special. He lettered in just about every sport there was. Do you know he still holds about a half dozen state athletic records?" He added proudly, "And you know Alabama's got more than its share of great athletes."

Sara sighed. "Did he play at the collegiate level?"

"Well, he got a slew of scholarship offers for football and basketball. Bear Bryant even wanted him at 'Bama, that's how good he was. Probably would've been a star in the NBA or the NFL. But he got sidetracked."

"How so?"

"Well, you know how so. His government asked him to defend his country in the war against communism."

"In other words, he got drafted and was shipped to Vietnam."

"That's right."

"Did he come back home afterward?"

"Oh, sure. His momma was still alive, but not for long. See, right about that time was when Rufus got in all that trouble. I actually think Rufus volunteered for the Army because of Josh. Maybe he wanted to be like his older brother, you know, a hero. Really I think he just wanted something to go right with his life for a change. After his daddy died there wasn't anything for him in this town. Of course, it ended up going about as wrong as it could. Anyway, Josh came to see me, to see if there was anything I could do. You know, the power of the press, but there wasn't anything I could do."

"Did Rufus killing the girl surprise you? I mean, had he ever been violent, that you knew?"

"He never hurt anyone that I know of. A real gentle giant. When I heard about the little girl I couldn't believe it. Now, if it had been Josh, I wouldn't have blinked twice, but not Rufus. But with all that, the evidence was clear as could be."

"Did Josh keep living there?"

"Well, now you take me to a particularly troubling part of this town's history."

"What's that?"

"I'd rather not say."

Sara thought quickly. What was the journalistic phrase? "It can be off the record."

"Is that right?" Barker sounded wary.

"Absolutely. It's off the record."

"I want you to know that I just recorded what you said. So if I read in some newspaper what I'm about to tell you, I'll sue you and your paper for every last cent you got," he said sternly. "I'm a journalist, I know how these things work."

"Mr. Barker, I promise that whatever

you're about to tell me will not be used in any way for a story."

"All right. Actually, I guess so much time has passed that it doesn't matter anymore — legally, anyway. But you can never be too careful in this old world." He cleared his throat. "Well, the story of what Rufus had done got around town, no way it wouldn't. A bunch of boys started drinking, got together and decided to do something. Now, they couldn't do anything to Rufus, he was in the custody of the United States Army. But they could do something about the other Harms living here."

"What did they do?"

"Well, what they did was they burned Mrs. Harms's house to the ground."

"Good God! Was she in it?"

"She was until Josh pulled her out. And let me tell you what, Josh went after those boys. They went at it right up and down the town's streets. I watched it from my office. You know, it must've been ten against one, but Josh put half of them boys in the hospital, until the rest beat him up bad, real bad. Never seen anything like it, hope I never do again."

"It sounds almost like a riot. Didn't the police come?"

Barker coughed in an embarrassed fashion. "Well, just so happens that it was rumored that a couple of the boys that were in on it, you know, who had burned the house down —"

"Were the police," Sara finished the sentence for him. Barker didn't say anything. "I hope Josh Harms sued for all the money the town had," she said.

"Well, actually, they sued *him*. I mean, the boys he put in the hospital did. Josh couldn't prove anything about the fire. I mean, I had my speculations, but that was all. And the police sort of put together this story about him resisting arrest and all. It was ten people's word against one, and a colored's word at that. Well, the long and the short of it was he spent some time in jail and they took everything he and his momma had, little enough that it was. She died soon thereafter. What happened to both her boys, I guess, was too much for her."

It was all Sara could do not to start screaming at the man. "Mr. Barker, that is the most disgusting story I have ever heard," she said. "I don't know much about your town, but I do know I would never want anyone I cared about to live there."

"It has its good points."

"Really — like welcoming home a war hero like that?"

"I know. I thought about that too. You fight for your country, get shot up and then come home to something like that, probably makes you wonder what the hell you were fighting for."

"You sound like you knew the truth. Didn't you use the power of the press that time?"

Barker sighed deeply. "This has always been my home, Ms. Evans, and you can only offend the powers that be so many times, even if they deserve it. Now, I can't say that I'm any great friend of the blacks, because I'm not. And I wouldn't lie to you and say I championed Josh Harms's cause, because frankly I didn't."

"Well, I guess that's partly what the courts are for: to keep people like those in your town from screwing people like Josh Harms. Please call me back with the name of Harms's lawyer."

She hung up the phone. Her whole body was tingling with rage from what she had just heard. But then, how many blacks had she known growing up in Carolina? The generations of squatters down the road? Or during harvest time when her father would bring in the part-timers to help? She had watched these men from the porch, sweat soaking the thin fabric of their shirts, their skin growing ever darker under the bite of the sun. She and her mother would bring them lemonade, food. They would mumble their thanks, never making eye contact, eat their meal and toil on into the darkness. Sara's school had been all white, despite the string of Supreme

Court cases demanding otherwise. These cases were the twentieth century battlefields of racial equality, replacing the Antietams, Gettysburgs and Chickamaugas of the last century. And some would argue with equal futility. And here at the Court there was one black justice, who occupied the so-called Thurgood Marshall seat, and currently one black clerk, out of thirty-six. Many of the justices had never had a minority person clerk for them. What sort of message did that send? At the highest court of justice in the land?

As she hurried down the hallway in search of Fiske, Sara wondered if they would ever really find out the truth. If the Army caught up to the Harms brothers before anyone else, the truth might very well die with them.

CHAPTER THIRTY-EIGHT

Fiske was standing outside his brother's office while Chandler was overseeing the progress of his evidence-collection team under close supervision of the Court's staff counsel. However, with now two dead clerks, concerns over confidentiality had taken a back seat to finding the killer or killers. When they finished with Michael Fiske's office, they would go down the hallway and start on Steven Wright's.

Fiske looked over at his brother's office door and then back at Wright's. He did so a couple more times as an idea began to percolate through his head. He went over to Chandler.

"Exactly where was Wright's body found?"

Chandler flipped open his notebook and started looking through his notes. "By the way, I got your car out of impound. It's at my office in a nice, legal parking space."

"Thanks for doing that for me."

"Don't thank me. With the tow and fine and all, it's gonna cost you about two hundred bucks."

"Two hundred bucks? I don't have that kind of money for a lousy parking ticket."

"Is that right? Well, maybe I can pull a few strings, you know, do you a favor. But you'll have to work it off. I got some painting that needs to be done at my house." Chandler cracked a smile and then stopped leafing through his notes. "Okay, here we are. Wright lived about a block from the Eastern Market metro station. His body was found in Garfield Park. That's at F and Second Streets. It's about a half dozen blocks from the Court."

"How did Wright usually get to and from work?"

"According to several people here, he either walked, took a cab or occasionally the metro."

"Was this Garfield Park on his way home?"

Chandler tilted his head as he studied his notes. "Not really. Normally he would've hung a left from Second onto E to go home. He wouldn't have continued on down to the park."

"Did he have a dog or anything? Maybe he went home and then took it for a walk in the park."

"He did have a dog, but he hadn't been home. At least we don't think he had. And if he was going to walk his dog, Marion Park is a lot closer to his home."

"That is strange."

Chandler's eyes narrowed as he thought of something.

"But Marion Park has something that Garfield doesn't."

"What's that?"

"A police substation right across the street."

"Whoever killed him might have known that."

"The substation's not exactly a big secret. We want our presence known there as a deterrent to crime."

"Does it look like he was killed at the park, or maybe somewhere else and dumped there?"

"The grass had blood on it. No shell casings — that we found yet, anyway. Shooter probably would've used a silencer, unless it was some random robbery. A silencer on a revolver is too tricky. If he used a semiautomatic, then we should find a shell casing unless it was picked up."

"Bullet still in the body?"

Chandler nodded. "Hope we lay our hands on a gun to match it against."

"Considering what happened at Mike's apartment, you should probably have someone posted at Wright's."

"Gee, now, why didn't I think of that."

"Sorry. Any idea when Wright left the Court last night?"

"We're still checking on that. After regular hours there's only one door open for entering and exiting. That door is constantly guarded and it closes up at 2 A.M. After that you need a guard to let you out. You can leave via the garage too, but it's also secured. However, Wright didn't drive, so the garage is irrelevant."

"Then someone must have seen him leave."

"My people are checking with the guards on duty last night."

"Doesn't this place have surveillance cameras?"

"You mean in the courtroom?" Chandler asked with a smile. "The answer is yes, but not everywhere and unfortunately not along this part of the hallway. But we're checking the tapes right now to see if there's anything relevant on them." Chandler scanned his notes once more. "At that time of night, really the only activity on this floor would have been a clerk working late."

"Anything in Wright's background helpful?"

Chandler shook his head. "No skeletons that we found so far. Motive is going to be tough on this one."

"But his wallet was missing."

"Yeah, I thought about that. A little too convenient."

"Like somebody wants to make us think both murders are connected?"

"You know, it actually could be some nut with a grudge against the Court."

"I believe the murders are connected but not for the reasons everyone probably thinks," Fiske said.

"How do you mean?"

"If Mike was killed for a reason someone doesn't want us to find out about, then killing another clerk and making it look related would be a great way to divert our attention."

Chandler looked intrigued. "So what's the *real* reason someone killed your brother and is trying to cover it up?"

Fiske hesitated again. Keeping the stolen appeal a secret was beginning to become very awkward. "I don't know, but I might have an idea why Wright was killed."

"Other than as a red herring?"

"Let's say his death might have served a dual purpose."

At that moment Sara joined them, trying very hard to conceal her excitement.

"John, can we talk for a minute?"

"Ms. Evans," Chandler said with a broad smile, "I hope your drive to Richmond was pleasant and uneventful."

"Let's just say it was different," she said quickly. "John, I really need to talk to you."

"Can I catch up with you later, Buford?"

"And you can tell me your theory."

As they walked off together, Chandler's smile faded. He was wondering if he had just lost his "unofficial" partner to Sara Evans.

Minutes after Sara had left her office, Justice Knight had stopped by to see her. She started to leave a written message when she saw the *Chance* bench memo with Wright's attached note. She sat down in Sara's chair and read the note. After she finished, it suddenly dawned on Knight what she had done. She had instructed Wright to work late, all night if necessary. He had done so, left the building late and someone had killed him. Her precious bench memo. She had never really focused on this chain of events before. A gush of air came out of her lungs so hard it almost choked her. She put the memo down and rushed from the room.

A minute later she raced past her astonished staff and locked the door to her office. She looked around the spacious, beautiful room, with even its own fireplace. Here she had sat and contemplated her little strategies, her philosophies of life. And it had cost a young man his life. She threw off her pumps, collapsed in a corner, covered her face and wept.

CHAPTER THIRTY-NINE

Back at her office, Sara spent the next thirty minutes filling Fiske in on everything she had found out. "When Barker calls back with the attorney's name, we can talk to him and maybe really start getting somewhere."

"That would be nice."

"Do you believe Michael went to see Harms in prison?"

"It really complicates matters that the guy's escaped."

Sara had a sudden terrifying thought. "You don't think Michael was somehow mixed up in that, do you?"

"My brother would not be part of anything illegal."

"I didn't mean intentionally."

"According to the newspaper reports, Harms escaped from a hospital in Roanoke *after* Mike's body was found. But I'm not saying that the timing is just coincidental."

"Do you have any brilliant deductions?"

"I think I know why Wright was killed."

"Why? Because he knew about Harms? About what Michael had done?"

"No, he was killed because he saw something. Something he shouldn't have."

Sara drew her chair closer to his. "What do you mean?"

"Wright's office — *your* former office — is right down the hallway from Mike's. Wright was going to be working all night."

Sara slumped in her chair. "Right. Because I told him he had to."

"No, because Knight told you to tell him he had to. Well, his body was found in a park that wasn't on his way home. Chandler told me that he was killed between midnight and two last night. If he was working all night here, what was he doing in that park?"

"You believe someone took him there and killed him?"

"More to the point, someone took him from inside the Court to the park and killed him."

Sara gaped. "Meaning the killer was here?"

Fiske nodded. "I don't know if the person works here, but I believe he was physically present here last night."

"What could Steven have seen that cost him his life?"

"I think he saw someone go into Mike's office. Yesterday, Wright heard Chandler tell everyone that the office was off limits to *everyone*. Whoever went into Mike's office might not have known that Wright was in *his* office. I assume you don't broadcast when you're working late."

"Like last night, often we don't even know

until the last minute."

"Right. So somebody goes into the office looking for something —"

"Like what?"

"Who knows? Copies of the appeal that Mike took. Telephone messages, something on his computer."

"But that's an awfully big risk. There's security here twenty-four hours a day."

"Well, if the person knew the police were going to search the office thoroughly the next morning, he'd only have a limited amount of time to do it."

"That makes sense."

"So Wright hears something, or he's finished his memo, he comes out, and runs right into whoever."

"If your theory is correct, do you think Steven knew the person who killed him?"

Fiske took a deep breath and sat back. "I think he had to. Otherwise he would've raised the alarm right away. And I saw Dellasandro lock the door to Mike's office. There's no sign of forced entry. The person had a key."

"But someone must have seen something, then."

"Not necessarily. If the killer is familiar with the layout of the Court, then he'd know ways to avoid being seen with Wright until they got out of the building."

"So it might be somebody he trusted."

Fiske looked at her. "Like one of the justices?"

Sara stared back, horrified. "I'll accept a lot, but I can't accept that." She had a sudden thought. "Maybe it was McKenna? Steven would have trusted him, FBI and all."

"How could McKenna be involved in this?"

"I don't know. He's the first one who occurred to me."

"Because he's not with the Court and he slugged me?"

Sara sighed. "Probably." Then she remembered something and tore through the papers on her desk until she found it. "I can tell you about what time Steven left." She picked up the memo Wright had left for her. Across the top of the memo was a date and time stamp. She flipped the papers around so Fiske could see it.

"The word-processing system automatically puts the date and time stamp on documents because we go through so many drafts. That way we can quickly tell what's current or not."

Fiske looked at the time stamp. "This was printed out at one-fifteen this morning."

"That's right. Steven finished the memo, printed it out, put it on my desk and then presumably left."

"And saw whatever he saw."

Sara suddenly looked puzzled. "Wait a

393

minute. Something doesn't make sense here. When a clerk works late, ordinarily what happens is one of the Court police officers will give the clerk a ride home, if you live nearby." She looked at Fiske. "The police here are really good to us."

"And at one-fifteen the metro's not running, is it?"

"No. Besides that, Steven lived barely a five-minute car ride from here. He's gotten rides home before."

"So the chances are very good that Wright got a ride home from somebody at the Court?"

"Leaving here at one-fifteen in the morning, I'd say it was a really safe bet."

"How about a cab, though? Maybe at that hour there weren't enough guards to spare to take him home."

Sara looked doubtful. "I guess it's possible."

"If a police officer did take him home, that should be easy enough to check. I'll tell Chandler."

"So where does that leave us?"

Fiske shrugged. "We need to see Harms's military file. I've got an old friend with the Army JAG. I'm going to call and see if he can help expedite the process. Until we know who's involved in all this, I want as few people as possible to know we're looking around."

Sara shuddered and wrapped her arms around herself.

"You know what?" she said. "I'm starting to become terrified of what the truth might be."

CHAPTER FORTY

While Sara went back to work, Fiske telephoned his lawyer friend at the JAG office, Phil Jansen, and relayed his request. Among other things, he asked Jansen to obtain a list of the personnel stationed at Fort Plessy during the time Rufus Harms was there.

When Fiske rejoined Chandler, he related his theory of why Wright had been killed. Chandler was impressed. "We'll check the cab companies too. We can only hope somebody saw or heard something."

Chandler stared intently at the young man. "So, did you find out anything interesting with Ms. Evans during your time together last night?"

"I think she's a good person. A little impulsive, but a good person. Very smart."

"Anything else? At our initial meeting, Ramsey said that she and your brother were close. She have any reason why he might have been killed?"

"You might want to ask her that."

"Well, I'm asking you, John. I thought we were a team." He moved closer to Fiske. "I've got way too much I don't understand on the front end of this case without having to watch my backside. You were a police officer; you should understand about covering somebody's backside."

Fiske said angrily, "I never let a partner down."

"Good to hear. So tell me about last night."

Fiske looked away, thinking how best to handle this. Withholding information was not the best course. So how could he do the right thing with Chandler and avoid destroying Sara's life and his brother's reputation?

"Can we get some coffee around here?"

"In the cafeteria. I'll even buy."

A few minutes later they were in the ground-floor cafeteria. The Court's afternoon session was in progress and thus the cafeteria was fairly empty.

Fiske sipped on his coffee while Chandler watched him.

"John, it can't be that bad, unless you tell me you're the one running around popping people."

"Buford, if I tell you something, then you have very specific rules as to what you do with that information and who else learns that information."

"That's true. And those rules are what's stopping you from coming clean?"

"What do you think?"

"I think let's talk hypotheticals, okay? Now, my job is to collect the facts and to use those facts to ultimately arrest somebody for a crime. If we're not talking facts, but just theories — like your theory of why Wright was murdered — then I can follow up that theory but I don't have an obligation to report it to anyone until it's proven correct by the discovery of facts to corroborate it."

"So we can talk theoretically and it'll just stay between you and me?"

Chandler shook his head. "Can't promise it will *stay* between you and me. Not if it becomes a fact."

Fiske looked down at his coffee cup. Sensing he was losing him, Chandler tapped his spoon against Fiske's cup.

"John, the bottom line here is finding out who murdered your brother and Wright. I thought that's what you wanted."

"It is. That's all I want."

Really? Chandler suddenly doubted that. "Then what's the problem?"

"The problem is you can hurt people at the same time you're trying to help them."

"Just your brother? Or somebody else?"

Fiske knew he had already said too much. He decided to go on the offensive.

"Okay, Buford, let's discuss theories for a minute. Let's suppose that somebody at the Court took an appeal before it was put into the Court's system."

"Why and how?"

"Apparently the *how* is easy. The *why* isn't."

"Okay, go on."

"Now let's suppose that somebody else at the Court saw this appeal, discovered that it wasn't on the system, but didn't say anything about it."

"I take it the *why* on that is also complicated?"

"Maybe not. Let's further assume that the person who took the appeal did so for a good reason. And that this person went somewhere, to visit the person who had filed the appeal."

"The eight hundred miles on your brother's car?"

Fiske stonily eyed the detective. "That's a fact, Buford, I'm not discussing facts."

Chandler took a drink of coffee. "Go on."

"And let's suppose that the person filing the appeal was a prisoner."

"Is that a fact or just speculation?"

"I'm not prepared to say."

"Well, I'm prepared to ask. Where is this prisoner?"

"I don't know."

"What do you mean, you 'don't know'? If he's a prisoner, he has to be in some prison somewhere, doesn't he?"

"Not necessarily."

"What the hell does that —" Chandler abruptly closed his mouth and stared across the table. "Are you saying this person escaped from prison?" Fiske didn't answer. "Please don't tell me that your brother got all suckered by some con's BS plea for help, went to the prison, helped bust him out and then the guy killed him. Dammit, please do not tell me that." Chandler's voice rose in his agitation.

"I'm not telling you that. That's not what happened."

"Okay. This appeal . . . do you know what it says?"

They had gone well beyond theories now, Fiske knew. He shook his head. "I've never even seen it."

"So how do you know it exists?"

"Buford, I'm not going to answer that question."

"John, I can make you answer that question."

"Then you're going to have to."

"You know you're taking a risk here."

"I do." Fiske finished his coffee and stood up. "I'll grab a cab back to pick up my car."

"I'll drive you. I do have other cases I'm working, even if this is the only one the world cares about right now."

"I think it would be better for both of us if you didn't drive me."

Chandler pursed his lips. "Suit yourself.

Your car's in the back lot. Keys are on the front seat."

"Thanks."

Chandler watched Fiske leave the cafeteria. "I hope she's worth it, John," the detective said quietly.

Chandler had put some inquiries of his own into play, and when he returned to his office he found a stack of paper on his desk. One standard line of investigation had been to obtain the phone records of Michael Fiske's office and home phones over the last month. The results were catalogued in the ream of paper. The phone call to his brother was on there. There were others to family. A dozen of them to a phone number that had been identified as Sara Evans's. That was interesting, he thought. Had both Fiske brothers fallen for the same woman? When Chandler got near the end of the list, his pulse quickened. After all the years on the job, that rarely happened anymore. Michael Fiske had called Fort Jackson in southwest Virginia several times, the last only three days before his body had been discovered. Fort Jackson, Chandler knew, housed a military prison. And that wasn't all. Chandler scattered the piles on his desk until he found what he was looking for. The telex had been sent nationwide asking for assistance on apprehending the man. When he had seen it earlier, Chandler hadn't thought much about it.

Now he intently studied the photo of Rufus Harms. He picked up his phone and made a quick call. Chandler needed one piece of information and he got it within a minute. Fort Jackson was approximately four hundred miles from Washington, D.C. Had Harms been the one to file the appeal John Fiske had mentioned? And if he had, why, according to Fiske's "theory," had his brother taken it?

Chandler looked back at the list of phone calls. His eyes flitted over one number without registering, perhaps because it was to some law office and there were several law-related calls on the list. But the name Sam Rider would have meant nothing to the detective even if he had focused on it for some reason. Chandler put down the phone list and contemplated bringing in Fiske and Sara Evans, and making them tell him what was going on. But then the instincts built up over thirty years kicked in with one precept clearly emerging: You can't trust anyone.

"Come on, John," Sara pleaded. They were in her office near the end of the work-day.

"Sara, I don't even know Judge Wilkinson."

"But don't you see? If someone at the Court *is* involved, this would be a perfect opportunity to find out some information because practically everybody from the Court will be there."

Fiske was about to protest again but then stopped. He rubbed his chin. "What time does it start?"

"Seven-thirty. By the way, have you heard from your JAG friend?"

"Yeah. There are actually two files that are applicable. Harms's service record, which contains not only his record of service, but also evaluations, personal info, enlistment contract, pay and medical histories. The second file, the record of his court-martial proceedings, would be with him at Fort Jackson. His lawyer's work product would be maintained at the JAG office that handled Harms's defense. That is, if they've kept it all these years. Jansen's checking. He'll send what he can."

As Sara started gathering her things to leave, Fiske remained sitting. "So what can you tell me about the Knights? Their pasts and all that?"

"Why?"

"Well, we're going to a party that they're hosting. She's a big part of the Court and he's a VIP in his own right. That qualifies them to be part of our investigation, don't you think?"

"You probably know more about Jordan Knight's past than I do. He's from your hometown."

Fiske shrugged. "True. Jordan Knight is big business in Richmond. At least he was until he entered politics. He made a lot of money."

"And a lot of enemies?"

"No, I don't think so. He's given a lot back to Virginia. Besides, he's a low-key, nice guy."

"Then he's an odd match for Elizabeth Knight."

"I could see how she'd bruise a few egos on the way up."

"More than a few. It came with the territory. Tough federal prosecutor turned tougher trial judge. Everybody knew she was being groomed for a seat on the Court. She's the swing vote on most of the major cases, which drives Ramsey crazy. I'm sure that's why he treats her the way he does. Kid gloves most of the time, but every once in a while he can't resist jabbing her."

Fiske thought back to the confrontation between the two justices at the conference. So that's what it was.

"How well do you know the other justices? You seem to know them well enough to believe they couldn't commit murder."

"Like in any other large organization, I know them mostly superficially."

"What's Ramsey's background?"

"He's the chief justice of the country's highest court and you don't know?"

"Humor me."

"He was an associate justice before being elevated to the top spot about ten years ago."

"Anything unusual in his background?"

"He was in the military. Army or Marines, maybe." She caught Fiske's look. "Don't even think it, John. Ramsey is not going around killing people. Other than that, just what's in his official bio."

Fiske looked puzzled. "I would have thought you'd know everything about the other justices by talking to the clerks."

"The clerks for one justice tend to stick together to a certain degree, although every Thursday afternoon there's a happy hour when we all get together. And periodically the clerks of one justice take another justice out to lunch just as a get-to-know-you sort of thing. Otherwise, each chamber is pretty self-contained" — she paused — "except for the famed clerk opinion network."

"Mike mentioned something like that to me after he first came to the Court."

Sara smiled. "I'm sure he did. The clerks are the mouthpieces for their justices. We send up trial balloons all the time, feeling each other out on a justice's position. For example, Michael used to ask me what

Knight needed in a majority opinion to join Murphy."

"But if Murphy is already writing the majority opinion, why does he need to court other votes?"

"You really are in the dark about how we work."

"Just a simple country lawyer."

"Okay, Mr. Simple Country Lawyer, the fact is if I had ten bucks for every time a majority opinion turned into a dissent because enough support wasn't garnered for it, I'd be wealthy. The trick is you have to craft an opinion that'll get five votes. And of course the opposition doesn't just sit idly by. One or more dissenting opinions might be circulated simultaneously. The use of dissenting opinions, or even the threat of them, is a fine art."

Fiske looked at her curiously. "I thought the dissenters were on the losing side. What kind of leverage could they have?"

"Let's say a justice doesn't like how a majority opinion is shaping up, so the justice either circulates a draft of a scathing dissent that may make the whole court look bad if it's published or that even undercuts the majority's opinion. Or better yet, and easier, the justice will let it be known that he intends to write such a dissent, unless the majority opinion is scaled back. They all do it. Ramsey, Knight,

Murphy. They go at it tooth and nail."

Fiske shook his head. "Like one long political campaign, always scrounging for votes. The legal version of porkbellies. Give me this and you got my vote."

"And knowing when to pick your battles. Let's say one or more justices doesn't like how a case was decided five years ago. Now, the Court doesn't lightly overturn its own precedent, so you have to think strategically. Those justices might use a case in the present to start laying the building blocks for overturning the precedent they didn't like years from now. That also goes for case selection. The justices are always on the outlook for just the right case to use as a vehicle to change a precedent they don't like. It's like a chess game."

"Let's hope one thing doesn't get lost in all the game playing."

"What's that?"

"Justice. Maybe that's what Rufus Harms wants. Why he filed his appeal. You think he can get justice here?"

Sara looked down. "I don't know. The fact is the individual parties involved in the cases at this level really aren't all that important. The precedents established through their cases, that's what counts. It all depends on what he's asking for. How it will impact others."

"Well, that really sucks." Fiske shook his

head and gave her a penetrating look. "A damn interesting place, this Supreme Court."

"So you'll come to the party?"

"Wouldn't miss it."

CHAPTER FORTY-ONE

Josh Harms assumed the police would now be covering the back roads, so he had taken the unusual tactic of driving on the interstate. It was dusk, though, and with the windows rolled up, they were okay; a police cruiser would have a tough time seeing inside. But despite all his precautions, he knew they were steering toward disaster.

Funny, he thought, after all the hell his brother had been put through, that he would even think about wanting to do the right thing at the risk of dying, of losing the freedom that never should have been taken away from him in the first place. He felt like both cursing and praising Rufus in the same breath. Josh's outlook on life wasn't complicated: It was him against everybody else. He didn't go looking for trouble, but he had a hair trigger when confronted with anybody looking to piss on him. It was a wonder he'd lived this long, he knew.

Still, you had to admire a person like Rufus, who could fight through all that, through people who didn't want to see the world change one iota since they were riding on top of it. Maybe the truth *will* set you free,

Rufus, he thought. Suddenly out of the corner of his eye he saw something in the truck's sideview mirror that made him ease his hand over and grip his gun.

"Rufus," he called back through the open window connecting to the camper, "we got a problem here."

Rufus's face appeared at the window. "What is it?"

"Stay low! Stay low!" Josh cautioned. He again eyed the police cruiser, which was a fixture in the truck's side mirror. "Trooper's passed us twice and then dropped back."

"You speeding?"

"Five clicks under."

"Something wrong with the truck, taillight out?"

"I ain't that dumb. Truck's fine."

"So what, then?"

"Look, Rufus, just because you've been in prison all these years doesn't mean the world's changed any. I'm a black man in a real nice-looking vehicle on the highway at night. Cops think I either stole it or I'm running drugs. Shit, going to the store for milk can be a real adventure." He looked in the side mirror again. "Looks like he's just about to hit his light."

"What we gonna do? I can't hide back here."

Josh didn't take his eyes off the mirror even as he slipped his gun under the seat. "Yep, any second now he's gonna hit that light, and we are done. Get down on the floor and pull that tarp on top of you, Rufus. Do it now." Josh pushed his baseball cap down low so that only the white hair of his temples showed. He stuck out his chin and pushed his bottom lip out, giving the impression that he had no teeth. He leaned over, flipped open the glove box and took out a tin of chew and put a big plug of it in his mouth, which made his cheek bulge. He let his strong frame collapse. Then he rolled down the window and stuck his arm out, motioning in long, slow waves for the police cruiser to pull over to the highway shoulder. Josh eased the truck off the road and stopped. The cruiser quickly pulled in behind the truck, its roof lights throwing off a startling, ominous blue into the darkness.

Josh waited in the truck. You let the boys in blue come to you, no hurried movement. He winced as the cruiser's searchlight beam reflected off the side mirror. A cop tactic to disorient you, he knew well. Josh heard the boots crunching on the bite of gravel. He could envision the trooper approaching, hand on his gun, eyes trained on the door.

Three times in the past, cops had pulled him over and then Josh would hear the tinkling of glass as the baton just happened to collide with a taillight, with the result that he had been cited for an equipment infraction. It was done just to piss him off, see if he'd do something that would warrant some jail time. It had never worked.

Yes sir, no sir, mister policeman, sir, even as he wanted to beat the man unconscious.

At least they had never planted drugs in his car and then tried to pin that on him. He had several buddies idling in prison right now after being hit with that shit.

"Fight it," his ex-wife Louise had always said.

"Fight what?" he had retorted. "Might as well be fighting God for all the good it'll do me."

As the footsteps stopped, Josh looked out the window.

The state trooper stared back at him. Josh noted that he was Hispanic.

"What's the matter, sir?" the trooper asked.

The chew bulging against his cheek with each syllable, Josh said, "Wanta git me on Luzzana." He pointed down the road. "Dis a'ight?"

The puzzled trooper crossed his arms. "Now where do you want to go again?"

"Luzzana. Bat' Rouge."

"Baton Rouge, Louisiana?" The trooper laughed. "You're a long way from there."

Josh scratched his neck and looked around. "Got me chil'ren on down dare ain't seen they's daddy in a while."

The trooper's expression turned serious. "Okay."

"Man say I gone git dare from dis here road."

"Well, the man didn't tell you exactly right."

"Huh, you know's how's I git dare, den?"

"Yeah, you can follow me, but I can't drive the whole way."

Josh just stared at the man. "My chil'ren, dey bin good. Dey wanta see Daddy. You hep me?"

"Okay, I tell you what, we're close to the exit you need to take to head on down that way. You follow me there, and then you're on your own. You stop and ask somebody else. How's that sound?"

"A'ight." Josh touched the bill of his cap.

The trooper was about to return to his cruiser when he glanced at the camper. He hit his light through the side window and saw the stacked boxes. "Sir, you mind my taking a look in the camper?"

Josh didn't flinch, although his hand edged toward the front of the seat, where his gun was. "Hell, no." The trooper went to the rear of the camper and opened the upper glass door. The wall of boxes stared back at him. Behind the stacks, Rufus huddled under the tarp in the darkness of the camper.

"What you got in here, sir?" the trooper called out.

"Food," Josh called back, leaning out the window.

The trooper opened one box, shook a soup can, opened the box of crackers and then replaced it, closed the box and then the camper window. He walked back to the driver's-side window.

"Lot of food. The trip isn't that long."

"Axed my chil'ren what dey want. Dey say food."

The trooper blinked. "Oh. Well, that's good of you. Real good of you."

"You got chil'ren?"

"Two."

"A'ight, den."

"Have a safe trip." The cop walked back to his cruiser.

Josh pulled back onto the road after the cruiser did.

Rufus appeared at the camper window. "I was sweating a damn river back there."

Josh smiled. "You got to take it cool. You play badass, they cuff you. You act too polite, they figure you scamming their ass and they cuff you. Now, you be old and dumb, they don't give a shit."

"Still a close call, Josh."

"We caught us a break with the Mexie. They're real big on family, kids. Talk that shit and they're cool with you. If he'd been white, we might have had us a big problem. Once he made up his mind to look, Whitie would've pulled everything out of that camper until he found your ass. Now, a bro' might've cut me some slack, but you never know. Sometimes, they got that uniform on, they start to act white."

Rufus stared at his brother with a look of displeasure.

"Now, the Asians, they the worst," Josh continued. "You can't say shit to them. They just stand there and look at you, not listening to a damn word, and then go off and do what they're gonna do. Might as well just shoot them mothers before they kung fu your ass. Yeah, it's real good we met up with Officer Pedro." Josh spit the chew out the window.

"You got everybody figured out?" Rufus said angrily.

Josh glanced at him. "You got a problem with that?"

"Maybe."

"Well, you live your life the way you want, I live mine the way I want. We see who makes it farther. I know you had it hard inside, but it ain't no picnic on the outside. I got me my own little prison right out here. And nobody's convicted me of a damn thing."

"God made all of us, Josh. We all his children. Ain't no good trying to divide us all up. I seen plenty of white folk beaten up in prison. Evil comes in all forms, all colors. Bible says so. I ain't judging nobody except on themselves. Only way to do it."

Josh snorted. "Look at you, saying that. After all Tremaine and them done to you. You telling me you don't hate them, want to kill 'em?"

"No. If I felt that way, that'd mean Vic took the love from my heart. Took my Lord away from me. He does that, that means he's controlling me. Ain't nobody on this earth strong enough to take God from me. Not old Vic, you or anybody else. I'm not dumb, Josh. I know life ain't fair. I know black folk ain't riding on top of the world. But I ain't adding to the problem by hating people."

"Shit. You got the gold card from God to hate every white person ever born."

"You're wrong. I hate them, it's like hating myself. I went down that road when I first went to prison. Hated everybody. The Devil had me, but the Lord took me back. Can't do it. Won't do it."

"Well, that's your problem. Sooner you get over that the better."

"That was a big oversight on your part, Frank. You take out Rider and his wife, but you didn't search his office?"

Rayfield's grip tightened around the phone. "Well, tell me exactly when I was supposed to do that. If I had done it before we killed him, he would've gotten suspicious and maybe gotten away. If we had gotten caught going through it now, there would've been questions I don't have answers for."

"But you just told me they ruled it a murder-suicide. The cops aren't going to investigate that anymore."

"Probably true."

"So you can hit his office. Like tonight."

"If the coast is clear, we'll do it."

"Have you found the letter Harms got from the Army?"

"Not yet —" He broke off as Tremaine burst into his office, waving a piece of paper. "Hold on."

Tremaine slid the paper in front of Rayfield, who went pale as he read it. He looked up at a grim Tremaine.

"Where'd you find it?"

"That SOB hollowed out one of the bed supports. Pretty slick," Tremaine grudgingly conceded.

Rayfield spoke into the receiver. In terse sentences he conveyed the contents of the letter.

"Was this your doing, Frank?"

"Look, if the guy had died in the stockade the way we planned, they would've done an autopsy, right? Well, this was the only way to cover that hole. We all agreed."

"But, Christ, Harms didn't die. Why didn't you have it expunged from the system later?"

"I did! Don't you think if I hadn't, it would've come out during the investigation? Rider wasn't stupid, he would've pounced on that as a defense."

"So if you took it out of the record back then, why did the Army send him that letter all these years later?"

"Who knows? Some dipshit clerk could have come across a piece of paper and put it back in, or these days entered it into a database. Once in the Army's official record, you never know if something's going to resurface, no matter how hard you tried to bury it. It's the biggest damn bureaucracy in the world. You can't account for everything."

"But it was your job to stay on top of it."

"Don't tell me what my job is. I tried to stay on top of it, but it's not like I could check on it every stinking day for the last quarter century."

The voice sighed. "So now we know what triggered Harms's memory."

"Any strategy comes with risks."

"Well, maybe Rider had a copy of this letter."

"I don't see how Rufus Harms could've had access to a copier, and the letter wasn't part of what he filed with the Court, we know that for a fact."

"But we can't be sure that he didn't. That's all the more reason for you to go over

Rider's office tonight."

Rayfield looked up at Tremaine and then said into the phone, "All right, we'll hit it tonight. Fast and hard."

CHAPTER FORTY-TWO

Senator Knight warmly greeted Fiske and Sara as they entered the foyer. Behind him, they could see the place was filled with the business and political elite of the nation's capital.

"Glad you could come, John," Jordan Knight said, shaking his hand. "Sara, you look radiant as always." He gave her a hug and they exchanged pecks on the cheek.

Fiske looked over at Sara. She had changed out of her business attire and into a light summer dress of soft pastel colors that accented nicely her suntanned skin. The bun was gone and her hair swept appealingly around her face.

She caught Fiske staring at her and he quickly looked away, embarrassed, before accepting a drink from one of the waiters. Sara and Jordan Knight did the same.

Jordan looked around, seemingly a little embarrassed himself. "I know the timing on this damn thing is atrocious." He eyed Sara closely when he said this. "I know Beth feels the same way, although she won't admit it."

Sure she does, thought Fiske.

Jordan pointed his drink toward an elderly

man in a wheelchair and spoke softly. "Kenneth Wilkinson unfortunately isn't long for this world. He's a scrapper, though, and he might fool us all. But he's lived a long, inspiring life. My mentor and my friend. I'm a better man for having known him."

"Didn't he introduce you and your wife?" Sara asked.

"That's another reason I owe him so much."

Fiske watched Elizabeth Knight methodically work the room, as polished and poised as any experienced politico. Fiske scanned the room again but didn't see any sign of Ramsey or Murphy. He wondered if they had boycotted the event. He did note several of the other justices looking nervous and uncomfortable. The fear that a madman wanted to mount your head in his trophy case could do that to you.

His eyes passed over Richard Perkins hovering in the background. There were armed guards everywhere and Fiske knew the hot topic of the evening was the two murdered clerks. Fiske's eyes narrowed as he spied Warren McKenna knifing through the crowd like a shark looking for flesh to devour.

"You two make a great team," Sara said.

Jordan Knight touched his glass to hers. "I think so too."

"Your wife ever think about running for political office?" Fiske asked.

"John, she's a Supreme Court justice. It's a lifetime appointment," Sara exclaimed.

Fiske kept his eyes on Jordan. "Wouldn't be the first time someone left the Court in pursuit of another job, would it?"

Jordan looked at him keenly. "No, it wouldn't, John. As a matter of fact, over the years Beth and I have talked about that. I'm not going to be in the Senate forever. I've got a seven-thousand-acre ranch out in New Mexico. I can easily see myself running that until the end of my days."

"And maybe your wife becomes the Virginia senator in the household?"

"I never presume to know what Beth will do. It actually adds a level of excitement to our marriage that I think is incredibly healthy." He smiled at his remark and Fiske felt himself smile in return.

Sara was raising her glass as a thought hit her. "Senator, can I use a phone?"

"Use the one in my study, Sara. It's more private."

She glanced at Fiske but said nothing. After she had gone, Jordan said, "She's quite a young woman."

"I wouldn't disagree with that," Fiske said.

"Since she's been clerking for Beth, I've come to know her quite well. I've been almost like a father figure, I guess you could say. She has a brilliant future ahead of her."

"Well, she's got a great role model in your

wife." Fiske almost choked on his drink as he said this.

"The absolute best. Beth does nothing halfway."

Fiske thought about this remark for a moment. "I know your wife is a real go-getter, but she might want to cut back on her schedule until the case is solved. You don't want to give some maniac a free shot."

Jordan studied Fiske over the rim of his glass for a moment. "Do you really think the justices might be in danger?"

Fiske didn't really think so, but he wasn't about to say that to Jordan. If he and Sara were wrong in their conclusions, he didn't want anyone letting down his guard.

"Let's put it this way, Senator, if anything happens to your wife, no one will care what I think."

Jordan's face slowly went pale. "I see your point."

Fiske noticed a line forming to talk to the man. "I won't take up any more of your time. Keep up the good work."

"Thank you, John, I intend to."

Senator Knight started to receive the other guests. He needn't have bothered to work the room, Fiske thought. His wife had probably already hit all the important players.

In Jordan Knight's study, Sara dialed home for messages. She had forgotten to check earlier, and she was desperately hoping to hear back from George Barker, the newspaper editor from Rufus Harms's hometown. Her hopes were rewarded when she heard the old man's deep voice on her answering machine. He sounded a little contrite, she thought.

She snatched a piece of paper from the notebook on the desk and wrote the name down: Samuel Rider. George Barker had left only the man's name; apparently, after twenty-five years, that was all the information his files had contained. She had to find out Rider's office address and telephone number right away. As she looked up, she saw the way to do it. The bookshelves on the far wall of the study held a set of current Martindale-Hubbells, the official directory of the legal profession, which purported to have the name, office address and phone number of virtually every attorney licensed to practice in the United States. It was divided by states and territories, and she decided to opt for the local jurisdictions first. As she looked through the index for the commonwealth of Virginia, her search was rewarded as she spotted the name Samuel Rider. Flipping to the page indicated, she found a brief bio of Rider. He had been in the JAG in the early seventies. That had to be the man.

She dialed the phone number to his office, but received no answer. She dialed Information for his home phone number, but it was unlisted. She hung up, thoroughly frustrated. She had to talk to the man. She thought a moment. The timing would be very tight, so there was only one way to do it. A phone directory was on the desk and she used it to look up a number. It took only a few minutes to arrange things. She and Fiske had a couple of hours before they could leave. With any luck they would be back by early tomorrow morning.

As Sara opened the door to the study, Elizabeth Knight was standing there.

"Jordan told me you might be back here."

"I had to make a phone call."

"I see."

"I guess I'll get back to the party."

"Sara, I need to talk to you in private for a moment."

Elizabeth Knight motioned her back into the study and then closed the door behind them. The justice had on a simple white dress, minimal makeup and a tasteful sapphire necklace. The white dress made her skin seem even more pallid. However, she wore her hair down and the dark strands were striking against the white background. When she made the effort, Sara thought, Elizabeth Knight could be a very attractive woman. She apparently picked those moments with great care. At this moment, Elizabeth Knight looked very uncomfortable.

"Is there something wrong?" Sara asked.

"I dislike delving into the personal lives of my clerks, Sara, I really do, but when it reflects on the image of the Court, then I feel that it is my duty to say something."

"I'm not sure I understand."

Knight collected her thoughts for a moment. Ever since the realization that she had, however unwittingly, condemned Steven Wright to death, her nerves had been in tatters. She felt like lashing out at someone, even if unfairly. It was not her habit to do such a thing, but the fact was she *was* upset with Sara Evans. And she did care about her. Thus, the young woman was going to feel the justice's wrath. "You're a very smart woman. A very attractive and smart young woman."

"I'm afraid I still don't —"

Knight's tone changed. "I'm talking about you and John Fiske. Richard Perkins reported that he saw you and Fiske leaving your home together this morning."

"Justice Knight, with all due respect, that is my personal business."

"It is certainly more than your personal business, Sara, if it reflects negatively on the Court."

"I don't see how that could possibly be the case."

"Let me see if I can make it clearer for you. Do you think it would sully the Court's reputation if it became known that one of its clerks was sleeping with the brother of her slain colleague on the day after his murder was discovered?"

"I am not sleeping with him," Sara said forcefully.

"That is quite beside the point. Public opinion is driven by perception rather than by fact, particularly in this town. If a newspaper reporter had seen you and Fiske leave your home this morning, what do you think the headline would've read? Even if it just recounted the actual facts of the reporter's observations, what do you think would be the likely perception of the reading public?" When Sara didn't answer, Knight continued. "Right now we don't need any additional adverse complications, Sara. We have quite enough of them to deal with."

"I guess I never thought that part through."

"That is exactly what you must do if you want to have anything other than a mediocre legal career."

"I'm sorry. I won't repeat the mistake."

Knight stared hard at her, then she opened the door. "Please see that you don't."

As Sara passed her, Knight added, "Oh, Sara, until the identity of the murderer is definitively ascertained, I wouldn't put your complete faith or trust in anyone. Whether you're aware of it or not, a large percentage of murders are committed by *family members*."

Astonished, Sara turned to face her. "You're not implying —"

"I imply nothing," Knight said sharply. "I'm only conveying a fact. You do with it what you will."

Bored, Fiske meandered through the apartment when he felt someone at his shoulder.

"There's a question I've been meaning to ask you."

Fiske looked around. Agent McKenna was staring at him.

"McKenna, I'm seriously considering a lawsuit against you, so get the hell away from me."

"Just doing my job. And right now I want to know where you were at the time your brother was murdered."

Fiske finished his glass of wine and then looked out the broad bank of windows. "Haven't you forgotten something?"

"What's that?"

"They haven't ascertained the time of death yet."

"You're a little behind in the investigation."

"Is that right?" Fiske said, a little taken aback.

"Between three and four A.M. Saturday. Where were you during that time?"

"Am I a suspect in this case?"

"If and when you become a suspect, I'll let you know."

"I was working at my office in Richmond until about four in the morning on Saturday. Now you're going to ask me if anyone can corroborate that, right?"

"Can anyone?"

"No. But I went to the Laundromat around ten that morning."

"Richmond's only a two-hour drive from Washington. You'd have plenty of time."

"So your theory is I drove up to Washington, killed my brother in cold blood, dumped his body in the middle of a heavily black area, with such skill that no one noticed me do it, drove back to Richmond and washed my underwear. And the motive is?" As soon as Fiske said the last sentence, his next breath caught in his throat. He had the perfect motive: five hundred thousand dollars in life insurance. *Shit!*

"Motives can always come later. You have no alibi, which means you had the opportunity to commit the murder."

"So you think I murdered Wright too? Remember, you told the justices that you think the two murders are related. I do have an alibi for that one."

"Just because I said something doesn't mean it's true."

"Fascinating. Do you take that same philosophy with you to the witness stand?"

"During the course of an investigation I've found it's not always good to show your hand. The killings could be completely unrelated, which means any alibi you have for Wright's murder means nothing."

As Fiske watched McKenna walk off, a very unsettling sensation went down his spine. Even McKenna wouldn't be so stupid as to try to pin the murder of his brother on him, would he? And why hadn't Fiske known about the autopsy results ascertaining the time of his brother's death? Fiske immediately answered that question: The information flow from Chandler had dried up.

"John?"

Fiske turned around and looked at Richard Perkins.

"Got a minute?" the man asked nervously. The two men went over to a corner. Perkins looked out the window for a moment as though preparing what he was about to say. "I've only been the marshal at the Supreme Court for two years. It's a great job, prestigious, not too much stress, pays quite well. I oversee almost two hundred employees, everybody from barbers to police officers. I worked at the Senate before that, thought I'd probably retire there, but then this opportunity came up."

"Good for you," Fiske said, but he wondered why Perkins was telling him this.

"Even though your brother's death didn't

430

take place at the Court I felt a real responsibility for his safety, for everyone who works at the Court. Now with Wright's death, I'm just reeling. I'm not used to handling things like this. I'm a lot better at payroll issues and overseeing the orderly functioning of bureaucracies than I am being in the middle of a homicide investigation."

"Well, Chandler is really good at his job. And of course you've got the FBI on the case too." Fiske almost bit his tongue when he said this. Perkins picked up on it.

"Agent McKenna seems to hold some kind of grudge against you. Have you ever met the man before?"

"No."

Perkins looked down at his hands. "Do you really think there's some crazy out there with a vendetta?"

"It's not out of the realm of possibility."

"But why now of all times? And why target clerks? Why not the justices?"

"Or other court personnel."

"What do you mean?"

"You might be in danger too, Richard."

Perkins looked astonished. "Me?"

"You're the head of security. If this person wants to show that he can pick people off at will, then he's flouting the security of the Court. He's flouting you."

Perkins seemed to consider this. "So you think the deaths are definitely connected?"

"If they're not, it's one helluva coincidence. Frankly, I don't believe in coincidences that big."

"And Chandler too?"

"Maybe. I'm sure he'll keep you informed."

As Perkins walked off, Elizabeth Knight powered by. It was as though the crowd automatically parted for her.

A hand pressed against his shoulder. "Meet me outside the building in ten minutes." It was Sara's voice, but by the time Fiske turned around he could only see her disappearing into the crowd.

Visibly frustrated, he looked around and picked up on Elizabeth Knight's movements again. She probably forgot Kenneth Wilkinson was even here, he thought. At his own party too. He was thus very surprised when Elizabeth went over to Wilkinson and spoke with him briefly. He watched as she wheeled him out onto the lighted and empty terrace, where he could see her kneeling beside the wheelchair, holding one of Wilkinson's hands and talking to him.

Fiske mingled a bit more and then couldn't keep himself from heading out to the terrace. Elizabeth Knight looked up and then quickly rose from her kneeling position.

"I'm sorry for interrupting, but I have to leave and I wanted to say hello to Judge Wilkinson."

Knight stepped back and Fiske went forward and introduced himself. He shook Kenneth Wilkinson's hand and passed along his congratulations for the elderly man's long career in public service. As he started back into the room, Knight stopped him.

"I assume you're leaving with Sara."

"Is that a problem?"

"I guess that's up to you."

"What's that supposed to mean?"

"Sara has a wonderful future ahead of her. But little things can sometimes disrupt careers with great potential."

"You know, Justice Knight, I think you have a real problem with me, and I'm not sure why."

"I don't know you, Mr. Fiske. If you're anything like your brother, then maybe I don't have a big problem."

"I'm not like anybody else. I try not to compare people or make nice, neat assumptions. They seldom prove true."

Knight appeared taken aback by this but said, "I actually agree with you."

"I'm glad we could agree on something."

"However, I do know Sara, and I care about her very much. If certain actions you take reflect negatively on her and thus on the Court, then you're right, I do have a problem with that."

"Look, all I'm concerned about is finding out who killed my brother."

433

She looked at him keenly. "Are you sure that's all?"

"If I weren't sure, well, you know what, it's a free country." Fiske thought he saw an amused expression pass across her face.

She crossed her arms. "You don't seem the least bit intimidated by a Supreme Court Justice, Mr. Fiske."

"If you knew something about me, you'd understand why."

"Perhaps I should make a point of finding out about you. Perhaps I already have."

"I guess that can be a two-way street."

Knight's expression turned dark. "Confidence is one thing, Mr. Fiske, disrespect is quite another."

"I've found that also to be a two-way street."

"I hope you appreciate my concerns for Sara. They are genuine."

"I'm sure they are."

She started to turn away and then looked back at him. "Your brother was a very special person. Highly intelligent, the consummate legal analyst."

"He was one of a kind."

"With that said, I'm not sure he was the most able lawyer in his family."

Knight walked away, leaving a surprised Fiske behind. He stood there for a minute trying to analyze her words. Then he left the terrace and made his way down in the elevator to the lobby. He looked around but didn't see Sara. A horn beeped and he saw her car ease up to the front door. He climbed in and looked over at her. "Where are we going?"

"To the airport."

"What are you talking about?"

"We're going to see Samuel Rider, Esquire."

"And who is Samuel Rider, Esquire?"

"Rufus Harms's attorney. George Barker called back with the name. I looked Rider up. He practices outside of Blacksburg, only a couple hours east of the prison. I tried his office, but there was no answer. His home phone's unlisted."

"So why are we flying out there then?"

"We have his office address. It'll be late by the time we get there, so it's a long shot he'll be in his office. But it's also not a big town: We should be able to find somebody there who can give us his home address or at least his phone number. And if we're right about his involvement, he could be in danger. If something happens to him, we may never find out the truth."

"So you really think he's the one who called the Court? The one who filed the appeal?"

"I wouldn't bet against it."

CHAPTER FORTY-THREE

Twenty-five minutes later Fiske and Sara arrived at National Airport, and Sara pulled into one of the parking garages. After that they made their way to the general aviation terminal. "Are you sure we can get a flight out?" Fiske asked.

"I chartered a private plane to take us there."

"You did what? Do you know how much that costs?"

"Do *you* know how much it costs?"

Fiske looked sheepish. "No, I mean it's not like I ever chartered a friggin' plane before. But it can't be cheap."

"It's about twenty-two hundred dollars for a round-trip flight to Blacksburg. I maxed out my credit card."

"Then I'll pay you back somehow."

"You don't have to do that."

"I don't like owing people."

"Fine, I'm sure I can figure out lots of ways for you to pay it off." She smiled.

A few minutes later they approached a small twin-engine jet sitting on the tarmac. Fiske watched as a boxy 737 lumbered down the main runway and then lifted gracefully into the air. Everywhere was the nauseating smell of jet fuel and the irritating whine of engines.

Sara and Fiske headed up the steps of the sleek jet, where they were met by a man in his fifties with short white hair and a wiry build. He introduced himself as the pilot, Chuck Herman.

Herman looked up at the skies. "I got the flight plan filed okay, but we're a little behind in the takeoff schedule. They had some delays earlier because of a software glitch in the control tower and everybody's paying for it."

"We're on a short time fuse, Chuck," Sara said. The later they arrived at Rider's office, the less likely it was that they'd find someone to help them. In addition, she couldn't be late for work again.

Herman looked proudly at his aircraft. "Not to worry. We're only talking a seventy-minute trip, and I can step on the gas if need be."

They all moved into the cabin and Herman indicated chairs for them to sit in.

"I'm sorry, but I couldn't get a cabin steward in here on such short notice. Do you two want anything?"

"A glass of white wine," Sara said.

"How about you, John? Can I get you anything?" Fiske declined. "The fridge is fully stocked with food. Please help yourself."

Ten minutes after takeoff, the flight became very smooth, like gliding on a calm pond in a canoe. Sara unstrapped her belt and looked over at Fiske. He stared out the window at the sinking sun.

"How about I fix up something to eat? And I've got some interesting things to tell you."

"Same here." Fiske unstrapped himself, followed her back and sat down at the table, where he watched Sara make up some sandwiches.

"Coffee?"

Fiske nodded. "Something tells me it's going to be a long night."

Sara finished making the food and poured out two cups of coffee. She sat down across from Fiske and looked at her watch. "The flight is so short we don't have all that much time. There aren't any rental car places at the airport in Blacksburg. We can take a cab to a rental place in town and get a car there, though."

Fiske took a bite of sandwich and swallowed it down with some coffee. "You mentioned some things that happened at the party."

"I had a run-in with Justice Knight." She recounted the story to Fiske. He then shared his own experience with Knight.

"A hard woman to figure out," Fiske remarked.

"Anything else?"

"McKenna asked me if I had an alibi for the time my brother was murdered."

"Are you serious?"

"I don't have an alibi, Sara."

"John, it's not like anyone believes that you could have murdered your own brother. And how would that tie in to Steven's death?"

"If the two are connected."

"So did McKenna have a theory as to what your motive might be?"

Fiske put his coffee down. It might be good to get somebody else's view, he thought. "No, but the fact is, I have a perfect motive."

Surprised, she put down her coffee. "What?"

"I found out today that Mike had taken out a half-million-dollar life insurance policy on himself and named me as the beneficiary. That qualifies as a top-rank motive, don't you think?"

"But you said you just found out today."

"Do you seriously think McKenna will believe that?"

"That's strange."

Fiske cocked his head at her. "What is?"

"Justice Knight said something along the lines that most homicides are committed by family members, and that I shouldn't trust anybody — meaning, I'm sure, you."

"Was she ever in the Army that you know?"

Sara almost laughed. "No, why?"

"I was just wondering if she could have

anything to do with Rufus Harms."

Sara smiled. "But now that we're on the subject, how about Senator Knight? He might have been in the Army."

"He wasn't. I remember reading in the Richmond papers during his first Senate campaign that he was physically unable to be in the Armed Forces. His political opponent at the time was a war hero and he tried to make a big deal out of Knight not serving his country. But he did, in an intelligence capacity, good record and all, and the whole thing went away." Fiske shook his head in frustration. "This is silly. We're trying to pound square pegs in round holes." He took a long breath. "I hope Rider can help us."

Dressed in overalls, the man pushed the bulky cleaning cart down the hallway and then stopped outside one office, noting the stenciled lettering on the frosted glass door: SAMUEL RIDER, ATTORNEY-AT-LAW. The man cocked his head and looked around, listening intently. The office building was small and Rider's law office was one of only a half dozen places of business on the second floor. At this hour, the town and the building were pretty much deserted.

Josh Harms tapped against the door and waited for a response. He tapped again, this time a little louder. Josh had left Rufus in the truck parked in the alley while he reconnoitered the area. He had found the cleaning supply closet and hatched his plan in case someone showed up. He tapped on Rider's office door once more, waited another couple of minutes, pursed his lips and gave a low whistle. Within twenty seconds, Rufus, who had been trailing him in the darkness of the hallway, joined him. Rufus wasn't wearing a cleaning uniform; there hadn't been one in the storage closet that came close to fitting him.

Josh pulled his lock-pick equipment and within a few seconds they were on the other side of the office door in the receptionist's area.

"We got to move fast. Somebody might show up," Josh said. Tucked inside his belt was his pistol, fully loaded, a round chambered.

"I'll look here and you go into Samuel's office and start looking around."

Rufus was already going through a file cabinet using the flashlight he had brought with him from the truck. Josh went into Rider's office. The first thing he did, after checking the street for activity, was close the drapes. He pulled out a flashlight of his own and started searching. He came to the locked desk drawer and jimmied it. He gave a low whistle as his hand closed around the packet that had been taped to the underside of the desk drawer. He went to the doorway. "Rufus, I got it."

His brother rushed in and took the papers. He scanned them under the flashlight's arc.

"You still ain't told me how having these pieces of paper is gonna help your butt any which way."

"I ain't thought that all the way through, but I'd rather have them than not have them."

"Well, let's get out of here before somebody has *us*."

They had barely made it to the receptionist area when they both heard the footsteps, two sets of them. They glanced quickly at each other. Josh pulled the pistol and punched off the safety. "Cops. They know we're here."

Rufus looked at him and shook his head. "It ain't the cops. And it ain't the Army. Building's deserted. If it was them they'd come in here sirens going and the next sound we'd be hearing is glass breaking when the tear gas canisters come through the damn window. Come on." Rufus led the way back into Rider's interior office and softly closed the door. All they could do now was wait.

CHAPTER FORTY-FOUR

Chandler walked around Michael Fiske's apartment. He knelt down and examined the gouge mark in the floor caused by John Fiske's swing with a tire iron. If the blow had found its mark, this mystery might have been solved. Chandler rose and shook his head. It was never that easy. His men were putting the finishing touches on the apartment. Black carbon dusting powder lay everywhere in piles like magic sprinkles, which in a way they were. They had taken Michael Fiske's prints for purposes of elimination. They would have to get his brother's as well. Since John Fiske was a lawyer licensed in Virginia, his fingerprints would be on file with the Virginia State Police. He should get Sara Evans's prints as well, he figured. She had undoubtedly been here too. He looked down the hallway. In the bedroom, perhaps? However, his inquiries had revealed only that the two had been good friends.

He had met with Murphy and his clerks. They had gone over all the cases Michael had been working on. Nothing really stuck out. That line of investigation would simply take too long. And people were dying.

John Fiske's unwillingness to confide in Chandler had cost him. As Fiske had earlier deduced, Chandler had cut off the flow of information to him. Chandler had played fair with the Feds, though, and passed along what he had to McKenna, including his newfound information on Rufus Harms's escape from prison and Michael Fiske's earlier calls to the prison. He had also informed McKenna of the missing appeal Fiske had told him about. McKenna had thanked him but had been unable to add any new information of his own. As if on cue, he heard a sound at the front door and the FBI agent walked into the room — after showing his ID card to the uniform outside and being added to the crime scene list, Chandler assumed. Crime scene. Well, it was one of sorts, Chandler said to himself.

"You're working late tonight, Agent McKenna."

"So are you." The FBI agent's gaze swept the area, starting at the center and marching outward grid by grid.

"So, is the director of the FBI just a little bit on your butt, or a lot, to get this thing solved?"

"Same as your boss. In the Bureau you get double kudos if you solve the crime in time for the evening news." McKenna flashed a rare smile, although it was as though his mouth didn't know quite how to manage it, because the effect came off as lopsided.

Chandler wondered if the man did it on purpose to throw people off. Because he'd had a weird feeling about the guy, Chandler had discreetly checked out Warren McKenna. His career at the Bureau was first-rate in all respects. He had been assigned to the Washington Metropolitan Field Office at Buzzard Point for eight years after transferring from the Richmond Field Office. Before his career at the FBI, he had done a brief stint in the military, then completed college. Since that time McKenna had done nothing except make positive impressions on his superiors. One curious thing Chandler had found out: McKenna had refused several promotions that would have taken him out of the field.

"You're lucky John Fiske hasn't slapped you with a lawsuit yet. He still might."

"Maybe he should," was McKenna's surprising reply. "I probably would if I were him."

"I'll be sure and tell him that," Chandler said slowly.

McKenna's gaze darted all over the place for a couple of minutes, seemingly absorbing every detail like a sheet of Polaroid, before he glanced back at Chandler. "What are you, anyway, his mentor?"

"Didn't know the man until a couple days ago."

"You make friends a lot faster than I do,

then." McKenna inclined his head at Chandler. "Mind if I look around?"

"Go ahead. Try not to touch anything that doesn't look like it's got a pound of print dust on it."

McKenna nodded and stepped carefully around the living room. He noted the mark on the floor.

"Fiske going after his purported attacker?"

"That's right. Only I didn't know he was purported."

"He is until we have a corroborating account. At least that's how I work."

Chandler unwrapped a piece of gum and popped it in his mouth, slowly chewing over both the agent's words and the gum.

"Sara Evans reported to me that she also saw a man flee from the building and that Fiske was chasing him. Is that good enough for you?"

"That's convenient corroboration. Fiske is one lucky guy. He should run out right now and play the lottery while he's so hot."

"I wouldn't call losing your brother being lucky."

McKenna stopped walking and looked at the pantry door, which was ajar and covered with print dust. "I guess it depends on how you look at it, doesn't it?"

"What the hell do you have against him? You don't even know the guy."

McKenna's eyes flashed at him. "That's

right, Detective Chandler, and you know what? Neither do you."

Chandler wanted to say something back but couldn't think of anything. In a way the man was right. This thought was interrupted by one of his men.

"Detective Chandler, we found something I think you might want to see."

Chandler took the sheaf of papers from the tech and looked down at it. McKenna joined him.

"Looks like an insurance policy," McKenna said.

"We found it on one of the shelves in the pantry. No food in there. Guy used it for storage. Tax returns, bills and stuff like that are in there too."

"Half a million bucks worth of life insurance," Chandler muttered. He flipped rapidly through the pages, passing by the legalese until he got to the end, where more specific information was set forth.

"Michael Fiske was the insured."

McKenna's finger suddenly stabbed at the bottom of the page. Chandler paled a little as he read the line the man had so energetically indicated. "And John is the primary beneficiary."

The two men looked at each other. "Would you like to take a walk and hear a theory of mine?" McKenna asked.

Chandler wasn't sure exactly what to do.

"It won't take long," McKenna added. "In fact, some of it you're probably thinking right now, I would imagine."

Chandler finally shrugged. "You got five minutes."

The two men walked out onto the sidewalk in front of the row house. McKenna took a moment to light up a cigarette and then offered one to Chandler. The detective held out his pack of gum. "I can be overweight or I can smoke. I like to eat, so there we are."

They strolled along the dark street as McKenna began talking. "I found out that Fiske doesn't have an alibi for the probable time his brother was murdered."

"Might be something in his favor. If he killed his brother, he would've worked hard to establish one."

"I disagree for a couple of reasons. First, he probably never thought he would become a suspect."

"With a half-million-dollar life insurance policy?"

"He might have thought we wouldn't find out. We go down a different trail and that's it. He waits awhile and then collects his money."

"I don't know about that. What's your second point?"

"If he had some perfect alibi — which there is no such thing if you're guilty — then a hole would come up in it somewhere, sometime, somehow. So why bother? He was a cop and now a lawyer. He knows all about alibis. He says he doesn't have one and then he doesn't have to worry about it blowing up in his face. And then he counts on everybody reaching the conclusion you just did, namely, that if he's guilty he would've concocted a good one."

McKenna took a long drag on his cigarette and looked up at the few stars visible in the sky. "So he's got motive and, by his own admission, opportunity. I checked him out. He's got a dip-shit law practice in Richmond, defending the scum of the earth. Guy never even went to law school. He's third-rate at best. Unmarried, no kids, lives in a shithole. A real loner. Oh, and he left the Richmond police force under a somewhat dark cloud."

"How do you mean?" Chandler asked sharply.

"Let's just say that there was a shooting incident that was never fully explained other than the fact a civilian and another police officer were dead as a result."

Chandler looked shaken, but recovered. "So why does he come up and offer his assistance in the investigation?"

"Again, a cover. Fiske's position would be, 'How could I have pulled the trigger? I'm up here working my butt off to find the person who murdered my brother.' "

"How does that explain Wright's death?"

"Who says it has to? Like you said, the two murders could be unrelated. If they are, then if I were Fiske I'd jump on it and argue that they are connected. See, he's got an alibi for Wright's murder."

Evans again, Chandler thought.

McKenna continued, "So if we believe they're connected, he's home free."

"And Sara Evans? Remember? She said she saw the guy running out of Michael Fiske's apartment building. You say she's lying too?"

McKenna stopped walking and so did Chandler. McKenna took a last puff of his cigarette and then crushed it out on the sidewalk with several twists of his foot. "Sara Evans too," McKenna repeated Chandler's words, eyeing the detective closely.

Chandler shook his head. "Come on, McKenna."

"I'm not saying she's in on the whole thing. I'm saying maybe she has a thing for Fiske and she's doing what he tells her to."

"They just met."

"Is that right? You know that for sure?"

"Actually, no."

"Okay, he convinces her he's done nothing wrong, but some people might try to frame him."

"Why do you have such a thing against Fiske?"

Now McKenna erupted. "He's got a smart mouth. He comes off as holier than thou, the defender of his brother's memory, only they seemed to have no contact recently. He and Evans spent the night at her house doing who knows what the day after his brother's body is found. He's got a shotgun for some reason. He's nosed his way into the investigation, which means he knows just about everything we do. He's got no alibi for the night of the murder and five minutes ago we found out he's a half million bucks richer because his brother is dead. What the hell am I supposed to think? Are you saying your cop radar's not even tingling over this?"

"Okay, you've made your point. Maybe I have been too lax with him. Rule number one: Don't trust anybody."

"Good rule to live by." McKenna paused and then added, "Or die by." He walked off leaving a very shaken Chandler staring after him.

CHAPTER FORTY-FIVE

Fiske knocked on Rider's office door. He squinted through the glass. "Dark inside."

"He's probably at home. We need to find out where that is."

"Well, the guy also might be eating dinner out, or out of town on business. He might even be on vacation. Or —"

"Or something could have happened to him," Sara said.

"Don't get overly dramatic." Fiske clasped the doorknob and it turned easily. He and Sara exchanged a significant glance. Fiske looked up and down the hallway. That's when he saw the cleaning cart and relaxed slightly. "Cleaning crew?"

"And they're cleaning in the pitch-dark because . . . ?" Sara responded.

"That's just what I was thinking." He pulled Sara away from the door and over to the cart. He rummaged around, before pulling out a pair of Vise-Grips from a tool-box.

Whispering, he said, "Go down near the exit stairs. If you hear anything, run to the car and call the cops."

She grabbed his arm and whispered back,

"I have a much better idea. Let's go call the police together right now and report a burglary."

"We don't know that it is a burglary."

"We don't know that it isn't either."

"If we leave, they could get away."

"And if you go in there and get killed, what exactly is that going to accomplish? You don't even have a gun — you have that thing, whatever the hell that is."

"Vise-Grips."

"Great, they could have guns and you have a tool."

"Maybe you're right."

"Lady is for sure right. Too bad you didn't listen."

Fiske and Sara whirled around.

Josh Harms stood there, his pistol aimed at them.

"Wall's mighty thin. Figured when we heard the door start to open, and then all that whispering, you two were going to go for the cops. Can't let you do that."

Fiske studied him. He was big but not bulky. Unless they had run into a routine burglary, this man had to be Josh Harms. He eyed the gun and then scrutinized Josh's features, trying to size up quickly whether he had it in him to pull the trigger. He had killed in Vietnam; Fiske knew that from reading the news reports. But killing them would have to be in cold blood, and Fiske just did not see that in Josh Harms's eyes. But that could always change. Mouth, do your magic, he told himself.

"Hello, Josh, my name's John Fiske. This is Sara Evans with the United States Supreme Court. Where's your brother?"

Behind him, from the open doorway leading into Rider's office, appeared a man of such huge proportions that both Sara and Fiske knew he could only be Rufus Harms. He had obviously heard Fiske's words.

"How you know all that?" Rufus said while his brother kept his pistol tightly on the pair.

"I'd be glad to tell you. But why don't we talk inside the office? You have that APB out on you and everything."

He motioned to Sara. "After you, Sara." Out of the Harms brothers' line of sight, he gave her a reassuring wink. He only wished he could feel as confident on the inside. They were confronted with a convicted murderer who had been in a hellhole for twenty-five years, which had probably not made him any nicer, and a wily Vietnam vet whose trigger finger was looking itchier with every passing second.

Sara walked into the office, with Fiske behind her.

Josh and Rufus eyed each other quizzically. Then they followed the pair inside and shut the door behind them.

★ ★ ★

The Jeep sailed through the back roads on the way to Samuel Rider's office. Tremaine was driving; Rayfield sat beside him. The two-seater Jeep was Tremaine's private vehicle. They were both off duty now and had decided against checking out a military vehicle from the motor pool. In case anyone came upon them while they were searching Rider's office, they had settled upon a cover story: Sam Rider, Rufus Harms's old military attorney, practiced in the area and had recently visited Harms in prison for an unknown reason. Rider and his wife had been killed. Harms and his brother could have committed the murders; perhaps Rider had mentioned to Harms that he kept cash or other valuables at his home or office.

Tremaine glanced over at Rayfield.

"Something wrong?" Tremaine asked.

Rayfield stared straight ahead. "This is a big mistake. We're taking all the risks here."

"You think I don't know that?"

"If we get the letter that Harms filed, along with Rider's letter, maybe we can forget about Harms."

Tremaine looked sharply over at him. "What the hell are you talking about?"

"Harms wrote that letter because he wanted out of prison. He killed the little girl, but he really didn't *murder* her, right? Well, he's out of prison. He and his brother are probably in Mexico right now waiting on a plane to South America. That's exactly what I'd be doing."

Tremaine shook his head. "We can't be sure of that."

"What else is he going to do, Vic? Write another letter to the Court and say, what? 'Your Honor, I wrote you before with this crazy story I can't prove, but something happened to my appeal, and my lawyer and the clerk who got it are now dead. So I escaped from prison, I'm on the run and I want my day in court.' That's bullshit, Vic. He's not going to do that. He's going to run like hell. He *is* running like hell."

Tremaine considered this. "Maybe. But on the off chance that he isn't as smart as you think he is, I'm going to do everything I can to blow him away. And his brother. I don't like Rufus Harms. I've never liked the guy. I'm getting my ass shot up in Nam and he's back in the States safe and sound, three squares a day. We should've just let him rot in the stockade, but we didn't," Tremaine added bitterly.

"Too late for that now."

"Well, I'm going to do him a big favor. When I find him, his next cell is going to be seven feet long, four feet wide and made of pine. And he ain't getting a damn flag on it." Tremaine punched the gas even more.

Rayfield shook his head and settled back

down in his seat. He checked his watch and then looked down the road. They were almost at Rider's office.

Sara and Fiske sat on the leather couch while the Harms brothers stood in front of them.

"Why don't we just tie them up and get the hell out of here?" Josh said to his brother.

Fiske jumped in. "I think you're going to find we're on the same side."

Josh scowled at him. "Now, don't go taking this the wrong way, but you're full of shit."

"He's right," Sara said. "We're here to help you." Josh snorted but didn't bother to respond.

"John Fiske?" Rufus said. He studied Fiske's features, remembering where he'd seen similar ones. "That clerk they killed was family, wasn't he? Brother?"

Fiske nodded. "Yes. Who killed him?"

Josh broke in: "Don't tell them nothing, Rufus. We don't know who they are or what they want."

"We came here to talk to Sam Rider," Sara said.

Josh looked over at her. "Well, unless you're gonna put on a séance or something you're gonna have a real hard time doing that."

Fiske and Sara looked at each other and then back at the brothers.

"He's dead?" Sara asked.

Rufus nodded. "He and his wife. Made it look like suicide."

Fiske noted the file clutched in his hand. "Is that what you sent to the Court?"

"You mind if I ask the questions?" Rufus said.

"I'm telling you, Rufus, we're your friends."

"Sorry, but I don't make friends nowhere near that easy. What'd you want to talk to Samuel about?"

"He filed that for you at the Court, didn't he?"

"I ain't answering no questions."

"Okay, I'll just tell you what we know and then you can take it from there. How's that sound?"

"I'm listening."

"Rider filed it. My brother got it and took it out of the Court's system. He came to the prison to see you. Then he ended up dead in an alley in Washington. They made it look like a robbery. Now you tell us Rider is dead. Another clerk was killed too. I think it's connected to my brother's death, but I'm not sure why." Fiske stopped talking and studied the two men. "That's all we know. Now, I think you know a lot more. Like why all this is happening."

"You know so much. You with the cops?" Josh demanded.

"I'm helping the detective in charge."

"See, Rufus, I told you. We got to get out of here. Cops probably on their way right now."

"No, they're not," Sara said. "I saw your name in the papers Michael had, Mr. Harms, but that's all I saw. I don't know why you filed it or what was in it."

"Why does a prisoner file something with a court?" Rufus asked.

"Because you want out," Fiske said. Rufus nodded. "But you have to have grounds to do that."

"I got me the best grounds of all: the simple truth," Rufus said forcefully.

"Tell me what it is," said Fiske.

Josh edged toward the door. "Rufus, I got a bad feeling about all this. We stand here talking to them and the cops are closing in. You've already said too much."

"They killed his brother, Josh."

"You don't know if he really is his brother."

Fiske pulled out his wallet with his driver's license.

"This'll at least prove we have the same last name."

Rufus waved it off. "I don't need to see that. You got the same way about you too."

"Even if they ain't in on it, what the hell can they do to help?" Josh asked.

Rufus looked over at Fiske and Sara. "You

both talk real good and quick. You got an answer to that one?"

"I work at the Supreme Court, Mr. Harms," Sara said. "I know all the justices. If you have evidence that shows you're innocent, then I promise you it will be heard. If not by the Supreme Court, then by another court, believe me."

Fiske added, "The detective on the case knows something is fishy. If you tell us what's going on, we can go to him and get him to explore that angle."

"I know the truth," Rufus said again.

"That's great, Rufus, but the fact is, in a court of law it's not the truth unless you can prove it," Fiske said.

Sara said, "What was in your appeal, then?"

"Rufus, don't you answer that, dammit!" Josh yelled.

Rufus ignored him. "Something the Army sent me."

"Did you kill the little girl, Rufus?" Fiske asked.

"I did," he said, looking down. "At least my hands did. The rest of me didn't know what the hell was going on. Not after what they done to me."

"What do you mean by that? Who did what to you?"

"Rufus, he's looking to trick you," Josh warned.

"Messed with my head, that's what," Rufus said.

Fiske eyed him sharply. "Are you pleading some sort of insanity? Because if you are, you don't have a chance in hell." He watched Rufus intently. "But it's more than that, isn't it?"

"Why you say that?" Rufus said.

"Because my brother took whatever was in that appeal very seriously. Seriously enough that he broke the law by taking it, and lost his life trying to help you. He wouldn't have done that for some twenty-five-year-old insanity plea. Tell me what it was that cost my brother his life."

Josh put one big hand on Fiske's chest and pushed him hard against the back of the couch. "Look here, Mr. Smart-ass, Rufus here didn't ask your brother to do jack-shit for him. Your brother was the one that blew this whole thing up sky-high. He had to come check Rufus out cuz he's some old colored man sitting in some old prison for some old crime. So don't sit there singing that song 'bout your 'righteous brother.' "

Fiske ripped the hand away. "Why don't you go to hell, you sonofabitch!"

Josh moved the pistol closer to Fiske's face and said menacingly, "Why don't I send you there first? I catch up with you later. How's that sound, whitebread?"

"Please don't," Sara implored. "Please,

he's just trying to help."

"I don't need no damn help from the likes of you."

"We're only trying to get your brother justice in a court of law."

Josh shook his head. "I can get me justice in a court all by myself. We done overwhelmed your white asses. Prisons full of us and you just too cheap to build more. So I can get me mor'n justice in a court. Problem is I can't get me none on the outside, and damn if that ain't where I spend most of my time."

"This ain't the way to handle things," Rufus said.

"Oh, so now you know the way to handle everything all of a sudden?" said Josh.

Fiske was growing more nervous. Josh Harms sounded like he was at the point where maybe even his brother would have no control over him. Should he make a jump for the gun? Josh was probably fifteen years older than he, but the man looked as strong as an oak tree. If Fiske made a grab and got tossed on his head, he would probably be eating several rounds from the 9mm.

The screeching of rubber against asphalt made them all look toward the window. Rufus hustled across and cautiously looked out. When he turned back from the window they all could see the fear in his eyes.

"It's Vic Tremaine and Rayfield."

"Shit!" Josh exclaimed. "What they carrying?"

Rufus took one long breath. "Vic's got a machine gun."

"Shit!" Josh said again as they all listened to the heavy boots clattering into the building. In another couple of minutes, maybe less, they would be here. He suddenly glared at Fiske and Sara. "I told you. They set us up. We been sitting here jawing with them while the Army surrounds this place."

"In case you didn't notice, we're not in uniform," Fiske said. "Maybe they followed you."

"We didn't come from the direction of the prison. When they see the two of us, they're gonna shoot, and that's it."

"Not if you give yourselves up, they won't."

"That ain't an option," Josh said loudly.

"It ain't an option," Rufus repeated. "They ain't gonna let me live, knowing what I know."

Fiske looked at Rufus Harms. The man's eyes darted left and right. He had admitted to killing the girl. Shouldn't that be an end to it? Why not let the Army put him back in his cage? But Mike had wanted to help him.

Fiske jumped up.

Josh covered him with his pistol. "Don't make this no harder than it is."

Fiske didn't even look at him; his eyes were

squarely on Rufus. "Rufus? Rufus!"

Rufus finally seemed to break out of his inertia and looked at him.

"Maybe I can get you out of this, but you have to do exactly what I say."

Josh said, "We can damn well get ourselves out of this."

"In about thirty seconds those two guys are going to come through that door and it'll be over. You can't match their firepower."

"How 'bout I put one of my bullets in you right now?" Josh said.

"Rufus, will you trust me? My brother came to help you. Let me finish what he started. Come on, Rufus. Give me a chance." A bead of sweat trickled down Fiske's forehead.

Sara couldn't even speak. All she could hear were those boots, all she could see was that machine gun, coming closer and closer.

Finally, almost imperceptibly, Rufus nodded.

Fiske launched into action. "Get in the bathroom, both of you," he said.

Josh started to protest until Rufus cut him off and pushed him toward the private bath adjoining the office.

"Sara, you go with them."

She looked at him, stunned. "What?"

"Just do what I say. If you hear me call your name, flush the toilet and then come out. You two" — he nodded at the brothers —

464

"stay behind that door. If you don't hear me say your name, Sara, stay put."

"And you don't think them Army boys might just want to come take a peek at the toilet, especially if the door's closed?" Josh asked sarcastically.

"Let me worry about that."

"Okay," Josh said slowly. "But let me give you another thing to worry about, smart boy. You sell us out and the first bullet I fire is gonna hit you right about here." Josh placed his pistol against the base of Fiske's skull. "But you won't even hear my pistol fire. You'll be dead before your damn ears tells your damn brain."

Fiske nodded at Josh as though accepting his challenge, which, in effect, he was. He looked at Sara; her face was pale. She leaned into him, shaking hard, trying, without success, to catch her breath, as the pounding feet drew closer.

"John, I can't do this."

He gripped her shoulders hard. "Sara, you *can* do this. You are going to do this. Now go. Go." He squeezed her hand and then she and the Harms brothers went into the bathroom and Sara shut the door behind them. Fiske looked around the office, fighting hard to get his composure. He spied a briefcase against one wall, grabbed it and unsnapped the lid. It was empty. He stuffed files from the top of Rider's desk into the briefcase. As the boots boomed down the hallway, he raced to the small conference table set up in one corner. As he sat down, he heard the outer door open. As he pulled a file from the briefcase and opened it, he heard the inner door start to open. He leaned back in the chair and pretended to study some of the papers as the door opened. He stared up into the faces of the men.

"What the hell —" he started to say until he saw the machine gun pointed at him and fell silent.

"Who are you?" Rayfield demanded.

"I was about to ask you that question. I'm here for a meeting with Sam Rider. I've been waiting ten minutes already and he hasn't bothered to show up."

Rayfield edged closer. "You're a client of his?"

Fiske nodded. "Flew in from Washington this evening on a chartered plane. The meeting's been planned for several weeks now."

"Little late for a meeting, isn't it?" Tremaine's eyes bored into Fiske.

"I have a very busy schedule. This was the only time I could meet." He looked at both men sternly. "And why is the Army bursting in here with machine guns in the first place?"

Tremaine's face flushed angrily, but Rayfield assumed a more diplomatic tone. "It's not our business, Mr. —"

Fiske started to say his real last name, but

then decided not to. Rufus had known these men by name. That meant these men were somehow involved with whatever had happened to Rufus. If that was true, they might have killed Mike.

"Michaels, John Michaels. I run a real estate development company and Rider is my land-use attorney."

"Well, you're going to have to get another lawyer," Rayfield said.

"I'm happy with Sam's work."

"That's not the point. The point is Rider's dead. He committed suicide. Killed his wife and then himself."

Fiske stood up, trying to make his expression as horrified as possible. It wasn't too hard, given the fact that he was trying to scam two armed men, with two more armed men in the adjoining room. If he failed, he would be the first casualty, if Josh Harms had anything to say about it.

"What the hell are you talking about? I spoke with him recently. He seemed fine."

"That's all well and good, but the fact is he's dead," Rayfield said.

Fiske sat down abruptly, looking numbly at the files in front of him. "I can't believe it," he said, slowly shaking his head. "I feel like an idiot. Sitting in the man's office waiting to hold a meeting. But I didn't know. No one told me. The door to his office was unlocked. Christ!" He pushed the files away, then looked up sharply. "So what are you two doing here? Why is the Army involved?"

Tremaine and Rayfield exchanged glances. "There's been an escape from the military prison nearby."

"Good Lord, you think whoever escaped is around here?"

"Don't know. Fact is, Rider was the escapee's lawyer. We thought he might hit this place for some cash or something. Who knows, the prisoner might have murdered Rider, for all we know."

"But you said it was a suicide."

"That's what the police think. That's why we're here. To look around, catch the guy if he's here."

Fiske watched with a sinking heart as Tremaine headed to the bathroom door.

"Susan, can you please come out here?" Fiske called in a loud voice.

Tremaine stared hard at Fiske as they all heard the toilet flush. And then the door opened partially and Sara came out, trying her best to look astonished. She did a pretty good job, Fiske thought, probably because she too was scared shitless.

"John, what's going on?"

"I told these gentlemen about our meeting with Sam Rider. You're not going to believe this, but he's dead."

"Oh, my God."

"Susan is my assistant." She nodded at both men.

"I didn't get your names," Fiske said.

"That's right," Tremaine shot back.

Fiske hurriedly continued: "These men are from the Army. They're looking for an escaped prisoner. They think the person might have had something to do with Sam's death."

"Oh, my God. John, let's just get back on the plane and get out of here."

"That's not a bad idea," Tremaine said. "We can search the place a lot faster with you two out of the way." He once again looked over at the bathroom door. Holding his gun with one hand, he reached out to push the door all the way open.

"Well, I can tell you there's no one hiding in there," she said with as straight a face as she could.

"If you don't mind, ma'am, I like to see these things for myself," Tremaine said curtly.

Fiske watched Sara. He was sure she was going to start screaming. Come on, Sara, hold on. Don't lose it.

Behind the door of the darkened bathroom, Josh Harms had his pistol pointed directly at Tremaine's head through the slight gap between the door and doorjamb.

Josh had already sized up the tactical advantages he had, slight though they were.

469

Vic Tremaine first, and then Rayfield, unless Rayfield got him first, which was a real possibility given Josh's very limited field of vision. Well, there was no way he could miss the little Sherman tank of a target Vic Tremaine represented. His hand tightened on the trigger as his brother loomed over his shoulder, pressing his bulk up as far as he could against the wall. But there was barely an inch of space between him and the door. As soon as Tremaine touched the wood, it would be over.

At that moment Fiske started to stuff the files in his briefcase. "I can't believe it. First two black guys almost run us over and now this."

Tremaine and Rayfield jerked around and stared at him. "What two black guys?" they said in unison.

Fiske stopped what he was doing and looked at them. "We were coming in the building and they ran by us, almost knocked Susan down."

"What'd they look like?" Rayfield asked, his voice strained as he edged closer to Fiske. Tremaine quickly moved away from the bathroom door.

"Well, they were black, like I said. Now, one of them looked like he was ex-NFL or something. You remember how big he was, Susan?" She nodded and then started breathing again. "I mean, he was huge. And the guy with him was pretty big too, six-two, six-three at least, but a lot leaner. They were running like the devil and they weren't young either. Forty-five, fifty if they were a day."

"Did you see which way they went?" Tremaine asked.

"They jumped in some old car and took off on the main road heading north. I'm not good with cars, I don't know the make or anything, but it was an old model. Green, I think." He suddenly looked frightened. "You don't think it was the escaped prisoner, do you?"

Tremaine and Rayfield didn't answer because they were rushing out the door. As soon as they heard the outer door open and the boots running down the hallway, Fiske and Sara looked at each other and then they both, as though tied together with string, collapsed onto the sofa. They reached for each other and huddled together.

"Glad I didn't have to shoot you. You think fast on your feet."

They looked up at the grinning face of Josh Harms as he jammed his pistol into his pants. "We're both lawyers," Fiske said hoarsely, still clutching Sara tightly.

"Well, nobody's perfect," Josh said.

Rufus appeared behind his brother. "Thanks," he said quietly.

"I hope you believe us now," Fiske said.

"Yeah, but I ain't gonna take your help."

"Rufus —"

"Everybody's tried to help me up till now, they're dead. Except Josh, and we all almost bought it tonight. I ain't having that on my conscience. You two get back on that plane of yours and stay the hell out of this."

"I can't do that. He was my brother."

"Suit yourself, but you're gonna do it without me." He went to the window and watched as the Jeep sped off, heading north. He motioned to Josh. "Let's get going. No telling when they might get the itch to come back."

As the two men started to turn away, Fiske reached in his pocket and took out something, which he held out to Rufus. "This is my business card. It's got my office and home numbers on it. Rufus, think about what you're doing. By yourself, you're not going to get anywhere. When you finally realize that, call me."

Fiske looked surprised as Sara lifted the card from him and wrote something on the back. She held it out to Rufus. "That's my home and car phone numbers on the back. Call either one of us, day or night."

Slowly, the huge hand reached out, took the card. Rufus slipped it in his shirt pocket. In another minute Sara and Fiske were all alone. They again stared at each other, completely drained. A full minute passed before

472

Fiske broke the silence.

"Well, I have to admit, that was pretty close."

"John, I never, ever want to do that again." Sara walked unsteadily to the bathroom.

"Where are you going?"

She didn't bother to look back at him. "To the bathroom. Unless you want me to throw up out here."

CHAPTER FORTY-SIX

An hour after his conversation with Warren McKenna, Chandler climbed out of his car and walked slowly to his house. It was a comfortable brick and siding split-level set in a neighborhood of like structures. A nice, safe place to raise kids — at least it had been twenty years ago. It wasn't as safe or as nice today, but then what was? he thought.

Many years ago, when he wanted to unwind after work, he would shoot a few hoops in the driveway with his kids using the basketball net he had hung over the garage doors. That net had long since rotted away and the hoop and backboard had been removed. Now he went into the small backyard, where he sat down on a weathered gray cedar bench, situated near a spreading magnolia and in front of a small in-ground fountain. His wife had pestered him into putting in the fountain and he had bitched and complained the whole time. It was only after he had finished the project that he had understood her insistence. Building the thing had been cathartic for him: the planning, the measurements, the selection of materials. It was a lot like detective work, meaning a jigsaw puzzle where, if you were equal parts competent and lucky, all the pieces fit.

After ten minutes of quiet he finally lurched to his feet, his coat thrown over his shoulder, and ambled into the house. He looked around the quiet, dark kitchen. It was well decorated, the whole house was, due entirely to the efforts of his wife, Juanita. Kids raised, doctor visits made, bills paid, flowers tended to, grass clipped, beds made, clothes washed and ironed, meals cooked, dishes cleaned — she did all those things while he worked horrendous hours on his way up. That had been their partnership. After the kids were gone, she had gone back to school, become a nurse and worked at a local hospital on the pediatric wing. Married thirty-three years now and still going strong.

Chandler had no idea how much longer he could continue being a detective. It was all getting to him. The stench of the work, the feel of his hands in rubber gloves, the taking of tiny, measured steps for fear of trampling a bit of evidence that might cost somebody his life or let a butcher go free. The paperwork, the slick defense attorneys asking the same questions, plotting the same verbal traps, the bored judges reading off the sentencing guidelines like they were parceling out test results. The robotic looks of the defendants who said nothing, showed no emotion, went to prison with all their buddies, their institution of higher learning, coming out much more accomplished criminals.

The ringing phone cut short these depressing thoughts.

"Hello?" He listened for a couple of minutes, gave a series of instructions and hung up. A slug had been found in the alleyway where Michael Fiske's body had been discovered. It apparently had ricocheted off one wall and gotten wedged in some trash that had fallen behind a Dumpster. From what Chandler had been told, the slug was in very good shape with little projectile deformity. The lab would have to confirm that it was actually the bullet that had killed the young clerk. That would be fairly easy to determine for a sickening reason: The slug would have blood, bone and brain tissue residue on it that could be linked pretty much conclusively to the head of Michael Fiske. With the bullet in hand, they could now search hard for the murder weapon. Ballistics could match the slug to the gun that had fired it with the reliability of matching fingerprints to a human hand.

Chandler rose and went into the living room, purposely leaving his own gun behind. He sat down in a recliner that matched his bulky proportions. The room was dark and he did not move to turn on a light. He had too many lights around him at work. Lights in his office beating down on him every day.

Harsher lights in the autopsy room, that made every piece of flesh enormous, ominously raw, memorable to the point of Chandler's excusing himself every once in a great while to go to the men's room, where his stomach showed its appreciation for the polished skill of official dismemberment. The popping lights of the photographers at a crime scene or a courthouse. Too many damn lights. Darkness was quiet, darkness was soothing. Darkness was how he wanted his retirement to be. Cool and dark. Like his fountain in the backyard.

Warren McKenna's words had disturbed Chandler, though he had tried hard not to show it. He couldn't bring himself to accept that John Fiske could murder his own brother. But, truth be known, wouldn't that be exactly what Fiske wanted Chandler to believe? But then he had something else to think about. Michael Fiske's phone calls to Fort Jackson. And now Rufus Harms's escape. Were they connected? Fiske was covering for Sara Evans, that was clear. Chandler shook his head. He would have to sleep on it, because his old brain was running on empty.

He started to get up and then stopped abruptly. The arms suddenly encircled his neck, startling him. His hands gripped the person's forearms as his eyes popped huge. His gun — where the hell was his gun?

"Working hard or hardly working?"

He immediately relaxed and looked up into Juanita's face. The edges of her mouth were crinkled into the beginnings of a smile. Her face always held that same look, as though she were about to tell a joke or laugh at one. That look never failed to cheer him up no matter how lousy his day had been, no matter how many bodies he had poked and probed.

He put a hand on his heaving chest. "Damn, woman, you sneak up on me like that again, the only thing I'm going to be working is my angel wings."

She sat down on his lap. She was wearing a long white robe, bare feet showing. "Come on, now, a big, strong fella like yourself? And aren't you being a bit presumptuous about those angel wings?"

He slid an arm around her waist, which, after three children, wasn't as small as on their wedding night, but then neither was his. They had *grown* together, he often liked to say. Balance was essential in life. One fatty and one skinny was just heading for disaster.

There was no one alive who knew him better than Juanita. Maybe that was really the one important product of a successful marriage: the knowledge that there was one other soul out there who had your number, all the way down to the last possible decimal place, out there with pi, maybe more; if that was possible, Juanita had his.

He smiled back at her. "Sure, I'm one big, strong guy, but sensitive, baby. Us sensitive types, you just never know what might knock us over. And after a life spent fighting crime, I thought the Lord would be up there right now sewing together a nice fancy pair of angel wings for me, size extra-large, of course. He's all-knowing, so He'll be aware of the fact that I've spread some in my old age." He gave her a kiss on the cheek and they held hands. She swept her fingers through his disappearing hair. She could sense that his humor was forced.

"Buford, why don't you tell me what's bothering you so we can talk about it and then you can come to bed? It's getting pretty late. Tomorrow's always another day."

Chandler smiled at her remark. "Hey, what happened to my poker face? As I look a culprit in the eye and wear him down without ever revealing what I'm really thinking."

"You stink at poker. So talk to me, baby."

She rubbed at his kinked-up neck and he reciprocated by massaging her long feet.

"You remember that young man I was telling you about? John Fiske? His brother was a clerk at the Supreme Court?"

"I remember. And now another clerk dead too."

"Right. Well, I was over at his brother's apartment tonight, going through it for evidence collection. McKenna, that agent from the FBI, showed up."

"The one you said was wound up like a grenade ready to blow? Couldn't figure him out?"

"He's the one."

"Mmm-hmm."

"Well, we found a life insurance policy that pays John Fiske half a million dollars upon his brother's death."

"So, they were family, weren't they? You have life insurance, don't you? I get rich if you die, right?" She lightly smacked the top of his head. "You better have, anyway. Promising me all this nice stuff my whole life and never delivering. I better be rich when your sorry butt kicks off."

They both laughed and exchanged lingering hugs.

"Fiske never told me about the insurance policy. I mean, come on, that's a classic motive for murder."

"Well, maybe he doesn't know about the policy."

"Maybe," Chandler conceded. "Anyway, McKenna laid out this whole theory that has Fiske killing his brother for the money, getting another clerk at the Court to help him because she's got a thing for him and then throwing all this misdirection at us, offering to help with the investigation and whatnot. Even lying about an intruder at his brother's apartment. I have to admit, he put together a

480

pretty convincing argument, at least on the surface."

"So John Fiske was at his brother's apartment?"

"Yep. Claims some guy hit him there and took off. Maybe stole some stuff from the apartment, something that tied in to the murder."

"Well, if John Fiske was at his brother's apartment and made up the story about this intruder person, and he knew about the life insurance policy, why didn't he search his brother's apartment for the policy? Why leave it for you to find and get suspicious?"

Chandler stared at her, wide-eyed.

"Buford, are you okay?"

"Damn, sweetie, I thought I was the detective in the family. Now, how the hell did I miss that one?"

"Because you're overworked and under-appreciated, that's why." She got up and extended her hand to his. "But if you come upstairs right now, I will show you some extra-special appreciation. Leave your sensitive side down here, though, baby, and just bring your other parts upstairs." She looked at him with heavy-lidded eyes that he knew did not indicate sleepiness.

Chandler quickly rose, took her hand and together they walked up the stairs.

CHAPTER FORTY-SEVEN

As the Jeep raced down the road, Tremaine scrutinized the passengers of each car they passed.

"The damn luck," Rayfield moaned. "We couldn't have missed them by more than a few minutes."

Tremaine ignored him, focusing instead on the car in front of them. The dome light of the car came on as they passed, revealing the driver and passenger. The passenger was unfolding a map.

As Tremaine stared at the car's interior he hit the brakes, ripped the Jeep to the left and went across the median. The vehicle bumped and jostled in the grassy ditch before the tires found asphalt again and they were heading back toward Rider's office.

Rayfield grabbed Tremaine's shoulder. "What the hell are you doing?"

"They suckered us. The guy and the gal. Their story was bullshit."

"How do you know that?"

"The light in the bathroom."

"The light? What about it?"

"It wasn't on. The bitch was in there in the dark. It hit me when I saw the dome light go on in the car back there. There was no light coming from under the bathroom door when she was in there. When she opened the door she didn't hit the light switch because the bathroom was already dark. She wasn't using the can. She was standing in the bathroom in the pitch-dark. And guess why?"

Rayfield's face went pale. "Because Harms and his brother were in there too." While he looked at the road ahead he had another thought. "The guy said his name was John Michaels. Could it have been John Fiske?"

"And the girl was Sara Evans. That's what I'm thinking. You better call and let the others know."

Rayfield picked up the cell phone. "We'll never catch up to Harms now."

"Yes, we will."

"How the hell can we?"

Tremaine drew on thirty years of Army training, studying what the other side would do in a particular scenario. "Fiske said he saw them get in a car. Opposite of a car is a truck. He said it was an old car. Opposite of that is a *new* truck. He said they were going north, so we go south. It's only been five minutes. We'll catch them."

"I hope to God you're right. If they were at Rider's office —" He broke off and looked anxiously out the window.

Tremaine looked over at him. "Then that means the Harms brothers ain't running.

That means they were looking for something Rider had. And that sure as hell is not good news for us." He nodded at the phone. "Make that call. We'll take care of Harms and his brother. They'll have to deal with Fiske and the woman."

Because of the high-profile nature of the case, the FBI had offered the use of its laboratory to perform the analysis on the slug found in the alley. After comparing tissue samples taken from Michael Fiske's remains, the slug was deemed to have been fired through his brain. The slug was a 9mm of a type typically carried by law enforcement personnel.

With that information, Agent McKenna sat down in front of a computer terminal at the Hoover Building and typed in a high-priority request to the Virginia State Police. Within a few minutes he had his answer. John Fiske had a 9mm SIG-Sauer registered to his name, a carryover from his cop days. Within minutes McKenna was in his car. Two hours later he turned off Interstate 95 and headed through the darkened streets of downtown Richmond. His car rumbled over the aged and uneven streets of Shockoe Slip. He parked in a secluded area near the old train station.

Ten minutes later he was standing in John Fiske's office, having picked the locks of the building and the lawyer's office with remarkable ease. He looked around the darkened space using a small light. He had decided to search Fiske's office first rather than his apartment. It only took a couple of minutes until he found it. The 9mm pistol was relatively light and compact. Wearing gloves, McKenna palmed it for a moment and then put it in his pocket.

He shone his light around the rest of the office. The beam caught on something and he went over to the bookcase. He picked up the framed picture. The flashlight kicked up too much glare on the glass covering the photo, so McKenna took it over to the window and looked at it under the moonlight.

The Fiske brothers looked like any others, standing side by side. Michael Fiske was taller and better-looking than his older brother, but the fire in John Fiske's eyes burned with a greater intensity. John had on his police uniform, so this had been taken a while back, McKenna knew. The older brother had seen much of life wearing that uniform, just as McKenna had in his career at the FBI. Sometimes those experiences gave you that fire, or else harshly took it away.

He put the photo back and left the office. In another five minutes the FBI agent's car was heading north once again. Two hours later, back at his home in a well-to-do northern Virginia suburb, McKenna sat in his small study and alternated sipping on a beer and pursing his lips around a cigarette. He held the pistol he had taken from Fiske's office. It was nicely maintained, a solid piece of work. Fiske had made a good choice in ordnance. As a cop he would have relied on this weapon to survive. Years ago policemen rarely had to pull their sidearm. That had changed.

Fiske had killed a man with this gun, McKenna knew. Fired the shot that had taken another's life. McKenna understood the complexities of that journey — a journey that was typically compressed within the span of a few seconds. The heat of the metal, the nauseating smell of exploded powder. Unlike in the movies, a bullet didn't blow a man backward several feet. A man fell where you shot him; made him crap and pee in his pants, plunged him to the dirt without a word. McKenna had killed a man too. It was quick, reflexive; he had seen the eyes bulge out, the body twist. Then McKenna had gone back to the spot where he had fired from and noted the two bullet holes on the wall on either side of where he had stood. The dead man had gotten off his own shots. They had miraculously passed on either side of the FBI agent. McKenna would later learn that the dead man had an eye disability that threw off his depth perception. McKenna had gone on, lived to see his wife and kids because the dead man had a wobbly pupil. On the drive home, McKenna had soiled his pants.

He put the pistol down and cast his thoughts forward now. His snitch in the clerks' office had paid off. Tomorrow, both Fiske and Evans would face some tough questioning. He would get hold of Chandler first thing, lay the facts before him, and let the pugnacious homicide detective do his duty. McKenna got up and walked around the room. On the walls were framed photos of him with a number of important people. Carefully arranged on a side table were the numerous awards and commendations Warren McKenna had earned with his wits and his courage as an FBI agent. He had led a long, productive career on the side of law enforcement, but that had not made up for one event that had caused him great shame ever since. It had happened so many years ago, and yet was still one of the clearest memories he possessed. What he had done back then was, today, compelling him to frame John Fiske for a crime.

He put out the cigarette and moved silently through the house. His wife had long since gone to bed. His two children were grown and on their own. He had done all right financially, although FBI agents never earned the big dollars, unless they gave up the badge. But his wife, a partner in a major D.C. law firm, had. Thus, the house was large, expensively furnished, and basically empty. He looked back in the direction of the den. His distinguished career, neatly tallied on that table, lastingly captured in those photos. He took a long breath as the darkness clung to him. Penance was a lifelong responsibility.

The plane touched down and taxied to a stop. Commercial jets and some private planes could not land at National after ten o'clock at night because of noise-level restrictions, but the small aircraft Fiske and Sara were flying in could take off and land pretty much wherever it wanted. A few minutes later Fiske and Sara were headed toward the parking garage at National Airport.

"We flew all the way out there, nearly got slaughtered and we came back empty-handed," Sara muttered. "Brilliant idea on my part."

"That's where you're wrong," Fiske said.

They reached the car and climbed in. "So what exactly did we learn?" she asked.

"Quite a few things. One, we saw Rufus Harms face-to-face. I think he's telling the truth, whatever the truth happens to be."

"You can't be sure of that."

"He came to Rider's office, Sara, when he should be doing his best to get out of the country. He came to get the appeal he had written. Why would he do that unless he believed it to be true?"

"I don't know," Sara admitted. "If it was his appeal, why not just write it again?"

"Rider had filed his own document with it. You saw that in my brother's briefcase. Now that Rider's dead, that was something Harms couldn't duplicate. He also mentioned something he got from the Army. A letter. Maybe he thought that would help, so he came to get both."

"That makes more sense."

"The Army guys were on a blood hunt. They didn't come there to look for Rufus Harms. They came there to search Rider's office."

"How do you know that?"

"They didn't even ask us if we'd seen anyone suspicious, anyone who looked like Rufus. I had to volunteer the information. And they weren't doing it in their official capacity. The middle of the night, machine guns. They weren't MPs or anything. They were of fairly high rank, judging from their age and attitude. Barging into civilian offices with machine guns at midnight, that's not how the Army does things."

"Maybe you're right."

"So I'm thinking whatever was in that appeal had something to do with those guys personally."

"But we don't even know who they are."

"Yes, we do. Rufus said their names at Rider's office. Tremaine, Vic Tremaine —

489

and the other guy's name is Rayfield. They're in the Army, which means they must be connected with Fort Jackson somehow. Rufus said they did something to him. I'm sure he meant back in the stockade."

"John, even if they somehow encouraged him to kill that little girl, or even ordered him to do it for some hellish reason, the most they'd get pinned on is some sort of accessory. And after all these years? If that's all Harms has, he has nothing, you damn well know that."

"The problem is we don't know enough about the actual events back then. If some people visited Harms in the stockade on the night the little girl was killed, there should be a record of that."

Sara looked skeptical. "After twenty-five years?"

"And then there's the letter from the Army that Harms mentioned. What sort of letter would the Army be sending a court-martialed con?"

"Do you think the letter somehow triggered this?"

"It could have had some information that Harms didn't know about before. I don't know what it could be or why he wouldn't have known it before, though."

"Wait a minute. If Tremaine and Rayfield are from Fort Jackson, why would they let that kind of a letter reach Harms? Isn't a prisoner's mail censored?"

Fiske thought for a moment. "Maybe it just slipped through."

"Or maybe it didn't come to the prison at all. Josh Harms seems to know all about it; maybe he got the letter, put two and two together and told Rufus about it."

"And then Rufus maybe fakes a heart attack somehow, gets taken to the nearest hospital and that's where Josh breaks him out?"

"That works."

"I just wish we knew what happened at Fort Jackson that day. It's pretty clear from what Josh and Rufus said that my brother visited him at the prison."

"Why not call or go to the prison? Then we can find out if Michael was there."

Fiske shook his head. "If those two guys are at the prison, they'll have covered that up, maybe transferred anyone who saw Mike out of the place. And we can't go to Chandler with it, because what would we say? Two Army guys are looking for a prisoner who escaped from their custody. So what?"

"Well, if Rayfield and Tremaine work at the prison, then Michael walked right into the lion's den. Even though you two weren't close, I'm really surprised Michael didn't try to call you for help. He might still be alive if he had."

Fiske froze at her words and then closed his

eyes. He said nothing more as they drove along.

When they reached Sara's cottage, Fiske went directly to the refrigerator and grabbed a beer.

"Do you have any cigarettes?"

She raised her eyebrows. "I didn't think you smoked."

"I haven't for years. But I really need one right now."

"Well, you're in luck." She pulled a chair over and set it next to the kitchen counter. She slipped off her pumps and stepped onto the chair's seat. "I've found that if I make it as difficult as possible to get to my little stash, I crave them less. I guess I have a real lazy streak."

Fiske watched as she stood on tiptoe and reached up over the highest cabinet, her fingers barely scraping the top edge.

"Sara, come on, let me do that. You're going to kill yourself."

"I've got it, John. Just about there." She stretched her body as far as she could and Fiske found himself staring at the tops of her exposed thighs as her dress had risen. She started to sway a bit, so he placed a hand on her waist to steady her. On the back of her right thigh was a small birthmark, almost perfectly triangular in shape and a dull red in color. It seemed to pulse with each of her exertions. He glanced down at her feet as he continued to hold on to her, the bottom of his hand resting lightly on the softness of her hip. Her toes were long and uncramped, as though she went barefoot often. He looked away.

"Got 'em." She held up the pack. "Camels okay?"

"As long as you can light one end, I don't really care." He helped her down, took out a cigarette, and then looked at her. "You in? You did all the work." She nodded and he nudged one out for her. They took a moment lighting up and Sara joined Fiske with a beer. They went out onto the small rear deck that looked out over the river and sat down in a faded wooden glider.

"You made a good choice in housing," he commented.

"The first time I saw it, I could see myself living here forever." She drew her legs up under her, tapped her cigarette against the deck rail, and watched as the breeze carried the ash away. She arched her long neck and took a long sip of beer.

"Impulsive of you."

She put the beer down and studied his face. "Haven't you ever felt that way about something?"

He thought about it for a moment. "Not really. So what's next? Husband, kids? Solely the career path?" He took a puff and waited for her to answer.

She took another swallow of beer and watched the car lights pass over the Woodrow Wilson Bridge in the distance. Then she stood up. "Want to go sailing?"

He looked up at her in surprise. "A little late for that, isn't it?"

"No later than our last boat trip. I've got the permit and the boat lights. We'll just do a lazy circle and come back in." Before he could answer, she disappeared into the cottage. Within a couple minutes she came back out wearing jean cutoffs, a tank top and deck shoes, her hair pulled back in a bun.

Fiske glanced down at his dress shirt, slacks and loafers. "I didn't bring my sailor suit."

"That's okay. You're not the sailor, I am." She had two fresh beers. They walked down to the dock. It was miserably humid, and Fiske quickly broke a sweat helping Sara ready the sails. While standing on the bow to rig the jig sail, Fiske slipped and almost tumbled into the water. "If you had fallen into the Potomac, we wouldn't need the moon to sail by, you'd be glowing all by yourself," Sara said, laughing.

The water was flat, no shore wind evident, so Sara fired up the auxiliary engine and they motored out into the middle of the river, where the sails finally caught a breeze and swelled with the warm air. For the next hour they moved in slow ovals across the river. The boat had a light, and the moon was at three-quarters and there were no other craft on the river.

Fiske took a turn at the helm, with Sara coaching him at the tiller until he felt comfortable. Each time they tacked into the wind, the mainsail would shudder and drop, Fiske would duck and Sara would swing the boom around and watch as the canvas filled again and propelled them along.

She looked over at him and smiled. "It feels magical to catch something invisible and yet so powerful, and compel it to do your bidding, doesn't it?" The way she said it, so girlish, with so much frank wonder, he had to smile. They drank beer and both smoked another cigarette after several humorous attempts at lighting up in the face of a stiff wind. They talked about things unrelated to present events, and both felt relieved to be able to do so even for a short time.

"You have a nice smile," Sara remarked. "You should use it more often."

By the time they headed back in, Fiske had a blister on the inside of his thumb from clutching the boom line.

They docked the boat and tied down the sails. Sara went up to the cottage and came back with more beer and a bag of chips and salsa. "Don't let it be said that I don't feed my guests."

They sat on the boat and drank, and whittled down at the chips. The wind started to pick up and the temperature dipped suddenly as a late night storm rolled in. They watched as the clouds turned black-edged and pops of lightning appeared on the horizon. In her tank top shirt, Sara shivered a little and Fiske put his arm around her. She leaned into him. Then a few drops of rain hit and Sara jumped up. With Fiske's help she pulled out the vinyl covers and snapped them into place across the open compartments of the boat.

"We better head in," she said.

They walked up to the cottage, running the last few feet as it started to pour.

"Long day tomorrow," Sara said, looking at the kitchen clock while patting her wet hair with a paper towel.

"Especially after no sleep last night," Fiske added, yawning. They turned the lights off and headed upstairs.

Sara said goodnight and went to her room. Fiske watched through the doorway as she opened the window, letting the breeze in along with some of the rain. A shaft of lightning flared across the sky and connected with the earth somewhere. The boom was deafening. So much power, Fiske thought. He went down the hallway to the other bedroom and undressed. He sat on the bed in his undershorts and T-shirt, listening to the rain. His room was stuffy, but he made no move to open a window. The house was too old to have central air, but it didn't have window-mounted air conditioners either. Apparently Sara preferred the river breeze to cool her. A clock hanging on the wall ticked the seconds at him. He caught himself measuring his pulse against it. His heart was pumping fast, gallons of blood gushing through him.

He pulled on his trousers, rose and went down the hallway. Her room was dark now, but the door was still open. The curtains kicked up and down with the bursts of wind. He stood in the doorway and watched her as she lay in bed, only a sheet over her.

She was watching him watching her. Was she waiting for him? Letting him come to her this time? He moved into the room, hesitantly, as though this was the first time he had entered a woman's bedroom. She didn't move or speak, neither encouraging nor discouraging.

He lay down next to her and she immediately moved next to him, as though refusing to give him the opportunity to rethink his decision, to flee from her. She wore no clothes. Her body was warm, her skin smooth; the breasts spongy and heat-filled; the scent of the outside air thick over them. Sara's hair was tangled and falling in her face. Her lips clenched and then opened; her fingers stroked him gently, everywhere.

Together, they worked his pants off and let them fall to the floor.

They kissed, lightly at first, and then with greater depth. She moved to raise his T-shirt, to rub his chest, his belly against hers. He moved her hand away and pulled his shirt back down. As the rain hit the roof and glanced off the windows, Fiske slid off his undershorts, lifted his body up, and eased himself down on top of her.

Sara awoke early, the first shafts of sunlight just dropping over the windowsill. Behind the storm had come waves of deliciously chilly air, and a sky that would transform fully from pink and gray to a deep blue in another hour. She put out her arm to touch him and felt the empty space next to her. She quickly sat up and looked around. Wrapping the sheet around her, she rushed down the hallway and checked the guest room. Empty. So was the bathroom. In a panic she reached the top of the stairs and stopped, a smile edging across her face.

She watched Fiske as he poured a cup of coffee and then returned to cracking eggs in a bowl, to which he then added grated cheddar cheese. Sara stood there, the smell of simmering onion reaching her nostrils. Fiske was fully dressed, his hair damp from the shower. As he turned to pull open the refrigerator door, he saw her.

Sara clutched the sheet a little tighter around her.

"I thought you might have left."

"Thought I'd let you sleep in. It was a late night."

A wonderful night, she wanted to say, but didn't. "You okay?" she asked as casually as she could, unable as yet to fully read the subtle messages behind his words, his movements and expressions. Especially about something as recent as their lovemaking. Was the choice of eggs over lying next to her until they both awoke a bad sign?

"I'm fine, Sara." He smiled, as if to show her that this was actually so.

She smiled back. "Whatever you're making smells wonderful."

"Nothing fancy. Western omelet."

"I usually have dry toast and kitchen sink coffee. It's a nice change. Do I have time to shower?"

"Make it fast."

"Not like last night." She smiled, flicked her eyebrows and turned away. The sheet was fully open in the back.

Fiske watched her go, aroused again at the sight of her naked body, the delicate, sensual tensing of her back, legs and buttocks. He sat down at the kitchen table and looked around the cozy space. He had stood on the rear deck for a while and watched the sun slowly rise over him. Dawn always seemed so much purer over water, as though these two essential elements of life, heat and water, produced a near-spiritual performance. He glanced back at the stairs as the sound of the shower started. He had watched Sara after she had fallen asleep. In the darkness of the night, their mingled scents a second skin, it had seemed as though he belonged next to her, and she to him. But then the blunt clarity of morning had come. Fiske lifted the coffee cup to his lips, but then quickly put it back down. If he had called his brother back right away, Mike would be alive right now. Fiske could never dodge that truth. He would, in fact, have to live with it forever.

CHAPTER FORTY-EIGHT

Elizabeth Knight also awoke at the crack of dawn, showering and dressing quickly. Jordan Knight still slept soundly and she made no move to wake him. She brewed the coffee, poured a cup, took her notebook and sat out on the terrace and watched the sun come up. She looked over every page of her materials for oral argument today, which included the last bench memo Steven Wright would ever author. His blood seemed to replace the ink on the page. As she thought this, she had to fight back the tears again. She swore to herself that he wouldn't die in vain. Ramsey would not carry this day, this case. Knight already had great incentive to make sure that Barbara Chance and women like her could sue the Army for damages for, in essence, condoning the cruel, sadistic and illegal behavior of its male personnel. The organization had not been invented that deserved immunity from such action. But now her motivation, her will to win, to beat Ramsey, had grown a thousandfold. She finished her coffee, packed her briefcase and took a cab to the Supreme Court.

★ ★ ★

Fiske rubbed his reddened eyes and tried to put the memory of the night before and its bewildering complexities out of his mind. He sat in a special section reserved for members of the Supreme Court bar. He looked over at Sara, who sat with the other clerks in a section of seats perpendicular to the bench. She looked over at him and smiled.

When the justices appeared from behind the curtain and took their seats, Perkins finished his little speech and everyone came to rigid attention. Fiske looked over at Knight. Her subtle movements, an elbow resting lightly here, a finger sifting through paper there, were those of nearly uncontrollable raw energy. She looked, he thought, like a rocket straining at its tethers, desperately wanting to explode. He looked over at Ramsey. The man was smiling, looking calm, in control. If Fiske were a betting man, though, his chips would be at the extreme right of the bench, directly in front of Justice Elizabeth Knight.

The case of *Chance v. United States* was called.

Chance's attorney, a hired gun from Harvard Law School, who made a practice of appearing before the Supreme Court with much success, launched into his argument with vigor. Until Ramsey cut in.

"You're aware of the *Feres* Doctrine, Mr.

Barr?" Ramsey asked, referring to the 1950 Supreme Court opinion first granting immunity from lawsuits to the military.

Barr smiled. "Unfortunately, yes."

"Aren't you asking us to overturn fifty years of Court precedent?" Ramsey looked up and down the bench as he said this. "How can we decide this case in favor of your client without turning the military and this Court on their heads?"

Knight did not let Barr answer. "The Court did not allow that argument to dissuade it from overturning the segregated school system in this country. If the cause is right, the means are justified, and precedent cannot stand in the way of that."

"Please answer my question, Mr. Barr," Ramsey persisted.

"I think this case is distinguishable."

"Really? There is no question that Barbara Chance and her male superiors were in uniform, on government property and performing their official duties when the sexual episodes occurred?"

"I would hardly call coerced sex, 'official duties.' But nonetheless, the fact that her superior used his rank to coerce her into what amounted to a rape, and —"

"And," Knight cut in, seemingly unable to remain quiet, "the superior officers at the base in question and the regional command were aware these events had taken place —

had been advised in writing of them, even — and had taken no action to even investigate the matter other than in a cursory fashion. It was Barbara Chance who called in the local police. They undertook an investigation which resulted in the truth coming to light. That truth clearly establishes a cause of action that would result in damages with respect to any other organization in this country."

Fiske stared from Ramsey to Knight. It was suddenly as though, instead of nine justices, there were only two. In Fiske's mind, the courtroom had been transformed into a boxing ring, with Ramsey the champ and Knight the talented contender, but still an underdog.

"We're talking about the military here, Mr. Barr," Ramsey said, but he looked at Knight. "This Court has ruled that the military is sui generis. That is the precedent you face. Your case deals with chain-of-command issues. An inferior personnel to her superior. That is just the issue that this Court has — several times in the past — addressed and unequivocally decided that it would not intrude upon the military's presumptive immunity. That was the law yesterday, and it is the law today. Which gets me back to my original statement. For us to hold for your client, this court must reverse its position on a long and deeply followed line of precedents. That is what you are asking us to do."

"And as I mentioned earlier, stare decisis is clearly not infallible," Knight said, referring to the Court's practice of adhering to and upholding its previous decisions.

Back and forth Knight and Ramsey went at it. For every salvo fired by one, there was an answer fired by the other.

The other justices, and Mr. Barr, Fiske thought, were reduced to interested spectators.

When the lawyer for the United States, James Anderson, stepped forward to deliver his argument, Knight did not even let him begin a sentence.

"Why does allowing a damage suit against the Army for condoning a hostile environment for women interfere with the chain of command?" she asked him.

"It clearly impacts negatively on the integrity of the relationship between superior and subordinate personnel," Anderson promptly replied.

"So let me see if I understand your reasoning. By allowing the military over the years to poison, gas, maim, kill and rape its soldiers with impunity, and stripping the victims of any legal recourse, that will somehow improve the relationship, the integrity, of the military and its personnel? I'm sorry, but I'm not quite getting the connection."

Fiske had to stop himself from laughing

out loud. His respect for Knight as a lawyer and judge increased tenfold as she finished her statement. In two sentences, she had reduced the Army's entire case to the level of absurdity. He looked over at Sara. Her gaze was trained on Knight, with, Fiske thought, a great deal of pride.

Anderson reddened slightly. "The military, as the chief justice has pointed out, is a unique, special entity. Allowing lawsuits to fly at will can only inhibit and destroy that special bond between personnel, the need for discipline that is at the very core of military preparation and readiness."

"So the military is special?"

"Right."

"Because it serves to defend and protect us?"

"Exactly."

"So we have the four branches of the Armed Forces which are already covered by that immunity. Why don't we extend this immunity to other special organizations? Like the fire department? The police department? They protect us. The Secret Service? They protect the president, arguably the most important person in the country. How about hospitals? They save our lives. Why not let hospitals be immune from suit in the event male doctors rape female personnel?"

"We are getting far outside the boundaries of this case," Ramsey said sternly.

"I think those boundaries are precisely what we're trying to determine," Knight fired back.

"I believe that *U.S. v. Stanley* —" Anderson began.

"I'm glad you mentioned it. Let me briefly recount the facts of that case," Knight said. She wanted this heard. By her fellow justices, several of whom were on the Court when the case had been decided, as well as by the public. To Knight, the *Stanley* case was one of the worst miscarriages of justice in history and represented everything that was wrong with the Court. That had also been Steven Wright's conclusion in his bench memo. And she intended to make those conclusions heard both today and when it came time to win a majority vote on this case.

When Knight spoke, her voice was strong and resonating.

"Master Sergeant James Stanley was in the Army in the fifties and volunteered for a program which he was told had to do with testing protective clothing against gas warfare. The testing was conducted in Maryland, at the Aberdeen Proving Grounds. Stanley signed up for it, but he was never asked to wear any special clothing or do testing with gas masks or anything. He only talked to some psychologists for great lengths of time about a variety of personal subjects, was given some water to drink during these sessions and that was it. In

1975, Stanley, whose life had gone downhill — inexplicable behavior, discharge from the Army, divorce — received a letter from the Army asking him to participate in a follow-up exam by members of the Army who had been given LSD in 1959, because the Army wanted to study the long-term effects of the drug. Under the pretense of testing clothing against gas warfare, the Army had slipped him and other soldiers LSD without his knowledge."

A collective gasp went up from the general public's seats as they heard this, and the spectators started talking to each other. Perkins actually had to bang his gavel, an almost unheard-of event.

As Fiske sat there and listened, it occurred to him how important this case was. Rufus Harms had filed an appeal with this Court. Was he also seeking to sue the Army? Something terrible had happened to him while in the military. Certain men had done something to him that had ruined his life and resulted in the death of a little girl. Rufus wanted his freedom, wanted justice. He had the truth on his side, Rufus had proclaimed. And yet even with the truth, under the current law, it didn't matter. Just like Sergeant Stanley, Private Rufus Harms would lose.

Knight continued, secretly well pleased with the audience's reaction. "The psychologist was employed by the CIA. The CIA and the Army had undertaken a joint effort on the study of the drug's effects, because the CIA had received reports that the Soviet Union had stockpiled the drug and the Army wanted to know how it might be used against its soldiers in wartime. That sort of thing. Stanley, who rightly blamed the Army for destroying his life, sued. His case finally made it to the Supreme Court." She paused. "And he lost."

Another gasp came from the public.

Fiske looked around at Sara. Her eyes were still fixed on Knight. Fiske peered over at Ramsey. He was livid.

"In effect, what you're asking is for this court to deny to Barbara Chance and similar plaintiffs one of the most cherished constitutional rights we possess as a people: the right to our day in court. Isn't that what you're asking? Letting the guilty go unpunished?"

"Mr. Anderson," Ramsey broke in. "What has happened to the men who perpetrated these sexual assaults?"

"At least one has been court-martialed, found guilty and imprisoned," Anderson again promptly replied.

Ramsey smiled triumphantly. "So hardly unpunished."

"Mr. Anderson, the record below clearly establishes that the actions for which the man was imprisoned have been going on for a very long time and were known to higher-ups in the Army, who declined to take any action. In point of fact only when Barbara Chance went to the local police did an investigation ensue. So tell me, have the guilty been punished?"

"I would say it depends on your definition of guilt."

"Who's policing the military, Mr. Anderson? To make sure what happened to Sergeant Stanley doesn't happen again?"

"The military is policing itself. And doing a good job."

"*Stanley* was decided in 1986. Since that time we've had Tailhook, the still-unexplained incidents in the Persian Gulf War, and now the rape of female Army personnel. Do you call that doing a good job?"

"Well, every large organization will have small pockets of trouble."

Knight bristled. "I rather doubt if the victims of these crimes would describe them as small pockets of trouble."

"Of course, I didn't mean —"

"When I alluded to extending immunity to police, firemen, hospitals, you didn't agree with that, did you?"

"No. Too many exceptions to the rule disproves the rule."

"You recall the *Challenger* explosion, of course?" Anderson nodded. "The survivors of the civilians on board the shuttle were entitled to sue the government, and the contractor that built the shuttle, for damages. However, the families of the military personnel on board were denied that right because of the immunity granted to the military by this court. Do you consider that fair?"

Anderson fell back upon the old reliable. "If we allow lawsuits against the military it will unnecessarily complicate the national security of this country."

"And that's really the whole ball of wax," Ramsey said, pleased that Anderson had raised the point. "It's a balancing act, and this court has already determined where that balance lies."

"Precisely, Mr. Chief Justice," Anderson said. "It's bedrock law."

Knight almost smiled. "Really? I thought bedrock law was the constitutional right of citizens of this country to seek redress of their grievances before the courts. No immunity from suit was granted to the military by any law of this country. Congress did not see fit to do it. In fact, it was this court in 1950 which invented, out of broadcloth, such specialized treatment, and they apparently did so, in part, because they were afraid that allowing such suits would bankrupt the U.S. Treasury. I would hardly call that bedrock."

"However, it is the controlling precedent now," Ramsey pointed out.

"Precedents change," Knight replied, "particularly if they're wrong." Ramsey's words truly irked her, since the chief justice had no problem overturning precedents of

511

long standing when it suited him.

Anderson said, "With all due respect, I think the military is better suited to handle this matter internally, Justice Knight."

"Mr. Anderson, do you dispute this court's jurisdiction or authority to hear and decide this case?"

"Of course not."

"This court has to determine whether serving your country in the military ironically carries the price of stripping away virtually all protections one has as a citizen."

"I wouldn't phrase it quite that way."

"However, I would, Mr. Anderson. It's really a question of justice." She locked eyes with Ramsey. "And if we can't deliver justice here, then I truly despair to think of where one could find it."

As Fiske listened to these impassioned words, he looked again at Sara. As though she somehow knew he was looking, she glanced at him.

Fiske had the strong sense that she was thinking the same thing he was: Even if they somehow solved this whole mystery and the truth finally came out, would Rufus Harms ever really find justice?

CHAPTER FORTY-NINE

Josh Harms finished his sandwich and then idly smoked a cigarette as he watched his brother doze in the front seat of the truck. They were parked on an old logging road in a dense forest. Driving through the night, they had finally stopped because Josh could barely keep his eyes open, and he didn't trust his brother to drive, since Rufus hadn't been behind the wheel of a vehicle for almost thirty years. Besides, when they were on the road, Rufus, for obvious reasons, had to be in the back of the truck. Rufus had kept watch while his brother had dozed and now Josh had taken up the sentinel.

They had talked during the drive about what they were going to do. Much to his own surprise, Josh found himself arguing that they shouldn't go to Mexico.

"What the hell's going on with you? I didn't think you'd want any part of that. You said you didn't," Rufus had said in wonderment.

"I didn't. But once we made up our mind — hell, once I made up *my* mind — then all I'm saying is we should stick to it. I don't like being no wimp on shit like that. If you're going to do something, then you should do it."

"Look, Josh, if Fiske hadn't thought real fast, we'd both be dead right now. I don't want you on my conscience."

"See, that's where you ain't thinking. Hell, it ain't going to get any worse than it is. Why don't we see what we can do to help it get better? You were right: They deserve what's coming to 'em. Seeing those two boys at Rider's office, I almost shot 'em down in cold blood, and I ain't never done nothing like that in my whole life. Fiske and that woman, they stood up for us. Maybe they're shooting straight."

Rufus had stared at him. "And you don't have a problem with them?"

"What the hell, you think I'm racist?" Josh had pulled out a cigarette as he said this, a grin lighting his face.

"I can't figure you out, Josh."

"You ain't got to figure me out. I ain't figured me out, and I've had a long time to do it. All you got to do is decide if you want to go to Mexico or you want to stick it out. And don't worry about me. If there's anybody that can take care of himself, then you're looking at him."

That had done it, and as soon as his brother woke up, they were going to head back toward Virginia, hook up with Fiske and see what they could do. If it was proof that was needed, then they could get proof, somehow, some way, Josh believed. They had the truth on their side, and if that still didn't count for something, then they might as well go ahead and get themselves shot up.

Josh eyed the surrounding woods. The leaves had already started to turn here, and the way the sunlight cut and dipped through the foliage presented a pleasing combination of colors and textures. He often sat in the woods when hunting; he'd find an old log and rest his bones, taking in the simple beauty of the country, a marvel that didn't cost you a dime. After coming back from Southeast Asia, he had avoided the woods for several years. In Vietnam, the trees, the dirt, everything around you meant death by some of the most ingenious methods the Vietnamese could devise. He checked his watch. Another ten minutes and they would have to be on their way.

He looked back out the window and squinted as the sunlight reflected off something and hurt his eyes. He sucked in his next breath instead of letting it go, spit his cigarette out the window, started the engine and put the truck in gear.

"What the hell," Rufus said as he was jolted awake.

"Get your gun and keep your damn head down," Josh hollered at him. "It's Tremaine."

Rufus gripped his pistol and ducked down.

Tremaine charged from the woods and opened fire. The first shots from the machine gun hit the tailgate of the truck, blowing out one of the lights and riddling the frame with holes. A cone of dirt kicked up in the truck's wake and momentarily blinded Tremaine, who stopped shooting and ran forward, trying desperately to get a clear field of fire on the truck.

Sensing what Tremaine was trying to do, Josh cut the wheel to the left and the truck went off-road and onto what appeared to be the dry remains of a shallow creek bed. It was a good move for another reason, as Rayfield came flying down the road in the Jeep from the other direction, trying to box the truck in.

Rayfield stopped to let Tremaine climb in and they went after the truck.

"How in the hell did they catch up to us?" Rufus wondered aloud.

"Ain't no sense wasting time thinking about that. They're here," Josh shot back. He glanced in the rearview mirror and his eyes narrowed. The Jeep was more nimble and better built to maneuver through the woods than the bulky truck.

"They're going to shoot out the tires and then they got us like sitting ducks," Rufus said.

"Yeah, well, Vic should've shot those tires out first thing. That was his second mistake."

"What was his first?"

"Letting the sunlight hit his binoculars. I saw that long before I spotted that little bastard."

"Let's hope they keep making mistakes."

"We count on ourselves, and hope that's enough."

Back in the Jeep, Tremaine hung out the side and fired his weapon. The machine gun wasn't really worth a spit long-range, although in close quarters it could take out an entire platoon of men in a few seconds; he wanted just two. He slipped the machine gun strap off his shoulder and pulled out his sidearm.

"Get as close as you can," he barked to a very nervous-looking Rayfield. "If I can take out one of their tires, they'll plow right into a tree and our problems are over."

Rufus looked back through the window in the camper and saw what Tremaine was attempting to do. He slid open the glass separating the cab from the interior of the camper and drew a bead on the Jeep. He had not touched a gun in almost thirty years, basic training with a rifle his last experience with a firearm. When he fired, the explosion pierced his ears, the truck's cabin immediately full of the sickening fumes of burned metal, flashed powder. The bullet shattered the rear glass door of the camper shell and then flew at the Jeep like an angry, metal-jacketed hornet.

Tremaine ducked back into his vehicle and the Jeep swerved a little.

"Hit anything?" Josh asked.

"Bought us a little time." Rufus's hand was shaking, and he rubbed at his ears. "I forgot how loud these things are."

"Try firing an M-16 for three years. They're real loud, especially when they explode in your face. Hold on."

Josh cut the wheel to the right and then to the left to avoid several trees that had toppled across the creek bed. Beyond was a mass of scrub pines, oaks and brambles. With the Jeep closing in, Tremaine was again taking up his shooting position. Josh cut the truck to the right and through a narrow cleft in the trees and brush, leaves and slender branches slapping and tearing at the truck. But the maneuver had its intended effect because Tremaine had to duck back inside the Jeep to avoid having his head torn off by a tree limb.

The Jeep slowed down. The narrow lane ahead opened up a little, and Josh decided to take advantage, hoping Rayfield was losing a little of his nerve.

"Hold the wheel," he shouted to his brother.

Rufus gripped the steering wheel hard, alternating between looking at his brother and eyeing where the truck was heading.

Josh pulled his pistol and scanned the trees ahead. They were on a fairly level bit of ground now, so the truck didn't rock as much. He gripped the pistol with both hands, doing his best to figure distance and speed, and then selected what he wanted: a thick oak branch high up on a forty-footer. The branch was at least twenty feet long and four inches thick, with other, smaller branches growing from it, and it hung directly over the narrow lane. What had drawn Josh's attention was the fact that the branch was so long and heavy it had started to crack where it was attached to the trunk.

Josh slid his arm out the window, kept it parallel to the truck, took aim and started firing. The first bullet hit the tree trunk directly above where the branch joined it. Having now gauged the trajectory, Josh continued to fire, and each bullet after that hit squarely at the juncture of branch and trunk as the truck hurtled closer. For him it wasn't that extraordinary a display of marksmanship. As a game, he had been shooting at tree branches since he was old enough to carry a .22 rifle. Scaring coons and squirrels, having fun. Still, he had never attempted it in a moving vehicle with two men shooting at him.

Rufus had to keep his eyes open to steer, but he scrunched up his face with each shot. His ears were ringing so loudly you could have shouted in his face and he would not have been able to hear you. The heavy branch dropped a couple of inches as its support weakened. Josh kept firing, as sprays of wood chips shot off the oak like steam from an old train engine.

Tremaine saw what he was doing. "Gun it, gun it."

Rayfield hit the gas.

Josh never took his eyes off the branch as he kept firing. It gave some more, and finally gravity took over and it cracked and swung down. A layer of bark clung to the tree, then the branch slapped hard against the trunk, broke free completely and started coming down. Josh slammed on the accelerator and took the steering wheel back, passing by the tree as he did so.

"Go, go," Tremaine screamed at Rayfield.

However, Rayfield slammed on the brakes as about a thousand pounds of tree branch smashed into the middle of the narrow lane directly in front of them. Tremaine was almost thrown from the vehicle.

"Dammit, why in the hell did you stop?" Tremaine looked ready to turn his pistol on the man.

Rayfield was breathing very hard. "If I hadn't, that damn thing would've crushed us. This Jeep doesn't have a hard top, Vic."

Josh looked up ahead and then to the right where the path opened up some. He braked hard, swerved to the left, swung the truck around and then headed right and gunned the motor. The truck broke free from the brush, lifted a little off the ground as it went over a shallow gully, and landed in a clearing. Rufus's head hit the top of the cab's interior as the truck came back to earth.

"Damn, what're you doing?"

"Just hold tight."

Josh slammed on the gas again and Rufus looked up in time to see the small shack ahead of them that his brother had spotted seconds before.

Josh looked back and saw what he expected to see. Nothing. But it wouldn't take Tremaine and Rayfield long to work the Jeep around the obstacle.

Josh looked past the shack at an angle and could see the road that lay beyond it. He had been right. Where there was a shack in the woods, there usually was a road. He pulled the truck around onto the other side of the old structure. Both brothers' hearts sank. There was a road there, all right. But it had a large steel barricade blocking any passage. And on either side of the barricade were impenetrable woods. Josh looked back. They were trapped. Maybe he could hoof it, but Rufus wasn't built for speed, and Josh wasn't leaving his brother behind.

Josh's eyes narrowed again as he looked at the shack. The Jeep would be on them in another minute or so. Even now he could hear the machine gun efficiently tearing the tree limb apart so the Jeep could shove it aside.

A minute later the Jeep scaled the gully and made its way to the clearing. Rayfield slowed down as they scanned ahead and immediately saw the shack.

"Where'd they go?" he asked.

Tremaine checked the area with his binoculars and spotted the road as it snaked off through the woods. "That way," he shouted, pointing ahead.

Rayfield hit the gas and the Jeep shot around the corner of the shack. Instantly both men saw that the road was blocked off and Rayfield slammed the Jeep to a stop. With a roar, the truck, which had been hidden on the far side of the shack, exploded forward and hit the vehicle broadside, knocking it over on its side and flinging Rayfield and Tremaine out.

Rayfield landed on top of a pile of rotted stumps, his head at a vicious angle. He lay still.

Tremaine took cover behind the overturned Jeep and opened fire, forcing Josh to back the truck up, his head below the dashboard. Finally the truck engine died, steam pouring out from the hood, the front tires flattened by the machine-gun fire.

Josh came out the driver's side while Rufus covered him. Josh lunged, dropped to his knees and rolled until he made it to the rear of the truck, and then he peered out. Tremaine hadn't moved from his position. Josh could see the tip of the machine gun. Tremaine was probably putting in another clip just as Josh was doing, and taking a moment to study the tactical situation.

Josh's heart was pounding, and he rubbed at his eyes to clear the dirt and sweat away. He had been in many battles on both foreign and American soil, but the last one had been almost thirty years ago. Besides, it didn't matter: Every time, you were terrified that you were going to die. When somebody was shooting at you, it didn't exactly make you think more clearly. You reacted more than anything else.

Josh had an edge, though. There were two of them and only one of Tremaine. Josh peered out once more and then sprinted from behind the truck and made it to the edge of the shack.

"Rufus," he hollered. "On the count of three."

"Start counting," Rufus shouted back, tremors of fear in his voice.

Three seconds later Josh opened fire on Tremaine, the bullets pinging off the Jeep's frame. Rufus hustled to the back of the truck. He was stopped there, however, when Tremaine managed to fire a burst between the truck and the shack. The air smelled of gunfire, and of the sweat of frightened men.

Josh and Rufus looked at each other, and then Josh cracked a smile, sensing the rising panic in his brother.

"Hey, Vic," Josh yelled out, "how 'bout you throw down that damn widowmaker and come on out with your hands up?"

Tremaine responded by blowing a chunk of wood off the shack a little above Josh's head.

"Okay, okay, Vic, I hear you. Now, you be cool, you hear me, little buddy? Don't you worry, we'll bury you and Rayfield. Ain't gonna leave you for the bears and shit to chew on. That's bad shit. Animals eating dead bodies. You saw that in Nam, didn't you, Vic? Or maybe you was running too fast the other way to see that." While he was talking, Josh was motioning for Rufus to stay put and then pointing around the shack to show his brother what he was going to do.

Rufus nodded to show he understood. Josh was going to try to flush the man into his brother's field of vision and let Rufus cut him down. Rufus gripped his gun and slipped in a new clip, grateful that his brother had taken the time to show him how. He was having trouble breathing; his arms felt heavy holding the gun. He was afraid that he would not have the nerve, the killer instinct, much less the skill to shoot the man down, even if Tremaine came at him, firing with that damn machine gun. Rufus had fought many men in prison in order to survive — with his hands only, even though his opponents had always been armed with a shiv or piece of pipe. But a gun was different. A gun could kill from a distance. But if he didn't shoot, his brother would die. And for once he could not pray to God to help him. He could not speak to his Lord for assistance in killing another.

In a half crouch, Josh made his way across the front of the shack, stopping at intervals to listen intently. Once he dared to raise his head up to one of the windows, in order to perhaps see through it and out the rear window to where the Jeep was, but the angle was wrong and his view was blocked. Josh was totally focused now. The fear was still there, it was very much there, but he had done his best to transform it into adrenaline, to heighten every sense he possessed. He pointed his pistol directly in front of him, knowing full well that if Tremaine had figured what his plan was, his best course of action would be to slip out from behind the Jeep and come around the shack the other way, with the result that he would meet Josh head-on somewhere in the middle. Machine gun against pistol, a hundred rounds to one, meaning Josh would die, and then so would Rufus.

He moved forward another foot. Then he heard the machine gun open fire again and listened as the bullets tore into the pickup truck. He raced forward and rounded the corner. While Tremaine was busy firing at Rufus, Josh could outflank him and silence the sonofabitch once and for all.

This plan vanished when he went around the corner, for Tremaine was standing there, his pistol pointed at Josh's head. An astonished Josh stopped so abruptly that his feet slid in the gravel and his legs went out from under him. This was fortunate, since the bullet slammed into his shoulder instead of his brain. His momentum carried him forward and his legs clipped Tremaine's, and they went down hard, both their pistols sailing out of reach.

Tremaine came up first; Josh, holding his bloody shoulder, was slower to rise. Tremaine pulled a knife from his belt. In the background the machine gun stopped firing. Josh yelled out as Tremaine lunged into him and both men hit the wall of the shack, shaking the primitive structure right down to its wooden joints. Josh managed to block Tremaine's arm with his forearm. His whole side hurt like hell. Whatever piece of ordnance was in him had gone beyond his shoulder to explore other parts of his body. He managed to kick at Tremaine and caught him once in the belly, but the man was up and was on Josh again in an instant. Josh felt the knife cut through his shirt and into his side, and he started to lose consciousness. The pain from this fresh wound was barely felt, so overwhelmed was it by the first. He could hardly make out the image of Tremaine pulling the knife free from his body and rearing his arm back for a final thrust. Probably at his throat, Josh dimly thought, as his brain started to shut down. The throat was quick and always fatal. That's what he would do, he thought, as the darkness started to close around him.

The knife never made its downward plunge. It stopped at its highest point and moved no closer to Josh Harms. Tremaine kicked and jerked as he was torn off the wounded man. Rufus was directly behind him. One hand gripped the wrist holding the knife. He smashed it against the shack until Tremaine's finger lock was finally broken and the knife dropped to the ground. Tremaine was solid muscle and superbly trained in hand-to-hand combat. But he was half Rufus's size. One on one, there were few men who could match Rufus. The big man was like a grizzly bear once he got hold of somebody. And he had a good hold of Vic Tremaine, the man who had made his life a nightmare he'd thought would never end.

As Tremaine tried to wedge a forearm against Rufus's windpipe, Rufus changed his tactic and lifted Tremaine completely off the ground, slamming his face again and again into the wall until Tremaine was groggy from the impacts, his face bloody. Finally Rufus put Tremaine's head right through the window, the jagged glass cutting deeply into the man's face. Then Josh screamed in pain from his wounds, and Rufus looked at him, his grip loosening a bit. Tremaine, sensing this, kicked out Rufus's knee and whipsawed an elbow into his kidney, dropping the big man to the ground. Tremaine rolled free, gripped his knife and lunged toward the defenseless man. The bullet hit him smack in the back of the head and dropped him on the spot.

Rufus heaved upward and looked at his brother, wisps of smoke still seeping from the barrel of the 9mm Josh held. Then he put the pistol down and lay back in the dirt. Rufus raced over and knelt next to him. "Josh! Josh?"

Josh opened his eyes and looked over at Tremaine's twisted body, both relieved and sickened by what he had done. Even the worst enemy in the world didn't look so terrifying dead. He looked back at Rufus. "You done good, little brother. Shit, better'n me."

"I'd be dead if you hadn't killed him."

"Ain't gonna let him get you. Ain't gonna let him . . ."

Rufus ripped open his brother's shirt and looked at the wounds. The knife had only cut a slice in his side. Probably hadn't hit anything vital, Rufus concluded, but it was bleeding like a bitch. The bullet, though, was something else. He saw the blood dripping from his brother's mouth, the rising glaze to his eyes. Rufus could stop the bleeding on the outside, but he could do nothing about what was going on inside. And that's what could kill him. Rufus took off his shirt and put it over his brother, who was now shivering despite the heat.

"Hold on, Josh." Rufus ran over to the Jeep and quickly looked through it. He found the first-aid kit and hustled back over to his brother. Josh's eyes were now closed and he didn't seem to be breathing.

Rufus shook him gently. "Josh, Josh, don't do it, keep your damn eyes open. Don't be going to sleep on me. Josh!"

Finally Josh opened his eyes and appeared lucid. "You got to get outta here, Rufus. All the shooting, people might be coming. You got to go. Now."

"*We* got to get out of here — that's right."

Rufus lifted Josh up a little and checked his back. The bullet hadn't gone through; it was still in him somewhere. Rufus started cleaning both wounds.

At one point Josh gripped his arm. "Rufus, get the hell out of here," he said again.

"You don't go, I don't go, so that's what we got."

"You still crazy."

"Yeah, I'm crazy as hell, let's leave it at

529

that." He finished cleaning and then dressing the wounds and tightly bandaged them. He gently lifted his brother, but the movement sent Josh into a coughing spasm, blood from his mouth pooling down his shirt. Rufus carried him over to the truck and laid him down next to it.

"Shit, Rufus, this thing ain't going nowhere," Josh said desperately, looking at the battered truck.

"I know that." Rufus pulled a bottle of water from the camper, twisted it open and put it to Josh's lips. "Can you hold it? You need to get some liquid in you."

Josh answered by gripping the bottle with his good hand and drinking a little.

Rufus rose and went to the overturned Jeep. He pulled the machine gun free from where Tremaine had wedged it between the seat and the metal side of the Jeep. The man had used wire, a piece of metal and a string to rig the trigger for full automatic fire while he set up his ambush of Josh. Rufus eyed the situation for a moment and then tried to push against the hood to right the vehicle, but he couldn't get any leverage that way, and his feet slipped in the loose gravel. He studied the situation some more. There was really only one way that he could see.

He put his back against the edge of the driver's-side seat and then squatted down. He dug his fingers into the dirt and gravel until they got underneath the Jeep's side, and then he clenched the metal tightly. He gave one good pull to gauge what he was up against. The Jeep was heavy, damn heavy. Thirty years ago, this wouldn't have been that much trouble for him. As a young man he had lifted the front end of a full-sized Buick, engine and all, clean off the ground by a good three feet. But he wasn't twenty anymore. He pulled again and he could feel the Jeep rise a little before settling back down. He pulled once more, straining and grunting, the muscles in his neck tensing hard beneath his skin.

Josh put the bottle down and even managed to lift himself partially off the ground by leaning against the shredded truck tire, as he watched what his brother was trying to do.

Rufus was tired already. His arms and legs weren't used to this anymore, not for a long time. He had always been strong, stronger than anyone else. Now, when he really needed it, when his brother would surely die if he couldn't turn this damn Jeep upright, would he not be strong enough?

He hunkered down again, closed his eyes and then opened them. He looked skyward where a big, black crow lazily circled. Not a care in the world, just long, unhurried brush strokes against the canvas of blue.

As sweat poured off Rufus's face he clenched his eyes again and did what he always did when he was troubled, when he thought he wouldn't make it. He prayed. He prayed for Josh. He asked the Lord to please grant him the strength he needed to save his brother's life.

He gripped the sides of the Jeep once more, tensed his massive shoulders and legs. His long arms began to pull, his bent legs began to straighten. For a moment, Jeep and man were suspended in a precarious equilibrium, moving neither up nor down — the Jeep unwilling to yield and Rufus just as stubborn. But then Rufus slowly started to fall back a little as the weight was just too much for him. Rufus sensed he would not have another chance. Even as the Jeep began to win the battle, he opened his mouth and let out a terrible scream that forced tears from his eyes. As Josh looked on at the impossible thing his brother was trying to do for him, tears started to fall down his exhausted face.

Rufus's eyes opened again as he felt the Jeep rise, inch by agonizing inch. His joints and tendons afire with what he was accomplishing, Rufus grunted and pulled and heaved and ignored the pain as it snapped perilous signals through his trembling body. The Jeep fought him every punishing inch. It creaked and groaned, cursing him. But then he was standing upright, and he gave the hunk of metal one last heave. Like a wave about to pitch onto a beach, the Jeep cleared the point of no return and fell hard to earth, rocking upon impact and then coming to rest on all four wheels.

Rufus sat down in the Jeep, his whole body shaking from his immense exertions.

Josh looked on in silent wonderment. "Damn," was all he could finally say about what he had just witnessed.

Rufus's heart was racing so hard now, he worried his success might prove to be an empty one. He clutched at his chest, breathed deeply. "Please," he quietly said, "please don't." A minute later Rufus slowly rose, shuffled over to his brother and carefully lifted him into the Jeep. He rearranged the cloth top, which had become dislodged when Tremaine and Rayfield had been thrown clear. He gathered up as many supplies as he could from the truck, including his Bible, and put them into the back of the Jeep along with the weaponry. He climbed in the driver's seat and then stopped and looked over at Tremaine and Rayfield. Then he stared up once again at the circling crow, which had now been joined by several brethren, large enough to be buzzards. In less than a day the two dead men would be picked to the bone if left out in the open.

Rufus climbed out of the Jeep and went over to Rayfield. He didn't have to check the man's pulse. The eyes didn't lie. That and the stench of released bowels. He slid first

Rayfield's and then Tremaine's bodies into the shack. He said a few simple words over both men before rising and closing the door. One day he would forgive them for all they had done, but not today. Rufus climbed back in the Jeep, gave Josh a reassuring look and started the Jeep. The engine didn't catch the first time, but it did the second. Gears grinding as Rufus got a quick lesson in driving a stick shift, the Jeep jolted forward, and the brothers left this impromptu battlefield behind.

CHAPTER FIFTY

The justices traditionally had a private lunch in the Court's second-floor dining room after oral argument. Fiske had left Sara in her office to catch up on some work. He had decided to use the opportunity to make some inquiries on his own. If his flow of information had been cut off from D.C. Homicide, Fiske decided he'd better make it up somehow. One possible source was Police Chief Leo Dellasandro.

As he walked along the hallway, he thought about the oral argument he just listened to. Even as a lawyer, he had never really understood how much power was wielded from this building. The Supreme Court over its history had taken some very unpopular positions on a myriad of significant issues. Many had been brave and, at least in Fiske's opinion, correct. But it was unnerving to realize that if a vote or two had gone the other way on some or all of those prior decisions, the country might be very different today. By any definition that seemed to be a precarious, if not perilous, state of events.

Fiske also thought about his brother, and how much good he had undoubtedly brought to this place, even in the role of a clerk. Mike Fiske had always been fair and just in his opinions and actions. And when he made up his mind, a person could not ask for a more loyal friend. Mike Fiske was good for this place. The Court had indeed suffered a great loss when someone had taken his life. But not as great as the Fiske family's loss.

Fiske made his way to Dellasandro's ground-floor office, knocked on the door, waited. He knocked again, and then opened the door and peered inside. He was looking at the anteroom to Dellasandro's office, where his secretary worked. That space was empty. Probably at lunch, Fiske assumed. He stepped into the office. "Chief Dellasandro?" He wanted to know if anything had turned up on the surveillance videos. He also wanted to know if one of the officers had driven Wright home.

He approached the inner office door. "Chief Dellasandro, it's John Fiske. I was wondering if we could talk." Still no answer. Fiske decided to leave the man a note. But he didn't want to leave it at the secretary's desk.

He slipped into Dellasandro's office and over to his desk. He picked up a piece of paper and, using a pen from the holder on the desk, scrawled out a brief note. As he finished and positioned the note prominently on the desk, he looked around the office for a moment. There were many ceremonial tokens on shelves and walls, attesting to a distinguished career. On one wall was a photo of a much younger Dellasandro in his uniform.

Fiske turned to leave. Hanging on the back of the door was a jacket. It had to belong to Dellasandro, obviously part of his Court uniform. As Fiske passed by it, he noticed several smudges on the collar. He rubbed it with his finger and examined the residue: makeup. He went out into the anteroom and looked at the photos on the desk there. He had seen Dellasandro's secretary once before. A young, tall brunette with quite memorable features. On her desk, there was a photo of her and Chief Dellasandro. His arm was around her shoulder; they were both smiling into the camera. Probably many secretaries had a photograph with their bosses. There was something in the eyes, how close they were standing together, however, that might suggest something more than a platonic working relationship. He wondered if the Court had specific rules on fraternization. And there was another reason why Dellasandro would be well advised to keep his pants on and his hands off his secretary: Fiske glanced back into Dellasandro's office at the photo on his credenza — of his wife and kids. A very happy-looking family. Only on the surface, obviously. As he left the office, he concluded that it pretty much summed up how this place and the world in general operated: Surface appearances could be very deceiving; one had to dig deeper to get to the real truth.

Rufus stopped the Jeep. "I'm going to flag down the first cop I see. Get you some help," Rufus said.

With an effort, Josh sat up. "The hell you are. Cops get hold of you, they find Tremaine and Rayfield, they'll bury you."

"You need a doctor, Josh."

"I don't need shit." With a lunge, he gripped his pistol. "We started this, we gonna finish it." He wedged the barrel of the pistol against his gut. "You stop for anybody, I'm gonna put a hole right here."

"You're crazy. What the hell you want me to do?"

Josh coughed up blood. "You find Fiske and that girl. I can't help you no more, maybe they can." Rufus looked at the gun. "Don't go thinking it — bullet's pretty damn fast."

Rufus put the Jeep in gear and pulled back on the road. Josh watched him, his eyes coming in and out of focus. "Stop that shit."

"What?"

"I see you doing that mumbling shit. Don't be praying for me."

"Ain't nobody telling me when I can talk to the Lord."

"Just keep me out of it."

"I'm praying for Him to watch over you. Keep you alive."

"Does it look like it's troubling me any? You just wasting your breath."

"God gave me the strength to lift this Jeep."

"*You* lifted this damn hunk of metal. Ain't no angels come down from no heaven and help you do shit."

"Josh —"

"Just drive." The intensity of his pain forced Josh to suddenly hunch forward. "I'm tired of talking."

While she was in her office, Sara received an urgent summons from Elizabeth Knight. She was surprised by this, because on Wednesday afternoons the justices were usually in conference, going over the cases heard on Monday. Each justice had two secretaries and a personal assistant. As she entered Knight's chambers, Sara greeted Knight's longtime secretary, Harriet, who had been with the justice through several careers. Normally cheerful and friendly, Harriet spoke in a cold tone. "Go right in, Ms. Evans."

Sara passed by Harriet's desk and paused at the door to Knight's office. She turned around and caught Harriet staring at her. Harriet quickly turned back to her work. Sara took a deep breath and opened the door.

Within the office, either standing or perched upon chairs, were Ramsey, Detective Chandler, Perkins and Agent McKenna. Seated behind her antique desk, Elizabeth Knight was nervously fiddling with a letter opener when she saw Sara.

"Please come in and sit down." Her tone was barely cordial, Sara thought.

She sat in an upholstered wing chair that had been, she thought, carefully positioned because it allowed everyone in the room to directly face her. Or confront her, perhaps?

She looked at Knight. "You wanted to see me?"

Ramsey stepped forward. "We all wanted to see you, and, more to the point, hear you, Ms. Evans. However, I will let Detective Chandler do the honors." Ramsey was as stern as Sara had ever seen him. He leaned back against the fireplace mantel and continued to stare at her, his large hands clasping and unclasping nervously.

Chandler sat down across from her, his knees almost touching hers. "I've got some questions I need to ask you, and I want the truth in return," he said quietly.

Sara looked around the room. Only half joking, she said, "Do I need a lawyer?"

"Not unless you've done something wrong, Sara," Knight quickly pointed out. "However, I think you should make the determination whether to have legal counsel present or not."

Sara swallowed with difficulty and then looked back at Chandler. "What do you want to know?"

"Have you ever heard the name Rufus Harms?"

Sara closed her eyes for a moment. *Oh, shit.* "Let me explain —"

"Yes or no, please, Ms. Evans," Chandler said. "Explanations can come later."

She nodded, then said, "Yes."

"Exactly how are you familiar with that name?"

She fidgeted in her chair. "I know that he's a military prisoner who escaped. I read that in the papers."

"Was that the first you'd heard of him?" When she didn't answer, Chandler continued, "You've been asking questions at the clerks' office about an appeal presumably filed by Rufus Harms. In fact, you did that before he escaped from prison, didn't you? What were you looking for?"

"I thought . . . I mean —"

"Did John Fiske put you up to it?" Knight asked sharply. She looked searchingly at Sara, the disappointment on her features making Sara feel even more guilty.

"No. I did it on my own."

"Why?" Chandler asked. From his vague conversation with Fiske in the Court's cafeteria, he already had a notion as to what the truth was. But he needed to hear it from her.

Sara let out a deep breath and looked once more at the army aligned against her. She wished that Fiske would suddenly appear to help her, but that was not going to happen. "One day I happened to see what looked like an appeal with Rufus Harms's name on it. I checked at the clerks' office, because I didn't recall seeing it on the docket. The clerks' office had no record of it."

"Where did you see this appeal?" Ramsey interjected, before Chandler could get the same question out.

"Just somewhere," Sara said, looking miserable.

"Sara," Knight said harshly, "it's no use covering up for somebody. Just tell us the truth. Don't throw your career away for this."

"I don't remember where I saw it, I just saw it. For maybe two seconds. And I only saw Rufus Harms's name, not what was in the filing," Sara said stubbornly.

"But if you suspected it was an appeal that was not logged into the system," Perkins said, "then why didn't you take it down to the clerks' office and have it logged in?"

How was she supposed to answer that? "It really wasn't convenient at the moment, and I didn't get another chance."

"Wasn't convenient?" Ramsey looked ready to erupt. "It's my understanding that you just recently inquired at the clerks' office about this 'missing' appeal. Was it still not convenient for you to have it logged in then?"

"At that point I didn't know where it was."

McKenna spoke up forcefully. "Listen, Ms. Evans, either you tell us or we find out from another source."

Sara stood up. "I resent your tone and I don't appreciate being treated this way."

"I think it's in your interests to cooperate," McKenna said, "and stop trying to protect the Fiske brothers."

"What are you talking about?"

"We have reason to suspect that Michael Fiske took that appeal for his own purposes, and that somehow you're involved in all of that," Chandler informed her.

"If he did and you knew about it but remained silent, that is a very serious ethical offense, Ms. Evans," said Ramsey.

"You're doing all of this running around, asking questions, because John Fiske put you up to it, didn't he?"

"This may come as quite a shock to you, but I can think and act all by myself, Agent McKenna," she said hotly.

"You know that Michael Fiske had a half-million-dollar insurance policy naming his brother as beneficiary?"

"Yes, John told me."

"And do you also know that Fiske has no alibi for the time of his brother's death?"

Sara shook her head and smiled tightly.

"You're wasting valuable time trying to pin Michael's murder on his brother. He had nothing to do with it, and he's trying as hard as he can to find out who did murder Michael."

McKenna put his hands in his pockets and studied her for a moment, changing his tactic. "Would you say the Fiske brothers were close?"

"What do you mean by 'close'?"

McKenna rolled his eyes. "Just the ordinary meaning of the word, that's all."

"No, I don't think they were particularly close. So?"

"We found the life insurance policy at Michael Fiske's apartment. Tell me why he insured his life for all that money and made his not-so-close older brother the beneficiary. Why not his parents? From what I've found out, they can certainly use the money."

"I don't know what Michael was thinking when he did that. I guess we'll never know."

"Maybe it wasn't Michael Fiske who did it at all."

Sara was momentarily stunned. "What do you mean?"

"Do you know how easy it is to take out a life insurance policy on somebody else? There's no photo identification necessary. A nurse comes to your house, takes some measurements and fluid samples. You forge a few signatures, pay the premiums through a dummy account."

Sara's eyes widened. "Are you suggesting that John impersonated his brother in order to take out the life insurance policy on him?"

"Why not? It would make it a lot clearer why two estranged brothers would have such a big financial pact."

"You obviously do not know John Fiske."

McKenna gazed at her in a way that she found unnerving. "The point is, Ms. Evans, neither do you."

McKenna's next words almost put her on the floor.

"Did you also know that Michael Fiske was killed by a slug fired from a nine-millimeter?" He paused for effect. "And that John Fiske has a nine-millimeter registered to his name? And this appeal, I'm sure he's telling you it's connected to his brother's murder, isn't he?"

Sara looked at Chandler. "I can't believe this."

"Well, none of it's been proven yet," Chandler said.

Perkins nodded thoughtfully, his arms crossed. "We received a phone call from the Office of Special Military Operations, Ms. Evans. A Master Sergeant Dillard. He said you had called about Rufus Harms, that you said an appeal had been filed by Rufus Harms with the Court and you were checking into his background."

"There's no law that says I can't make a

phone call to clarify something, is there?"

"So you admit having called him," Perkins said triumphantly, looking first at Ramsey and then at Knight. "That means you admit to having used Court facilities and Court time on some personal investigation into some escaped convict. And you happened to have lied to the military, since no such appeal is on file here, as you pointed out."

"Your offenses are quickly adding up," added McKenna.

"I admit to no such thing. As far as I'm concerned, it was Court business and I had a perfect right to do it."

"Ms. Evans, are you going to tell us who exactly had that appeal?" Ramsey was staring at her just as he had peered down at the lawyers during oral argument that morning. "If someone at this Court stole an appeal before it was filed — the very idea is unthinkable — and if you know who it was, you have a duty to this institution to tell us who it was."

They all knew the answer to that question, Sara realized, or at least they thought they did. However, she wasn't providing any clarification. Summoning a reserve of strength she was unaware she possessed, she rose slowly. "I think I've answered enough questions, Mr. Chief Justice."

Ramsey looked over at Perkins and then at Elizabeth Knight. Sara thought she could see a slight nod pass among all of them.

"Then, Sara, I have to ask you to voluntarily resign your clerkship, effective immediately," Knight said, her voice breaking as she made this announcement.

Sara looked at her with very little surprise. "I understand, Justice Knight. I'm sorry it's come to this."

"Not nearly as sorry as I am. Mr. Perkins will escort you out. You may gather your personal belongings from your office." Knight abruptly looked away.

As Sara turned to go, Ramsey's voice boomed out again. "Ms. Evans, be advised that if your actions cause this institution any harm whatsoever, all appropriate action will be taken against you and any other responsible parties. However, if I am reading the situation correctly, I think the harm has already come to pass, and may well be irreversible." His voice rose dramatically. "If so, then may your conscience haunt you with that damnable fact for the rest of your natural life!"

Ramsey's face was red with indignation; his gaunt body seemed ready to burst through his suit. Sara could read it all in his smoldering eyes: A scandal on his watch. At the one institution that had been above scandal in a town constantly and infamously mired in it. His place in history, his long-earned career of jurisprudence, to be blemished by the blunders of an insignificant clerk; the history of his professional life reduced to a series of explanatory footnotes. If she had struck down his entire family right in front of him, Sara Evans could not have devastated the man any more. She fled the room before she burst into tears.

CHAPTER FIFTY-ONE

Fiske was waiting for Sara in her office. When she appeared in the doorway, he rose and started to speak, but then Perkins appeared behind her. Sara went over to her desk and started cleaning it out, while Perkins watched from the doorway.

"Sara, what happened?"

"This is none of your concern, Mr. Fiske," Perkins said. "However, I will let Detective Chandler and Agent McKenna know you're here. They have something to ask you."

"Well, why don't you run off and tattle on me so I can talk to Sara in private."

"I am going to escort Ms. Evans from the building."

Sara continued to pack her things into a large shopping bag and then picked up her purse and laid it on top in the bag. As she passed Fiske, she whispered, "I'll meet you in the garage."

As she went by Perkins, he said, "I'll also need all of your keys to this building."

Sara put her bag down, fished through her purse, pulled the keys off her key ring and tossed them to Perkins.

"It's not like I'm enjoying any of this,"

Perkins said indignantly. "The Court's in shambles, we're surrounded by a media army, people being murdered, the police swarming everywhere. It's not like I wanted you to lose your job."

Sara wordlessly pushed past him.

On the way down the main hallway, the group slowed as Chandler and McKenna approached from the other way.

"I need to talk to you, John," Chandler said.

Fiske looked at Sara. "I'll catch up with you, Sara."

She and Perkins walked off.

"You want to ask me something?" Fiske said.

"That's right."

"Would this be about my brother's life insurance policy?"

"Yes it would," Chandler said grimly. "McKenna thinks you might have taken it out yourself in your brother's name without his knowledge and then killed him."

"You found the policy in my brother's apartment?" Chandler nodded. "Well, then he obviously knew about it."

Chandler looked over at McKenna with an inquiring look. However, McKenna remained silent.

"Look, I didn't know my brother had taken out the policy. The insurance agent talked with me. I'll give you her name. She actually met with my brother, if you're really thinking I set this whole thing up myself." He looked at McKenna and saw the man's face darken. "Sorry to pop your balloon, McKenna. The money's going to our parents — Mike knew that's what I'd do with it. Talk to the insurance agent, she can confirm it. Unless you think I'm also in cahoots with her. Why stop there? I've probably got all nine justices in the back of my pocket too. Right?"

"So you talked your brother into taking out a life insurance policy to help your parents. But you and only you are the beneficiary. That's still terrific motivation to kill him," McKenna said. He turned to Chandler. "You want to ask him or do you want me to?"

Chandler looked at Fiske. "Your brother was killed by a nine-millimeter slug."

"Really?"

"You own a nine-millimeter pistol, don't you?"

Fiske looked at both men. "Been talking to the Virginia State Police?"

"Just answer the question," McKenna said.

"Why answer it, if you already know the answer?"

"John —" Chandler began.

"All right, yes. I own a nine-millimeter. SIG-Sauer P226, to be specific, with a fifteen-round mag."

"Where is it?"

"In my office, back in Richmond."

"We'd like to have it."

"For ballistics?"

"Among other things."

"Buford, this is a waste of time —"

"Do we have your permission to go to your office and get the gun?"

"No."

McKenna said, "Well, we'll have a search warrant issued in about one hour."

"You don't need a warrant. I'll give you the gun."

McKenna looked stunned. "But I thought you just said —"

"I don't want them breaking into my office to get it. I know how cops can be sometimes. They're not the most gentle souls, and it'd take me forever to get reimbursed on the cost of fixing my door." Fiske looked at Chandler. "I assume I'm not part of the unofficial team anymore, but a couple of things: Did you talk to the guards on duty the night Wright was murdered, and have the video cameras been checked?"

"I would advise you to say nothing to him, Chandler," McKenna said.

"Advice duly noted." Chandler looked at Fiske. "For old times' sake. We talked to the guards. Unless one of them's lying, none of them gave Wright a lift home. One of them offered, but Wright declined."

"What time was that?"

"About one-thirty A.M. or so. The film from the video cameras was checked and showed nothing out of the ordinary."

"Did Wright give a reason for not wanting a ride home?"

"The guard said he just walked out the door and he didn't see him after that."

"Okay, let's get back to the gun," McKenna said. "I'm going with you to your office."

"I'm not driving anywhere with you."

"I meant I'll follow you down."

"Do whatever you want, but I want a uniformed Richmond police officer there, and I want him to take the gun into custody and then have it transferred to D.C. Homicide. I will not let you be anywhere near the chain of custody."

"I really don't like what you're implying."

"Fine, but that's the way it's going to be, or you can go get your warrant. It's up to you."

Chandler spoke up, "Okay, anybody in particular?"

"Officer William Hawkins. I trust him and so can you."

"Done. I want you to leave right now, John. I'll arrange things with Richmond."

Fiske looked down the hallway. "Give me a half hour. I need to talk to somebody."

Chandler put a hand on Fiske's shoulder. "Okay, John, but if the Richmond police don't have your gun in about three hours or so, then you got a big problem with yours truly, understood?"

Fiske hustled off to the garage in search of Sara.

A couple minutes later, Dellasandro joined Chandler and McKenna.

"I'd like to know what the hell is going on around here," Dellasandro said angrily. "Two clerks murdered and now another fired over some missing appeal."

McKenna shrugged. "Pretty complicated."

"That's real encouraging," Dellasandro said.

"I'm not paid to be encouraging," McKenna shot back.

"No, you're paid to find out who's doing this. And you too, Detective Chandler," Dellasandro replied.

"And that's what we're doing," Chandler snapped.

"Okay, okay," Dellasandro said wearily. "Perkins filled me in earlier. You really think John Fiske killed his brother? I mean, okay, he had the motive, but, damn. Five hundred thousand sounds like a lot, but it's really not these days."

McKenna answered. "When you've got zip in your bank account, anything seems like a lot. He's got the motive, he's got no alibi, and in a few hours we'll see if he has the murder weapon."

Dellasandro looked unconvinced. "And what about Wright's death? How does that tie in?"

McKenna spread his hands. "Look at it this way. Sara Evans may have somehow been duped into helping Fiske. Evans and Wright shared an office. It's not out of the realm of possibility that Wright overheard something or saw something that made him suspicious about those two."

"But I thought Fiske has an alibi for the time of Wright's death," Dellasandro said.

"Yeah, Sara Evans," McKenna said.

"And all this stuff with this escaped convict Harms and the questions Evans was asking?"

Chandler shrugged. "I can't claim we have it all figured out, but that could be just another red herring."

McKenna said, "I don't think, I know. If there was anything to it, they would've told somebody. Evans couldn't even tell us what was in the appeal. Maybe Michael Fiske took some appeal, so what? John Fiske pops him for the money and he uses this missing appeal as a bunch of mumbo-jumbo to dupe Evans and everybody else."

"Well, I'm not letting my guard down until we know for sure," Dellasandro said. "The people in this building are my responsibility and we've already lost two of them." He looked over at McKenna. "I hope you know what you're doing with Fiske."

"I know exactly what I'm doing with him."

Fiske caught up with Sara in the parking garage. It didn't take her long to explain what had happened.

"Sara, I hoped I would never have to tell you this, but Chandler boxed me into a corner the other day. I'm sure I'm the reason you just lost your job."

Sara put the shopping bag in the trunk of her car. "I'm a big girl. I'm responsible for my own actions."

Fiske leaned up against the car. "Maybe I can go and talk to Ramsey and Knight, try and explain things to them?"

"Explain it how? What they're alleging I did, I did." Sara closed the trunk and joined him. "I assume they told you about your gun?"

Fiske nodded. "McKenna's giving me an armed escort to my office so I can hand it over." He looked at her closely. "So what are you going to do now?"

"I don't know. But I've suddenly got a lot of free time on my hands. I'll try to find out about Tremaine and Rayfield."

"You sure you still want to help?"

"At least I won't have ruined my career for nothing. What about you?"

"I don't have any choice in the matter."

He looked at his watch. "How about I come by your place around seven tonight?"

"I think I can manage dinner. Buy some food, a nice bottle of wine. I might even get real ambitious and dust. We can celebrate my last day at the Court. Maybe go for another sail." She paused and touched his arm. "And finish it off the same way?"

"I can bag Richmond and stay with you. I know how you must be feeling."

"But what about Chandler and Mc-Kenna?"

"I don't have to do what they say."

"If you don't go, McKenna will probably push for the electric chair. Besides, to tell you the truth, I feel really good."

"Are you sure?"

"I'm sure, John, but thanks." She stroked his face. "Tonight you can be with me."

After Fiske left, Sara was about to get in her car when she realized she had left her purse, with her car keys, in the bag in the trunk. She popped the trunk and reached in the bag to get her purse. As she lifted it out, the photo on top caught her eye. She had taken it from Michael Fiske's office before the police had searched it. It suddenly occurred to her that she did have something very important to take care of. She got in her car and pulled out of the garage.

She had just been fired as a Supreme Court clerk. Oddly, she didn't feel like bursting into tears, or slipping her head in an oven. She felt like going for a drive. Down to Richmond.

She needed to see somebody. And today was as good a day as any.

When she drove past the columned facade of her old place of work, a great wave of relief swept over her. It was so sudden that it left her breathless. Then, bit by bit, she was okay. She accelerated down Independence Avenue and didn't look back.

CHAPTER FIFTY-TWO

Fiske hurried down to Knight's chambers and, surprisingly, was allowed in. Knight sat behind her desk. Ramsey was still there, slumped in a chair. He quickly rose when Fiske entered.

Fiske plunged in. "I want you to know that anything Sara did or didn't do was to protect my brother. All she's trying to do now is help me find who killed him."

"And you're sure that question wouldn't be answered by your simply looking in a mirror?" Ramsey said forcefully.

Fiske paled. "You're way off the mark, sir."

"Am I? The authorities don't seem to think so. If you are a murderer, then I hope you spend the rest of your life in prison. As for your brother's actions, they reside not far down the ladder from taking someone's life, at least in my book."

"My brother did what he thought was right."

"I find that statement positively laughable."

"Harold —" Knight began, but he cut her off with a sweep of his hand.

"And I want you" — he pointed at Fiske —

"to get out of this office and out of this building before I have you arrested for trespassing."

Fiske looked at the two of them. The anger he was feeling right now was the culmination of the last three days of sheer hell. It was as though everything bad that had ever happened to him had been caused by Harold Ramsey. "I've seen the nice little sign over the front door of this place: 'Equal Justice Under Law'? I find that laughable."

Ramsey looked ready to attack Fiske. "How dare you!"

"I've got a client on death row right now. If I ever have the 'honor' of appearing before you, can you tell me you'll actually care whether my guy lives or dies? Or will you just be using him and me to overturn a precedent that pissed you off ten years ago?"

"You insufferable —"

"Can you tell me that?" Fiske shouted. "Because if you can't, then I don't know what you are, but you're sure as hell not a judge."

Ramsey was livid. "What do you know about anything? The system —"

Fiske smacked his chest. "I'm the system. Me and the people I represent. Not you. Not this place."

"Do you realize the magnitude of the issues we deal with here?"

"When's the last time you sat and 'judged' a battered wife? Or a molested child? Have you ever watched a man die in the electric chair? Have you? You sit up here and you never even see a real person. You don't hear from any live witnesses, you never hear from any of the people you'll destroy or help by your actions. All you get is a bunch of high-powered lawyers throwing a bunch of paper at you. You have no idea of the faces, the people, the heartbreak and pain behind any of it. To you it's some intellectual game. A game! Nothing more." Fiske stared at the man. His voice shook as he said, "You think the big issues are so hard? Try dealing with the little ones."

"I think you should leave," Knight said, almost pleadingly. "Right now."

Fiske stared at Ramsey for a few seconds longer and then, calming down, he looked at the woman. "You know, that's good advice, Counselor, I think I'll take it." Fiske turned to the door.

"Mr. Fiske," Ramsey boomed out. Fiske slowly turned back. "I have several good friends at the Virginia state bar. I think they should be apprised of the situation. I would think that appropriate action should be taken against you, perhaps resulting in suspension and subsequent disbarment."

"Guilty until proved innocent? That's your idea of how the criminal justice system should work?"

"It's my strong opinion that it's only a

matter of time until you're found guilty."

Fiske started to say something else, but Knight, one hand on the phone, said, "John, I would much prefer if you left without the assistance of the guards."

After Fiske was gone, Ramsey shook his head. "Beyond all doubt, the man's a psychopath."

He turned and looked at Knight. She sat there, staring straight ahead. "Beth, I just want to let you know that you're welcome to use one of my clerks until you find a replacement for Sara."

She looked over at him. The offer of a clerk seemed very nice. On the surface. A spy in her camp underneath that surface?

"I'll be fine. We'll just have to work harder."

"You put up a good fight at oral argument today, though I do wish you wouldn't take it personally. It's a little unseemly when we bicker back and forth like that in public."

"How can I not take the cases personally, Harold? Tell me how." Her eyes were swollen, her voice suddenly hoarse.

"You have to. I never lose sleep over a case. Even a death penalty one. We don't decide guilt or innocence. We interpret words. You have to think of it in those terms. Otherwise you'll burn out."

"Maybe burning out early is a preferable

alternative to having a long, distinguished career that only challenges my *intellect*." Ramsey glanced sharply at her. "I want to hurt, I want to feel the pain. Everyone else does. Why are we an exception? Dammit, we should be agonizing over these cases."

Ramsey shook his head sadly. "Then I'm afraid you'll never endure. And you have to if you want to make a real difference up here."

"We'll see. I may surprise you. Starting today."

"You don't have a chance of overturning *Stanley*. But I admire your tenacity, even though it was wasted today."

"The votes haven't been counted yet that I recall."

Ramsey smiled. "Of course, of course. A formality only." He put his hands in his pockets and stood in front of her. "And just so you know, I also am aware of your plans to reexamine the issue of the rights of the poor —"

"Harold, we've just lost our third clerk. A third human being. One whom I care greatly about. The place is in shambles. I don't feel like talking about Court business right now. I may never feel like it again, in fact."

"Beth, we must move on. True, it's been one crisis after another, but we will persevere."

"Harold, please!"

Ramsey would not back down. "The court goes on. We —"

Knight stood up. "Get out."

"I beg your pardon?"

"Get out of my office."

"Beth —"

"Get out! Get out!"

Without another word, Ramsey left. Knight stood there for another minute or so. Then she quickly left her office.

After his confrontation with Ramsey, Fiske entered the Court's underground garage and went straight to his car. He felt numb. He had gotten Sara fired, was being set up for murdering his brother and had just told off the chief justice of the United States. All in less than an hour. In any realm other than total lunacy, that would be called a bad day. He sat in his car. He had no desire to drive to Richmond and watch McKenna try to put the finishing touches on the destruction of his life.

He pushed his fists against his eye sockets. A groan escaped from him and then he jerked forward as he heard the sound. His eyes widened as he saw Elizabeth Knight tapping on the car window. He rolled it down.

"I would like to talk to you."

He composed himself as best he could. "What about?"

"Can we go for a short drive? I don't think

I'd risk bringing you back in the building. I'm not sure I've ever seen Harold quite that upset."

Fiske thought he saw a trace of a smile on the woman's face as she said this. "You want to go for a drive in my car?" he asked.

"I don't have a car here. Is there a problem with yours?"

Fiske looked at her expensive dress. "Well, my car's interior is basically rust covered with a veneer of grime."

Knight smiled. "I grew up on a ranch in East Texas. When my family drove to the little shacks that constituted the town we lived near, we did so on a backhoe with me and my six siblings hanging on for dear life and enjoying every minute of it. And I *would* like to talk to you."

Fiske finally nodded and Knight slipped in the front seat.

"Where to?" Fiske asked as they left the garage.

"Take a left at the light. I hope you don't have anything pressing. It was rude of me not to ask."

Fiske thought of McKenna waiting for him. "Nothing important."

After he made the turn, Knight started speaking. "You shouldn't have come back and said those things, you know."

"I hope you didn't come here just to tell me that," Fiske said sharply.

"I came to tell you that I feel terribly about Sara."

"Join the crowd. She tried to help my brother and then me. I'm sure she just loves the day she ran into the Fiske brothers."

"Well, at least one of you anyway."

"What does that mean?"

"Sara liked and respected your brother. But she didn't love him, although, quite frankly, I think he was in love with her. But her heart lies elsewhere."

"Is that right? And she told you this?"

"John, I really don't like to admit to any gender bias, but I also refuse to ignore some basic realities: I doubt if my eight male colleagues have any clue whatsoever, but it's clear to me that Sara Evans is very much in love with you."

"Your womanly intuition?"

"Something like that. I also have two girls of my own." She noted his curious look. "My first husband died. My daughters are grown and on their own." Knight put her hands in her lap and looked out the window. "However, that's not really why I wanted to talk to you," she said. "Turn right, up here," she said.

As Fiske did so, he asked, "So what is on your agenda? You people seem to always have one."

"And you find that somehow wrong?"

"You tell me. Seeing the games you people

play doesn't give me warm fuzzies."

"I can respect that point of view."

"I'm in no position to really judge what you do. But, to me, you're not judges, you're policymakers. And what that policy will be depends on who lobbies hard enough to get five votes. What does that have to do with the rights of one plaintiff and one defendant?" As soon as Fiske had finished speaking he had a sudden, depressing thought: He had no room to complain about the Court and how it operated. He spent all his time dodging the truth on behalf of his clients. In a way, that was worse than anything the Court did or didn't do in the name of justice.

They drove in silence for a minute until Knight broke it. "I started out as a prosecutor. And then became a trial judge." She paused. "I can't tell you that your feelings are wrong." Fiske looked mildly surprised. "John, we could debate this until we're both sick of it, but the fact is there is a system in place and one must work within that system. If that means playing by its rules and, on occasion, bending them, so be it. Perhaps that's an oversimplified philosophy for a complex situation, but sometimes you have to go with your gut." She looked at him. "Do you know what I mean?"

He nodded. "My instincts are pretty good."

"And what do your instincts tell you about

Michael and Steven's deaths? Is there anything to this story of the missing appeal? If there is, I would really like to know about it."

"Why ask me?"

"Because you seem to know more than anyone else. That's why I wanted to talk to you in private."

"Are you really hoping that I killed my brother and I'm using this appeal as a red herring? That way the Court doesn't get a black eye."

"I didn't say that."

"You said as much to Sara at your party."

Knight sighed and sat back. "I'm not sure why I did. Perhaps to scare her away from you."

"I didn't kill my brother."

"I believe you. So this missing appeal may be important?"

Fiske nodded. "My brother was killed because he knew what that appeal said. I think Wright was killed because he was working late, came out of his office and saw someone at the Court going through my brother's office."

She turned pale. "You believe someone at the Court murdered Steven?" Fiske nodded. "Can you prove that?"

"I hope so."

"That can't be, John. Why?"

"There's a guy who's spent half his life in

568

prison who'd like to know the answer to that."

"Does Detective Chandler know all this?"

"Some of it. But Agent McKenna has pretty much convinced him I'm the bad guy."

"I'm not sure Detective Chandler believes that."

"We'll see."

As Fiske dropped Knight back at the Court, she said, "If everything you suspect is true and someone at the Court is involved in this . . ." She stopped, unable to continue for a moment. "Do you realize what this could do to the Court's reputation?"

"I'm not sure of a lot in life, but I'm certain of one thing." He paused and then said, "The Court's reputation isn't worth an innocent man dying in prison."

CHAPTER FIFTY-THREE

Rufus looked anxiously over at his brother, who had just finished an exhausting coughing fit. Josh tried to sit up a little, thinking that would help his breathing. His insides, he knew, were all but destroyed. Something important to keeping him alive might burst at any moment. He still held the pistol against his side. But it didn't look like a bullet would be needed to end his life. At least, not another one.

It was fortunate for them that Tremaine and Rayfield hadn't come in an Army vehicle. But the Jeep did have one crushed side from being broadsided by the truck and this would draw unwanted attention to them. At least it had a cloth top, which prevented anyone from getting a good glimpse of what was inside.

Rufus didn't know where he was going, and Josh moved in and out of lucidity too much to really help him. Rufus flipped open the glove box and pulled out a map. He studied it quickly and traced the route to Richmond with his finger. He had to get to the highway. If he had to he would stop and ask directions. He pulled the little card out of his shirt pocket and glanced at the names and telephone numbers. Now he just had to find a phone.

When Fiske and McKenna arrived at Fiske's office, the FBI agent said, "Let's get to it."

"We wait for the police," Fiske said firmly.

Just as he said that, a police cruiser pulled up and Officer Hawkins climbed out.

"What the heck's going on here, John?" Hawkins asked, perplexed.

Fiske pointed at McKenna. "Agent McKenna thinks I killed Mike. He's here to get my gun so he can do a ballistics test."

Hawkins looked at McKenna with hostile eyes. "If that's not the biggest bunch of bullshit I ever heard . . ."

"Right, thanks for your official assessment — Officer Hawkins, is it?" McKenna said, coming forward.

"That's right," Hawkins said grimly.

"Well, Officer Hawkins, you have the consent of Mr. Fiske to search his office for a nine-millimeter pistol registered to his name." He looked at Fiske. "I'm assuming you are still giving that consent." When Fiske didn't respond, McKenna looked back at Hawkins. "Now, if you have a problem with that, then let's go talk to your boss and you can start planning another career outside of law enforcement."

Before Hawkins could do something foolish, Fiske grabbed his sleeve and said, "Let's just go get this over with, Billy."

As they walked into the building, Fiske commented, "Your face looks a lot better."

Hawkins smiled, embarrassed. "Yeah, thanks."

"What happened?" McKenna asked.

Hawkins looked at him sullenly. "Guy decided to take a ride on drugs. He was a little difficult to arrest."

There was a stack of mail and packages in front of Fiske's office door. He picked them up and unlocked the door. They went inside and Fiske walked over to his desk and dropped the stack of mail on it. He slid open the top drawer and looked inside. He stuck his hand in and fumbled through the contents before looking up at both men. "It was right in this drawer. I actually saw it the day you came to tell me about Mike, Billy."

McKenna crossed his arms and eyed Fiske sternly. "Okay, has anybody else had access to your office? Cleaning crew, secretary, delivery people, window washers?"

"No, nobody. Nobody else has a key, except for the landlord."

Hawkins said, "You've been gone, what, two days or so?"

"That's right."

McKenna was looking at the door. "But there's no signs of forced entry."

Hawkins said, "That doesn't mean anything. Person who knew what they were doing could pick that lock and you'd never even know it."

"Who knew you kept the gun here?" McKenna asked.

"Nobody."

"Maybe one of your clients took it so he'd have a piece of ordnance to knock over a bank with," McKenna said.

"I don't interview clients in my office, McKenna. They're usually in prison by the time I get the call."

"Well, it looks like we have a little problem here. Your brother was killed by a nine-millimeter slug. You have a nine-millimeter Sig registered to you. You admit it was actually in your possession as of a few days ago. Now that pistol is missing. You have no alibi for the time of your brother's death and you're a half million bucks richer because of his death."

Hawkins glanced over at Fiske.

"A life insurance policy Mike took out," Fiske explained. "It was for Mom and Dad."

"At least that's your story, right?" McKenna added.

Fiske edged closer to McKenna. "If you think you have enough to charge me, then do it. If not, get the hell out of my office."

McKenna wasn't fazed. "I believe Officer Hawkins has your consent to search your entire office for the gun, not just the drawer you said it was in. Now, friend or not, I would expect him to carry out his sworn duty."

Fiske backed off and looked over at Hawkins. "Go ahead, Billy. I'm going down to the corner café for something to drink. You want anything?" Hawkins shook his head.

"I could use a cup of coffee," McKenna said, following Fiske out. "It'll give us a chance to have a little talk."

Sara pulled her car into the driveway. She took a deep breath. The Buick was there. As she got out of the car, the smell of cut grass hit her. It was comforting, taking her back to high school football games, lazy summers in the peace of the Carolinas. When she knocked on the door, it was jerked open so quickly she almost fell off the stoop. Ed Fiske must have watched her drive up. Before he could slam the door in her face, she held the photo out to him.

There were four people in the photo: Ed and Gladys Fiske and their two sons. They all wore broad smiles.

Ed looked questioningly at Sara.

"Michael had it in his office. I wanted you to have it."

"And why's that?" His tone was still cold, but at least he wasn't screaming obscenities at her.

"Because it seemed like the right thing to do."

Ed took the photo from her. "I got nothing to say to you."

"But I have a lot to say to you. I promised someone something, and I like to keep my promises."

"Who? Johnny? Well, you can tell him that it's no good sending you over to try to mend things."

"He doesn't know I'm here. He told me not to come."

He looked surprised. "So why are you here?"

"That promise. What you saw the other night wasn't John's fault. It was mine."

"It takes two to tango and you ain't telling me no different."

"May I come in?"

"I don't see why."

"I'd really like to talk to you about your sons. I think you need to know some things. Some information that might make things a little clearer. It won't take all that long and I promise you, after I'm done, I won't ever bother you again. Please?"

After a long moment, Ed finally moved aside and let her pass. He closed the door noisily behind them.

The living room was much the way it had been the first time she had seen it. The man liked things tidy. She imagined his garage full of tools kept in the same manner. Ed motioned to the sofa and Sara sat down. He went into the dining room and carefully placed the photo among the others there. "You want something to drink?" he asked grudgingly.

"Only if you're having something."

Ed sat down in a chair across from her. "I'm not."

She looked at him closely. Now she could more clearly see the rough outlines of both sons in his face, his build. The mother was there too, though more in Michael than in John. Ed started to light up a cigarette and then stopped.

"You can smoke if you want. It's your house."

Ed replaced the pack of smokes in his pocket and slid the lighter back in his pants pocket. "Gladys wouldn't let me smoke in the house, just outside. Old habits are hard to break." He crossed his arms, waiting for her to start talking.

"Michael and I were very close friends."

"I'm not sure how close you could've been after what I saw the other night." Ed's face started to flush.

"The fact is, Mr. Fiske —"

"Look, just call me Ed," he said gruffly.

"All right, Ed, the fact is we were close friends. That's how I saw it, but Michael wanted more than that."

"What do you mean?"

Sara swallowed hard, her own face reddening. "Michael asked me to marry him."

Ed looked shocked. "He never said anything to me."

"I'm sure he didn't. You see" — she hesitated for a moment, very nervous about what his reaction would be to these next words — "you see, I told him no." She shrank back a little, but Fiske just sat there, trying to digest this.

"Is that right? I take it you didn't love him."

"I didn't — not like that, anyway. I'm not sure why I didn't. He seemed perfect. Maybe that's what scared me, sharing my life with someone like that, trying to keep my standards up that high for a lifetime. And he was so caught up in his work. Even if I had loved him, I'm not sure there would have been room for me."

Ed looked down. "It was hard raising those two boys. Johnny was good at most everything, but Mike . . . Mike was flat-out great at anything he wanted to do. I was working all the damn time and didn't really see it that good when they were growing up. I see it a whole lot better now. I bragged a lot on Mike. Too much. Mike told me Johnny wouldn't have nothing to do with him, and wouldn't really say why. Johnny really keeps to himself. Hard to get him to talk."

Sara looked past him, out the window, where a cardinal flitted by and settled on the branch of a weeping willow.

She said, "I know. I've spent a lot of time with him the last few days. You know, I always thought I'd be able to tell, almost instantly: This is the person I want to spend my life with. I guess that notion seems silly. And unfair. Doesn't it?"

A tiny smile creased the man's face. "The first time I saw Gladys, she was waitressing at this little diner across from where I worked. I walked in the door with a bunch of my buddies one day and from the moment I saw her I didn't hear a word they said. It was like it was just me and her in the whole damn world. Went back to work and made a mess of a Cummins diesel engine. Couldn't get her out of my head."

Sara smiled. "I'm well acquainted with the stubbornness of John and Michael Fiske. So I doubt if you just left it at that."

Ed smiled too. "I went back over to that diner for breakfast, lunch and dinner for the next six months. We started going out. Then I got up the courage to ask her to marry me. I swear to God I would've done it that first day, but I thought she'd think I was crazy or something." He paused for a moment and then said with finality, "We've had a damn good life together too." He studied her face. "Is that what happened to you when you saw Johnny?" Sara nodded. "Did Mike know?"

"I think he figured it out. When I finally met John I asked him if he had any idea why the two of them didn't seem to be close. I thought that might have been part of it, but they seemed to have drifted apart before then." Sara tensed. "So that night in the boat, what you saw was me pushing myself on your son. He had been through the most hellish day imaginable and all I could think about was myself." She looked directly at him. "He turned me down flat." She thought of last night, the tenderness she and John Fiske had exchanged, both in and out of her bed. And then the morning after. She thought she had figured it all out. That had been a good feeling. Now she was close to overwhelmed by the sense that she knew nothing about the man or his feelings. She let out a troubled laugh. "It was a very humbling experience." She pulled a tissue from her pocketbook and dabbed at her eyes. "That's all I came to tell you. If you want to hate anyone, hate me, not your son."

Ed studied the carpet for a minute and then stood. "Just finished cutting the grass. I'd like an iced tea, how about you?" With a surprised look, Sara nodded.

A few minutes later Ed came back with glasses of ice and a pitcher of tea. As he filled the glasses he said, "I've thought a lot about that night. I don't remember all of it. Had a damn bad hangover the next day. As mad as I was, I never should've hit Johnny. Not in the damn gut."

"He's pretty tough."

"That's not what I meant." Ed took a swallow of tea and sat back, chewing on his lip. "Did Johnny ever tell you why he left the police force?"

"He said he had arrested some young kid for a drug offense. That the kid was so pathetic and everything, that he decided to start helping people like that."

Ed nodded. "Well, he didn't actually arrest him. That boy died at the scene. And so did the officer that backed Johnny up on that call."

Sara almost spilled her tea. "What?"

Ed looked a little uncomfortable now that he had opened this subject, but he continued. "Johnny never really talked about it, but I got the story from the officers who arrived after it all happened. Johnny stopped the car for some reason. It was stolen, I think. Anyway, he called in for backup. He got the two boys out of the car. Found the drugs. That's when his backup came. Right before they were going to search them, one of the boys dropped like he was having a seizure. Johnny tried to help him. His backup should've kept his gun on the other, but he didn't, and the other fellow pulled a gun and killed him. Johnny managed to fire, but the boy put two rounds into him.

"They both went down, facing each other. The other boy had just been faking it. He jumped up and took off in the car. They caught him a little while later. The other fellow and Johnny were about a foot apart, both bleeding like crazy."

"Omigod!"

"Johnny stuffed a finger in one of the holes. It stopped the bleeding a little. Well — and I heard some of this from him while he was in the hospital half out of his head — the boy said some things to Johnny. I'm not exactly sure what, Johnny never would say, but they found the boy dead and Johnny next to him, his arm around him. Must've dragged himself over there or something. Some of the cops didn't exactly like that, what with one of their own lying dead because of the kid. But they checked everything out and Johnny was cleared. It was the other cop's fault. Anyway, Johnny almost died on the way to the hospital. As it was, he was in there for about a month. Whatever load the boy was carrying in that pistol ripped Johnny's insides to shreds."

Sara suddenly thought back to Fiske's pulling his shirt back down before they made love. "Does he have a scar?"

Ed looked at her funny. "Why do you ask?"

"Something he said."

He nodded slowly. "From his gut to his neck."

"Too old for skinny-dipping," Sara said to herself.

"Guess they could've done some plastic surgery, but Johnny had had enough of hospitals. Besides, I think he figured if they couldn't fix him on the inside, what the hell did it matter what he looked like on the outside?"

Sara's face took on a stricken look. "What do you mean? He fully recovered, didn't he?"

Ed shook his head sadly. "Those bullets ripped him bad, bounced around inside him like a damn pinball. They patched him up, but just about every one of his organs was damaged for good. Maybe they could make it all right if Johnny wanted to spend a bunch of years in the hospital, have transplants and stuff like that. But that ain't my son. Docs say eventually things inside him are just going to stop working. They said it was like diabetes — you know, how a person's organs get worn out and all?" Sara nodded as her own stomach started to churn. "Well, the docs said those two bullets will eventually cost Johnny about twenty years of his life, maybe more. And there wasn't really nothing they could do about it. Back then we didn't care. Hell, he was alive, that was enough. But I know he thinks about it. He pumped iron, ran like a damn demon, got himself in good

582

shape, at least on the outside. Quit the police force. Wouldn't even take damn disability, although he was sure as hell entitled. Became a lawyer, works like a dog for what amounts to chickenshit, and gives me and his momma most of it. I got no pension and Gladys's medical bills added up to more than I made in my whole life. Hell, we had to mortgage this place again after spending thirty years paying it off. But you do what you got to do."

As Ed paused, Sara glanced over at the table where John Fiske's medal for valor sat. A little piece of metal for all that pain.

"I tell you all this so you'll see Johnny doesn't really have the same goals as you and me might. Never got married, never talks about having no kids of his own. Everything is sped up for him. He figures if he makes it to fifty, he's the luckiest man on earth. He told me that himself." Ed Fiske looked down, his voice catching. "Never figured I'd outlive Mike. I hope to God I don't outlive my other boy."

Sara finally found her voice. "I appreciate your telling me this. I realize it was hard for you. You don't really know me."

"Depending on the situation, sometimes you can know a person better in ten minutes than someone you've crossed paths with all your life."

Sara rose to leave. "Thank you for your

time. And John really needs to hear from you."

He nodded solemnly. "I'll do that."

As her hand touched the doorknob, Ed spoke one last time. "You still love my son?"

Sara walked out without answering.

At the small café down from his office building, Fiske bought his coffee and sat down at an outside table. McKenna did the same. At first Fiske chose to completely ignore the hovering FBI agent and idly watched the passersby while he drank his coffee. He slipped on his sunglasses as the sun cleared the top of the building across the street and drew both men's shadows across the bricks. McKenna silently munched on some crackers he had bought and fingered his Styrofoam cup of coffee.

"How's the gut? Sorry I had to punch you like that."

"The only thing you're sorry about is that you didn't hit me harder."

"No, really. I saw the shotgun and got concerned."

Fiske looked up at him. "I guess you thought I might be able to somehow open the car door, pull the shotgun out, swing it around and get off a shot before you could blow me away from a distance of, what, six inches?"

McKenna shrugged. "FYI, I read up on

your police record. You were a good cop. Right up until the end, anyway."

"What the hell is that supposed to mean?"

McKenna sat down at the table. "Nothing, other than there being some questions about that last event in your record. Care to fill me in on it?"

Fiske took off his glasses and stared at the man. "Why don't you put a bullet in my head instead? I think that would be more fun for me."

McKenna leaned his chair back against the side of the building and lit up a cigarette. "You know, if you're so anxious to prove your innocence, then you might want to start being a little more cooperative."

"McKenna, you're convinced I killed my brother, so why should I bother?"

"I've worked a lot of cases over the years. Half the time my original theory didn't turn out to be right. My philosophy is: Never say never."

"Boy, you really sound sincere."

McKenna assumed a friendlier tone. "Look, John, I've been doing this stuff a long time, okay? Nice, neat little cases aren't the norm. There are twists on this one and I'm not ignoring them." He stopped and then added as casually as he could, "So why was your brother interested in Rufus Harms, and what exactly was in the appeal?"

Fiske put his sunglasses back on. "That

doesn't fit into your theory of me killing my brother."

"That's only one of my theories. I'm down here following that up by looking for your suddenly vanished nine-millimeter. While I'm waiting on that, I'm looking at it from another angle: Rufus Harms. Your brother took the appeal, it looks like he visited the prison."

"Chandler told you that?"

"I have a lot of information sources. You and Evans have both been snooping around into Harms's background. He escaped from a prison in southwest Virginia. And you two took a chartered plane to that area last night. Why don't you tell me about that? Where'd you go and why?"

Fiske sat back, stunned. McKenna had put them under surveillance. That wasn't unusual, yet somehow Fiske hadn't even thought about the possibility. "You seem to know so much — why ask me?"

"You might have some information I could use to solve this case."

"Ahead of Chandler?"

"When people are getting killed, what does it matter who stops it first?"

That statement made a lot of sense, Fiske knew. On the surface, at least. But of course it mattered a great deal who stopped it. People in law enforcement kept score, just like people in other lines of work. Fiske stood up. "Let's check in with Billy. By now he's probably found those two bodies I stuffed in my file cabinet last week."

Hawkins was just finishing up when they returned.

"Nothing," he said in response to McKenna's look. "You can search it yourself if you want," he added defiantly.

"That's okay, I trust you," McKenna said amicably.

Fiske was staring at Hawkins. "What's that, Billy?" Fiske pointed at his neck and collar.

"What's what?"

Fiske touched Hawkins's collar with his finger and then held it up for the man to see.

Hawkins blushed a little. "Oh. Damn, that was Bonnie's idea to cover the bruises. That's why my face doesn't look so beat up. I've never been hit that hard in my life. I mean, the guy was big, but so am I."

McKenna said, "I would've emptied my clip in the bastard."

Fiske stared openmouthed at McKenna as he said this.

Hawkins nodded. "I was tempted. But anyway, the guys would give me hell if they knew, but it's so hot outside and you start sweating, and the stuff just comes off on your clothes. I don't know how women do it."

"Then you're saying it's —"

"Yeah, it's makeup," he said sheepishly.

Despite the revelation that had just occurred to him, Fiske tried his best to appear calm. He unconsciously rubbed his still-tender shoulder.

McKenna was staring at him.

Just then the phone rang. Fiske picked it up. It was the nursing home where his mother lived.

"I read about Michael in the paper. I'm so sorry, John." The woman had worked at the home for years and Fiske knew her very well.

"Thanks, Anne. Look, right now is a real bad time —"

"I mean, Michael was just here and now he's gone. I can't believe it."

Fiske tensed. " 'Here,' as in at the nursing home?"

"Yes. Just last week. Thursday — no, Friday."

The day he disappeared.

"I remember because he usually comes on Saturday."

Fiske shook his head clear. "What are you talking about? Mike didn't visit Mom."

"Sure he did. I mean, not nearly as often as you did."

"You never told me that."

"Didn't I? Well, I guess if you have to know, Michael didn't want you to know."

"Why in the hell didn't he want me to know? I'm sick and tired of people not telling me things about my brother."

"I'm sorry, John," the woman said, "but he asked me not to say anything and I honored his request. That's all. But now that he's gone, I . . . I didn't think it would hurt for you to know."

"He saw Mom on Friday? Did he talk to you?"

"No, not really. He seemed a little nervous, actually. I mean, sort of anxious. He came really early and only stayed about a half hour."

"So they talked?"

"They met. I don't know how much they actually talked. Gladys can be difficult sometimes. When do you think you might stop by to see her? I mean, she couldn't possibly know about Michael, but still she seems very depressed for some reason."

It was clear to Fiske that the woman believed a mother's link to her children could trump even the grip of Alzheimer's. "I'm really busy right —" Fiske broke off what he was saying. It would be a miracle if his mother could remember anything of any conversation she might have had with Mike that could possibly help them. But if she did?

"I'll be right over."

Fiske hung up the phone, picked up his briefcase and stuffed the stack of mail in there.

"Your brother visited your mom on the day he disappeared?" McKenna asked. Fiske nodded. "Then she might be able to tell us something."

"McKenna, my mom has Alzheimer's. She thinks John Kennedy is still president."

"Okay, what about somebody who works there?"

Fiske wrote down an address and phone number on the back of one of his cards. "But leave my mom out of it."

"You're going to see her, aren't you? How come?"

"She's my mother." Fiske disappeared out the door.

Hawkins looked over at McKenna. "You ready to leave? Because I want to lock up. Don't want anybody else coming in here and stealing any more stuff."

The way Hawkins said it made McKenna blink. The guy couldn't know that he had taken the gun, could he? Still, he felt guilty about it. But he had bigger things to feel guilty about. Far bigger.

CHAPTER FIFTY-FOUR

Sara was stopped at a red light on her way to Fiske's office when she saw him drive through the intersection heading west. She didn't have time even to blow her horn. She thought about flagging him down, but a glimpse of his tense face stopped her. She turned right and followed him.

Thirty minutes later she slowed as Fiske's car turned into the parking lot of a long-term care facility located in the West End of Richmond. Sara had been here once before, with Michael, to visit his mother. She kept her car hidden behind a broad-leaved evergreen next to the entrance and watched as Fiske stepped out of his car and hurried inside.

Fiske met up with Anne, the woman who had just called him, who apologized again and led him to the visitors' lounge, where Gladys sat docilely in her pajamas and slippers. When Fiske appeared, she looked up and silently clapped her hands together.

Fiske sat down across from her, and Gladys put out her hands and tenderly touched his face. Her smile broadened, her eyes wide and catching absolutely nothing of reality.

"How's my Mike? How's Momma's baby?"

He gently touched her hands. "I'm fine. Doing good. Pop's good too," he lied. "We had a nice visit the other day, didn't we?"

"Visits are *so* nice." She looked behind him and smiled. She often did that. It was hard keeping her attention. She was an infant now, the cycle complete.

She touched his cheek again. "Your daddy was here."

"When was that?"

She shook her head, "Last year sometime. He got leave. His ship went down. Japs done it."

"Really? He's okay, isn't he?"

She laughed long and loud. "Oh yes, that man is A-okay." She leaned forward and whispered conspiratorially, "Mike, honey, can you keep a secret?"

"Sure, Mom," Fiske said hesitantly.

She looked around, blushing. "I'm pregnant again."

Fiske took a deep breath. This was a new one. "Really? When did you find out?"

"Now, don't you worry, sweetie, Momma's got enough love to go around for all of you." She pinched his cheek and kissed his forehead.

He squeezed her hand and managed a smile. "We had a good talk the other day, didn't we?" She nodded absently. This was crazy, he thought, but he was here and he might as well try. "I had a good trip. You remember where I went?"

"You went to school, Mike, just like every day. Your daddy took you on his ship." She frowned. "You be careful out there. Lot of fighting going on. Your daddy's out fighting right now." She punched a fist in the air. "Get 'em, Eddie."

Fiske sat back and stared at her. "I'll be careful." Looking at her was like watching a portrait that was fading daily under unforgiving sunlight. Eventually, he would come to visit and all the paint would be gone, the only image left would come from his memory. And so life goes. "I have to get going. I'm, uh, I'm late for school."

"So pretty." She looked past him and waved. "Hello, there." Fiske turned around and froze as he saw Sara standing there.

"I'm pregnant, honey," Gladys told her.

"Congratulations," was all Sara could think to say.

Fiske stormed down the hallway to the exit, Sara trailing him. He threw open the door so hard it smacked against the wall.

"John, will you stop and talk to me?" she pleaded.

He whirled around. "How dare you come and spy on me."

"I wasn't spying."

"It's none of your damn business." He

pulled out his keys and got into his car. She jumped in.

"Get the hell out of my car."

"I'm not budging until we talk about this."

"Bullshit!"

"If you want me out, throw me out."

"Damn you!" Fiske shouted, before climbing out of the car.

Sara followed him. "Damn *you,* John Fiske. Will you please stop running away and talk to me?"

"We've got nothing to talk about."

"We have *everything* to talk about."

He pointed an unsteady finger at her. "Why the hell are you doing this to me, Sara?"

"Because I care about you."

"I don't need your help."

"I think you do. I know you do."

They stood there staring at each other.

"Can't we go somewhere and talk about this? Please." She slowly walked around the car and stood next to him. Touching his arm, she said, "If last night meant half as much to you as it did to me, we should at least be able to talk." She stood there, convinced that his response would be to climb in his car and drive out of her life.

Fiske looked at her for a moment, dropped his head and wearily leaned against his car. Sara's hand slipped down to his and tightened around it. Fiske looked beyond her to a car parked on the road and the two men inside. "We'll have the Feds along for a ride." His manner and tone were now resigned. At least it wasn't McKenna back there.

"Good, I'll feel very safe," she said, her gaze refusing to leave his, until finally she saw she hadn't lost him, at least for now.

They climbed in their cars and Sara followed Fiske to a small shopping mall about a mile away, where they sat at an outdoor table and sipped lemonade in the heat of the late afternoon.

"I can understand how you could hold that against your brother, although it's not his fault," Sara said.

"Nothing was ever Mike's fault," Fiske said bitterly.

"It's not like your mother can help herself. It could just as easily be that she called Michael by your name."

"Yeah, right. She chose not to remember me."

"Maybe she calls you that because you visited her a lot more than Michael did and that's her way of reacting to it."

"I'm not buying that."

Sara looked angry. "Well, if you want to be jealous of your brother even now that he's dead, then I guess that's your right."

Fiske settled a very cold gaze on her. She expected him to erupt. Instead, he said, "I am, was, whatever, jealous of my brother.

Who wouldn't be?"

"But that doesn't make it right."

"Maybe it doesn't," Fiske said, his voice tired. He looked away. "The first time I visited Mom and she called me Mike, I thought it was a temporary thing, you know, she was having a real bad day. After two months of it . . ." He paused. "Well, that's when I cut Mike off. For good. Everything that had ever ticked me off about him, no matter how stupid, I just blew up into a huge picture of this evil sonofabitch with no heart, nothing good. He had taken my mother away from me."

"John, the day we came to see you at trial, I went with Michael to see your mother."

He tensed. "What?"

"Your mother wouldn't even talk to him. He brought her a gift, she wouldn't take it. He told me she was always like that. He assumed that it was because she loved you so much, that she didn't care about him."

"You're lying," Fiske said in a hushed tone.

"No, I'm not. It's the truth."

"You're lying!" he said again, more forcefully.

"Ask some of the people who work there. They know."

A few minutes of silence passed. Fiske's head was bowed. When he looked back up, he said, "I never really thought about him losing his mother too."

"Are you sure about that?" Sara asked quietly.

Fiske stared at her, his hands clenched. "What do you mean?" he said, his voice shaking.

"What stopped you from talking to your brother? Michael told me you had shut him out, and you just admitted that. Even so, I can't believe you never knew how she treated him."

For a full minute Fiske said nothing. He stared at Sara, perhaps through her; his eyes revealed nothing of what he was thinking. Finally, he closed his eyes and said in a barely audible tone, "I knew."

He looked at her. The terrible pain on his features made her tremble.

"I just didn't want to care," Fiske said. Sara gripped his shoulder tightly. "I guess I used it as an excuse not to have anything to do with my own brother." He took another deep breath. "There's something else. Mike did call me, before he went to the prison. I didn't call him back. Not until it was too late. . . . I killed him."

"You can't blame yourself for that." Sara's words had no effect, she could see that, so she changed tactics. "If you want to blame yourself, then do it for the right reason. You unfairly cut your brother out of your life. You were wrong to do that. Very wrong. Now he's gone. That's something you'll have to live with forever, John."

Now he looked at her. His face grew calmer. "I guess I've been living with it already."

Since he had confided in her, Sara decided it was only fair to reciprocate. "I saw your father today." Before Fiske could say anything, she hurried on. "I promised you I would. I told him what really happened."

"And he believed you," Fiske said skeptically.

"I was telling the truth. He's going to call you."

"Thanks, but I wish you had kept out of it."

"He filled in some gaps for me."

"Like what?" Fiske said sharply.

"Like what happened to make you stop being a cop."

"Dammit, Sara, you had no need to know that."

"Yes, I did. A great reason."

"What is it?"

"You know what!"

Neither of them spoke for several minutes. Fiske looked down at the table too, and fiddled with his straw. Finally, he sat back and crossed his arms. "So my dad told you everything?"

Sara glanced up at him. "About the shooting, yes." Her tone was cautious.

"So you know I'm probably not going to be alive and kicking when I'm sixty or maybe even fifty."

"I think you can beat any odds someone throws at you."

"And if I don't?"

"If you don't, that doesn't matter to me." He leaned forward. "But it matters to me, Sara."

"So you give up the life you do have?"

"I think I'm leading my life exactly how I want to."

"Maybe you are," she quietly conceded.

"It would never work, you know."

"So you've thought about it?"

"I've thought about it. Have you? How do you know this isn't another impulse decision? Like buying your house?"

"It's what I feel."

"Feelings change."

"And it's so much easier to admit defeat rather than work at something."

"When I want something, I work very hard at it." Fiske had no idea why he said that, but he saw the devastated look on Sara's face.

"I see. And I guess I have no choice in the matter?"

"You really don't want to have to make that kind of a choice." She said nothing and Fiske remained quiet for a moment. "You know, my dad didn't tell you everything, because he doesn't know everything."

"He told me how you almost died, how the other officer did die. And the man who shot you. I can understand how that could change your life. How it could make you do what you do. I think it's very noble, if that's the right word."

"That's not even close. Do you really want to know why I do what I do?"

Sara could sense the sudden change of mood. "Tell me."

"Because I'm scared." He nodded at her. "Fear drives me. The longer I was a cop, the more it became 'us against them.' Young, angry, attitude, with a pistol to back it all up." Fiske stopped speaking and watched through the glass partition as people inside bought refreshments. They appeared carefree, happy, pursuing some tangible goal in their lives; they were everything he wasn't, couldn't be.

He looked back at Sara. "I kept arresting the same guys over and over and it seemed like before I filed the paperwork they were back on the streets. And they'd blow you away like stepping on a cockroach. See, they lived the game of 'us against them' too. You lump people together. Young and black, catch 'em if you can. Blues coming at you? Kill 'em if you can. It's quick and you don't have to make choices about individuals. It's like a drug addiction."

"Not everybody does that. The whole

world isn't made up of people like that."

"I know that. I know that most people, black, white or whatever, are good people, lead relatively normal lives. I really want to believe that. It's just that as a cop I never saw any of that. Normal ships didn't sail by my dock."

"So did the shooting make you rethink things?"

Fiske didn't answer right away. When he did, he spoke slowly. "I remember dropping to my knees to check the guy, who it turned out was faking a seizure. I heard the gun go off, my partner scream. I pulled my pistol at the same time I was turning. I don't know how I got a round off, but I did. It hit him right in the chest. We both went down. He lost his gun, but I kept mine. Pointed it right at him. He wasn't more than a foot from me. Every breath he took, blood kicked out of the bullet hole like a red geyser. It made this swishing sound I still hear in my sleep. His eyes had started to freeze up, but you never knew. All I knew was that he had just shot my backup, and he had just shot me. My insides felt like they were dissolving." Fiske let out a long breath. "I was going to just wait for him to die, Sara." Fiske stopped talking as he recalled how close he had come to being another blue in a box, buried and mostly forgotten.

"Your father said you were found with your

arm around him," Sara gently prompted.

"I thought he was trying to grab my gun. I had one finger on the trigger and one finger stuck in the hole in my gut. But he didn't even put his hand out. Then I heard him talking. I could barely make out what he was saying at first, but he kept saying it until I did."

"What did he say?" Sara asked gently.

Fiske let out a breath, half expecting to see blood kick out of his old wounds, his tired, betrayed organs calling it quits on him forty years early. "He was asking me to kill him." As if in answer to her unspoken question, Fiske said, "I couldn't. I didn't. It didn't matter, though, he stopped talking a few seconds later."

Sara slowly sat back, unable to say anything.

"I actually think he was terrified he *wasn't* going to die." Fiske shook his head slowly, the words becoming more difficult to put together. "He was only nineteen. I'm an old man already, next to him. His name was Darnell — Darnell Jackson. His mother was a crack addict, and when he was eight or nine she would whore him out for drug money."

He looked at her. "Does that sound horrible to you?"

"Of course it does. Yes!"

"To me, it was the same old shit. I saw it all the time. I'd become immune to it, or at least

I thought I had." He licked his dry lips. "I didn't think I had any compassion left. But after Darnell, I got some back." He flashed a troubled smile. "I call it my steel-jacketed epiphany. Two slugs in my body, a kid dying in front of me, wanting me to finish him off. It's hard to imagine one event having enough force to make you question everything you've ever believed. But it happened to me that night." He nodded thoughtfully. "Now I think of the whole future of the world solely in the context of Darnell Jackson. He's my version of nuclear holocaust, only it won't be over in a few seconds." He looked at her. "That's the terror that drives me."

"I think you really do care. You do a lot of good."

Fiske shook his head, his eyes glimmering. "I'm not some rich, brilliant white attorney running around nobly saving the little Enises of the world. And it took a lost kid blowing up my insides with a cannon to make me even give a damn. How many people do you think really care?"

"You can't be that cynical, can you?"

Fiske stared at her a moment before answering. "Actually, I'm the most hopeful cynic you'll ever meet."

CHAPTER FIFTY-FIVE

"You did the right thing, Beth. As much as it hurts. I still can't believe it about Sara, though." Jordan Knight shook his head. They were in the back seat of his government limousine, which was threading its way through bumper-to-bumper traffic toward their Watergate apartment. "Maybe she just cracked. The pressures are enormous."

"I know," Elizabeth Knight said quietly.

"It all seems so bizarre. A clerk steals an appeal. Sara knows about it but keeps quiet. The clerk is then murdered. Then the clerk's brother comes under suspicion. John Fiske just doesn't strike me as the murderous type."

"He doesn't strike me that way either." Her discussion with John Fiske had only deepened her fears.

Jordan Knight patted his wife's hand. "I've checked on Chandler and McKenna. Both are rock-solid. McKenna has an excellent reputation at the Bureau. If anybody can solve this thing, I think those two can."

"I find Warren McKenna rude and obnoxious."

"Well, in his line of work I suppose he

sometimes has to be," he pointed out.

"That's not all. There's just something about him. He's so intense, but he almost seems to be" — she paused, searching for the right word — "playacting."

"In the middle of a murder investigation?"

"I know it sounds crazy, but it's just how I feel."

The senator shrugged and stroked his chin thoughtfully. "I've always said a woman's intuition is worth more than a man's best judgment. I guess in this town we're all on a stage. Sometimes one does grow tired of it."

She eyed him closely. "The New Mexico ranch beckons?"

"I've got a dozen years on you, Beth. Every day becomes a little more precious."

"It's not like we're not together."

"Time together in D.C. is not really the same. We're both so busy here."

"My appointment to the Court is a lifetime one, Jordan."

"I just don't want you to have any regrets. And I'm trying my best not to have any."

They both fell silent and looked out the window as the car traveled along Virginia Avenue.

"I heard you and Ramsey went at it tooth and claw today. Do you think you have a chance?"

"Jordan, you know I don't feel comfortable talking to you about these things."

Jordan reddened. "That's one thing I hate about this town, and our jobs. Government should not interfere in the covenant of marriage."

"Funny talk, coming from a politician."

Jordan laughed deeply. "Well, as a politician, I have to get up on the damn soapbox every now and then, don't I?" He stopped and took her hand. "I appreciate your going forward with the dinner for Kenneth. You took some heat for it, I know."

Elizabeth shrugged. "Harold takes any opportunity, no matter how trivial, to tweak me, Jordan. I've built up a very strong resistance." She gave him a kiss on the cheek, while he lovingly stroked her hair.

"We really have prevailed, despite all the odds, haven't we? We have a nice life, don't we?"

"We have a wonderful life, Jordan." She kissed him again and he put a protective arm around her.

"I say tonight we cancel all of our appointments and just stay home. Have some dinner, watch a movie. And talk. We don't get to do that much anymore."

"I'm afraid I won't be good company."

Jordan squeezed her tightly. "You're always good company, Beth. Always."

When the Knights arrived at their apartment, Mary, their housekeeper, handed a phone message to Elizabeth. A curious expression crossed her face as she looked at the name on the paper.

Jordan appeared in the hallway rubbing his hands together. He looked at Mary. "I hope you have something nice planned for dinner."

"Your favorite. Beef tenderloin."

Jordan smiled. "I think we're going to have a late dinner. Tonight the missus and I are going to relax completely. No interruptions." He looked at his wife. "Anything wrong?" He noted the paper in her hand.

"No. Court business. It never ends."

"You don't have to tell me that," he said dryly. "Well, I'm for a hot shower." He went down the hallway. "You're welcome to join me," he called over his shoulder.

Mary went off to the kitchen, a smile on her lips at the senator's remark.

Elizabeth took the opportunity to slip into the study and dialed the number on the message.

"I'm returning your call," she said into the phone.

"We need to talk, Justice Knight. How's right now?"

"What is this about?"

"What I'm about to tell you will come as quite a shock. Are you prepared for that?"

For some reason, Elizabeth Knight sensed that the man was enjoying this. "I really don't have time for the cloak-and-dagger rhetoric that obviously amuses you."

"Well, I'm going to give you a crash course in it."

"What are you talking about?"

"Just listen."

And she did. Twenty minutes later she threw the phone down, raced out of the room and almost knocked down Mary, who was coming down the hallway. Elizabeth raced into the powder room, where she splashed water on her face. She gripped the edges of the sink, composed herself, opened the door and moved slowly down the hallway.

She could still hear Jordan in the shower. She looked at her watch. She went out into the lobby and down the elevator to the reception area of the building and waited over by the main entrance. Time seemed to pass slowly. Actually only ten minutes had gone by since her phone call. Finally, a man she didn't recognize, but who clearly knew her by sight, appeared and handed her something. She looked down at it. When she looked back up, he had already disappeared. She put what he had given her into her pocket and hurried back up to her apartment.

"Where's Jordan?" she asked Mary.

"I believe he's in the bedroom getting dressed. Are you all right, Ms. Knight?"

"Yes, I . . . my stomach was just a little upset, but I'm fine now. I decided to stretch my legs and do some window shopping downstairs, get some fresh air. Would you mix up some cocktails and put them out on the terrace?"

"It's starting to rain."

"But the awning's up. And I feel very claustrophobic all of a sudden. I need the air. It's been so hot and humid lately, and the rain has made things so cool. So very cool," she said wistfully. "Make Jordan's favorite, will you?"

"Beefeater Martini with a twist, yes, ma'am."

"And the dinner, Mary . . . please make sure it's absolutely wonderful. Just perfect."

"I will, ma'am." Mary headed to the bar with a puzzled look on her face.

Elizabeth Knight squeezed her hands together to fight the waves of panic. She just had to stop thinking about it. If she was going to make it through this, she had to merely act, not think. Please, God, help me, she prayed.

CHAPTER FIFTY-SIX

Fiske stared moodily out the car window at the dark clouds. He and Sara were halfway to Washington, and neither one had said much on the drive up.

Sara turned on the wipers as the rain started to fall. She looked over at him and frowned. "John, we've got a lot of information to work with. We might want to use the next hour making some sense of it all."

Fiske glanced at her. "I guess you're right. Do you have pen and paper anywhere?"

"Don't you have that in your briefcase?"

He undid his seat belt, pulled his briefcase from the back seat and popped it open. He pushed through the stack of mail until his hands closed around a bulky package. "Christ, that was fast."

"What?"

"I think this is Harms's service record." Fiske tore it open and started reading. Ten minutes later, he looked at her. "It's in two different parts. His service record, portions of the record of court-martial, and the personnel list from Fort Plessy during the time Harms was stationed there." Fiske pulled out a section marked MEDICAL RECORDS. He studied the pages and then stopped. "Would you like to guess why Rufus Harms was so insubordinate, wouldn't take orders, was always in trouble?"

"He was dyslexic," Sara answered promptly.

"How the hell did you know that?"

"A couple of things. Even the little I saw of it, the handwriting and spelling on the appeal was so bad. That's a sign of dyslexia, although it's not conclusive. But when I talked to George Barker, remember he told me that story about Rufus fixing his printing press?" Fiske nodded. "Well, he recalled Rufus saying that he didn't want to look at the manual for the printing press, that the words would just mess him up. I went to school with a girl who had dyslexia. She once told me more or less the same thing. It's like you can't communicate with the world. Although, from our encounter last night, it looks like Rufus has conquered his disability."

"If he can survive in prison all those years with people trying to kill him, he can do anything he sets his mind to." Fiske looked back at the records. "Looks like he was diagnosed with it after the murder. Probably during the court-martial proceedings. Maybe Rider discovered it. Preparing a defense requires some client cooperation."

"Dyslexia is not a defense to murder."

"No, but I know what is."

"What?" Sara asked excitedly. "What?"

"First, a question: Leo Dellasandro — is he having an affair with his secretary?"

"Why are you asking that?"

"He had makeup on his coat collar."

"Maybe it was from his wife."

"Maybe, but I don't think so."

"I really doubt he was having an affair, because his secretary just got married."

"I didn't think they were."

"So why did you ask me?"

"Just covering all the bases. I don't think Dellasandro got it from his wife either. I think he was wearing it."

"Why would a man — a chief of police, no less — be wearing makeup?"

"To cover the bruises he got when I hit him in my brother's apartment." Sara's breath caught as Fiske continued. "I haven't seen Dellasandro since that night. He wasn't at the meeting at the Court after Wright was murdered. I've been with Chandler a lot and the man never came by to check up on the investigation. At least while I was there. I think he was avoiding me. Maybe afraid I'd recognize him somehow."

"Why in the world would Leo Dellasandro have been at your brother's apartment?"

In response, Fiske held up a sheaf of papers. "The list of personnel stationed at Fort Plessy. Luckily, it's alphabetized." He turned toward the end of the roster. "Sergeant Victor Tremaine." He turned another page. "Captain Frank Rayfield." He flipped back through some pages and stopped. "Private Rufus Harms." Then he went back near the beginning, circled a name with his pen, and said triumphantly, "And Corporal Leo Dellasandro."

"Good God. Then Rayfield, Tremaine and Dellasandro were the men in the stockade that night?"

"I think so."

"How did you know Dellasandro was in the military?"

"I saw a photo of Dellasandro in his office. He was much younger, in uniform. His *Army* uniform. I think the three of them went there to teach Rufus Harms a lesson. I think we'll find they all fought in Vietnam, and Rufus didn't. He wouldn't follow orders, was always in trouble."

"But what the hell did they *do* to Rufus Harms?"

"I think they —"

The car phone rang. Sara glanced at Fiske and then picked it up. Her face went pale as she listened. "Yes, I'll accept the call. Hello? What? Okay, calm down. He's right here." She handed the phone to Fiske. "Rufus Harms. And he doesn't sound good."

Fiske gripped the phone. "Rufus, where are you?"

Rufus was inside the Jeep parked next to a pay phone. He had one hand on the phone, the other on Josh, who was now slipping into longer periods of unconsciousness, but still had the pistol wedged against his side. "Richmond," he answered. "I'm two minutes from the address on the card you gave me. Josh is hurt bad. I need a damn doctor and I need him quick."

"Okay, okay, tell me what happened."

"Rayfield and Tremaine caught up to us."

"Where are they now?"

"They're dead, dammit, and my brother's about ready to join 'em. You said you'd help me. Well, I need help."

Fiske glanced in the rearview mirror. The black sedan was still back there. He thought quickly. "Okay, I'll meet you at my office in four hours tops."

"Josh ain't got four hours. He's shot the hell up."

"We're going to take care of Josh right now, Rufus. I'm meeting you, not Josh."

"What the hell you talking about?"

"I'm going to call a buddy of mine who's a cop. He'll get an ambulance. They'll take care of him. MCV Hospital is only a few minutes from my office."

"No police!"

Fiske yelled into the phone, "Do you want Josh to die? Do you?" Fiske took the silence as Rufus's surrender to whatever help Fiske could give him. "Describe the car to me and give me the intersection where you are right now." Rufus did so. "My friend will have help there in a few minutes. Leave Josh in the car. As soon as you hang up, walk to my office building. It's open. Go in the front door and go down the flight of stairs on your left. You go through another door. There's a door on your right marked 'Supplies.' It's unlocked. Get in there and sit tight. I'll be down quick as I can. I also want you to take your brother's wallet because I don't want him to have any ID. If they know it's Josh, they're going to start looking for you nearby. That includes my office. The police cordoning off the area would throw a real wrench in my plan."

"What if somebody sees me? Maybe recognizes me?"

"We don't have much choice now, Rufus."

"I'm trusting you. Please help my brother. Please don't let me down."

"Rufus, I'm trusting you too. Don't let me down."

When Rufus hung up, he looked at Josh. He slipped a gun under his shirt and reached out to touch his brother. He thought Josh was completely unconscious now, but when Rufus brushed his shoulder gently with his finger, Josh opened his eyes.

"Josh —"

"I heard." The voice was weak; everything about him was now.

"He wants me to take your wallet, so they won't know who you are just yet."

"In my back pocket." Rufus slid it out. "Now get going."

Rufus considered this for a moment. "I can stay with you. We go together."

"No good." Josh spit up some more blood. "Docs'll sew me up. I been hurt a lot worse than this." Josh moved a shaky hand out, touched his brother's face, brushed away the wetness from his eyes.

"I'm gonna stay with you, Josh."

"You stay, all this is for nothing."

"I can't leave you alone. Not like this. Not after all these years away."

With a painful grimace, Josh sat up. "You ain't leaving me alone. Give it to me."

"Give you what?"

Josh said, "The Bible."

Without taking his eyes off his brother, Rufus slowly reached behind the seat and handed him the book. In return, Josh held out the pistol that had been wedged against his ribs for all these hours. Rufus looked at him questioningly. "Fair swap," Josh said hoarsely.

Rufus thought he saw a smile flicker across his brother's lips before Josh closed his eyes, his breathing shallow but steady. One large hand gripped the Bible so tightly the spine of the book twisted.

As Rufus climbed out of the Jeep, he

looked back once more, and then left his brother behind.

Fiske finally reached Hawkins at home. "Don't ask me why or how, Billy. I can't tell you who it is. For now he's a John Doe. Stall the paperwork and drive the Jeep to the hospital." Fiske hung up.

"John, how are we going to meet Rufus with the FBI right behind us?" Sara said.

"I'm meeting Rufus, you're not."

"Wait a minute —"

"Sara —"

"I want to see this through."

"Believe me, you will. You have to make a phone call for me, to my friend at the JAG."

"What about? And you still haven't told me what you think happened in that stockade twenty-five years ago."

He put one hand on top of hers. "*U.S. v. Stanley*. An innocent soldier and LSD," Fiske said, watching her eyes go wide. "Only worse," he added.

After making a quick stop at Sara's home, they drove to National Airport and parked. Fiske tugged the trench coat around him and pulled his hat down tightly over his head as the rain began to fall harder. He opened a big umbrella and covered Sara with it. They went to the general aviation terminal, and then out the other side to the boarding area, where they climbed in a sedan with tinted windows. A couple minutes later the car pulled away from the curb.

Behind them were two FBI agents, one of whom was already communicating this development to his superiors. Then he went over to the service counter to determine the destination of the flight Fiske and Sara were about to get on. The other agent went out and watched as the sedan pulled up to the private jet.

Inside the sedan, Fiske and the driver, Chuck Herman's copilot, were busy switching places. The driver put on the trench coat and hat. From a distance he would look like Fiske. Their plan was to have Sara stay on the plane for an hour, during which time she would attempt to contact Fiske's JAG friend, Phil Jansen. Then she would leave. They knew the FBI would question her about Fiske's disappearance, but they would have no grounds to detain her.

The FBI agent watched as a thin, white-haired man came down the steps from the plane and greeted Sara and the man whom he assumed was Fiske as they climbed out of the car. The group went up the steps and into the plane. The sedan pulled away. The FBI agent kept his eyes on the plane as the sedan passed by him and continued on to the main road leading out of the terminal.

Driving the sedan, Fiske let out a deep

breath as he pulled onto the George Washington Parkway. Within ten minutes he was headed south on Interstate 95 toward Richmond. Traffic was heavy; it was almost three hours before he pulled the car up to his office building. He had already checked in with Billy Hawkins. Josh Harms was in surgery at MCV. It didn't look good, Hawkins had told him. Fiske parked the car and went around to the office's rear entrance, just in case.

He made his way to the lower level and approached the supply room. Please be there, he urged Rufus. He tapped on the door. "Rufus?" he said quietly. "It's John Fiske."

Rufus cautiously opened the door.

"Let's get out of here."

Rufus gripped his arm. "How's Josh?"

"He's in surgery. All you can do is pray."

"That's all I been doing."

They went out the rear entrance, walked quickly to Fiske's car and climbed in.

"Where we going?" Rufus said.

"You want to tell me about the letter from the Army?"

"What about it?"

"They wanted to follow up on the phencyclidine testing, right?"

Harms stiffened. "Phen-what?"

"You know, PCP."

"How did you know about that?"

"Same thing happened to another guy in the Army named Stanley, who was in a bogus program. They used LSD on him."

"I wasn't in no damn PCP program, even if they said I was." He pulled out the letter and gave it to Fiske.

Fiske took a moment to read it and then looked at him. "Tell me about it, Rufus."

Harms sat back as much as he could. He was so large that his knees touched the dash and his head brushed the car's ceiling. "They'd been out to get me for a while. Tremaine and Rayfield."

"And Dellasandro? Corporal Leo Dellasandro?"

"Yeah, him too. I guess they didn't take too kindly to me sitting nice and snug in the States, even if it was in the stockade."

"They didn't know about your dyslexia?"

"You seem to know a damn lot."

"Go on."

"I'd had plenty of run-ins with that group before. Tremaine got thrown in the stockade with me one night for drinking. He told me real directly what he thought about me. I guess they planned this thing out. They came in the stockade one night. Leo had a gun. They made me close my eyes, get on the floor. The next thing I knew, they stuck something in me. I opened my eyes and saw the needle coming out of my arm. They all stood there laughing, waiting for me to die. I could tell from what they said, that was their plan. OD me on the stuff."

"How the hell did you go from getting shot up with PCP to escaping from the stockade?"

"My whole body seemed to swell up like somebody was pumping air in me. I remember getting up and it felt like the room wasn't big enough to hold me. I tossed 'em all aside like they were made of straw. They had left the door unlocked. The guard on duty came running up, but I hit him like a truck and then I was running free." His breathing had accelerated, his huge hands clasping and unclasping, as though reliving what he had done with them so long ago.

"And you ran into Ruth Ann Mosley?"

"She was there visiting her brother." Rufus slammed his fist down onto the dash. "If only God had struck me down before I got to that little girl. Why'd it have to be a child? Why?" Tears streamed down the man's face.

"It wasn't your fault, Rufus. PCP can make you do anything, anything. It wasn't your fault."

In answer Rufus held up his hands and bellowed, "These did it. No matter what shit they put in me, ain't nothing gonna change the fact that I killed that beautiful little girl. Ain't nothing on this earth gonna make that go away. Is it? Is it?" Rufus's eyes blazed at Fiske, but then he closed them and slumped back, as though lifeless.

Fiske tried to keep calm. "And you remembered nothing, until you got the letter?"

Finally Rufus came around. "Hell, all those years the only thing I remembered from that night was sitting in the stockade reading the Bible my momma give me. The next thing I knew I'm next to this dead little girl. That's all." He wiped the tears away with his sleeve.

"PCP can do that too. Screw with your memory. Probably the shock of it all too."

Rufus took a heavy breath. "Sometimes I think that crap's still in me."

"But you pleaded guilty to the murder anyway?"

"There was a bunch of witnesses. Samuel Rider said if I didn't take the deal, they'd convict me and then they'd execute me. What the hell else was I supposed to do?"

Fiske thought about that for a moment and then said quietly, "I guess I would've done the same thing."

"But when I got that letter, it was like somebody turned this big light on inside my head, and some part of my brain that had been all dark got real bright and everything came back to me. Every damn little bit."

"And so you wrote the letter to the Court and asked Rider to file it for you?"

Rufus nodded. "And then your brother came to see me. Said he believed in justice, wanted to help me if I was telling the truth. He was a good man."

"Yes, he was," Fiske said hoarsely.

"The thing was, he had brought my letter

with him. Rayfield and old Vic weren't going to let him go. No way. I went crazy when I found out. They took me to the infirmary, tried to kill me there. I got to the hospital and Josh busted me out."

"You said Tremaine and Rayfield are dead."

Rufus nodded. He took another deep breath, watched the rain falling over the darkened Richmond skyline and then looked over at Fiske. "Now you know everything I know. So what are we going to do?"

"I'm not sure," was all Fiske could manage to say.

CHAPTER FIFTY-SEVEN

An hour after Fiske had driven off, Chuck Herman smiled as he passed Sara in the plane aisle. "This is the only time I've ever been paid *not* to fly."

"This is Washington, Chuck. They pay farmers not to grow crops too," Sara said dryly.

She picked up the cell phone for the tenth time and dialed Phil Jansen's home number. His office had already told Sara that Jansen had left for the day. Luckily, Fiske had given her Jansen's home number too. She was relieved when Jansen finally answered. She quickly introduced herself and explained her connection to Fiske.

"I don't have much time, Mr. Jansen, so I might as well get to the point. In the past has the Army been involved in PCP testing programs?"

Jansen's voice tensed. "Why exactly are you asking that, Ms. Evans?"

"John thinks that Rufus Harms was involuntarily given PCP when he was in an Army stockade at Fort Plessy twenty-five years ago. He thinks the exposure to PCP caused Harms to go berserk and kill a little girl. He's been in prison for the crime ever since."

Sara recounted all that she and Fiske had deduced, along with what they had learned from Rufus at Rider's office. Sara continued, "Rufus Harms recently received a letter from the Army asking him to participate in a follow-up test to determine the long-term effects of PCP. That's what happened to Sergeant James Stanley, right? The Army sent him a letter. That was the only reason he knew the Army had given him LSD. Well, we think a group of Army personnel forcefully administered PCP to Harms in the stockade, but not as part of any program. We think they intended to use the drug to kill him. Instead he broke free and committed the murder."

Jansen said, "Wait a minute. Why did the Army send him a letter saying Harms was in the program, if he wasn't?"

"We think whoever gave Harms the PCP enrolled him in the program."

"And why would they do that?"

"If they killed him with the PCP and there was an autopsy, presumably the substance would have been found in his bloodstream."

"Yes, it would," Jansen said slowly. "So they enrolled him in the program to cover that up. The coroner would chalk it up to an unfortunate reaction to the drug. I can't believe this."

"Right. So such a program existed?"

"Yes," Jansen conceded. "It's public information now. All declassified. It was run jointly by the Army and CIA in the seventies. They wanted to determine if PCP could be used to 'build' super soldiers. If Harms was listed in the program's records, he would have recently received a follow-up letter." Jansen paused for a moment. "What are you and John going to do now?"

"I wish we knew." Sara thanked Jansen and hung up.

She waited awhile longer and then left the plane and walked across the tarmac to the terminal. She was immediately stopped by the two FBI agents.

"Where's Fiske?" one of them demanded.

"John Fiske?" she asked innocently.

"Come on, Ms. Evans."

"He left a while back."

The agents looked startled. "Left. How?"

"I assume he drove. Now, if you'll excuse me."

She smiled as the stunned men took off at a dead run toward the plane. They had no grounds to detain her. She took the opportunity to hop on the shuttle bus to the garage and got her car. She drove out of the airport and headed south. A sudden thought hit her and she pulled off the road and into a gas station. Keeping the motor running, she opened Fiske's briefcase and took out the packet of documents they had received from St. Louis. She wasn't sure how closely Fiske had examined them, but it had occurred to her that it was possible the Army might have put a copy of the letter they had sent to Rufus Harms in his official file — although technically it had been closed upon the occasion of his court-martial. It was worth a look.

A half hour later she sat back, disappointed. She started returning the papers to the briefcase when her hand closed around the personnel list from Fort Plessy. She leafed through the pages, noting the names of Victor Tremaine and Frank Rayfield. Then her eye sadly passed over the name of Rufus Harms. So many years of his life gone.

As she was thinking this, she was continuing to turn pages, running her eye down the personnel list; as soon as she saw the name, she froze. When she finally broke out of her trance, she did so with such force that she bumped her head against the window. She threw the file down and slammed the car into gear, burning rubber on the slick pavement as she sped out of the gas station. She glanced down at the floorboard where the personnel list had landed, where the name Warren McKenna seemed to stare back at her, taunting her. She never looked back, so she didn't notice the car that had followed her from the airport.

CHAPTER FIFTY-EIGHT

Harold Ramsey leaned back in his chair, a grave look on his face. "I never imagined that anything like this could have happened here."

McKenna and Chandler sat in Ramsey's chambers. McKenna watched the chief justice closely. They seemed to make eye contact for a moment, and then McKenna looked away and glanced over at Chandler.

"Well, we don't have any solid proof one way or another about whether Michael Fiske actually stole an appeal, or if there even was an appeal," Chandler said.

Ramsey shook his head in disagreement. "After the discussion with Sara Evans, can there be any doubt?"

Discussion? Inquisition was more like it, Chandler thought. "It's still speculation. And I would advise against going public with this information."

"I agree," McKenna said. "It could complicate the investigation."

"I thought you were convinced that John Fiske was behind it all," Ramsey said. "If you're changing your position now, I don't see how we're any farther ahead than we were two days ago."

"Murders don't just solve themselves. And this one is a little more complex than usual. And I never said I had changed my position," McKenna said. "Fiske's gun was missing from his office. No big surprise there. Don't worry, things are falling into place."

Ramsey looked unconvinced.

"I really don't see why waiting a bit will hurt," Chandler said. "And if things turn out the way we hope, maybe the public never has to know."

"I don't see how that is possible," Ramsey said angrily. "But I suppose it won't make this disaster any more horrible by taking your advice. For now. What about Fiske and Evans? Where are they?"

"We have them under surveillance," McKenna answered.

"So you know where they are right now?" Ramsey asked.

McKenna maintained his stone face. He wasn't about to admit that in fact both Sara and Fiske had managed to elude his FBI surveillance team. McKenna had just gotten that message a minute before he had stepped into this meeting.

"Yes," McKenna answered.

"Where are they?" Ramsey asked.

"I'm afraid I can't give out that information, Mr. Chief Justice." He added quickly, "As much as I'd like to accommodate you. We really need to keep that confidential."

Ramsey looked sternly at him. "Agent McKenna, you promised to keep the Court informed about the progress of this case."

"I did. That's why I'm here right now."

"The Court has its own police force. Chief Dellasandro and Ron Klaus are out right this very minute trying to solve this thing. We have our own investigation ongoing and it's in the best interests of everybody that we have full disclosure. Now please answer my question. Where are they?"

"What you say makes a lot of sense, but I'm afraid I still can't divulge that information," he said. "FBI policy, you understand."

Ramsey arched his eyebrows. "I think I should speak to someone else at the Bureau, then," he said. "I don't like going over people's heads, Agent McKenna, but this is a unique situation."

"I'd be glad to give you some names to call at the Bureau, starting with the director himself," McKenna offered pleasantly.

"Do you have anything of actual importance to report," Ramsey said dryly, "or is that it?"

McKenna stood up. "We're trying as hard as we can to get to the bottom of this. And I'm convinced that, with a little luck, we will."

Ramsey stood up too, towering over them. "A word of advice, Agent McKenna. Never leave anything to chance. Anyone who does that usually lives to regret it."

Sara unlocked the door to her cottage and hurried inside. From her car she had tried phoning Fiske's home and office; then had tried Ed Fiske too, but he had heard nothing from his son. She threw her purse down on the kitchen table, went upstairs and changed out of her wet clothes and into jeans and a T-shirt. She was nearing panic and she wasn't sure what to do. If Dellasandro was in on this, that was bad enough. He was privy to what was happening with the investigation. The fact that FBI Agent Warren McKenna was also involved was potentially cata- strophic. He was practically running the damn investigation. She could now see the subtle manipulations of the FBI agent at every juncture in the case. Fiske implicated, herself forced to quit the Court; all of it building motive for John's killing his brother. It was all untrue, and yet, for someone just looking at the bare facts, it would make sense.

She tried Chandler's office. She wanted to know definitively if Agent McKenna had been stationed at Fort Plessy, or if it had been simply someone else with the same name. She couldn't believe two McKennas would be involved here, but she needed to be sure. Unfortunately, Chandler wasn't in. Who else could she call who would have that informa- tion? Jansen might be able to find out, but it would probably take him a while. She tried his number anyway, but there was no answer. Who else? It suddenly hit her. She dialed the number. After three rings a woman answered. It was the housekeeper.

"Is he in? It's Sara Evans."

A minute later Jordan Knight's voice came on the line.

"Sara?"

"I know this is terrible timing, Senator."

"I heard what happened today." His tone was cold.

"I know what you must think, and I'm sure nothing I could say would change your mind."

"You're probably right about that. However, for what it's worth Beth feels terrible about what happened. She was one of your strongest supporters."

"I appreciate that." Sara held the phone away from her ear as she struggled to hold her nerves in check. Every second counted now. "I need a favor."

"A favor?" Jordan sounded perplexed.

"Some information on someone."

"Sara, I hardly think this is appropriate."

"Senator, I will never, ever call you again, but I really need to know the answer to my question, and with all your information resources, and your personal clout, you're the only person I can think of to ask. Please? For old times' sake."

Jordan pondered this for a moment. "Well, I'm not at my office right now. I was just settling down to a late dinner with Beth, in fact."

"But you could call your office, or maybe the FBI."

"The FBI?" he said loudly.

She hurried on. "A phone call would be all that it would take. I'm at home. You can even have the person call me back directly. You and I won't even have to speak again."

Finally, Jordan relented. "All right, what's your question?"

"It's about Agent McKenna."

"What about him?"

"I need to know if he ever served in the Army. Specifically at Fort Plessy during the seventies."

"Why in the world do you need to know that?"

"Senator, it would take me far too long to explain."

He sighed. "All right. I'll see what I can do. I'll have someone from my office check and then call you. You'll be at home?"

"Yes."

"Sara, I hope you know what you're doing."

"If you can believe it, Senator, I really do."

"If you say so," he replied, not sounding convinced.

When he went back into the dining room about fifteen minutes later, Elizabeth looked up at him. "What in the world did Sara want?"

"The strangest thing. You know that FBI

agent fellow? The one you were complaining about?"

She tensed. "Warren McKenna? What about him?"

"She wanted to know if he had ever served in the Army."

Elizabeth Knight dropped her fork. "Why would she want to know that?"

"I don't know. She wouldn't tell me." Jordan looked over at her curiously, noting her tension. "Are you all right?"

"I'm fine. This has just been the day from hell."

"I know, honey, I know," he said soothingly. He looked down at his cold meal. "I guess our relaxing evening just went out the window."

"What did you tell her?"

"Tell her? I told her I'd check. And that I'd have somebody get back to her. That's what I was doing, calling my office. I guess they can check on the computer or something."

"Where is Sara?"

"At home, waiting for the answer to her question."

Elizabeth got up, her face pale.

"Beth, are you all right?"

"A headache just hit me. I need some aspirin."

"I can get it for you."

"No, that's all right. Finish your dinner. Then maybe we can finally relax."

A worried-looking Jordan Knight watched his wife go down the hallway. Elizabeth Knight did indeed get some aspirin, since she did have a very real headache. Then she slipped down the hallway to her bedroom, picked up the phone and dialed a number.

"Hello," the voice said.

"Sara Evans just called. She asked Jordan a question."

"What was the question?"

"She wanted to know if you had ever been in the Army."

Warren McKenna loosened his tie and took a sip of water from the glass on his desk. He had just returned from the meeting at the Court. "And what did he tell her?"

"That he'd check and get back to her." Elizabeth did her best to fight back the tears.

McKenna nodded to himself. "Where is she?"

"She told Jordan she was at home."

"And John Fiske?"

"I don't know. Apparently she didn't say."

McKenna grabbed his coat. "Thanks for the information, Justice Knight. It might prove to be even more valuable than one of your opinions."

Elizabeth Knight slowly hung up the receiver and then picked it up again. She couldn't leave it like this. She dialed Information and got the number. The call was answered. "Detective Chandler, please. Tell him it's Elizabeth Knight and it's urgent."

Chandler came on the line. "What can I do for you, Justice Knight?"

"Detective Chandler, please don't ask me how I know, but you have to get to Sara Evans's house. I think she's in grave danger. Please hurry."

Chandler didn't waste time asking questions. He raced out of his office without even hanging up the phone.

Elizabeth Knight slowly put down the receiver. She had thought her work at the Court was pressure-filled, but this . . . She knew that no matter how this turned out, her life was going to be devastated. For her, there was no way out. How ironic, she thought, that justice would end up destroying her.

The figure was outfitted in dark clothing, a ski mask pulled over his face. He had followed Sara down to Richmond and then trailed her and Fiske and the FBI agents back to Washington. He was very grateful that she had lost the FBI agents; it would make his job much easier. Crouching down, he made his way over to the car and opened the driver's-side door. The dome light came on when he did so, and he quickly twisted the control to dim it. He looked at the windows of the house. He saw Sara pass by once, but she didn't look outside. He pulled a small flashlight from his pocket and swept the beam around the car's interior. He saw the papers on the floorboard, glanced at them and noted the encircled name. He gathered up the files and put them in a knapsack he was carrying. He pulled a pistol from his holster and attached a silencer to the muzzle. Looking up at the house again, he saw no sign of Sara this time. But she was in there. Alone. He put out the light and headed toward the house.

Sara had been nervously pacing the kitchen, constantly checking her watch and waiting for a phone call from Jordan Knight's office. She stepped out onto the rear deck and watched as a jet slid past under the canopy of dark clouds. Then she looked down at her sailboat as it nudged against the rubber tires that were affixed to the dock to act as buffers between the smooth fiberglass and the rough wood. She had to smile as she thought back to the events of last night. The smile disappeared as she recalled what she and Fiske had discussed after their encounter at the nursing home. She pressed her bare toes against the damp wood, and took a moment to breathe in the soothing smells of the wet, rustic surroundings.

She went inside and up the stairs, stopping at the doorway of her bedroom and looking inside. The bed was still unmade. She sat down on the mattress and picked up one edge of the sheet as she recalled their lovemaking.

She thought of how Fiske had pulled his T-shirt back down. The scar went from navel to neck, Ed had told her. As if it could ever actually make a difference to her. And yet Fiske obviously believed it could.

She listened as another jet passed overhead and then the complete silence returned in its wake, as though all sound had disappeared into a Pratt & Whitney-made vacuum. The silence so profound she could clearly hear the side door of the cottage open. She jumped up and raced to the stairs. "John?" There was no answer, and when the downstairs light went out, a shiver of fear hit her spine. She ran into her bedroom, shut and locked the door. Her chest heaving, her own pulse bursting in her eardrums, she looked around desperately for a weapon, because there was no way to escape. The window was small and even if she could manage to wriggle through, the grade of the land was such that the room was two stories off the ground, with a concrete sidewalk down below — and breaking both her legs didn't seem like a good idea.

Her sense of desperation turned to panic when the sounds of the footsteps reached her. She now cursed herself for not having a phone in the bedroom. She held her breath as she saw the doorknob slowly turn until the lock halted the movement, but both the lock and the door were very old. As something hit the door with a solid blow, she instinctively jumped back, a small scream escaping her lips. She scanned the room before her gaze settled on the four-poster bed. She raced over and grabbed one of the pineapple-shaped finials off one of the bedposts. Thank God she had never gotten around to having the bed actually canopied. The finial was solid wood and weighed at least a pound.

She held it in one upraised hand and stepped quickly over to the door. It shook as another blow landed, the lock bending under the force of it; the doorframe started to splinter. After that impact she reached over, quietly unlocked the door and then stood back. With the door unbolted, the next blow sent it and the man flying into the room. Sara's arm came down swiftly and the finial hit flesh. She raced through the doorway and down the hallway. The man she had struck lay on the floor holding his shoulder and moaning.

Sara knew that Rayfield and Tremaine were dead. Then the man she had just hit was either Dellasandro or — she shuddered at the thought of the man being in her home — Warren McKenna. She navigated the stairs in two jumps, grabbed her car keys off the table and threw open the door on her way to the car. She let out a shriek of terror.

The second man stared back at her, calmly, coolly. As he stepped forward, Leo Dellasandro pointed a pistol directly at her. The man in black came racing down the stairs holding his shoulder, his gun trained on her as well. Dellasandro closed the door. Sara looked at the man behind her. It must be McKenna. But then her expression changed. This man wasn't nearly big enough to be the FBI agent.

The ski mask came off and Richard Perkins glared at her. Then he smiled at her obvious astonishment and pulled some papers from his knapsack. "You must have overlooked my name on the Fort Plessy service roster, Sara. How sloppy of you."

She stared at him angrily. "The marshal of the Supreme Court and the chief of its police, parties to a despicable crime."

"Harms killed that girl, not me," Dellasandro said.

"Have you made yourself believe that, Leo? You killed her, not Rufus, just as sure as if your hands were around her neck."

Dellasandro's face turned ugly. "That sonofabitch. If I had my way I would've pumped him full of lead instead of some damn drug. He was a disgrace to the uniform."

"He was dyslexic," Sara screamed at him. "He didn't follow orders because he couldn't understand them, you idiot. You destroyed his life and that girl's for nothing."

A smirk appeared on Dellasandro's face. "I don't see it that way. Not at all. He got what he deserved."

"How's the face, Leo? John really popped

640

you. He knows everything, of course."

"We'll just have to visit him too."

"You, Vic Tremaine and Frank Rayfield?"

"You're damn right," Dellasandro said with a sneer.

"Your buddies are dead." Sara's smile emerged as Dellasandro's faded. "They ambushed Rufus and his brother, but just like last time they couldn't finish the job," she added tauntingly.

"Then I hope I get the chance to do it for them."

Sara stared him up and down and finally shook her head in disgust. "Tell me something, Leo. How did vermin like you ever get to be a police chief of anything?"

He slapped her across the face, and would have hit her again if Perkins hadn't stopped him. "We don't have time for this crap, Leo." He gripped Sara by the shoulder. That's when the phone rang.

Perkins looked at Dellasandro. "Fiske?" He looked again at Sara. "Fiske is with Harms, isn't he? That's why you had to split up, isn't it?" Sara looked away as the phone rang again. Perkins stuck his pistol under her chin and his finger tightened on the trigger. "I'll ask you one more time. Is Fiske with Rufus Harms?" He pushed the gun harder against her skin. "In two seconds your head will disappear, I swear to God. Answer me!"

"Yes! Yes, he's with him," she said in a

strangled voice as the metal pushed against her windpipe.

He shoved her to the phone. "Answer it. If it's Fiske, pick a place to meet. Make it somewhere around here, but private. Tell him you've found some more information. You say anything to warn him, you're dead." She hesitated. "Do it! Or die!" Sara could see now that the mild-mannered Perkins was actually the more dangerous of her two captors. She slowly picked up the phone. Perkins stood next to her listening, his gun pressed against her temple. She took a quick breath to try to calm herself.

"Hello?"

"Sara?" It was Fiske.

"I've been trying to reach you everywhere."

"I'm with Rufus."

Perkins pushed the gun against her head as he listened. "Where are you?" she asked.

"We're halfway to D.C. At a rest stop."

"What's your plan?"

"I think it's time we went to Chandler. Rufus and I have talked it over."

Perkins shook his head and pointed at the phone.

"I don't think that's such a good idea, John."

"Why not?"

"I've . . . I've found out some things that you need to know first. Before you go to Chandler."

"Like what?"

"I can't tell you over the phone. It could be bugged."

"Come on, I kind of doubt that, Sara."

"Look, I tell you what, give me the number where you're at and I'll call you from the car." She looked over at Perkins. "We can arrange to meet someplace. Then we can go to Chandler. The FBI has the tag number of the car you're in. You have to get rid of it anyway."

He gave her the number and she wrote it down on a pad by the phone and ripped off the top sheet.

"Are you sure you can't tell me over the phone?"

"I talked to your friend at the JAG," Sara said, whispering a silent prayer for what she was about to say next. If Fiske reacted the wrong way, she was dead. She had to trust him. "Darnell Jackson told me all about the PCP testing."

Fiske stiffened and looked over at Rufus, who sat in the car at the darkened rest stop. *Darnell Jackson.* He answered quickly. "Darnell's never let me down before."

Sara let out an inaudible breath. "I'll call you back in five minutes." She hung up and looked at the two men.

Perkins grinned malevolently. "Good job, Sara. Now let's go see your friends."

CHAPTER FIFTY-NINE

After Sara called him back with the meeting place, Fiske made one more phone call. The news was not good. Not good at all. Then he got in the car and looked at Harms. "He's got Sara."

"Who's got her?" Harms asked.

"Your old buddy. Dellasandro. He's the only one left."

"What you talking about, the only one left?"

"Rayfield and Tremaine are dead. That leaves Dellasandro. Sara tipped me off without him catching on —" Fiske stopped and stared at Rufus, who was staring back at him quizzically. Fiske spoke haltingly. "Rufus, how many men were in the stockade that night?"

"Five."

Fiske slumped back. "I only know about the three I just mentioned. Who are the other two?"

"Perkins. Dick Perkins."

Fiske thought he might be sick. "Richard Perkins is the marshal of the Supreme Court."

"I ain't seen him since that night and damn

glad of it. Except for Tremaine, he was the worst of the bunch. He'd come in and beat me with his damn baton. He's the one who shot me up with the PCP."

"And the fifth man?"

"Didn't know him. Never seen him before."

"That's okay. I think I know who it is." Sara had not told him about finding the man's name on Fort Plessy's personnel roster, but Fiske had finally figured it out himself. Warren McKenna's image appeared starkly in his thoughts. That's why the FBI agent was trying to frame him. It all made sense. Fiske started up the car.

"Where we going?"

"Sara just called back. She . . . they want us to meet them at a place off the GW Parkway in Virginia. I tried to get hold of Chandler, but he wasn't in. I left a message telling him where we'll be. I just hope he gets it in time."

"And we're going to go?"

"If we don't, they'll kill Sara. If you want to stay behind, you can."

In response, Rufus slid a pistol out of his pocket and handed it to Fiske. "You know how to use one of these things?"

Fiske took the pistol, pulled back the slide and made sure a round was chambered. "I think I can manage," he said.

It was well after midnight now and the

parkway was deserted. At various points there were pull-offs with picnic areas and small parks where, during the day, families would gather for barbecues and quality time. But now, as Fiske pulled the car down the road, the area was dark, isolated and, he knew, deadly. He eyed the exit signs until he found the one he wanted. At the same time that he saw the sign, he spotted Sara's car parked in the otherwise empty parking lot. Large trees served as a backdrop to the grassy picnic area. Beyond them Fiske could make out the deeper darkness that was the Potomac River.

Rufus was crouched in the back seat, his eyes level with the bottom edge of the window. His gaze swept the darkened landscape. "Somebody's in the car. Can't tell if it's a man or woman, though," he said.

Fiske squinted and then nodded in confirmation. They had devised a plan of sorts on the way up. Now that the lay of the land had been established, they could implement that plan. He pulled ahead a little until they passed a bend in the road that took them beyond the line of sight from Sara's car. Fiske pulled to a stop. The back door of the car opened, and Rufus quickly disappeared into the surrounding trees and headed through the woods toward the parking lot.

Fiske drove into the parking lot and pulled up a couple of spaces from Sara's car. He looked over and was relieved to see her in the driver's seat. He pulled his gun and slowly got out. He looked over the top of his car. "Sara?"

She looked at him, nodded and smiled tightly. The smile disappeared when the man next to her rose up and pointed a gun against her head. They both got out the driver's side. Dellasandro locked one arm around her neck, his free hand holding the gun tightly against her temple.

"Over here, Fiske," Dellasandro said. Fiske did his best to look shocked. "Where's Harms?" Dellasandro said.

Fiske made a show of rubbing his cheek. "He had a change of heart. Didn't want to go to the cops. Hit me and took off."

"And left you the car? I don't think so. Give me the answer I want or your girlfriend gets a chunk of lead in her brain."

"I'm telling you the truth. You know he's been in prison all these years. He didn't take the car because he can't even drive."

Dellasandro considered this for a moment. "Come over here. I want your hands way, way up in the air."

Fiske slipped the pistol in the back of his waistband and put his hands up in the air. He stepped slowly around the car and walked toward them. When he got close enough, he saw the ugly bruise on Sara's cheek. "Are you all right, Sara?"

She nodded. "I'm sorry, John."

"Right, right — look, just shut up," Dellasandro said. "Exactly where did Harms get away from you?"

"When we got off the interstate. We came up Route One."

"That was pretty stupid of him to go off like that. He'll never get far."

"Well, like they say, you can lead a horse to water . . ."

"Why don't I believe a word you're saying?"

"Maybe because you've been a lying sack of shit all your life and you figure everybody is the same way."

Dellasandro pointed his gun at Fiske's head. "It's gonna be so much fun blowing you away."

"Kind of hard disposing of a couple bodies."

Dellasandro glanced toward the river. "Not when you've got the best of Mother Nature to help you."

"And you don't think Chandler will suspect anything?"

"What's to suspect? The cops think you killed your brother for the insurance money. The chick here got fired today because of you and your dumb brother. Her whole career ruined. You two meet up, things get violent. Maybe you kill her and then pop yourself. Maybe it's the other way around. Who cares?

They'll find her car, and a few days or weeks later, they'll find your bodies floating some-where — what's left of them, anyway. Case closed."

"Actually, that's a good plan. And since I know there's no way you could have thought of it, where are your partners?"

"What are you talking about?"

"The other two guys in the stockade that night."

"Perkins is one," Sara blurted out. "He's here too."

"Shut up!" Dellasandro yelled.

"I actually knew that one. I think I can guess who the other one is."

"Run your theories by the fish. Let's go."

They all started to move toward the river-bank. Fiske glanced back at Dellasandro. "Don't even think about it, Fiske. I could blow you away from fifty yards, much less two feet. And if your plan is to have that stupid lummox jump me from the trees, well, then just bring him on."

Since that was their plan, Fiske's heart sank. Then a bullet hit the dirt next to Dellasandro's leg. He shouted and moved the pistol away from Sara's head.

Fiske hit him hard in the belly, doubling him over, and then clocked him in the head with his fist. Before Dellasandro could recover, Rufus exploded from behind a tree and hit him with the force of a runaway tank.

The man sailed down the bank and into the water from the impact. Fiske pulled his gun. Rufus was about to go after Dellasandro when more shots zipped past them and everybody hit the ground.

Fiske had one protective arm over Sara. "You see anything, Rufus?"

"Yeah, but you ain't going to like it. I think those shots came from two different places."

"Great, both his backups are here. Shit!" He clenched his pistol. "Look, Rufus, here's the plan. We'll fire two shots each and draw their fire in return so we can see where the muzzle flashes are coming from. Then I'll cover you and you take Sara and get the hell out of here. Make it to her car and go." Before Sara could say anything, he added, "Somebody's got to go get Chandler."

Rufus said, "I can stay behind. I owe these suckers a lot more than you."

"I think you've carried the ball long enough." Fiske aimed his gun. "You fire left and check left, one-two-three, now!" Sara covered her ears as the shots rang out. A few seconds later their fire was returned.

Fiske and Rufus quickly analyzed the muzzle flashes. Fiske said, "One of them's aiming wild. Maybe we hit him. Okay, I'm going to fire in both directions. Keep your gun ready, but don't shoot. I'm going to move to my right about ten yards. I'll draw the fire my way. Give me to the count of twenty and then when you hear the first round go, hit it."

Fiske started to move away, but Sara clutched at his hand, unwilling to let him go.

Fiske wanted to say something confident, cocky even, to her, to show he wasn't scared. But he was. "I know what I'm doing, Sara. And I guess fifty years of living is better than nothing."

She stared at him as he crawled off, convinced it would be the last time she would see him alive.

A minute later the shots began. Rufus half carried Sara as they raced for the car. They made it and Rufus threw open the door and pushed Sara inside before climbing in.

Fiske moved slowly through the underbrush, the smell of hot metal and flamed gunpowder clinging to him. His spirits had faded to nothing. He had counted his shots carefully, but, unknown to him, his clip had not been full to begin with; he had no more ammo. As he heard the car crank up, he smiled grimly. With his thoughts distracted for a moment, his ears still ringing from the shots he had fired, he didn't hear the sound behind him until it was too late.

Dellasandro, dripping filthy river water, pointed the gun at him. Fiske couldn't speak, his mouth too dry. He also couldn't breathe, as though his lungs had sized up the situation and decided to stop working a few seconds before the slug would force them to. Two bullet holes in him, the third would do the trick. Darnell Jackson had been facing Fiske's gun, had been off balance after killing Fiske's partner; Dellasandro would have no such problems. Fiske looked in the direction of the river. A week in that water and not even his father would be able to identify him. He looked back at Leo Dellasandro: his last image before death.

When the shot came, Fiske watched in stunned silence as Leo Dellasandro pitched forward and lay still.

Fiske looked up. What he saw made him wish Dellasandro had been able to get off his own round. McKenna looked down at him. Fiske could only shake his head. Why couldn't it have been Chandler? Why couldn't he catch a damn break just this once? And then he saw Dellasandro's pistol where it had landed very near to him.

"Don't try it, Fiske," McKenna said sharply.

"You sonofabitch!"

"Actually, I thought you'd want to thank me."

"Why? For killing your accomplice before you kill me?"

In response, McKenna pulled another pistol from his pocket. "Here's your pistol. I just happened to find it."

"Right. Some way, someday you're going to get what's coming to you."

McKenna glanced at Dellasandro. "Actually, in a way, I just did."

The man's next actions absolutely astonished Fiske.

McKenna flipped the gun around and handed it to him, grip first. "Now don't go and shoot me." He put a hand out and helped Fiske up. "Chandler's on his way. I managed to catch him at Evans's house. I got there just as Perkins and Dellasandro were leaving with Sara. I figured they were trying to use her to set you up. I followed along as your unofficial backup. A little better than the last one you had. I *never* let my guard down."

Fiske just stared at him, unable to speak.

"Perkins took off. He was the other guy firing. I tried to hit him, but he was too far off. I also fired the shot to distract Leo. I figured Rufus was around here somewhere."

"I thought you were one of the guys in the stockade that night," said Fiske.

"I was."

"Then what are you doing? Clearing your conscience? If you are, you're the only one of the five to do it."

"I wasn't one of the five."

"But you just said you were in the stockade that night."

"There were *six* men there that night other than Rufus."

653

Fiske looked bewildered. "I don't understand."

"I was the guard on duty that night, John. It took me twenty-five years to figure out what happened, but I couldn't have done it without you and Sara. I think the PCP angle hit me right after it did you at your office. I never even knew about the drug testing at Fort Plessy, although I guess it wasn't something they broadcast."

"Whether anybody else knew or not, I don't think anyone back then cared about what happened to Rufus Harms."

"Actually, I cared." McKenna looked down. "I just didn't have the balls to do anything about it until it was too late. I could have stopped this whole thing." His body seemed to sag for a second as his mind went back to the past. "But I didn't."

Fiske studied the man for a moment, still reeling from this last development. "Well, you're doing something about it now."

"Twenty-five years too late."

"Rufus is going to be free, isn't he? That's all he cares about."

McKenna looked up. "Rufus is free now, John. No one will ever put him back in prison. If they try to, they have to go through me first. And believe me, they won't be able to."

Fiske looked toward the road. "What about Perkins?"

McKenna smiled. "I know exactly where Perkins is going. We can call Sara in the car and let her know. As soon as Chandler gets here, we'll go."

"Go? Go where?"

"Perkins is going to see the fifth person who was in the stockade that night."

"Who? Who was it?"

"You'll find out. Soon you'll know everything."

CHAPTER SIXTY

When the woman opened the door, Richard Perkins burst in past her. "Where is he?"

"In his study."

Perkins raced down the hallway and threw open the door. The tall man looked back at him, a calm look in his eyes.

Perkins shut the door. "Everything's gone to hell and I'm getting out of here."

Jordan Knight sat back and shook his head. "If you run, they'll know you're guilty."

"They know I'm guilty now. I kidnapped Sara Evans. Leo is probably dead by now."

"You followed her ever since she left the Court today. I hoped, when I contacted you, it would all have been taken care of. But it's still only her word against yours."

"Why would she make up something like that?"

Jordan rubbed his chin. "Think about it. She was fired today. You escorted her out the door. She makes wild accusations against you; perhaps you can invent some others to bolster your position."

"Rufus Harms is still out there. I saw him."

Jordan's face darkened. "Ah, the cele-

656

brated Mr. Harms."

"He killed Frank and Vic."

"Two fewer people to worry about, then."

"That's damn cold-blooded of you. You were the one who told them to kill Michael Fiske. You got all this started."

Jordan looked thoughtful. "I still don't know how Rufus Harms was able to identify me in that appeal. He knew all of you. I wasn't even in the Army."

"He didn't ID you."

Knight looked shocked at first; then there was a glint of hope in his eyes.

Perkins explained, "I talked to Tremaine. Rayfield lied to you. You weren't named in the appeal. Just the four of us."

"So I'm the only unknown." Jordan stood up and looked at Perkins. God, that meant he still had a way out. Only one more thing, one more person to deal with, and this nightmare was over. He almost trembled at the thought of it.

"Who knows for how long. God, all this for what? We shoot the bastard up with PCP and it comes down to this."

"You actually shot him up, Richard."

"Don't act high and mighty now. It was your idea to use the PCP, Mr. CIA."

"Well, naturally — I was there conducting the testing. And listening to all of you complain about Harms. Just trying to do you a favor." He eyed Perkins with an unnerving calmness. "I'm very anti-drug now, of course."

"Stumping to the end? How about anti-murder? How do you feel about that, Senator?"

"I never killed anybody."

"How about that little girl, Jordan? How about her?"

"Rufus Harms pled guilty to that crime. As far as I'm concerned, that plea hasn't changed."

"Well, it will soon enough if we don't do something."

"Are you certain you want to run?"

"I'm not hanging around for the ax to fall."

"I suppose you'll need money?"

Perkins nodded. "I don't have a nice little retirement package like we put together for Vic and Frank. I have the bad habit of always living beyond my means."

Jordan took a key from his pocket and unlocked his desk drawer. "I have some cash here. The rest will have to be by check. I can give you fifty thousand, to start."

"That sounds good. To start."

Jordan turned and pointed a pistol at Perkins.

"What the hell are you doing, Jordan?"

"You burst in here, clearly out of your mind, telling of these outrageous crimes you've committed, including kidnapping Sara Evans, for what purpose I don't know.

You threaten me. I manage to get out my gun and kill you."

"You're crazy. No one will believe that."

"Oh, they will, Richard." Jordan pulled the trigger and Perkins dropped to the floor. He heard a scream from the hallway. Jordan moved to the body, quickly searched Perkins, found his gun, placed it in the dead man's hand and fired a shot into the wall. "It's all right," he called out, rising from the floor and putting the pistol down. "I'm all right." He opened the door and froze as Rufus Harms stared back at him. Behind Rufus were Chandler, McKenna, Fiske and Sara.

Jordan finally pulled his gaze from Rufus and looked at Chandler. "Richard Perkins burst in here making wild threats. He had a gun. Fortunately I was a better shot."

McKenna stepped forward. "Senator, you don't remember me, do you? I mean, outside the FBI?" Jordan stared at him without recognition. McKenna edged closer to the man. "Perkins and Dellasandro didn't remember me either. It's been a long time and we've all changed a lot. Besides, everybody was pretty drunk that night. Everybody except you."

"I have no idea what you're talking about."

"I was the guard on duty the night you and your friends came calling on Rufus at Fort Plessy. It was my first and last time pulling guard duty at the stockade. Probably why nobody remembered me."

Jordan Knight flinched. "Am I supposed to know what you're talking about?"

"I let you in to see Rufus because I was a greenhorn scared private and I had a captain ordering me to. And then Rufus came busting out of his cell, knocked me down and changed everybody's life forever. For twenty-five damn years I've wondered what really happened in there. I kept quiet about all of you because I was scared. Rayfield was the most senior. He probably would've remembered me. Guess no one mentioned my name to him. Lucky. Rayfield fixed it up so I wouldn't get in trouble, but he made it clear I had better keep my mouth shut about all of you being in there. And I never knew what had happened anyway. And by the time I got the courage to say something, it was all over, and Rufus was in prison. I've lived with that guilt all these years. But I got off easy." McKenna looked over at Rufus. "I'm sorry, Rufus. I was weak, a coward. It probably doesn't make any difference to you, but there hasn't been a day gone by that I didn't hate myself for it."

Jordan cleared his throat. "Very touching, Agent McKenna. However, if you think you saw me in the stockade that night, you're mistaken."

"CIA records will show that you were at Fort Plessy conducting PCP tests on soldiers stationed there," McKenna pointed out.

"If you can get those records, get them. Even if I was there, so what? I was in the intelligence service back then. That's no secret. The public is aware of that."

"I wonder if your constituents would be bothered by the fact that you were administering PCP to soldiers," Chandler said heatedly.

"Even if I did — and I'm not admitting anything — the program was perfectly aboveboard and legal, as my wife could certainly tell you."

"*U.S. v. Stanley?*" Sara said bitterly.

Jordan's gaze did not leave McKenna. "Quite a coincidence that you claim to have been in the stockade and now you're involved in this matter," he said.

"It was no coincidence, it was intentional," was McKenna's surprising reply. "After I left the Army I finished college, and then went to the FBI academy. But I kept tabs on you and the others. Guilt is very strong motivation. Rayfield and Tremaine moved around with Rufus. That I found suspicious, but not conclusive. Perkins and Dellasandro moved around with you. They had positions in your various businesses. I got myself transferred to the Richmond Field Office so I could be close to you. When you jumped into politics they again went with you. When you went to D.C., you got Dellasandro and Perkins jobs at the Senate. So I got transferred to D.C.

661

When you were given a seat on the Senate Judiciary Committee a few years ago, you got them their positions at the Court. Real nice of you. It must be part of the payback, the agreement all of you made. Rayfield and Tremaine baby-sat Rufus. You took care of Perkins and Leo. I bet if we checked their accounts, we'd find some nice little retirement funds somewhere.

"When I got wind of Michael Fiske's murder, I jumped on it only because it was at the Court. When I discovered Rufus was connected somehow, I prayed all those years of following you were going to pay off. Now the truth has finally come out."

"Absurd speculation, you mean," Jordan Knight countered. "From your own words, it's obvious you have some deranged vendetta against me. I find it outrageous that you've come into my home making all these accusations, particularly after I've had a man try to murder me, forcing me to kill him. And other than Detective Chandler, who has to investigate this act of obvious self-defense, I want the rest of you to get the hell out of my home."

McKenna pulled a cell phone from his pocket, spoke into it and listened to the response. "I'm placing you under arrest, Senator Jordan. I'm sure Detective Chandler will do the same."

"Get the hell out of here. Now!"

"I'm going to read you your rights now."

"I'll have you in the FBI equivalent of Siberia by dawn. You have no proof of anything."

"Actually, I'm basing my arrest on your own words." While everyone watched, McKenna knelt under the desk kneehole, probed for a moment and pulled out a listening device. "Your statements came through loud and clear in the surveillance van parked outside." He looked at Fiske. "Knight was the one who told Rayfield to kill your brother."

Jordan was furious. "That is completely illegal. There's not a judge in this city who would have given you a warrant for that. I'm not going to prison, you are."

"We didn't need a warrant. We had consent."

"Bullshit!" Jordan roared. He looked like he was about to attack the agent. "I demand you give me those tapes immediately. You're an imbecile if you think anyone will believe that I gave such consent."

"You didn't, Jordan. I did."

The blood drained from Jordan's face as his wife stepped into the room. She didn't even look at Perkins's body. Her gaze remained fixed on her husband.

"You?"

"I live here too, Jordan. I gave that consent."

"In God's name, why?"

Elizabeth held his gaze for a moment, then touched the sleeve of Rufus Harms. "This man is why, Jordan. This man is the only reason strong enough to make me do what I did."

"For him? He's a child killer."

"It's no good, Jordan. I know the truth. And damn you for what you've done."

"What I've done? All I've ever done is serve my country." He stabbed a finger at Rufus. "This man never did shit for anything or anybody. The bastard deserved to die."

Moving faster than his bulk would seem to have allowed, Rufus reached Jordan, his big hands encircling the senator's neck as he slammed him up against the wall.

"Damn you!" Rufus screamed. His grip tightened and Jordan started turning red.

McKenna and Chandler trained their guns, but couldn't bring themselves to shoot. They looked helpless. They grabbed Rufus, but it was like pulling on a mountain.

"Jordan," Elizabeth screamed.

"Rufus, stop," Sara yelled.

Jordan was nearly unconscious.

Fiske stepped forward. "Rufus, Rufus?" Fiske took a quick breath and then just said it. "Josh didn't make it." Rufus instantly loosened his grip on Jordan's throat and stared at Fiske. "He's dead, Rufus. We both lost our brothers." Fiske was visibly trembling and Sara put a hand on his shoulder. "If you kill him, you'll go back to prison and Josh will have died for nothing." Rufus relaxed his grip even more as tears wound down his face. "You can't do it, Rufus." Fiske took another unsteady step forward. "You just can't."

As the two bereaved men looked at one another, Rufus simply let go, and a gasping Jordan Knight slumped to the carpet.

Jordan did not look at his wife as he was led away in handcuffs by McKenna. An hour later the forensics team had completed its work and Perkins's body was removed. Chandler, Rufus, Sara and Fiske remained behind. Elizabeth Knight was in her bedroom.

"So how much did you know about the truth, Buford?" Fiske asked.

"Some of it. McKenna and I had talks. At first I think he really believed you were involved, or at least he genuinely didn't like you." Chandler smiled. "But after he learned Rufus was somehow connected, his opinion changed. I didn't like the idea of him setting you up for the fall, though. And he pushed the buttons on Sara getting fired."

"Why?" Sara asked.

"You two were getting close to the truth. That meant you both were in danger. McKenna knew the people involved were capable of a lot. But he didn't have any proof.

He had to make them think you two were the primary suspects. And every time we were around Perkins and Dellasandro, McKenna made it clear he thought Rufus's appeal was bogus and John was the killer. He took your gun and made sure Perkins and Dellasandro knew it was missing. He hoped that meant they would feel safe and might slip up. Also it was meant to keep you two safe."

"I don't think it accomplished the last part," Sara said with a shiver.

"Well, he didn't count on you losing his surveillance team either. Once McKenna got Justice Knight to agree to the bug, he just had to spring the trap. McKenna had already told Justice Knight that he knew her husband from Fort Plessy, so when the senator told her he had to call to get that information, she knew he was lying."

"So Justice Knight's quick thinking probably saved my life," Sara commented.

Chandler nodded in agreement. "When everything went down, McKenna knew Perkins would make a run for it and would need Jordan's help. It worked out okay. Jordan killing Perkins was not in the game plan. But I'm not going to lose any sleep over that." Chandler looked at Rufus Harms. "I need to take you into custody, but it won't be for long."

"I want to see my brother."

Chandler nodded. "I can arrange that."

"I'll go with you, Rufus," Fiske said.

As they walked to the door, Elizabeth Knight met them in the hallway.

"Justice Knight, you did a very brave thing tonight. I know how painful it was for you," Chandler said.

Elizabeth reached out her hand to Rufus Harms. "It can't possibly be worth anything to you after all you have suffered, Mr. Harms, but I am so sorry for everything. So very, very sorry."

He took her hand gently. "It's worth a lot, ma'am. To me and my brother."

As they headed out the door, Elizabeth Knight looked at them all and said with finality, "Good-bye."

The group headed to the elevator. When the three men stepped on the elevator car, Sara hesitated. "I'll catch up with you later," she said. As the elevator doors closed, she raced back to the apartment. Mary opened the door.

"Where's Justice Knight?"

"She went into the bedroom. Why —"

Sara flew past her and burst into the bedroom. Sitting on the bed, Elizabeth Knight looked up at her former clerk. The justice's hand was clenched in a fist; a prescription bottle lay empty next to her.

Sara walked slowly over to her, sat down and took her hand. She opened it and the pills spilled out. "Elizabeth, that's not the way to deal with this."

"Deal with it?" Elizabeth said hysterically. "My life just walked out that door in handcuffs."

"Jordan Knight just walked out that door. Justice Elizabeth Knight is sitting right here next to me. The same Justice Knight who will be leading the Supreme Court into the next century."

"Sara . . ." The tears spilled down her face.

"It's a lifetime appointment. And you have a lot of life left." Sara squeezed her hand. "I'd like to help you with your work, your very important work. If you'll have me back."

Sara put her arms around the woman's trembling shoulders.

"I don't know if I can do this . . . survive this."

"I'm certain that you can. And you won't be doing it alone. I promise."

Elizabeth clutched at the young woman's shoulder. "Will you stay with me tonight, Sara?"

"I'll stay as long as you want."

CHAPTER SIXTY-ONE

On the strength of his being the possessor of the Silver Star, Purple Heart and Distinguished Service Medal, Josh Harms was entitled to burial with modified honors — the highest an enlisted man could attain — at Arlington National Cemetery. However, the Army representative who had come to speak to Rufus about the arrangement seemed bent on talking him out of it.

"He got shot up, saved a bunch of the men in his company, won himself a box full of medals," Rufus said, eyeing the man's uniform, the single row of colored metal on it. "A lot mor'n you got."

The man twisted his lips. "His record was not the cleanest in the world either. He had a real problem with authority. From what I could gather, he didn't like or respect one thing about the institution he was representing."

"So you think burying him up there with all them generals and such would be disrespectful?"

"The cemetery is running out of space. I think it would be a nice gesture to reserve those spaces for soldiers who actually were proud to wear the uniform, that's all I'm saying."

"Even though he earned it?" Rufus said.

"I'm not disputing that. But I can't believe your brother would *want* to be buried there either."

"I guess he'd spend all of eternity telling those dead brass exactly what he thinks of them."

"Something like that," the man said dryly. "So then we're in agreement? You'll arrange burial for him elsewhere?"

Rufus eyed the man. "I made up my mind."

Thus, on a cool, clear day in October, former Sergeant Joshua Harms, USA, was laid to rest at Arlington National Cemetery. From an angle, the ground was so covered with white crosses that it looked like an early snow had fallen. As the honor guard fired off its salute and the bugler launched into taps, the simple coffin was lowered into the ground. Rufus and one of Josh's sons received the flag, folded tricornered, from a somber and respectful Army officer, while Fiske, Sara, McKenna and Chandler looked on.

Later, as Rufus prayed over his brother's grave, he thought about all of the bodies buried here, most in the name of war. There were both men and women who had this as their final resting place, although, histori-

670

cally, it was the men who were the instigators and chief wagers of armed conflict. For those who traced their history through the Book of Genesis and beyond, as did Rufus, the bodies buried here could blame the existence of wars on the man called Cain and the mortal blow he struck his brother Abel.

As Rufus finished his prayer, his talk with his Lord and his brother, he rose and put an arm around the nephew he had never seen until today. His heart was sad, but his spirits were lifted. He knew that his brother had passed on to a better place. And for as long as Rufus lived, Josh Harms would never be forgotten. And when Rufus went to join his Lord he would also, once again, embrace his brother.

CHAPTER SIXTY-TWO

Two days later, Michael Fiske was buried at a private cemetery on the outskirts of Richmond. The well-attended funeral service included each justice of the United States Supreme Court. Ed Fiske, dressed in an old suit, his hair neatly combed, awkwardly stood next to his surviving son and received condolences from each of the jurists, together with many of Virginia's political and social elite.

Harold Ramsey spent an extra minute giving comfort to the father and then turned to the son.

"I appreciate all that you did, John. And the sacrifice that your brother made."

"The ultimate one," Fiske said in an unfriendly tone.

Ramsey nodded. "I also respect your views. I hope that you can respect my views as well."

Fiske shook the man's hand. "I guess that's what makes the world go round."

Looking at Ramsey made Fiske think of what lay ahead for Rufus. Fiske had encouraged him to sue everybody he could think of, including the Army and Jordan Knight.

There was no statute of limitations on murder, and the ensuing cover-up orchestrated by Jordan and the others had broken numerous other laws.

Rufus had refused Fiske's advice, however. "All of 'em except for Knight are in a far worse place than any judge on this earth could send 'em to," he had said. "That's their true punishment. And Knight's got to live with what he done. That's enough for me. I got no reason to get mixed up with courts and judges no more. I just want to live as a free man, spend a lot of time with Josh's children. Go see my momma's grave. That's all."

Fiske had tried to get him to change his mind, until he realized that the man was right. Besides, Fiske thought, according to the precedents established by the Supreme Court, Rufus couldn't sue the Army anyway. Not unless Elizabeth Knight could use the Barbara Chance case to give military personnel the same basic rights as the rest of the country's citizens. To do that, she had to get past Ramsey. As he thought about it, though, Fiske concluded that if anyone could do it, Elizabeth Knight could. He'd like to be a fly on the wall of the Supreme Court in the coming years.

But there were two things Fiske — with the assistance of JAG attorney Phil Jansen — was going to accomplish for Rufus: an honorable discharge, and a full military pension and benefits. Rufus Harms wasn't going to scrape for an existence, not after all he had been through.

As Fiske finished this thought, Sara walked up with Elizabeth Knight. Sara had returned to the Court as Knight's clerk. The place was slowly returning to normal. Or as normal as it was going to get with Knight and Ramsey in the same building.

"I feel deeply responsible for all of this," Knight said.

She and the senator, Fiske knew, were divorcing. The government, the Army in particular, wanted to keep all of this quiet. Important strings in Washington were being pulled. That meant that Jordan Knight might not go to prison for all that he had done. Even with Elizabeth Knight's consent, the legality of the electronic surveillance of the man had already been drawn into serious question by the senator's very skillful lawyers. In a private meeting with McKenna, the FBI agent had told Fiske that the wiretap had been a risky strategy, since they did not have the consent of one of the parties being taped, but it was the only way McKenna could think of to implicate Jordan Knight. But without the recording, Chandler and McKenna really had nothing to take to court. The thought that Jordan would go unpunished made Fiske want to visit the man late at night with his 9mm. But the man had suffered, and would continue to do so. The wiretap had carried some leverage. Jordan had resigned his senate seat and, more devastatingly, lost the woman he cherished. He still had his New Mexico ranch, though. Let it be your seven-thousand-acre prison, Fiske thought.

"If there's anything I can ever do for you . . ." Elizabeth Knight said.

"You have the same offer from me," Fiske said.

Thirty minutes after the last mourners were gone, Fiske, his father and Sara watched as the chairs and green carpet were removed. The coffin was lowered, and the slab was laid over the vault. Then the dirt was shoveled on top. Fiske spoke with his father and Sara for a few minutes and told them he would meet them back at his father's house. He watched them drive off. When he looked back over at the fresh hump of earth, he was startled. The cemetery workers were gone now, but on his knees next to the new grave, eyes closed, Bible clutched in one hand, was Rufus Harms.

Fiske walked over and put a hand on the man's shoulder. "Rufus, you okay? I didn't even know you were still here."

Rufus didn't open his eyes, and he didn't say anything. Fiske watched as his lips moved slightly. Finally, Rufus opened his eyes and looked up at him.

"What were you doing?"

"Praying."

"Oh."

"How about you?"

"How about me, what?"

"Have you prayed over your brother yet?"

"Rufus, I haven't been to Mass since high school."

Rufus gripped Fiske's sleeve and pulled him down next to him. "Then it's time you started up again."

His face suddenly pale, Fiske looked at the grave site. "Come on, Rufus, this isn't funny."

"Nothing funny about saying good-bye. Talk to your brother, and then talk to your Lord."

"I don't remember any prayers."

"Then don't pray. Just talk, plain words."

"What exactly am I supposed to say?"

Rufus had already closed his eyes and didn't answer.

Fiske looked around to see if anyone was watching. Then he turned back, looked over at Rufus, awkwardly put his hands together and, embarrassed, finally let them dangle at his sides. At first he didn't even close his eyes, but then they just seemed to do so on their own. He felt the moisture from the ground soak through his pants legs, but he didn't move. He felt the comforting presence of Rufus next to him. He didn't know if he could have remained here without it.

He focused on all that had happened. He thought of his mother and his father. The insurance money had given Gladys Fiske her first trip to the beauty parlor in years, and some new clothes to admire herself in. To her he was still Mike, but at least she remembered one of them. Ed Fiske would soon be driving a new Ford pickup, the loan on the house paid off. He and his father were planning a fishing trip for the next year, down in the Ozarks. A lot to be thankful for.

With a smile Fiske thought of Sara, gratefully, even with all the complexities that came with the woman. Fifty, sixty, maybe seventy years old? Why not give himself the benefit of the doubt? He had a life to live. Potentially a very satisfying one. Particularly when it included Sara. Then he tilted his head up and smelled the wet air, caught the scent of leaves burning somewhere. The air also carried to him an infant's cry, followed by the silence of the dead around him. Growing more comfortable, he squatted back on his haunches, easing himself more firmly into the embrace of the ground, the cool touch of the dirt now welcome somehow.

Finally, with difficulty, he thought of his brother. He was so tired of grudges held. He now focused on reality. On the truth. On his baby brother, a person he would have done anything for. He recalled the pride he shared with his mother and father for the exceptional human being they had jointly raised. For the good man Mike Fiske had grown into, graceful faults and all, just like the rest of them. A brother who had shown, through his actions, that he respected John Fiske, cared about him. Loved him. Through the half dozen feet of dirt, past the bound flowers on top, inside the bronze coffin, he could clearly see his brother's face, the dark suit he had been buried in, the hair parted on the side, the hands folded across the chest, the eyes closed. At rest. At peace. The limbs stilled much too early. The exceptional mind shut down far from its potential.

It did not take long for the tremors to start. The two-year void that John Fiske had artificially forced upon the pair was nothing compared to the one he was suddenly stricken with now. It was as though Billy Hawkins had just walked through the door and told him that Mike, the other half of his life growing up, was dead. Only he wouldn't have to identify the body. He wouldn't have to search for and falsely share grief with his father. He wouldn't have to watch as his mother called him by another's name. He would not have to risk his life to find his brother's killers. But he would have to do something else. The one task left was the hardest of all.

He felt the burn in his chest, but it was not the underbelly of his scar come calling. This pain was not capable of killing him, but it was worse by legions than that inflicted on him by the two bullets. The things he had found out about his brother lately only highlighted how unfair Fiske had been in shutting him out. But if he had tried, Fiske would have realized all those things while Mike was still alive. Now his brother was dead. John Fiske was kneeling in front of his grave. Mike was not coming back. He had lost him. He had to say good-bye and he didn't want to. He desperately wanted his brother back. He had so much he wanted to do with him, suddenly so much love he wanted to convey. He felt his heart would burst if he didn't get it out.

"Oh God," he said with an outward breath. He couldn't do this. He felt his body start to give on him. The tears suddenly poured with such force he thought his nose was bleeding. He started to go down, but a strong hand grasped him, easily held him up; Fiske's body felt light, fragile, as though he had left part of it somewhere else. Through the blur of tears he looked at Rufus. The man had one hand under Fiske's arm, thrusting him up. Yet his eyes were still closed, his head looking to the sky; the lips still rising and falling in the narrowest of ranges as he continued his prayers.

Right then John Fiske envied Rufus Harms, a man who had lost his own brother, a man who really had nothing. And yet in the most important way, Rufus Harms was the richest man on earth. How could anyone believe in anything that much? Without doubt, without debate, without an agenda, with all his substantial heart?

As Fiske looked at the calm face of his friend next to him, he thought how very fine it must be to know for certain that your loved one is in a better place, embraced and held for all time by the phenomenon of unassailable good. So comforting a notion at the precise time you needed to feel it. How often did such timing occur in life? Death as joyous. Death as the beginning. Meaning life was both more and less precious because of it.

Fiske looked away from Rufus and stared down at the grave, the image of a pale hand under a white sheet coming back to him, and then leaving, like a bird in search of food. He dug his knees into the earth, closed his eyes, bowed his head, placed his hands firmly together and started making his peace. With his brother below. And with whatever lay above.